"This really slapped."

-RJ Bayley

"A wild ride between our world and a magical realm."

– LukeJAnthony

"The writing is imaginative and very inviting, with vivid settings and captivating prose."

– J. Roman

"A captivating and well-written story with humor, action, and an engaging plot."

– TheCrimsonEclipse

"A phenomenal merging of Celtic mythology and modern storytelling."

– Ingelina

"A story worth reading for anyone who loves Celtic lore or fantastical adventures."

– PathOfPen

"The story is intricately woven, drawing on deep roots of mythology while skillfully integrating game mechanics."

– Dessel4

"A fantastic isekai adventure with a unique twist that keeps the pacing fresh and exciting… A well-researched, immersive portal fantasy rooted in Celtic mythology."

– VMJaskiernia

Longwinded One Press
www.longwinded.one

First Edition, November, 2025

ISBN 979-8-9893883-4-9

If you have made it this far, you know that this is not historic fiction. You know that I believe LitRPG to be more than systems and overpowered narrators. This is book two of a series that could be longer than three books. Calling it a saga makes me sound like an ass, but at the time of naming the series, I wasn't sure if trilogy was going to be accurate. Once again, if you have made it this far, you aren't one of those third-person snobs and you don't mind non-crunchy, light-hearted LitRPG. You are my people, and I very much appreciate you following me on this journey. Enjoy!

THE BREAKING OF ANNWN

A LITRPG ADVENTURE

THE FOUR TREASURES SAGA, BOOK TWO

BY THE LONGWINDED ONE

DEDICATION

For Eden.

For years, I have had a children's book in mind that I wanted to dedicate to you. But this book came to life first, and now you are too old for a children's book. Years have not diminished my love for you. I am in awe of all that you do. You will forever be my "Pumpkin Muffin."

"You best retrieve your army, my lad.
This war can't start without us."

- Lir Dofainn

PRONUNCIATION GUIDE

Abhartach (OWR-hah-tukh)
Aillén (AHL-yen)
Annwn (AN-oon)
Aoibhinn (Eev-een)
Aonbharr (AYN-var or EEN-var)
Arianrhod (AH-ree-an-rhod)
Baile Toradh (BAL-yeh TOR-uh)
Bairic (BAH-rik)
Bánánach (BAW-naw-nukh)
Beithir (BEH-hir)
Belenus (BEH-len-uss)
Béstin (bay-shteen)
Bhean sí (Van shee)
Boatswain (BOH-suhn)
Bren Búachaill (brehn BWAWK-hil)
Breo-Banríon (breh-oh ban-ree-uhn)
Briomhaith (BREE-vah)
Brú na Dallta (Broo nuh DALL-tuh)
Caarunach (KAH-roo-nakh)
Caer Ibormeith (KYER ih-VOR-meth)
Cai Maccán (kai MAHK-kawn)
Caileach (KAL-yukh)
Cailleach Bhéara (KAL-ee-akh VAY-ruh)
Camulos (KAH-moo-los)
Caoineag (Kwee-nak)
Caolán (KAY-lawn or KWEE-lawn)
Caoránach (KEE-ruh-nukh)
Captaen (KAWP-tan)
Cathscian (KAH-skee-an)
Cé Gwalch (KAY Gwahlkh)
Cessairian (KESS-uh-ree-uhn)
Cethlenn (Keh-len)
Claíomh Solais (KLEE-uv SOH-lish)
Cluain Toradh (Cloon TOR-uh)
Cnoc Aine (Knuk AWN-ya)
Comhthíreach (KOH-heer-ukh)
Cruachan (CROO-uh-khawn)
Currach (KUR-ukh)

Deichtine (JEKH-tin-eh)
Deoghabha (DAY-uh-wuh)
Dian Cécht (DEE-an KAY-kht)
Diarmuid (Dear-mid)
Dubhlinn (Duv-lin)
Dún na Fola (Doon na FULL-uh)
Dweomer (dwimmer)
Eadríne (EE-dree-neh)
Efa (EH-va)
Eiocha (EH-yuh-kha)
Éire (AIR-uh)
Erelith (AIR-uh-lith)
Ériu (AIR-yoo)
Ethlinn (ETH-lin)
Fachan (FAHK-an)
Falias (FAHL-yas)
Fea (Fay-uh)
Fiacha (fee-akh-uh)
Fíadan Ellyllon (FEE-ah-din ETH-lath-on)
Fibula Fathaigh (FIB-yoo-la FAH-hee)
Findrias (FIN-ree-as)
Flide (flied)
Flideion (FLIDE-ee-on)
Fragarach (FRAH-guh-rahkh)
Fuilgeir (FWIL-gair)
Gaible (GAH-bil-eh)
Gaoth (gwee)
Garbánach (GAR-vawn-ahk)
Gealltóir (GYAL-tor)
Géis (gaysh)
Goibhniu (GWIV-nyoo)
Gorias (GOR-EE-us)
Gráinne (GRAWN-ya)
Grianainech (GREE-uh-NEH-akh)
Ildatbach (ILL-dath-bakh)
Imbas Forosnai (IM-bas FOHR-uh-snee)
Indech (IN-jukh)
Inis Fer Falga (IN-ish FAYR FAWL-guh)
King Neit (KING NAYT)
Leic na Beatha (Lek nuh BAH-ha)
Lía Fáil (LEE-uh foyl)

Lir Dofainn (Leer DOH-in)
Lough Dearg (Lokh Jarrig)
Lough Solais (Lokh SOH-lish)
Mag Mór (Mag MOHR)
Mag Rein (MAHG RAYN)
Mag Tuired (MAHG TOO-ruh)
Manannán mac Lir (MAH-nuh-nawn MAHK LEER)
Manau (MAH-nah-oo)
Maponos (MAH-po-nos)
Mná na Mara (Mraw nuh MAH-rah)
Móralltach (MOHR-ahl-tukh)
Morias (MOHR-ee-us)
Morlaithen (MOHR-lay-then)
Morvra (Mor-vrah)
Muireann (MWIR-in or MWIR-awn)
Murias (MUR-ee-as)
Neartór (NAR-tore)
Nemedian (NEV-uh-dee-uhn)
Ogma (OHG-mah)
Oilliphéist (ill-if-aysht)
Oirneth (Or-nehth)
Oisín (Uh-sheen)
Port Cóelrenna (Port KWEEL-reh-nuh)
Rónán (ROH-nawn)
Searbhán (SHAR-van)
Segais (SEH-gish)
Senias (SHEN-ee-uhs)
Seodra Nuada (SHOH-drah NOO-uh-dah)
Seolán Neimhe (SHOH-lawn NEV-uh)
Sétanta (Shay-TAHN-ta)
Síorláidir (SHEER-lah-dyur)
Slí Draíochta (SHLEE DREE-ukh-tuh)
Súg (soog)
Tadg mac Nuadat (tie-g Mahk NEW-ah-Da)
Tairseach (TAR-shukh)
Taranis (TAH-rah-nis)
Teutates (TOO-tah-tehs)
Tine Sí (CHIN-eh SHEE)
Tir fo Thuinn (TEER foh HIN)
Tir Tairngire (TEER TARN-gir-uh)
Trow (tr-oh)

Tuatha Dé Danann (TOO-uh-huh day DUN-uhn)
Túr Crochta (Toor KROKH-tuh)
Uaimh an Bhróin (OO-iv un VROH-in)
Uisneach (ISH-nukh)

TUATHA DÉ DANANN & CHANGELINGS

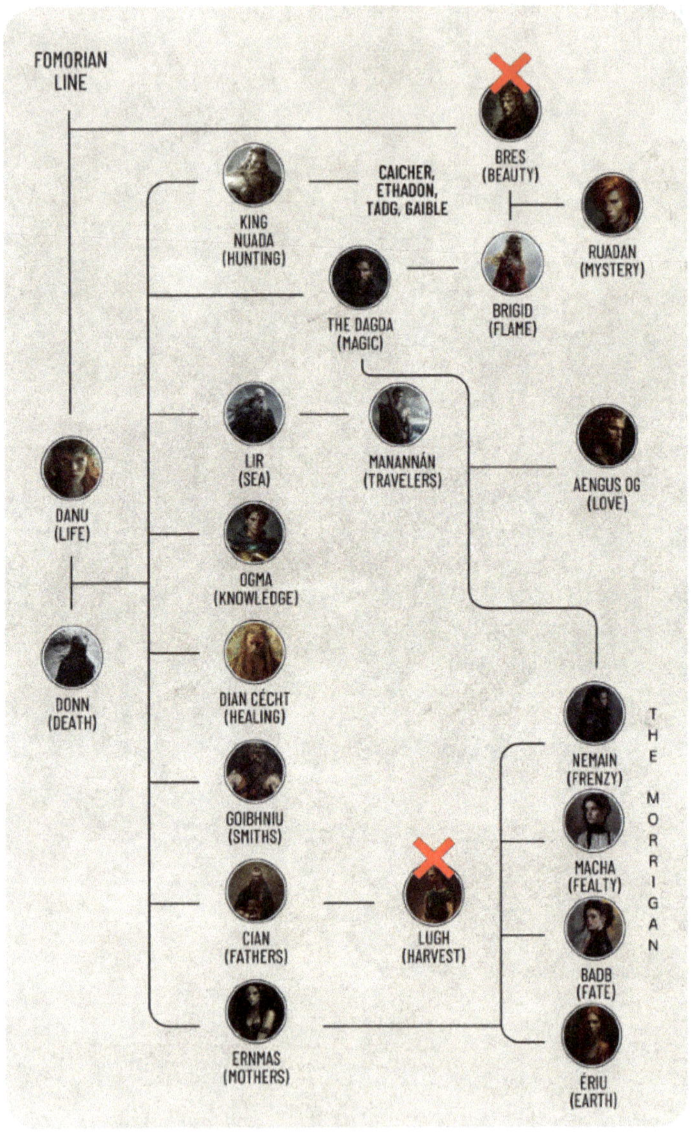

EXPANDED FOMORIAN LINEAGE

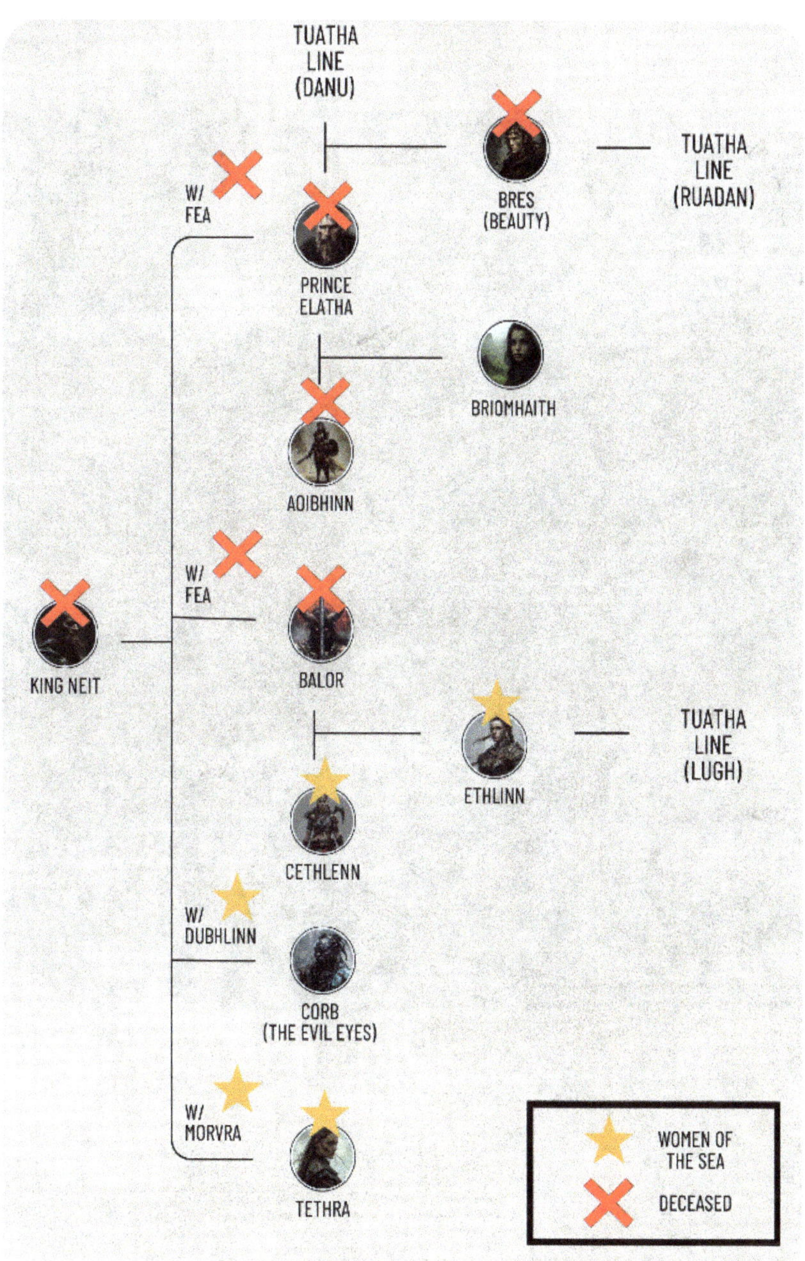

MAP OF ANNWN

Falias "Hightower"
Tech Duinn
Goibhniu's Cave
Inn for a Pint
Murias "Deepwater"
Cruachan
Tír Tairngire
Well of Secrets
Tairseach
Mag Mell
Mag Mell "Midlands"
Cnoc Áine
Port Ildathach
Abhainn Dallta
Brú na Dallta
Loch na Rélais
Cluain Toradh
Eastern Segais Reddishorah!
Inis Fer Falga "Deep Realm"
Heart-shaped Pool
Well of Wisdom
Port Coelrenna
Findrias "Cloudfair"
Straits of Segais / Well of Drowning (Crosswaters)
Slí Dísiochta
Gorias "Flamebright"
Lough Dearg
Emain Ablach
Hook Head "The Sacred Cape" (The Drowning Pool)
Annwn

TABLE OF CONTENTS

PART 1:

CROSSING THE THRESHOLD

CHAPTER 1:

BACK AT THE RANCH

Day 13 of Midwinter, Sunrise
Caisleán Saighead, Gorias
Annwn

"Where am I?" I asked to a dark room.

"You are in the House of Elrond," a husky, yet familiar voice replied. "And it is ten in the morning on July the thirteenth if you wanted to know."

"What?" I asked, still groggy.

"You and me both are lucky to be here. If only a few more hours had passed, you would have been beyond the aid of Lord Elrond."

I picked up my pillow and threw it at the large man sitting next to my bed. My fuzzy brain was slowly focusing on the room around me. I had gleaned, based on the decor, that I was in my old room in Castle Arrow. My whole body hurt.

I scowled at Morias. "Didn't one of your poet friends say something about absinthe making the heart grow fonder?"

"That's 'absence,' my dear Fíadan... Though I would imagine absinthe might also do the trick." His eyes danced as he tried to hold in a chuckle.

"Sage," I began, continuing to test the mobility of my stiff joints. "My fondness for you hasn't quite reached "stupid literary quote" level. You haven't been absent that long."

"Aye, but you have." Morias hefted his sizable body up to stand, then leaned in to gently raise my aching body into a seated position. "That particular quote is fairly accurate for the situation that we find ourselves in."

A sharp pain rippled down the right side of my back. I grimaced and reached back with my left hand, groping for the injury I knew must be in my right wing. Morias rested his hand gently on my shoulder, pausing my search. I froze at the expression on his face.

"We did everything we could..." Morias trailed off, not meeting my eyes.

I twisted to look over my shoulder. The top half of my wing was...missing, severed, and bandaged at what should have been the midway point.

I growled under my breath. Why hadn't Morias, or someone, anyone else, fixed it? I staggered to a standing position on my bed, glaring and daring him to continue.

He cleared his throat. "The vault and the medical stores were sacked when the Fomorians invaded. Most of the survivors have since been rounded up or killed, but it will take time to find and organize all of our supplies."

"What about your magic rings? The Dagda..." I trailed off, dizzy at having exerted myself too quickly.

"When they found you, I was still in rough shape," he said, sitting heavily in his chair. I looked more closely and realized he seemed thinner than usual. I could see a black eye and several cuts in and around his beard.

"The Queen's Guard found you beneath a pile of dead Fomorians at the gate. They told me...they said had they not found you when they did, you would surely have drowned in the lake of Fomorian blood you lay in."

I swayed again and eased myself back down to my bed. My mind swirled with all the things I didn't know. "Swish and Stick?"

"They are here." Morias pointed to the nightstand next to my bed. A knot of tension I hadn't realized I felt eased when I saw the Silverwhite blades.

"Where is Bren? What happened to Nemain and The Dagda?"

"Slow down, Ellyllon. There is much to tell you. But you need your rest first." The big man paused and chuckled to himself. "They counted twenty-one dead Fomorians around the gate that you cut yourself through."

I kicked feebly at the bed covers and scoffed. "Wasn't quick enough, apparently…" In all of my years of service, I had never had my wings this badly damaged. Even so, past experience told me the wing would grow back, but it would take a farthing long time to do it. There would be no flight in my foreseeable future.

"So have you just been sitting here waiting for me to wake up?"

"No." Morias stood and made his way over to a folded set of clothing and equipment. "I have only recently been released from medical care myself. You've had excellent care, I am told. It seems Erelith has barely left your side these last two days."

"I don't know who that is."

"Erelith is the new lead Queen's Guard here at Castle Arrow. It is an honor that she watched over you personally." I rolled my eyes, remembering the Ellyllon we had met on the pier many days earlier.

The sage brought the clothes over to my now disheveled bed, setting them in front of me. I immediately recognized them as Bren's…his léine, trews, cloak, meshmail, and dagger. A simple seashell and a tri-part ring sat atop the stack.

I felt myself flush with emotion, realizing what Morias must be trying to tell me. No, not Bren, I thought. My heart pounded and I heard a rushing in my ears.

"Wait, Fíadan! Please wait. Bren is alive and well." I took a deep breath, my panic easing.

"But why do you have his stuff?" I staggered out of bed, reaching for my own nearby clothes. "I want to see him," I demanded.

"Sit down, Fí." Morias' voice was sharp, and the rebuke surprised me enough that I complied without thinking.

I eyed him suspiciously. "You aren't the boss of me, Sage."

"Nor would I want to be… Now, listen. Please!"

I stayed seated but began pulling my clothes on as he talked. My head wasn't quite as swirly-twirly as it was when I first woke up.

"While you were battling the Fomorians at the gate, Bren rescued me from Balor, but at a nearly fatal cost."

"But he is alive?"

"Yes… He earned his domain just before he and Balor fell from the wall."

My eyes must have registered my shock because Morias was quick to continue.

"We know that he earned his domain because…" he smothered a laugh before continuing. "Well, let's just say that Nemain saw him up to his usual hijinks on the Old Orchard Trail north of the Heart-shaped Pool."

I smiled at that. It was hard to tell what kind of trouble Bren was getting into out in the wide world. For all I knew, he could have been out wrestling with ogres! I was sad to have missed whatever it was.

"Nemain caught him wrestling with an ogre before getting arrested by Tadg's men."

A laugh burst out of me. "So Nemain and Bren made it. And you said the Queen's Guard came to find me... which means The Dagda and the fiacha successfully rescued them. The fact that I was sleeping in my bed here in the castle also means that Aengus led the townspeople into the keep. So, what am I missing? Why is your face doing that thing it does when you are worried?"

"There are other…" Morias began, before stopping mid-sentence. "Wait. What face do you mean?"

"You wrinkle your face…like this." I did my best impression of him, bringing my eyebrows as close together as I could and scrunching my face as if I'd eaten something sour.

Morias drew back. "Oh. Well…I didn't realize my face looked quite like that."

"It's okay," I said. "I like not having to guess what mood you are in."

"Anyway…" Morias said after a moment of awkward silence. "I was GOING to tell you that we have some other crucial business to attend to here in Gorias."

"We?" I looked curiously at Morias. "Does the boss have something else for me to kill?"

Morias sighed. "Fíadan, when are you going to stop pretending that you are some simple tool to be wielded? We both know it isn't true."

He shook his head at my glare. "What we have done here in Gorias is just the beginning of something much, much larger."

He opened the door to the hallway, before turning back to face me. "Erelith will be by shortly to give you a tour of the castle's current setup. It has changed greatly since you were last here, and it is important for you to see the chess pieces in motion… and how fragile the board is presently." He opened his mouth to say something else, then stopped. Thankfully, he knew how I felt about his long-winded speeches.

"And where are you going?" I asked.

"The Dagda gave me leave to explore the lab of the former Gorias Sage, Urias. It was ransacked by the Fomorians."

I puzzled over this. The laboratory space had been abandoned since the Sages were killed, and Morias fled to Ériu. That was a long time ago, even by my standards.

Morias must have seen the look on my face. "I have… a theory about something Urias was working on when he was killed. I will join you in the council chamber when you have finished making the rounds with Erelith."

With that, Morias left me alone to finish getting dressed. It was quiet and surreal being back in the room I had abandoned after Bres was deposed. It brought back feelings of a time that I wasn't ready to face. It made me feel vulnerable, like prey.

I threw on my clothes and grabbed Swish and Stick, relishing the feel of the blades sliding into their sheathes. Just having the Silverwhite blades near me helped to shift the uncomfortable feeling. I wasn't prey. No, I was the predator.

A knock sounded at my door. It was time to go. As I headed to where Erelith waited in the hallway, I eyed the seashell on my bed. Something from a past conversation between Bren and Ruadan came back to me, something I'd missed before.

Part of me knew the shell wasn't just a token, but rather a tether between Fern and Bren, between Bren and me... and maybe, to something far more important than any of us.

CHAPTER 2:

IN THE WIND

Day 14 of Midwinter, Sunrise
Brú na Dallta
Annwn

I walked down the quiet hallway that led to my father's chamber. Despite the late hour, I knew he would be awake, unable to rest after even the town's successful defeat of the Bodach. There would likely be none sleeping in the town after the unexpected invasion of the Old Powers.

My brothers, Ethadon and Caicher would be nearby in adjacent rooms, likely flanked by numerous changeling guards and a handful of faithful Ellyllon.

Despite all of it, I needed to see that my family was safe, that they had survived the attack of the clawed demons that had plagued my nightmares as a child. Even as my feet carried me down the hall, I scolded myself for caring. After all, they had been the ones to toss me aside and imprison me with Bren.

In the war that raged across Annwn, there was no greater enemy to my father than Bren's brother, Cai, the new warlord of the Fomorian horde. It had been my declaration of friendship with Bren that had sealed my fate. He'd been suspicious at my release, and in his mind, my defense of Bren had only confirmed that I must be a traitor.

Yet he didn't know the conflict that raged in my heart. Father was strong, and I had looked up to him and sought his approval at every moment of my life. I had never questioned the rightness of my father's decisions or actions until Bren opened my eyes to the dangers of his absolute power.

My family had declared war on the Fomorians, but we had also turned our backs on the fae. All my life, I believed in the laws of Annwn, the most important being that the gods never die. But my father had murdered his nephew and stolen his domain. He'd attempted to gain control of the Four Treasures.

I was complicit in another of his crimes, the capture and imprisonment of the Breo-Banríon. The former Fiery Queen was beloved in the land, even beyond her home of Gorias. She was my kin, and I had willingly marched her into the proverbial lion's den, believing blindly in Father's vision for Annwn.

I had thought of little else since my time in the Deep Realm. Though I had done many regrettable things, believing them to be for the good of the realm, marching Brigid into Falias wounded me the deepest now that my eyes had been opened.

She lived still, locked in the tower. Brigid lay in a forced torpor she might never wake from. I didn't know why Father hadn't killed her as he did Bres. Was it the power of her domain that stayed his sword? Or had it been easier for him to murder Bres simply because he had the blood of the Fomorians running through him?

Thoughts swirled in my mind, and something inside me changed. I stopped in the dark hallway and thought about my actions. Just ahead, I would find my father surrounded by his loyal advisors. None would dare contradict him in his war plans. My proud and envious brothers would be near, imbibing our father's worst qualities.

I stood frozen in the hall, hearing the familiar voices of my family murmuring just ahead, knowing that when the next battle came, my love would drive me to protect them. But I also knew that if I stepped into that room, they would lock me up again, just as I had done to Brigid.

Ahead, beyond the maze of hallways and corridors in the compound, the harbor bell rang, signifying the coming of the Fomorian fleet. Father would answer this call to arms. I could hear him shout for someone to lash on his armor. He must be nearly ready. Soon, they would exit the building using the hallway I was standing in. I should have been worried about being discovered, but instead, I felt… numb. My body felt like a vessel adrift in the sea, without wind or waves and lacking momentum and bearing.

A glimmer of light near the doorframe caught my eye. Leaning down, I saw a scabbard containing a familiar handle. I had taken the bloody, well-worn blade I was currently carrying off of one of the soldiers who had fallen fighting the Bodach. While that blade was mundane in nature, the sword on the floor was not.

No, this was one of the renowned King's Guard sabers. I picked up the sword, which had a short cross guard. The scabbard mirrored the curved tip of the one-sided blade inside. Turning it, I saw that the pommel read "Gealltóir." Vowkeeper. I smiled. That would do.

I gently placed my borrowed blade next to the door so those behind me would find it. Gripping Vowkeeper, I turned and began walking back the way I'd come.

When I exited my father's section of the building, I hooked back around to the rear of the complex instead of heading toward the harbor. There were no guards at the rear entrance. All of them had rushed toward the sound of battle. I knew I would eventually run into someone loyal to my father, but where I was going, I would also find friendly faces.

Popping out into the morning light, I took in the landscape of the partially walled-in pasture. To my left were the stables of the king. A thundering of hooves sounded. It was accompanied by a whinny that was music to my ears. Gaoth, the fastest warhorse in all of Annwn, halted his cantor just steps from where I stood. From behind him came the familiar hearty laugh of the stable master.

"I knew you must be near," Bairic said. "Old Gaoth here has been inconsolable since last evening, probably wonderin' why ya hadn't come to see him yet."

I felt a smile stretch across my face. The man was an old friend. He was charged with tending the mounts of the king and his immediate family. My brothers and I had spent countless hours in the stables tending to the horses, and even more in the saddle, posting according to Bairic's instruction.

He was the only man I knew, other than Morias, to have ever openly disagreed with Father and kept his job. Their disagreement had been about Gaoth. Father had been adamant the warhorse go to my eldest brother, Caicher.

Bairic insisted that Gaoth would only let me ride him. And up until Bren had stolen away on Gaoth from the Heart-shaped Pool, he had been right. Unfortunately for my brother, Father had insisted Caicher try to ride the stallion named for the wildest part of nature. A few broken ribs later, Caicher managed to convince Father that perhaps Bairic had been right all along.

I clasped the giant forearm of the man. "You are a sight for weary eyes, my friend."

Bairic gripped my hand, his eyes looking me up and down. I knew I must look haggard after the events and revelations of these last few days.

"What? Has your old man not included you in his war?" Clearly, he thought that I was bothered by not being on the front line with the Overking and my brothers.

I forced a laugh and shook my head. "I'm afraid I may have permanently fallen out of Father's good graces this time."

"Nonsense, lad," Bairic said. His big hand rose to stroke the side of Gaoth's muzzle. "Your father loves his family more than anything else in this here crazy world of ours. And there ain't nothing you can do about that."

"Even if I oppose his war?"

The big man paused at my words. He turned, studying me. More time passed, and it became clear to me that he wasn't simply thinking about what I had said. He seemed to be carefully weighing his next words. "So, one of ya has got some sense after all."

I raised my eyebrows at that statement and he tensed. Then I smiled and slapped him on the arm. The tightness of his weathered face eased, and he reached forward to gently set Gaoth's lead in my hand.

I held his eyes. "You realize you're going to get in trouble if you let me take him, right?"

Bairic gave me a sad smile and shrugged. "Where will you go?"

"I need to get back to Falias before Father returns."

"Don't go through Murias. It's faster to go through Deepwater, but someone will recognize and detain you there."

I thought about that. He was suggesting that I take Gaoth the long way around Tech Duinn, through the Midlands. "Mag Mell presents its own challenges."

"If ya can stay away from the fachan and the trow, Gaoth should get ya there in under two moons." He looked at the prancing warhorse with pride in his eyes.

I wondered how long the battle would rage here in the harbor, and if Father would choose to stay on another night in Brú na Dallta. Not likely, after the events of the previous night. Taking the longer route would be close.

I noticed Bairic studying me in a manner that I was unaccustomed to. Seeing my gaze, he cleared his throat. "Something is different with you, my boy. I can't quite put my finger on it."

"That makes two of us," I muttered.

He laughed and urged Gaoth closer to the stables. We both began getting my mount ready to ride. "What's so pressing back in Hightower, if ya don't mind me asking?"

"There is a sin I need to atone for," I said, intentionally trying to keep it vague. The less Bairic knew, the better it was for his own well-being. I swung myself up, resting my weight upon the familiar saddle. He nodded and handed me the reins.

"Be careful with our beautiful boy here," Bairic said, reverently resting his palm on Gaoth's broadside. "And be careful with your own arse. War changes a man. Be sure it is changing you for the better."

I nodded, then turned, urging Gaoth into a full cantor. His hooves thundered, spiriting me away from my home. As the world passed by me at impossible speeds, Bairic's words echoed in my mind. I wondered, not for the last time, how this journey would change me.

CHAPTER 3:

GOD OF HARMONY

< CAI >

Day 14 of Midwinter, Sunset
The Deep Realm
Annwn

I watched as my brother disappeared into the waves with the Cup Bearer of Lir. It was ironic, as during the war with the Tuatha, it had always been a concern of mine that certain members of their court had access to water-bound minions who knew the secret location of our protected isles.

Neit had never been worried about it. He said that Lir had always taken extra care to keep our refuge secret, even from members of his own family. He had worked to ensure our safety, raising his minion, Muirdris, by hand on the lichen native to the Deep Realm, and laying protection spells upon the shores of the islet. When it had become too dangerous for Lir to hold onto our secret, he had fled into the waves, far away from the prying eyes of Overking Nuada.

Neit's relationship with the Sea had preceded the birth of Lir's family, dating back to the time of the first Síorláidir of the land and sea, Eiocha. It was she who pulled a grievously injured Neit into Tir fo Thuinn. Annwn had changed him in ways that were unexpected to both he and the Síorláidir. Not only were his wounds healed, saving his life, but his height and strength increased.

Since that day, Neit had attempted to expand his family, only to be thwarted at every opportunity by the ruling members of the new gods of Annwn, the Tuatha Dé Danann. His son and grandson were killed, likely by servants of the Overking. A lesser man would have sought revenge, but Neit had focused only on the protection of his people. I knew Neit. He had been a hard man, and not responding to these acts of violence had taken all of his strength.

Some, like Balor and Corb, saw Neit's restraint as weakness, but I knew the toll that it took on him. Neit was a man of war, but a wise one who had known that acting on his impulses would make things worse for his people. It was excruciating for him.

Not long after his son died, only four years ago, I came through the Heart-shaped Pool. Tethra found me and brought me to the grieving man who would become my father. She believes I reminded the king of his lost son, Prince Elatha, and that my presence filled a hole in his heart. According to her, Elatha had been cut from the same material as his father—they walked softly, carried a big stick, and feared nothing.

Strange, because I fear everything. I feel a never-ending pit in my stomach when I march my adopted family into battle. I fear I won't be able to protect the soon-to-be appointed Queen Tethra and how much I've missed out on connecting with my real family, whom I have little memories of. They are fears born from the edges of my influence.

Neit once told me that being brave wasn't about not having fears, which everyone had. Instead, it was about what you did with those fears. I have taken that to heart, perhaps too much so. That is the difference between the god of chaos and the god of harmony….to protect those I love, I will always do what needs to be done.

The Inis Fer Falga, Isle of the Protected Men, hummed with activity. The sky was black with smoke from the pyres that burned our dead. The pyres were both a Fomorian tradition and a necessity, an attempt to keep the abhartach at bay. I have seen those blood-suckers awaken in the bodies of the fallen. That was to be avoided.

I was alone with my thoughts. Tethra was overseeing the funeral preparation for King Neit, and Ruadan was around somewhere doing what only Ruadan could do. My thoughts turned to what Bren had told me about his newly learned fairy trance skill and its rejuvenating effect. I had wanted to attempt it since he'd explained it to me, in hopes it might alleviate the constant pain that wracked my body.

Hearing Bren's recounting of our last moments before our genesis, I had been able to piece together some of what had happened in Hy-Brasil. The darkness of the mysterious woman in black had wrapped itself around my torso, leaving me with agonizing dark scars and a hole in my memory. For four years, I had relied on súg to combat the pain, but I had given the last of the magical golden sap to Bren to heal the wounds he'd sustained battling Caoránach the oilliphéist in Lough Dearg.

I lowered myself to my knees, in the way I had seen modern-day Christians pray. I rested my elbows on the stone around the railing of the lighthouse. This was the highest point in the islet and one I had visited many times as I wrestled with recent decisions.

I closed my eyes and focused. My energy boons quickly identified the wounds on my chest and back. I watched the familiar sight of my life force slowly leaking from the scars. I had seen this before when I utilized the boons from my domain classification, Mancer Savant. This time, though, I felt at peace. There was no urgency, no offensive or defensive need for the energy I was summoning.

Bren had said that the fairy trance felt both similar and different from using the energy for our boons. He told me to watch the flow in the environment for as long as it took to understand its natural state. Then, I was to plug myself into the flow, with my body in the center.

Just when I thought I was beginning to recognize patterns in the flow of energy, I was interrupted by the god of magic.

Name: Cai Maccán
Race: Síorláidir
Current Power Rank - Level 15

Current Progression Status:
Physical Progression +43
Mental Progression +53
Spiritual Progression +50

Domains: Harmony and Harvest
Domain Classification: Mancer Savant

You have been gifted with the following Harmony boons:
Control Energy
Graceful Agility
Dark Vision
Energy Resonance
Empathic Influence
Spiritual Augur
Transform Energy
Divination of Balance

You have been gifted with the following Harvest boons:
Maximum Yield
Perfect Aim

You have one blood-borne curse:
Life Leak (Permanent)

Innate Racial Abilities:
Rapid Regeneration

Advanced Identification
Magic Sense

One magic item is in your possession.
Fragarach

Item abilities unlocked:
Trust Tongue

One relic is in your possession.
You have acquired:
The Spear of Victory

Relic abilities unlocked:
Armor Piercing
Return to Sender

I sighed. So much had changed in the last two weeks. When Bren had earned the mantle of Chaos, my own had suddenly shifted to Harmony. I knew now that we represented a duality. What affected one would affect the other. All my boons appeared to have shifted to match my new domain. Only my domain classification seemed unaffected, though I imagine a sage or the god of magic would be able to explain the unnoticed evolution of Mancer Savant during the change. I took another moment to run through the most noteworthy parts of my power rank notification.

Domain Classification:
Mancer Savant- Masters the pure essence of energy
manipulation.

Energy Resonance:

Enhances the Control Energy and the Transform Energy
boons by allowing for multiple kinds of energy absorption
at the same time, in perfect harmony.

Empathic Influence:
Influence emotions and thoughts positively by
manipulating bodily energies. This boon can foster
cooperation among allies and help to pacify foes. This is
not a charm spell.

Magic Sense
Your attunement to magic not only allows you to detect
spells, artifacts, and Power Rank Notifications, but it also
grants you awareness of others' attempts to analyze your
own abilities.

Spiritual Augur
When used with the Magic Sense ability, this boon allows
you to push past magical protections surrounding power
rank notifications.

Transform Energy:
Convert one type of energy into another—such as heat to
light—or amplify or diminish energy in the environment.

Divination of Balance:
Foresee potential disharmonies in the future. This allows
for corrections to maintain balance in the world.

Maximum Yield
This boon ensures every action, whether harvesting crops
or defeating foes, yields the greatest possible result in any
situation.

Perfect Aim
Your precision allows you to identify and exploit weak points with unerring accuracy.

Curse: Life Leak
This curse causes life energy to slowly seep away through scars inflicted by necrotic trauma, weakening the afflicted over time.

CHAPTER 4:

UNDER THE SEA

< BREN >

Day 14 of Midwinter, Sunset
At Sea, Well of Wisdom
Annwn

I traveled like a rocket through the water behind Nechtan. I had started to ask the Cupbearer of Lir if there was a way we could keep Fern's Shell of Promise dry while we were traveling, but he had only let me get out a syllable before glancing down at the shell, grunting, and magically propelling me after him. I'll give him credit though, he must have either recognized the shell or knew what I was going to say because I was as dry as a Methodist hootenanny.

I couldn't really tell which way we were traveling. Several times I felt gravity shift directions. The water where we were traveling was dark. Thankfully, my Night Vision boon allowed me to see just how fast we were traveling, and because of that I only felt mildly carsick… or is it seasick in this case?

The landscape of the sea was fascinating. I tried to imagine what it would look like if it were totally drained of water. There were hills and mountains, valleys, and huge, dark crevasses. It was as mysterious as any place above sea level that I could ever remember seeing, and I was seeing it at super speed. There were fish and huge creatures that could only be from Aquaman's worst nightmares, but they left us completely alone. I also thought I saw the faint outline of a female mirroring our nautical path in the water. It had to be the other Cup Bearer, Connla, I thought. We traveled like this for 20-30 minutes, and I had no problems breathing or fighting against the waves or currents.

After a particularly scary giant invertebrate passed by, I shifted my focus to a glowing light in the distance. As we got closer, I realized we were approaching an open underwater area that had a similar sheen to that of the Deep Realm. I popped out into breathable air inside of a vast room where the walls were either nonexistent or invisible. All I could see around me were vertical planes of water running from the floor to the ceiling.

Nechtan didn't come in with me but simply flung me. I stumbled to a stop on a mostly flat sea floor. Thankfully, it was dry inside the space, but it was a little disconcerting being surrounded by massive walls of water. As I looked around and felt the Well of Wisdom loom over and around me, I wondered if this was what Moses felt like when he parted the Red Sea.

There wasn't a soul in the enormous room with me. I turned to wave in the direction Nechtan, Connla, and I had come from, but when I looked into the water I realized it was opaque. There was no semi-translucent water layer covering up an aquatic landscape. Instead, there was a dark wall of undulating liquid that appeared to give off a faint glow. Looking around, I could see the same scene play out around the entire room.

"Hello?" I yelled into the airplane-hanger-sized room. There was no answer. I began to walk around the perimeter of the room, eyeing intently the various colors emanating from the water. When I looked more closely I could see the vaguest outlines of shapes moving inside of the water.

I focused harder and realized the various colors seemed to represent different scenes, and inside those scenes were different people and different landscapes. There must have been hundreds. This was a portal room, I realized, only the portals in question had no discernible borders. There were no wardrobes in this room, no Stargate, just an unseen transition from one portal to another on the surface of the vertical water. I did a double take in the direction of one scene when I realized the people and objects inside had changed from what had been there mere seconds before.

That scene in particular drew my attention, and I began to walk toward it. I could see darkness inside, but it was a different darkness than that of the underwater landscape. Inside the darkness were glowing points of light representing magic. I could see a variety of colors, illuminated by my racial ability that allowed such arcane identification. There were silvers and coppers, and even a few golds. Someday I needed to figure out what each of these colors meant.

All of these thoughts passed through my mind, as they often did, while I willingly wandered into danger. I realized too late that I was passing through the portal, into the dark room, as my whole leg disappeared into the space. The inertia of my motion carried the rest of me forward.

Upon standing fully in the dark room, I found the brightness level comfortable, like the inside of Isengard from the Peter Jackson movies. The dark stone walls and polished stone floor gave both the acoustics and visuals a vault-like vibe.

The room reminded me of the treasure room in Gorias, though this room was coated in a thick layer of dust. There were fewer gems and currency caches in this vault. Instead, sparse displays of weapons and a single suit of armor hung on the wall. The smooth floors were covered in dirty area rugs. Strange, almost holographic lights pulsed along the ceiling. A brazier flared to life in front of the armor as I stepped closer.

Now that I was close, I realized calling it a suit of armor was a little generous. It appeared to have a shoulder guard set attached to a significant-looking belt by crossing leather straps. Ornate golden metal plates connected to the straps in the sternum and lower abdomen areas. This was armor meant to protect the wearer from killing blows, but nothing more. To either side of the armor were gauntlets. Activating my Advanced Identification skill, I could feel my Battlesmith domain knowledge feeding the boon information.

> **Seolán Neimhe**
> **This Neartór Disc Armor once belonged to the sky god, Taranis. Its name means "Heaven's Channel." Originally designed to focus the raw fury of thunder and lightning, the disc armor amplifies the wielder's ability to attract and harness the weave.**

Before the description of the item had even finished, I had taken it off of the wall and affixed the belt to my waist. The rest of the pieces went on easily enough, and once I was completely adorned in the Sky God's armor, I felt a slight hum throughout my body. I caught a yellow glow emanating from the abdominal disc and watched as a solitary spark arced to the right gauntlet. The amount of energy that I could draw on from my Control Energy boon had just doubled. It was as if the very weave was drawn to me. Instinctively, I reached for the nearest sword and lifted it into the air. Then I mouthed the words, "I have the power!" Eat your heart out, He-Man.

The technicolor holographic lights that flashed on the ceiling began to elongate and stretch in my direction. It gave the room an odd hue, reminding me of the sky before a tornado. The brazier on the floor of the chamber began to flare in my direction, only the fire was not true fire. This was clearly a magical light source, and it was almost like the magic felt compelled to get closer to me.

"I see you've found Eiocha's hidden armory." The voice came from behind me, near where I had entered the room. I turned to see a gray-haired man garbed in a tattered blue robe standing near the portal. "Be careful with that, lad. You could suck this room dry of magic, and then where would we be? You would pop like a ripe fruit."

I didn't need to ask if this man was Lir. Not only did every part of him scream god of the Sea, but I was having a hard time untangling myself from the various points of energy trying to attach itself to me.

"How do I turn it off?" I asked. I was beginning to feel a bit overwhelmed by the seemingly unending energy assault.

The man chuckled, and that instantly irritated me. I clenched my teeth together and tried my best to get a handle on the sheer amount of ambient energy trying to force itself into me. My eyes closed on instinct and I exhaled.

"Interesting," I heard Lir say. "Not all can wield the personal effects of the Síorláidir."

And with the utterance of that word, Síorláidir, I lost all concentration. My eyes flicked open to look at the man, and the brightness of the weave almost blinded me. The energy began to bombard my body, leaving me a limp, helpless vessel for unrelenting magic.

CHAPTER 5:
TOURS BY ERELITH

< FÍADAN >

Day 13 of Midwinter, Sunrise
Caisleán Saighead, Gorias
Annwn

"You must be Elsa," I muttered to the Ellyllon at my door. She was clothed head to toe in a full-body black suit of armor, leaving only her face visible. It was a stark contrast in all of its pale glory.

"Erelith, my Captaen."

She had a mess of hot pink hair barely wrangled by a delicate arrangement of flowers. Her wings were iridescian, an extremely rare pattern in Ellyllon culture. They glimmered with all the colors of the rainbow. She was both strikingly beautiful and delicate... everything I hated.

"I was afraid you would be the one with crooked hair," I motioned with my hands at the side of my head, thinking of the earlier Ellyllon's side ponytail. "She was a peach."

"Nimeth is dead, my Captaen."

"What?" I drew back, shocked. "And stop calling me 'Captaen.' I'm no one's Captaen now."

The beautiful fairy inclined her head. "Nimeth died by Fomorian hands. She refused to be taken prisoner in the invasion."

I nodded, considering. "Good for her."

"What?" Erelith asked, sounding confused.

I shrugged. "She died in service, not taking any chet from those stilted sea-farts."

Erelith appeared to be at a loss for words.

I sighed quietly. It was as I had expected. This generation of Ellyllon was soft. The King's Guard that I had served with would have been proud to die in service to Bres.

"Anyway…" she said, motioning at me to follow. "I am to take you around the castle so you can see the work that has been done while you have been… recovering."

I took a moment to take another look around my old room. There were so many memories here. Despite my refusal to return, Brigid and Bres had managed to preserve the room. It looked exactly as it had the day I had left. I could see no damage from the Fomorian raid. It was a time capsule from a better time.

I shook myself free from my nostalgia, pocketed Bren's seashell and ring, and followed the very colorful Queen's Guard out of the room and around the massive castle. Erelith's features remained impassive, unchanged by even my most outlandish comments.

The castle was abuzz with activity. There were changeling and Ellyllon soldiers everywhere. Some were clearly on duty, based on their armaments, while others were cleaning and clearing debris. Some wielded a hammer and nails. Townspeople milled about, seeming to have free rein of the grounds. Each appeared to have a specialty that they employed to repair the damage the recent incursion and battle had caused.

Each member of the guard or the community that we saw saluted as we passed. At first, I believed they were paying their respects to the highest-ranking Queen's Guard, which would have been customary, but by the tenth or eleventh salute, I had the uncomfortable realization they were addressing me.

"What is going on?" I asked the walking rainbow leading me around. I was starting to feel like this was less of a tour and more of a parade. "Why are all of these people being… nice to me?"

"They just wish to show their gratitude, my captaen."

"I told you to stop calling me that!" The word had not been used to describe me in a very long time, and I itched at the sudden change.

More townsfolk passed by and saluted. From the look of the burn marks on their clothing and the heavy leather aprons, these had the look of blacksmiths. "Captaen!" they said in unison. I frowned.

"Why do you look so angry?" Erelith asked with genuine confusion.

"That is your title, not mine. The better question is, why are you so comfortable with them disrespecting you?"

She took a long moment to consider my question, though her face remained completely unmoved. "You are the last King's Guard."

"So what?" I interrupted. I had lived countless moons in seclusion. The old times had faded from people's hearts and tongues long ago. "Why does that matter now?"

"Because you give them something to believe in again…You give us all something to believe in." The fairy waited until another group of people had passed, then continued. "I know you exiled yourself after the Fall of Gorias. I suspect that you pushed the memory of your time in the Guard so far from your mind and assumed that even the others had forgotten…and many did. They forgot about your sacrifice. But now they are remembering that you have been here all along."

"I don't need a pep-talk from you, kid," I muttered, feeling the familiar weight of old regrets pressing in.

"Don't you feel it?" she asked, her neutral expression softening just slightly. "A new age is dawning."

I scowled at her, even though I knew she was right. I had felt it since the night of the Cold Moon.

"It matters," Erelith continued. "Because the Silverwhite blades represent something we wish we could all be."

"What?" I asked. I found myself truly curious about what she might say.

"Fearless and honorable." Her voice caught, and for the first time, I saw the faintest flicker of emotion in her eyes. "Selfless."

I looked at the young Ellyllon. Her face betrayed no shame at having let slip how she felt. It was all too serious for my liking.

"You forgot wise and benevolent," I cracked.

She smiled softly and began walking. I followed, glad she hadn't pressed her point. I respected her more for it. She led me from one end of the castle to the other. Once I became accustomed to the attention, the parade began to feel more like the tour it was meant to be, and I saw the state of things.

Not all workers were focused on repairs. Many worked to strip the dead of their pilfered booty. I saw Morias there, overseeing the organization of the items and the coin. The treasure vault was being filled again.

Badb assisted with the collection of stolen items from their own troops. It seemed that even those under the influence of the god of frenzy were not immune to the lure of greed. What they couldn't do was hide that greed from the god of fate.

Nemain's job appeared to be rounding up the survivors of both armies, which she then redistributed into companies under each banner, the red of Gorias and the green of Findrias. After the ground troops were organized to her liking, I knew she would shift her focus to the Gorias navy.

I grimaced, seeing Nemain's fiacha shadowing her wherever she went. They wore their cruelty on their faces as they made sure the soldiers followed Nemain's every command. They seemed to have gained a mystique, based on the changelings' fearful whispers about what they had seen of the brutalized remains of the Fomorians who had crossed blades with those Ellyllon.

In stark contrast, I witnessed a rare, but not unwelcome, sighting of Aengus Og in the courtyard. The handsome god was enlisting and initiating a whole continent of townsfolk into the Gorias military. He mingled and laughed among the people there. He embraced them and appreciated them, and they loved him like a brother for it.

I didn't see the third sister in or around the castle. But then, Macha had never been one to get her hands dirty. She was more at home in the throne rooms and courthouses than on the battlefield. Funny, that... Politics had always made me feel grimier than any dirt or blood.

Erelith was about to lead me back into the castle when a cheer went up among the new recruits. "Captaen!" someone shouted.

The cheering spread like wild magic in a summer storm, and before long, everyone in the courtyard had joined in. The shouting cheers coalesced into a unified chant of "Captaen! Captaen!"

I suddenly became very self-conscious of my broken wing. I found myself unable to raise my eyes to meet those of the frenzied soldiers, but I did finally peek up, making eye contact with Nemain. The edge of her mouth was curled up in a cross between a smile and a sneer. I didn't know what her expression meant, but I did wonder if Nemain's frenzy domain hadn't added to the reaction of the people in the courtyard.

Erelith seemed to sense my discomfort. She turned to lead me back into the interior of the castle, away from the chanting.

We made our way toward the meeting room where Bren, Morias, Tadg, and I had learned about the death of Bres. The walls still held the scorch marks from where Brigid had called on her fire domain to stop me from attacking her Queen's Guard.

"I am to leave you here," Erelith started to say something else, but I held out a finger to stop her. I had heard my fill of Captaens for the day. She stared at my face for a moment, then quietly took her exit.

I wasn't alone in the room. I turned to the god of fealty and the god of magic, who sat at the far end of the long table. Macha and The

Dagda waited patiently for me and the rest of the Tuatha Dé Danann to join the first council meeting presided over by someone other than Brigid or Bres.

I bowed low to the patriarch of Gorias and heard his voice echo in my mind.

CHAPTER 6:

THE BALLAD OF BOLD BREN THE BARE

< TADG >

Day 14 of Midwinter, Sunset
Outskirts of Cluain Toradh
Annwn

I rode until well into the night, finally forced to slow when I could no longer see more than an arm's length in front of Gaoth. Though I was sure the horse could see well enough in the dark, I could not, and some dangers in the Midlands gave no second chance. I needed to see any enemies coming.

I'd hoped to reach the great farmlands and orchards of Cluain Toradh while staying clear of its sprawling namesake, the farm Baile Toradh. I needed a safe place where I could let my trusty mount graze and water himself. A thick grove of peach trees in the northern orchards would provide me some cover.

I'd ridden hard all day, my chest and ribs aching despite Gaoth's sure footing. The hours had melted together eventually, allowing my thoughts to spiral out of control. I found myself thinking about my time with Bren before and after Inis Fer Falga.

When his head had popped up over the side of The Whiskey Wind, I had been filled with hope. Never before had someone risked themselves so overtly for my benefit. While my brothers had defended me as a child, I had always known that their defense had merely been a defense of our family name and therefore themselves.

Bren, however, was a true friend, something I hadn't expected. I didn't fault him for lashing out at me in the prisons of the Deep Realm. I deserved much worse than his burst of energy magic. He could have tortured or killed me, but as quickly as it had come, his rage had eased. He could have even simply left me to rot in prison, but instead, he had taken me out and delivered me unto destiny's door. The moment had changed me.

Even now, I felt conflicted—torn between being the son my father expected and the man I seemed to be becoming. If I had walked away from Bren and his cause, I might have kept my father's respect. But I would've stayed blind.

Father had always said a ruler must always choose the righteous path, no matter the cost. He was my father, larger than life, and the leader of our people. I had followed him so blindly, trusting that he knew what was best. I had the uncomfortable realization that everyone thinks their path is righteous, but that didn't make it so. When I looked back at his decisions and my own part in them, I knew I'd been following the wrong man. This new path that I was on, both physical and spiritual, felt like a betrayal, but also…right.

The days ahead would be dangerous. I traveled through lands where the fae would not take kindly to a lone changeling traveler, let alone one so close in proximity to the crown. I had to remain hidden, traveling swiftly and silently around Tech Duinn. I had no intention of getting close to the hills and crags surrounding that fire-breathing mountain, as those were the home of the giants and the ogres.

Even the plains nearby contained all manner of fae whose allegiances had been questionable even before the Slaugh Doctrine had soured them further on the throne. The small villages and hamlets in these lands were filled with changelings so far removed from the Tuatha that they would be more closely aligned with the wild fae than with the laws and order of Falias. I was hoping to avoid all manner of living and nonliving creatures on my eastern path.

I was shaking from my thoughts as Gaoth's sure footing caught a root in the path. The warhorse's slight stumble caused pain to ripple through my ribs. I'd been mostly able to ignore the small bit of discomfort that each breath caught me, but now and again, a sudden movement or shift of weight brought sharp pain that took my breath away.

I took that moment to focus on my most recent power rank notification. It had come after we battled the Bodach. Father had commissioned Uncle Ogma to gift his sons with a Basic Identification anointment when they came of age.

Name: Tadg mac Nuadat
Race: Changeling
Current Power Rank - Level 21

Current Progression Status:
Physical Progression +26
Mental Progression +23
Spiritual Progression +21

I focused on my physical progression, drilling into my injuries:

Current Physical Injuries:
Broken Ribs x2, Left Side
Small Lung Puncture, Left Lung
Minimal Lung Collapse, Left Lung

No surprise there. I had assessed myself immediately after the enraged Bren had left my cell in the Deep Realm. My injuries had not gotten any worse. The healing process was simply painful.

I marveled at the power rank notification. It had been years since I ranked up from Level 19 to 20. But in the span of the last three weeks, I had noticed a sizable difference in my experience earned. Could it be related to my recent adventuring with the god of Chaos?

I would have parsed that out more in my mind, but the reality of my physical environment pulled my attention back into the present. Gaoth was closing in quickly on Baile Toradh. The sheer scale of the farm had always impressed me, no matter how many times I had seen it.

The old trees of the farm extended as far as I could see. They had been planted in orderly rows and columns, meaning I would need to move far into the trees to be obscured from view. I dismounted, walking Gaoth between the low-lying branches. We made our way behind a particularly large tree.

"Thank you, my friend," I said to the horse, placing my hand on his warm shoulder. Gaoth nuzzled me with his nose, blasting me with a breath of hot air. He turned to clop to the nearby stream, drinking long and deep. I smiled, calling "Don't go far, I need your eyes and ears."

Gaoth's ears twitched in acknowledgment. Done drinking, he stepped further into the trees, moving out of my visual range. The trees concealed what little light the moon supplied. It was nearly pitch black where I stood, and only the hours spent in gradually increasing darkness aided my eyes.

I carefully removed my breastplate and attempted to stretch my back and legs without further stressing my aching ribcage. In the near silence of the woods, my ears caught a surprising sound. It came from farther south, into the orchard. The smoky scent of a campfire made its way to my nose, hanging low under the canopy of the peach leaves.

I stood still, weighing my options. It would be so easy to do nothing, to simply sit at the base of the tree and close my eyes or gather up Gaoth and make my way farther east. But the truth is, I found myself tired of riding and curious. At this distance, the sound was formless. It could be almost anything here in Mag Mell. The only thing to be done was to investigate.

I crept stealthily toward the noise, taking note of the features of each peach tree so that I could find my way back to Gaoth. As I drew near, the sounds took on a clarity and revealed themselves to me. A company of six men and women had made camp for the night in a clearing up ahead.

A laughing voice called out "Oisín! Sing it already."

I stood in the darkness of the trees, some distance away, and watched as a bard, who must be Oisín, strummed a beautiful cittern. The wood of the instrument was a deep mahogany color, and it had wear marks where hours of constant hand movements had smoothed and faded the wood.

The four changeling men and two women around the fire had the look of warriors. The group listened intently and some even sang along as Oisín's voice rose.

I'll tell ye a tale from the old orchard trail,
Where the moss grows thick and the roots never fail.

As the bard's fingers flew over his cittern, I studied the people around the fire. They carried weapons and sported armor, though most had taken off their protection for the day. The women flanked one man, who sat staring into the fire. Looking more closely, I could see the man had a very prominent birthmark in the middle of his forehead. He looked familiar for some reason.

We crept through the brambles and what did we see?
A man in the mud, rollin' wild and free
With an ogre half-covered with tooth and with hair,
And standing there grinning was bold Bren the Bare!

Though I hadn't been listening very closely to the song the bard was singing, the last line caught my attention. "And standing there grinning was bold Bren the Bare?"

My attention now caught, I continued to listen. The song went on to talk about Bold Bren the Bare washing himself in a pool of water while being watched by the Morrigan's raven before being arrested by the "king's men." Could this song be about Bren Búachaill?

The bard's voice rose in volume as several of the changeling warriors clapped and stomped their feet in tune.

So mind where you wander and try not to stare,
Where there's mud on the ground and some fruit in the air,
For gods only know what you'll find over there—
You might just run into our bold Bren the Bare!

There was no doubt in my mind now. The song could only be about my friend, now apparently a folk hero. I chuckled to myself and then went cold as I realized the man with the birthmark was no longer staring into the fire. His gaze was focused directly on me.

CHAPTER 7:

WOMEN OF THE SEA

< CAI >

Day 14 of Midwinter, Sunset
The Deep Realm
Annwn

The fallen that weren't burned immediately were paraded through the Deep Realm as heroes. At the head of the procession rode the body of King Neit. I did not escort our dead but met Tethra and the other Fomorian warriors at the "Hanging Tower" in Túr Crochta, the city's center.

"So now, what?" Ruadan asked me. He hadn't left my side for hours.

"Now Tethra becomes queen, and we wait to see how Hightower responds."

He raised his eyebrows. "You know how they are going to respond."

"I do," I admitted.

"And is it intuition or that new-fangled boon of yours making this particular prediction?"

"The Divination of Balance boon is not so cut and dry. It only allows me to see disharmonies... it doesn't show me how to fix or change them." I thought about what the boon had shown me. Our invasion of Brú na Dallta seemed to have thrown everything into chaos.

Ruadan nodded. He watched as the larger men and women marched into Túr Crochta, where they reverently laid our many dead. "So are we farthed or not?"

"Pretty much. But then again, Bren is off with the Cupbearer. Perhaps he will bring back good news."

"You're waiting on the god of chaos to bring you good news? We are definitely farthed."

I shook my head at him, smothering a chuckle. I could always count on Ruadan to lighten the mood, even on such a dark day as this. "Come on, Red. It's time to pay our condolences to Dubhlinn and Morvra."

We walked to the end of the parade route, near the line of dispersing warriors. Tethra stood there, surrounded by four women. Three were human, the fourth a Fomorian.

I approached the women, inclining my head in respect. "Hail, Mná na Mara." This was the customary greeting for the "Women of the Sea," a highly venerated group of wives, mothers, and daughters of kings, or in one case, a future queen. These women had earned my respect. While every woman in the upper echelon of Fomorian society was eligible to be a member, simply being a woman was not sufficient. Each member of the Mná na Mara was a warrior in her own right.

Together they made up Tethra's retinue. The first of these were the last surviving widows of former King Neit. Dubhlinn was the mother of Corb. Morvra was the mother of Tethra. The third human, Cethlenn, was the wife of Balor. Their Fomorian daughter, Ethlinn, was the mother of Lugh. I felt a pang, remembering the Tuatha I had killed in self-defense back on Emain Ablach.

These were the women who had the pulse of the people in the Deep Realm. While the king may have led the army and made important decrees, it was the Mná na Mara who worked the political magic behind the scenes.

Unfortunately, I knew that most of these women were no fans of mine. Despite adhering to a strict warrior's code, Cethlenn and Ethlinn would never forgive me for killing their kin. While they knew Lugh had aligned himself with the Tuatha, over the Fomorians, and had died in fair combat, they had never fully accepted me as one of their own. The grace of being an adopted son, even one of their beloved king, only went so far.

Dubhlinn followed the lead of her son, Corb, who had followed Balor on the offensive. Dubhlinn had therefore been vocally opposed to the plans of the former king and I.

Ultimately, though the whole Mná na Mara had supported our invasion of Brú na Dallta, my only true allies in this influential group were Tethra and her mother, Morvra.

"Hail, Maccán," the women said in one voice. They did not address Ruadan. He was even more of an outsider here than I was, maybe more now than ever before, for it was the king who had officially welcomed him in at my recommendation. He remained a step behind me, keeping his head bowed.

"We wish to pay our respects, Mistress Dubhlinn and Mistress Morvra." The pair nodded in acknowledgment. I knew it was one of many such exchanges they would have had throughout what had been a long day. I turned to my adopted sister, catching her striking midnight eyes.

"Lord Tethra, I wonder if we might have a word about the ceremony."

Tethra nodded, then turned to the Mná na Mara to say her goodbyes. The three of us walked together in the direction of the throne room.

After a few quiet moments, I asked the question weighing on my heart. "Will there be any challengers?"

As we entered the stone hall at the center of the great stalactite, Tethra slowed, appearing to take in the details of the room.

"Dubhlinn thinks we should separate the ceremony from the funeral."

"Of course she does," Ruadan grumbled. "It must chap her arse that Corb wasn't considered."

"To be fair, with Elatha and Balor dead, Elatha's family killed, and Balor's family intertwined with the Tuatha, Corb was next in line." I had never met Elatha or his family. Whoever had killed the Prince had made sure to leave no loose ends. His wife Aoibhinn and his daughter Briomhaith had disappeared, leaving only bloodstains in Briomhaith's bedchamber. Their story remained one of tragedy and mystery.

My mind drifted to those family members that I did know and the heated debates that were held in this very room. "Except Corb is just as culpable as Balor in terms of going against his king's wishes."

"Dubhlinn will not interfere with the ceremony." Tethra gave me a pointed look. "Why do you ask of challengers?"

Tethra knew me so well… and she knew of my boon, and likely suspected the reason for my asking was my fear of the immediate future, one I could see was awash in disharmony.

"Up overhead, I was trying out a form of meditation that my brother had mentioned. In clearing out all the distractions, I began to see… tendrils. It is the best way I can describe it. It is as if reality is hazy. The tendrils went off into the distance, out to sea."

"Is that how you typically see disharmonies?" my future queen asked.

"That is typically how you see a crazy person," Ruadan quipped.

Tethra gave Ruadan a dirty look. "I wonder if these tendrils are trying to show you how Nuada will try to bring doom to our islands."

"I wondered the same thing," I admitted. "I do think they represent a fleet sailing toward Inis fer Falga, but…"

"Why is there always a but?" Ruadan rolled his eyes and perched on one of the stone half-tables.

"The tendrils are here now, in THIS room," I continued, feeling a chill run up my spine.

"I see. Whatever is going to happen is going to happen in this room." Tethra nodded to herself. "I trust your foresight, Béstin. It has served us well. But have you checked the Diviner lately?"

"The bloody thing doesn't work on Nuada any longer," Ruadan muttered. "I've been trying all afternoon. Maybe I have a kink for spying on people… Any chance I can borrow that thing when the war is over?"

It was my turn to roll my eyes. Before I could reply, the pallbearers of King Neit entered the throne room. We watched in silence as they placed his ornate casket on the pyre at the center of the room, just below the huge, candle-filled chandelier. Light from the large opening above the chandelier streamed down into the room. I knew smoke would vent out the opening when the king's pyre was lit.

When the pallbearers exited the room, Tethra picked up our conversation. "I don't see how this information helps us."

"Agreed," I said. "Just…be ready for anything during the ceremony."

Tethra shook her head. Her face remained serious for a brief moment before she shot me a quick smirk. "You know, it's not too late to nominate you instead of me."

"You really think that will be good for his ego?!" Ruadan joked, shooting me a double pistol salute.

"I don't want it any more than you do," I admitted. "But at least you know you will have one loyal subject." I smiled, looking at Ruadan. "Make that one and a half." Ruadan turned his pistol fingers into middle fingers.

A bell rang across the city, the faint sound audible even through the heavy double doors of the throne room. We looked around at each other in silence, knowing that our time together was over. Soon the room would fill up with dignitaries and relatives of the former king.

I studied Tethra's strong arms and beautiful blond braids, the gleam of Orna, her infamous sword. I looked at my friend and confidant, the future queen of the Fomorians, watching in fear as the hazy tendrils grew, coalesced, and encircled both her and Ruadan.

CHAPTER 8:

EIOCHA'S ARMORY

< BREN >

Day 14 of Midwinter, Sunset
At Sea, Well of Wisdom
Annwn

I managed to wrestle the gauntlets off first. From there, I disconnected the belt and shoulder guards. Lir simply watched with an air of amusement, though I noticed he didn't get any closer during the energy flare-up.

"I'm… Bren," I tried to say, teetering on shaky legs… and was that burnt toast I suddenly smelled?

Lir looked me up and down. "Are you well?"

"I think so." I glanced back down at the armor. "Did someone actually wear that armor?"

"Not since the founding of the great cities."

I thought maybe he was speaking about Falias, Gorias, Murias, and Findrias, but things were still a little fuzzy in my shell-shocked brain. "I want to know more about…what's-his-name… but I'm having a hard time focusing right now." My vision swam.

Lir came forward and took the sword from my hands. He gently leaned it back on the wall and led me to a chair. "Taranis was a Síorláidir. Like you, it would seem."

"Like me…" I chuckled. "Before you tell me anything else about the sky god, can you please start with what Síorláidir means?"

"You don't know what you are?" Lir's lips twitched. He seemed genuinely amused by my complete and utter confusion. My physical disorientation seemed to add to his amusement.

"I haven't really had a chance to learn about my…uh…recent changes. I was saving a long list of questions for Morias for the next time I see him." I paused, thinking about my friend and caretaker. The last time I had seen Morias, he was unconscious atop the parapet in Gorias. Thanks to Nemain, I at least knew he and Fíadan were still alive.

Lir nodded. "You can ask me your questions if you like."

"No offense, but so far your brothers and sisters haven't really given me much reason to trust members of your family."

"Hence why I left."

That statement gave me pause. I hadn't considered what Lir's reason for leaving the court of the Overking might be until now, but it made sense. Before I could think better of it, I blurted, "You know, your brother is a real dink."

Lir looked confused. "I'm afraid I don't know what a 'dink' is."

I ignored him. I didn't think I could define it either, come to think of it. "Let's just say that Nuada locked up his own son just because he admitted to being my friend."

"My brother does not forget perceived slights," he said. I raised my eyebrows, letting him know I thought this was maybe a bit of an understatement. Unfazed, he continued, "You asked about the Síorláidir?"

I nodded.

"I once thought that the Síorláidir were the lost powers of the realms. They were the gods of this world before the coming of my family."

"What do you mean you 'once thought' they were the lost powers?"

He smiled. "That is what I believed… until a Síorláidir came to visit me at Tir fo Thuinn and nearly exploded himself playing with the sky god's armor."

"Har de har har," I muttered, realizing he was talking about me. I waved at him to keep talking.

"Mother Danu was among their number, as was Father Death."

"Donn?" I asked, trying to remember the Tuatha patriarch's name.

"Indeed. My brothers and I called them the 'Greater Gods,' or the 'Old Powers.' They represent the dualistic nature of the realms"

"Danu represents life and Donn represents death. The same duality exists between my brother and I. We are Harmony and Chaos." I had cobbled together some rudimentary knowledge of my own duality in the last two weeks, so I actually knew what he was talking about. Sort of. "What were some of the others?"

Lir motioned to the armor sitting in a heap in front of me. "Taranis was the god of the heavens. His counterpart was Eiocha, the embodiment of the land and sea. Eiocha built this room, as a refuge, when the Síorláidir began to disappear."

I shook my head as I tried to wrap my mind around a second pantheon of gods in this crazy world. Then I had a thought… was there only one pantheon at a time? It seemed like it. The Síorláidir were the first generation of gods in Annwn. Lir and his Tuatha brothers and sisters came about as the old gods were disappearing. "Does that mean Danu and Donn were the last of the dualistic gods?"

"Until the night of the Cold Moon, yes." Lir paused, looking away from me. He scanned the room, appearing to take inventory of each weapon, bit, and bauble lying around. "I've never been able to enter this gateway before."

He stood and extended a hand, helping me to my feet. I staggered at first, as a wave of dizziness came and went, leaving me feeling mostly normal. "You mentioned Tir fo Thuinn. Is that the underwater room I was just in?"

Lir had stepped away from me and appeared to be assessing the various items in the room. His voice was distracted. "Yes. Its name roughly translates to 'The Land Under the Waves.' It is a means to and from Annwn for those in need."

"A portal room," I said, pondering his words. "Why haven't you come into this room before?"

Lir glanced back at me, looking troubled. "The 'portals' change and fluctuate according to the needs and the deeds of those across the realms. Though I have seen this gateway before, it has never presented an opportunity for my entry." As he spoke, he carefully examined weapons and other items, lifting and discarding each in turn, before continuing his circumnavigation of the room.

And me? I found myself eyeing a nearby flask Lir had already assessed and discarded. My thoughts drifted, again, to Morias. He had always carried a flask with him. The last time I had seen that flask, it had contained magic water that he made me drink. Never mind that it was water he had wrung out of his clothing after a swim in the Heart-shaped Pool. I shuddered, remembering, then reached out and pocketed the flask. Clearly, it wasn't of interest to Lir.

I heard a clatter from the other side of the room. "You don't see this every day," Lir said. He reached into the cold forge, pulling out a dark staff with a large knot on the end. "A Lustrum alloy shillelagh." He tossed the staff and I caught it with ease.

I turned the imperfect staff around in my hands, testing the properties. Though it appeared to have been forged intentionally crooked, the length and weight felt… somehow right. The gnarled, misshapen knot on the end made for a great handhold, and also, I suspected, a brutal hammerhead.

The staff had looked black at first, but now that I angled it in the light, I could see a rainbow of colors within the darkness. With a start, I realized the staff was made of the same alloy as the meshmail

Ruadan had given me in Gorias. I used my Advanced Identification boon to get more information:

Cast Lustrum Shillelagh
Lustrum is an alloy made from cold iron mixed with smelted Duinnite ore. It contains some of the lightness and durability of grown Silverwhite, but allows the metal to be forged or shaped. This weapon was cast from an ancient Blackthorn shillelagh and retains each thorn scar and knot of the original.

Your domain classification, Battlesmith, allows you the ability to modify this weapon with little or no equipment. This item is a lustrum shillelagh. Would you like to MODIFY this item?

I mentally focused on NOT modifying the ancient weapon. Instead, I placed the tip to the ground and transferred some of my weight onto the non-wooden, very metal walking stick. It was a weird weapon to want to hold on to, but in a strange way, it felt very me.

"Bren," Lir called. He stood next to the portal leading back to the large underwater room. "Grab the armor and come with me. There is something I need you to do."

CHAPTER 9:
THE NEW COUNCIL

< FÍADAN >

Day 13 of Midwinter, Midday
Caisleán Saighead, Gorias
Annwn

I had slipped Bren's ring on while I was nervously fidgeting in the courtyard. It seemed I had somehow activated it when I saw the Dagda…allowing me to get my first-ever power rank notification.

Name: Fíadan Ellyllon
Race: Fairy
Current Power Rank - Level 52

Current Progression Status:
Physical Progression +52
Mental Progression +42
Spiritual Progression +10

Innate Racial Abilities:
Fairy Trance
Gloaming Gaze

Fae Speech
Flight (Unavailable)

Four magic items are in your possession.

You have acquired:
The Silverwhite short sword, Swish
The Silverwhite dagger, Stick
The Rings of Identification
The Green Gem of Riftwalking (0 charges)

Item abilities unlocked:
Unbreakable- Swish and Stick
Soulbound- Swish and Stick
Veil Rift- The Green Gem of Riftwalking

You have one pact:
Protect the family line of Gorias (failed)

I looked up from the ring to see The Dagda approaching. He assumed a double-kneed bow in front of me so that we were mostly at eye level. Macha scoffed behind him.

"It is strange hearing your voice in my head, Lord," I told him.

He took my hands in his. "I see you have the ring I gave to Morias all those years ago."

"Technically, I think I stole it from Bren, but he isn't using it at the moment."

"Come, let's get off of our knees. I'm unaccustomed to assuming this position. I find it isn't particularly comfortable." Rising, he kept one of my hands in his. Together we walked back to his original, seated position next to the frowning Macha.

"That was not very dignified, uncle," she said.

"He didn't ask you," is what I tried to say, but of course, nothing came out. Stupid Morrigan and their even stupider boons!

The Dagda, seeing that I was under the influence of Macha's domain, hid a smile with a small cough.

The entryway door opened, and a line of council members made their way to their seats. Nemain was there, thankfully without her fiacha. Badb entered as well, Morias at her side. And Aengus brought up the rear… and what a rear it was!

There were six members in all from across Emain Ablach. Two members of the Gorias nobility, three members from Findrias, and the lone Sage. I moved to stand, but The Dagda squeezed my hand as if signaling me to stay. I froze, understanding his intent. If I remained at the table, it would mark another first for me… though I had attended many council meetings over the years, I had never been included as an actual participant until now.

Macha cleared her throat as though she were about to call the meeting to order, then seemed to think better of it. She turned to the Dagda. "Uncle, would you care to start us off?"

The room quieted as he began to speak. "First, let me say, that I'm pleased to have our relatives from the east here among us. Without your aid, none of us would be sitting here right now. Second, I would like to thank Fíadan and Nemain for the risks they took, especially beneath the wall." His eyes lingered on the space my wing should have been. "Without your courage and sacrifice, Morias would still be in chains…or worse."

"As would many of our guards and Ellyllon," Aengus added, his expression serious. The Dagda nodded, turning to face his son.

"Thirdly, I would like to thank my son. Without his help, we would have never been able to gain entry to the last redort." His eyes twinkled at the fatherly pun. Nemain groaned quietly.

"Finally, I would like to thank he who has truly lived up to his name, Bren Búachaill, the Protector. Without his swift action in Findrias and upon the wall, Balor would have seen the whole castle burn."

"Speaking of our long-lost savior," I interrupted. "Can we get a status on him from our eyes in the sky?" The council members turned as one to Nemain.

"Bren is well enough," she said finally. "Though I do not understand his actions fully."

"That makes seven of us," I quipped. I couldn't help myself.

Macha glared at me again. "Last I saw him, he had just stowed away on a Fomorian vessel. I believe Tadg had been captured, and Bren sought to free him."

"Ruadan is with them," Badb chimed in.

"That's right," Nemain finished. "Ruadan and Bren were on the shores of Inis Fer Falga when I saw them go underground."

Macha's eyes widened. "You have been to the Isle of the Protected Men!" She cast her eyes around the table, barely able to contain her excitement. "Then, you can direct the fleet to their very door."

Nemain looked to The Dagda as if for clarity on the type of protection magic that was laid upon those islands. He nodded somberly.

I took the shell out of my pocket and slid it across the table to Nemain. "The next time you spy on him, would you have one of your Crow-verts give him this?"

"You really need to work on your diplomacy, Ellyllon." Macha's tone was degrading, but she wasn't wrong. I really wanted to get angry with her, but I found that her words made more sense to me the longer I thought about them. I thought hard for a moment.

"Gossip Gulls, then?" I asked. "Creeper Corps?"

A guffaw burst out of Aengus, but a look from his mother quieted him. Still, the handsome man couldn't manage to hide a grin.

Nemain took the shell. "I will deliver this Shell of Promise to our hero of Harmony."

"About that..." Morias said, barely beating The Dagda to a rebuttal. "I don't believe Bren is the god of Harmony."

The Dagda nodded. "The Sage is correct. I believe Bren has recently been granted the domain of chaos."

That actually made a lot more sense to me. The craziest chet happened when Bren was around. Random evil fae and Old Power attacks. Ending up on Tadg's horse. Bumping into The Dagda in Ériu.

"That means he really is a part of a duality, with his brother," Badb thought aloud.

"I have a theory on this very topic, one that I would like to explore further in the lab of the former Sage, Urias," Morias said, his voice solemn. "I ask for Fíadan's assistance in this task… with the council's permission, of course."

Macha rolled her eyes. "Fine, Sage. Let us return to more important things. For example… the communications beacon of Gorias is not working. We have no way to communicate with the other castles."

"As discussed, I will work on that." The Dagda said with a sigh. "It is a magical communication system, and I will repair it." It was obvious from his expression that this topic had come up before.

"Are we not going to talk about the most important thing?" Aengus asked, his voice harsher and angrier than I had ever heard it. The council members turned to him in surprise. None of us could remember the last time Aengus had raised his voice.

"Where is Brigid? Where is my sister?"

CHAPTER 10:

DIARMUID OF THE LOVE SPOT

< TADG >

Day 14 of Midwinter, Sunset
In the Wild, Midlands
Annwn

"Come, join us at our fire," said the man with the birthmark on his forehead. At his words, the strumming music stopped. The remaining five pairs of eyes turned in my direction. I stepped out from behind the tree as smoothly as I could, trying not to spook the group of warriors.

"I heard the music," I began, my voice trailing off. "And thought I might share your fire if you are so inclined."

"Someone actually came toward your music instead of running away," one of the women said with a laugh. The others chuckled, one elbowing the bard good-naturedly. The bard, Oisín, gave the woman a look of mock outrage, but even from here, I could see his eyes gleaming with mirth…and, I realized the effects of some type of alcohol.

The man with the birthmark, clearly their leader, kept his eyes on me. It was clear that he was unsure whether I was friend or foe. My next words would be critical in avoiding unnecessary violence.

My mind flicked back to the song the bard had been singing. "Was that song about a man named Bren Búachaill?"

The bard set carefully set down his beautiful cittern and began to rise. The leader stopped him with a word, "Sit." The other four changelings quieted immediately, their faces sober.

"Who are you, friend, and from where have you come?" The stoic man remained seated, with his hand casually easing nearer the hilt of his sword, which was resting on the ground in its sheath.

My mind feverishly raced through possible answers. I knew the best course of action would be to give an alias and a false destination, but I found the idea strangely disturbing. Even after everything I had discovered, it was not in me to deny the name given to me by my father.

"Tadg," I said, stepping closer to the man, keeping my hands loose and unthreatening at my sides. "I left Brú na Dallta at dawn." These partial truths answered his questions, without giving so much as to put me at risk. "I find myself wearied after a long day of riding and appreciate your hospitality."

The man nodded, his eyes still sharp. "I am Diarmuid. These are members of our fianna." He motioned around the group, starting with the two women. "This is Gráinne and Muireann, and these lads are Rónán and Caolán. The bard there is Oisín."

I managed to keep my face from betraying any emotion at the man's use of the term "Fianna." I saw now just what I had blundered into. The fianna were bands of independent warriors who traveled around Annwn righting wrongs and settling scores according to the warrior-chief's unique brand of honor. There were multiple fianna roaming the Midlands, some of which I had dealings with during my time at the Heart-shaped Pool. Generally, the fianna did good deeds and saved the Falias military countless days in maintaining domestic order.

"Pleased to meet you," I said, slowly stepping nearer the fire. "I had hoped to travel farther, but the darkness is thick, and I was forced to stop for the night."

"Did you say that you came from Brú na Dallta this Sunrise?" Gráinne scooted closer to Diarmuid as she spoke. "That is a long ride."

I nodded at the woman, then crouched down by the fire. It was difficult to keep my expression relaxed as my broken ribs screamed in protest at the movement. I needed to keep my injuries a secret, just in case I ended up in a confrontation with this group.

The fire warmed my chest, and it occurred to me suddenly that I had left my breastplate at the edge of the woods. That was good in one respect... while I'd be without its protection, the quality of the armor was such that it would likely have given away my pedigree.

Diarmuid raised an eyebrow. "Beautiful sword you have there," he said, his tone dry.

Dwal... armor or no armor, I had forgotten I was carrying the former sword of a king's guard. I nodded and partially pulled Vowkeeper out of the sheath so that the man could see the saber's blade. The others leaned forward, curiosity getting the better of them.

Even Oisín roused, though his curiosity seemed to have nothing to do with the gleaming blade. "I must know, lad, did you know our Bold Bren the Bare?"

I nodded again. "He is a friend."

The group laughed at that. I wondered how many times they had heard Oisín's retelling of Bren's time at the north of the Pool. "I would go so far as to say that 'Bold Bren' is the reason I find myself in Cluain Toradh this night."

Oisín took a long draft of his canteen before trying unsuccessfully to hide a small burp. "What is he? Is he Tuatha?"

I shrugged. "I wish I knew." Oisín's face fell.

I felt strangely bad about disappointing the bard. "What I can tell you is that I once saw him go into a fairy trance."

Oisín smiled at my words. I had a feeling his mind was already working on a new verse for his song. I turned to Diarmuid and quickly changed the subject. "Where is your fianna headed?"

Gráinne spoke up again. She had moved even closer to Diarmuid, enough to make me suspect they were more than just fellow members of the fianna. "We are traveling to meet up with the rest of our group. They are stationed outside of Cruachan."

While Gráinne spoke, Muireann sidled up closer to Diarmuid as well. The two women were practically sitting on top of the man, but he seemed unfazed by their attention.

Diarmuid must have seen the surprised look on my face or the way my eyebrows had risen at the mention of Cruachan. "Never fear, our people know enough to stay clear of the temple there." He stared at me, then spoke again, as if he'd made a decision.

"We may be traveling in the same direction, but we do not share your pace." The words hung in the air in an unspoken question. Why was I traveling in haste?

Untruths had never come easy to me, so again, I told a partial truth. "There is something I must do… something that only I can do." The words surprised me as they left my lips. Why was I sharing even this much?

A flickering light in the trees my attention. The four warriors stood and drew their weapons, obviously having seen the light as well. Looking around, I saw that even Oisín had risen, leaving only Diarmuid seated. He was still looking at me. His head slowly turned to the light, taking his eyes off of me only at the last moment.

The light was spherical, brightening at the center where oranges and yellows danced about like a living flame. Wisps of white light trailed the ball, making it look almost like a comet in the sky brought to Annwn and caught in a twirling vortex.

"Tine Sí," said a hushed voice. Fae Fire, I mentally translated.

"It is an omen!" Oisín announced. He had been the only one, other than Diarmuid and I, who had not drawn a weapon. His eyes were locked on the fiery ball of light. Where before I had seen merriment in his expression, he now looked serious, almost reverent.

Gráinne chuckled. "You think everything is an omen."

I myself had never seen Fae Fire this close before. Yes, I had seen it at a distance before a battle, and once… I paused, remembering. It had been the night of the Cold Moon. I had seen the Fae Fire dancing over the Heart-shaped Pool.

"Oisín's right," Diarmuid said. Again, I was struck by the feeling that he reminded me of someone I knew. I couldn't place who it was, but I knew that whoever it might be, Diarmuid's hair wasn't right, and his beard was too short.

I found myself intentionally avoiding looking too closely at the mark on his forehead. When my eyes happened to pass close to it, I sensed a strange vibration in the weave. I had spent enough time around magic-rich individuals to know a magic spot when I saw it.

Diarmuid stood. "It seems that Tadg's coming to our fire this sunset has garnered the attention of the very spirit of the air." The fairly light danced through the camp, then away into the woods as quickly as it had come. Diarmuid stepped closer to me as he continued to address the fianna.

"The lights mean us no harm, friends. Sit back, and rest. Oisín, play another song." He nodded his head in my direction. "Tadg and I will walk together a bit. I see now the gravity of our meeting this night."

Diarmuid stepped past me, heading back the way I had come. Either he wanted to discover what lay back at my camp, or he was hinting it was time for me to leave.

"I know who you are," he said as soon as we were alone among the trees.

"I thought you might." I tried to keep my tone even, doing my best to hide my worry. "I was stationed at the Heart-shaped Pool for many moons. If your fianna is based out of the Midlands, we have likely crossed paths a time or two."

Diarmuid drew to a stop. His face was harsh in the moonlight. "Your father is an enemy to those that I love. The Slaugh Doctrine has caused many fae to flee to Ériu."

I remained silent, unsure if I should share my recent awakening with the man.

"Your silence is telling, princeling. But I believe something big is coming and based on the arrival of the Fae Fire tonight, I wonder if you might not have an important part to play in it."

I shrugged. "Likely not." But was I lying to myself? The more I thought about Brigid, the more I realized that she could well be the lynchpin to a resistance victory. Did I want what I had always thought of as the opposition to win? I realized that I didn't know.

"I have seen that look before," Diarmuid said.

"What look is that?"

He ignored my question. "It isn't easy, is it, cousin?" He paused, seeming amused. "If I had told the fianna who you are, anything might have happened. They would have run you off, taken you captive, or worse."

He smiled. "But I believe WE can be better, Tadg mac Nuadat, and so instead, I will encourage you on your way. Don't make me regret my decision."

CHAPTER 11:

EXILES NO MORE

< CAI >

Day 14 of Midwinter, Sunset
Túr Crochta, The Deep Realm
Annwn

My adoptive father's funeral began in the usual Fomorian fashion. As the king's people paid their respects and left offerings, a low chanting began to thrum through the room. The voices of the prominent women began to rise in a communal song. It began with unheard and unknown words, evolving into a refrain of words and phrases that spoke of the deeds of the passed king.

These sacred songs, called "keening" by our people, could last for hours. It was believed the songs would hold the Bánánach at bay for the funeral. The wailing conveyed the shared pain of the loved one's passing and helped alleviate the grief of the community.

The sound had another purpose. As I listened, the volume of the women's keening reached a climax, inviting the Caoineag, the bhean sí, or as she is known by those in Ériu, the banshee, to share in their grief.

As the keening song rose to its penultimate note, the wail of the Caoineag spirit joined it, silencing the other singers as it brought the song to its end. I opened my eyes, looking for the mysterious spirit, but she had already gone. Her presence, though brief, was a mark of respect and acknowledgment of the worthiness of King Neit.

His absence felt surreal. Neit had been a constant guiding presence for his people. Though I only had a few years with him, I knew he had lived over a thousand times longer with his people. The deeply held secrets and special moments between Neit and these people were more numerous than one could count.

Though my own time with him had been relatively much shorter, I had held a special place in his life. Together we had been planning a better future for our people.

I turned to watch as Tethra came down the stairs into the throne room. She looked strong and graceful in the ceremonial golden armor that I knew she hated wearing. It felt strange to see her in anything but the green leather armor she favored. It had always seemed like it was a part of her.

As she approached the pyre where the patriarch lay motionless and pale, a Fomorian warrior handed her a lit torch. Before she could set the flames to the pyre, the double doors to the hall creaked open and slammed against the walls on both sides. A powerful gust of air shot forward, extinguishing the torch. A veritable company of large men and women entered the room amid gasps and hushed conversations.

Everything happened so quickly that I needed a moment to process it. No guards converged on the crowd of men. None of the Fomorian warriors at the funeral sought to defend either the room or the man being honored. I realized why when I saw the dark-skinned man leading the group of warriors. He wore Balor's horned helm, which could mean only one thing. Corb was home, and he was now the wielder of the Evil Eyes.

Corb's voice boomed, silencing the hushed whispers across the large room. "I see it is not too late to pay respects to MY father."

Dubhlinn ran forward to wrap her arms around her son's waist. As the shock of Corb's appearance wore off, a smattering of applause rang through the room. Many Fomorians looked conflicted as to whether to celebrate or condemn his arrival.

Tethra stood near her father's pyre, looking too stunned for words, and that prompted my tongue to move on its own accord. "You are just in time to pay your respects to both Father and our future queen."

Corb leveled his glowing red eyes on me. I could feel the malice behind the metal and magic. He immediately stepped forward, towering over me. His new helmet put him close to three feet taller than me. He sneered. "The adopted son mourns for his 'father.'" His tone was condescending. "And now the illegitimate son backs his illegitimate sister."

The room erupted into shouts and side conversations. I took a step toward the huge man. Corb only smiled down at me, seeming to have expected this reaction.

Tethra's voice rang through the room, calling for order. When the noise had quieted down, she turned to address her older brother. "It is funny that you talk about illegitimacy, as it was the man we all celebrate today who exiled you." There were more murmurs from the crowd in the throne room. "Cai holds more claim over this throne than you do."

Corb's wicked eyes darted from Tethra to me. "You do not belong here, Béstin." His use of Tethra's pet name for me came out mocking. It wasn't nearly as endearing when he said it. "And neither does your fire-haired pet."

Ruadan had been standing behind me, but at Corb's words, shot forward to stand next to me, as if lending his support. His expression was cold and out of character for my normally cheerful friend.

Corb's massive hands snapped out, clutching Ruadan's face. There was a sickening crack and Roo's body fell limp beside me. Shocked, I fell with him, trying to catch his body before it could hit the ground.

An audible collective gasp came from the onlookers. And before I had even hit the floor with Ruadan, I felt rage well inside me.

Ruadan was dead. If the full weight of his body hadn't given it away, the lack of swirling energy that I constantly saw around living people and places would have. Ruadan's body was inert and devoid of any energy except residual heat.

Tethra surged forward, placing herself between Corb and me before I could rise and draw Fragarach. As I stood, she raised her arms, holding me back. She stared at me, then down to Ruadan's body, repeating, "He's not really dead. He's not really dead."

Corb stood behind her, still smirking. "She's right, you know. Not only can he not die, but that one likely has copies of himself on every continent and every island in this world… but not here, not anymore. He will not be able to spy on us any longer."

"Ruadan wasn't a spy!" I shouted. "He stole the Spear of Victory for us and fought beside us at Brú na Dallta. How dare YOU, of all people, challenge HIS loyalty?"

Corb looked unsurprised by my outburst. He casually strolled to his father's open coffin, placing a hand on it. "It is not Ruadan I wish to challenge… There is no longer a need." He paused to let the meaning of his words sink in and then drew his blade.

"I challenge Tethra's legitimacy for the throne. I challenge her skill and combat prowess in single combat." His malevolent gaze swept the room. "I wish to have the most skilled and wise heir lead our people into the future. Here, on the precipice of war, I, Corb of the Evil Eyes, say that I am your champion and rightful king."

Several cheers rose from both Corb's soldiers and from Fomorians who had been loyal to Neit. I cast my eyes around the room. The earlier haze I had seen no longer wrapped itself around Ruadan. It had grown thicker, its tendrils wrapping around both me and Tethra.

Tethra saw me studying her and in her eyes, I could see the recognition of what I had warned her about. I shook my head at her, begging her silently not to do what I knew she would.

"I accept." Her simple words rang through the room. The room erupted into shouts, the noise rising into a cacophonous nightmare.

There were so many people shouting that I couldn't make out wisdom from the frenzy.

Tethra reached for Orna, turning to face her challenger. Desperate, I leaped to the top of a nearby stone half-table. I reached out to the nearly endless vibration energy in the room. I flattened the sound waves themselves from the vibrations coming out of the mouths of each person present and the vibrations bouncing off of the carved stone walls of the room.

In less than a second, the sound level went from uproarious yelling and screaming to complete silence. All eyes were on me. I had the floor to say whatever I wanted, but the only thing I wanted was to protect Tethra.

She glared at me, not knowing any more than I did what I was about to say. I searched my brain for the right words. I couldn't say anything to undermine Tethra's strength. It would be political suicide.

I cleared my throat. "Many of us are still sleep-deprived from war. Many of us carry with us the injuries from only a few short hours ago. This test of arms would be better served after the funeral of our king." I thought back to what Tethra had said about Corb's mother's official stance on this very transition of power. "As Dubhlinn said earlier today, let us separate the celebration of death from the coronation."

There were shouts of agreement from the crowd and skeptical looks from many of the Mná na Mara. To my surprise, it was Tethra's mother, Morvra, and Dubhlinn who stepped forward. Morvra offered a hand up to me, a polite gesture that clearly communicated "Get off the table." Her hand felt like iron in mine, but her eyes were kind. Her eyes held mine, seeming to peer through me. I felt a silent gratitude in her gaze.

Dubhlinn spoke, grabbing the attention of the room. "Maccán's words are sound. Let each moment of import have its own time in the sun." She nodded to Morvra.

Morvra turned from me and said the words I was hoping to hear. "Today, we honor our former leader. In two days' time, we will convene to settle this challenge and honor our new leader."

Just like that, it was decided. Tethra and Corb both lit the pyre of the king. And as the Fomorians dispersed from the great hall, I watched as the ashes of my adopted father burned away into the night.

CHAPTER 12:

SQUID PRO QUO

Day 14 of Midwinter, Sunset
At Sea, Well of Wisdom
Annwn

Lir and I stepped back into Tir fo Thuinn from the armory of Eiocha. In my hands, I held the disc armor and the shillelagh.

"That armory was an interesting find," murmured Lir. "We have no other surviving record of Taranis or Eiocha practicing their smith skills."

I stopped long enough to carefully place the armor and shillelagh on the sea floor before turning to face the god. Enough was enough. "Are we really going to just keep chatting about history, pretending there isn't a war going on? You sent for me to discuss your brother's war, and now that I'm here, you don't seem to want to talk about it." I gestured around the cavernous room. "What are you even doing down here? Where have you been?"

Lir inclined his head and sighed. "I suppose we should get down to business. Please forgive an old man's meandering. It would seem that when someone lives as long as I have, their sense of urgency changes somewhat." He gazed around the room. A long pause filled the air until I couldn't stand it anymore.

"You're doing it again," I blurted. "Why am I here? What is it that you need me to do for you?"

Lir gave me an amused look, either oblivious to my growing impatience or simply not caring. "Which question would you like me to answer first? What I'm doing down here, where I have been, or what I must ask of you?"

I felt my face growing hot with frustration. Even my ears were burning. "Well, as for where you've been, I guess you've been down here, probably staring into these water gateways." I waved a hand at the various scenes playing out around us. "So, I guess let's start with what you're doing down here in the first place, and your thoughts on the Overking's declaration of war on the Fomorians and the fae."

Lir looked as though I had slapped him. "I abhor it. It is the culminating act of a desperate man. My brother has changed… something I first began to notice 1,500 of your years ago, though I never expected him to stray so far."

"That number rings a bell." I thought back to my conversations with Morias. "That was when the sages were killed, and Morias came to Ériu. Right?"

Lir nodded. "Yes. Those were very troubling times."

"Is that why you left Falias? Because you noticed the Overking had changed?" It sounded a bit far-fetched that a god would leave for such a simple reason as his brother acting weird.

Lir frowned at me. "There is that name again, "overking.' Before Nuada, Bres simply used the title of High King. It implied nobility and responsibility. When Nuada began to change, he took the title Overking, which implies rulership and his expectation of servitude from those he ruled."

"Yep, that sounds pretty fitting for your bro. No offense."

"You may doubt me, but he wasn't always like this," Lir insisted. "When he led us in the battles of Mag Tuired, he was a sight to behold." Lir smiled sadly, seeming lost for a moment.

"Was that before or after he killed all of Bres' Ellyllon and kicked his half-brother off of the throne?" I demanded. I couldn't help but feel rage and sorrow as I thought about what had happened to Fíadan's comrades in arms.

Lir looked pained but nodded. "Fair point. Perhaps within my brother, there were always the underpinnings of a tyrant, and we were just too enamored with him to notice it."

"Now what? You can't mean to stay down here forever. The world is going to chet up there!"

"That is why I sent for you." Lir stepped closer. He pointed in the direction of the various portals. "These weren't meant to be windows into the wide world, but rather passageways… highways, I believe you call them. But through these aqueous lenses, I have witnessed the subjugation of my brothers and sisters. I have watched as the Fomorians were forced to sneak into the mortal world to further their families and preserve their race. And I have seen countless refugees abandoning the land of magic for the land of the aged. It is time for those with eyes to act."

I felt goosebumps ripple across my arms at his words. "Does this mean you will help us to defeat Nuada?"

"Not exactly." He abruptly began to rustle through the pile of armor at my feet. When he found the belt, he expertly removed the two straps connecting the shoulder sets and sternum disc. He handed the reduced belt to me. "Put this on."

I had no idea what was going on, but took the belt and cautiously reattached it to my waist. "I feel a charge in the air, like before."

Lir looked me up and down, appearing satisfied. "Yes. You will begin with the belt. As you are ready, you will work your way up, eventually gaining the ability to don the full set. You will need it for where I will send you."

I took a step back, raising my hands. "Woah, woah, woah. I'm already on a mission. I need to find allies for the Fomorians. I don't have time to go on some kind of side quest!"

Lir stepped closer to the massive wall of water. He beckoned me to follow. "If you are seeking allies for your brethren, you will complete this 'quest' for me."

I followed the man, curious despite my doubts. As we walked, I couldn't help but glance at the opaque centers of the doorways. Occasionally, I could see a place I recognized. In one portal, I saw the carved homes and buildings of the Deep Realm. Masses of people stood in the open areas above the water. A procession of large men and women marched through the underground city toward the Hanging Tower, a massive stalactite.

In another, I saw the white caps of the Green Mountains and the púca I had met on my brief journey back to Earth. The huge, extended family had been fleeing the violence and persecution of the Tuatha. I saw my little buddy, Jamie, running and playing with the other púca children. The sight awakened a warm feeling inside of me, as it was Jamie who had renewed my faith in my own intentions and abilities.

Lir stopped in front of a portal that opened into a beautiful, medieval town. The brownstone brickwork of each building appeared ancient and weathered, even while seeming impervious to time. Balconies and elevated porches overlooked the streets.

I realized, with a start, that the city contained no traditional streets like I would have expected in a medieval urban landscape. Instead, it was built more like Venice. Where I would have expected traditional roadways, were only waterways. Small longboat-style water taxis traversed the town, ferrying people to stairs and walkways that ended at the water's edge. The boats' prows extended far above the water. In some cases, the ferrymen and passengers even appeared to use the long prow to enter and exit the vessels.

"This is the Deep Water port of Murias, home to the largest navy in Annwn," Lir said with reverence. "This is where the next leg of your journey begins."

Incredulous, I turned to face the god. "Uh… Unless you're suggesting I hijack the whole navy and bring it back to Cai, I don't really understand. What exactly do I need to do?"

Lir ignored my question. "After my brother took the crown, he gathered those immediate family members he deemed most dangerous to his rule. We were required to remain in Falias. Nuada wanted us close by, where he could watch us."

My head was spinning. "Who exactly did he force to remain in the capital?"

Lir looked surprised at my question. "It is easy to forget how little you understand of Annwn. There were five of us. Myself, of course, and Ogma, who holds dominion over the domain of Knowledge. Dian Cécht, the god of Healing. You can imagine the value of having the two of them around. Next, the smith god, Goibhniu, who formed the Silverwhite blades for King Bres. Finally, there is The Dagda, though Nuada allowed the god of magic to remain in Gorias, mostly out of fear of his power."

"Why are you telling me all of this?" I asked. While I knew this was important context, I also didn't particularly see how it was relevant in this particular moment.

"You are seeking allies, if I am not mistaken. Yes?"

I nodded.

"I am not the only Tuatha Dé Danann to defy my brother's wishes and go into hiding. My brother Goibhniu has disappeared, and I fear the worst."

I suddenly realized where he was going with what had seemed like an off-topic history lesson. I sighed. "You want me to find him, don't you?"

It was Lir's turn to nod. "If you can find him and convince him to aid you, you will have my gratitude… and I will lend the Fomorians the strength of the sea."

I turned to the Murias portal. It appeared to open into the water itself. "The sea," I remarked absently, watching the dark water lap against the rocks and stones that made up the foundation of Murias.

Lir's voice snapped me out of my musing. "Bren. 'Now is no time to think of what you do not have. Think of what you can do with that there is.'"

I recognized his words, a quote from one of Morias' favorite books, Hemingway's The Old Man and the Sea. He'd talked about it so much, that I had actually given in and read the thing. I turned back to Lir, digging the next phrases of the passage from the depths of my mind. "'But every day is a new day. It is better to be lucky. But I would rather be exact.'"

A brief flicker of surprise passed over Lir's face before it broke into a grateful smile. I held his gaze as I continued. "I will find your brother, but there will come a time to reclaim what I 'do not have.' When that time comes, I will call on you for the strength and speed of the sea."

I thought of my existing strengths and about what might lie before me. Then I reviewed the notifications from my last Power Rank level up.

Name: Bren Búachaill
Race: Síorláidir
Current Power Rank - Level 12

Current Progression Status:
Physical Progression +44
Mental Progression +37
Spiritual Progression +48

Domain: Chaos
Domain Classification: Battlesmith (Enhanced)

You have been gifted with the following boons:
Control Energy
Erratic Agility
Dark Vision

Pain Sponge
Spiritual Augur
Battlefield Forge

You have one blood-borne curse:
Mark of the Bodach (Permanent)

Innate Racial Abilities:
Rapid Regeneration
Advanced Identification
Magic Sense

Two magic items are in your possession.
You have acquired:
Seolán Neimhe
Cast Lustrum Shillelagh

CHAPTER 13:
LABORATORY OF URIAS

Day 13 of Midwinter, Sunset
Caisleán Saighead, Gorias
Annwn

The opinion of the council, or more accurately, Nemain, was that Brigid remained in Falias, for some reason. Of course, the lack of an immediate way to contact Hightower meant that no one really knew for sure. The Dagda couldn't sense anything afoul with Brigid's magical domain. Princess Prophecy didn't offer up any useful information, and Captain Cloaca remained quiet. Morias, Aengus, and I weren't buying it.

Eventually, the council meeting had ended, after which Morias led me up into the southernmost tower. Before his death, this had been the library and laboratory of the Gorias Sage, Urias. He had been active during the years I had served High King Bres. He had been a strange, bald man. Fat, like Morias, but not as likable.

As we ascended the spiral staircase, which I would normally have flown up, I could see this area had been maintained. While it didn't look like the army of cleaners had made it this far after the invasion, it was clear that Brigid and Bres had kept Urias' room much the same as they had kept mine. Unchanged.

"So… this is your new playground?" I joked.

"Indeed," Morias replied. "I have not been in a true laboratory since before I took the Stone to Ériu."

"Planning to move in?"

"Not likely, my dear." The sage puffed out his breath as we trudged up the stairs. His round face was red with exertion. "Urias was an… eccentric individual. Before the unfortunate events of the last season, I would not have desired to disturb…"

"Ah, who are you kidding?" I interrupted with a snicker. "This has got to be a know-it-all's wet dream."

Morias turned and looked at me, his brows raised. I knew it wasn't because I was wrong, but rather that my sense of humor was always tough on the big guy. That's part of what made him so fun to needle.

Taking pity on him, I softened my words. "I mean, Urias was the first Prime Sage."

"That is a term I haven't thought about in many years," he said, finally reaching the top of the tower stairs.

Morias had earned the title of Prime Sage when the capital had shifted to Falias. But this particular room was the workspace of the first Prime Sage.

"What exactly are we doing up here anyway? I figured you would want to hoard all of this 'really interesting chet' for yourself."

"Truth be told, my dear, I have already been through a good portion of the books that Urias left out. I have reviewed the various experiments Urias was working on before his death…Consequently, did you know that the reason the cider here in Gorias is so tasty is because the Sage designed a special cultivar of apple with a higher sugar content?"

I was torn between being annoyed by how easily distracted the old man was with fun facts and finding myself truly interested in this particular topic. After all, the cider here in Gorias was my favorite.

"Did Urias invent Cidercrisp apples?"

Morias nodded, clearly delighted at my interest. "He first called them 'Senias Gold.'" He chuckled, and his obvious enthusiasm made me smile. I wanted to be annoyed, but the sound of Morias' laugh had usually marked good times… and lightened any bad ones. I knew he was laughing at this particular moment because Urias had chosen to name his winning variety of apples after the Sage of Findrias, Senias.

"Apparently," Morias said, still chucking, "Senias and Urias had gotten into a wee bit of a competition."

"And Urias created a better apple than Senias… Yeah, yeah, I get it, you old crazy person."

The Sage quieted at my tone. He sighed. "Fine, Fíadan. Have it your way. Down to business."

He walked through the entryway, carefully stepping between desks filled with papers and bottles of various liquids. I had been in this lab before a handful of times. With a pang, I realized it honestly didn't look any different than it had when Gorias was the capital and Bres was our king.

I followed Morias as he stepped through the mess of furniture. We entered a section of the lab that was a veritable maze of book stacks—literal towers of books, stacked haphazardly above my head in no observable pattern.

"The reason we are here together, Fí," Morias began, "is because I discovered that Urias had an obsession that was even sweeter than his cider."

"I don't like pretty talk," I reminded him. "Just what was the baldie working on that has you so worked up?"

"Dualities… and the Síorláidir." He paused when I wrinkled up my nose at him. I may have exaggerated my confusion a bit. "It occurred to me that the last time anyone discussed a duality, it was in reference to the old gods."

"So… what…"

"Something is happening in Annwn. It is unseen, and it harkens back to an older time. The coming of two new Síorláidir is no coincidence, my old friend."

I looked around again at the piles of books. It had to be said. "Did Urias have something against bookshelves?"

"I vaguely remember some of his eccentricities," Morias said. "His organizational methods were…uncommon. I only recently remembered that he had written copious notes and journals on the subject of the Síorláidir."

"Is that what these books are about?" I asked, eyeing the towering monuments of old tomes.

"Yes, some of them. None of the Sages or Tuatha are old enough to remember the Greater Gods, other than Danu and Donn. Some of these books and notes refer to a contemporary source that may be able to tell us about these early gods."

"Contemporary… that means 'bad art,' right?"

"What?" Morias just looked at me like the question had awakened him from a bad dream… or maybe my question was the bad dream. He shook his head at my smirk.

"I'm talking about the first Sage, the one that came before the four. The Sage that saw the landing of the Cessairian, Nemedian, and all those in between. The one that survived the afflictions of Éire land. The one who made the four."

"Made the four?" Though I tended to zone out the longer Morias talked, I found myself paying close attention. I had always been curious about the origins of the sages. "Do you mean… somehow these books were written by this first Sage?" My mind whirled. "And they'll tell us where the four sages came from?"

He paused. "No."

I threw up my hands in exasperation. My hand slapped into the side of a nearby stack of books, sending it cascading to the side, where it promptly toppled into another stack of books, sending the second stack flying…and so on, and so on. I was reminded of a long-ago game of dominoes I had played in Lady Strom's back garden before Aengus had taken up residence there.

When the sound of crashing books died down, I peeked at Morias, expecting him to be angry, but he just shook his head and extended an open book to me. The old, leather-bound book was opened about halfway. The right-hand page showed a crude drawing of a well.

"This single diagram, drawn the day before Urias died," Morias said, "speaks of a sunken well that leads to the library of Fintan the Wise. The reason I asked you to come is because of your vast experience living here in Emain Ablach." He pointed to the drawing. "Are you familiar with any sacred sites associated with magical wells around the Gorias coast… and I mean drinking wells, not the great oceans."

I glanced briefly at the page. "That's the Drowning Pool," I said matter-of-factly, finding a tiny thrill of satisfaction as Morias' eyes went wide. I shrugged. "But your guy Urias was a chet artist. It looks nothing like that. It's way down under the waves."

Morias leaned closer, looking as excited as I had ever seen him. "Where, Fí? Where is this Drowning Pool?"

"On the south coast, in the middle of the Sacred Cape."

"How did you find it?" he asked, his voice filled with wonder. "According to Urias, the well fell beneath the waves when the seas rose in Annwn."

"And by seas, you mean Wells… when the Wells covered the well."

He stammered a bit before recovering. "Yes…Yes. Well. Now you see why I didn't lead with that. It can be a bit confusing."

"I can take you there if you want," I offered. "But I don't exactly have great memories of that place."

Morias must have seen something in my expression because he didn't say anything. He was good like that. Despite his long-winded nature, he always knew when to shut up. He waited patiently for me to continue.

"It was during my blue period, okay?" I finally blurted. "Isn't that what that crazy painter called it? His blue period?"

"Are you saying you painted blue-themed portraits and landscapes?" he asked.

"What?" I said, confused. "No… After Bres was deposed, I was really sad and really angry. I went around Emain Ablach a bit. I killed anything that attacked me. It was my blue period." I held his eyes, willing him to understand. "But it was also red and black."

Morias seemed to choose his words carefully. His expression was sad. "I should have been there for you, Fíadan. I'm very sorry."

I forced myself to shrug and faked a bright smile. "Chet, don't get all soppy on me, Sage. Anyway… do you want me to take you there?"

He smiled sheepishly. "How do you feel about a little swim?"

CHAPTER 14:

CRUACHAN

Day 15 of Midwinter, Sunset
Cruachan, Midlands
Annwn

I hadn't lingered long after my chat with Diarmuid. Once Gaoth had properly watered and fed himself, and the darkness of the night lightened enough, we were on our way. It had been a grueling day and night was beginning to close in again when we made it to the outskirts of Cruachan.

The ancient temple of Cruachan was a sprawling monument that dated back to before the Sages. While little is known of its origins, all were aware of the malevolent force that took up residence there around the time the four cities were founded.

Over the years, travelers had shared whispered stories of the foul smells and strange noises that emanated from the double doors leading inside. Pilgrims had avoided the sanctum and halls inside of Cruachan for all of recorded history, knowing that whatever had claimed the temple as its home still resided within the walls of the massive structure. Still, many a weary traveler had taken advantage of the temple's dark reputation, seeking shelter from both enemies and weather in its exterior grounds.

Gaoth slowed to a canter as we passed the first crumbling structure on the perimeter of the temple grounds. It became immediately clear to me that a group of people had quickly extinguished a fire in the area and hidden in the rubble.

Hiding meant one of two things. Either the people were afraid or they intended an ambush. I was banking on the former based on my conversation with Diarmuid.

"Greetings," I bellowed from atop Gaoth. I briefly considered my breastplate, which was in plain sight. The sight of its heraldry wouldn't alleviate the concerns of anyone hiding from view. "I mean you no harm. I have just come from the company of Diarmuid and your fianna."

A few heads rose cautiously from behind old buildings that had been worn away by time. One head was lower to the ground than I had expected. A boy with a curly mop of hair. Of the group, he appeared to be the boldest, as he quickly emerged from his hiding space and began toward me.

"Sétanta," a woman called from across the ancient street. "Get back! Don't go near him."

I dismounted and slowly approached the boy.

"Hello there, lad," I said, crouching down to his level. "Do you like horses?" The boy spared me a glance before his eyes wandered to Gaoth standing behind me. The boy studied the warhorse intensely.

"I like all animals," he announced, his dark eyes never leaving the horse. I could see a group of twelve or so people beginning to step out into view. The woman who had said Sétanta's name came to stand beside him and took his hand.

I stood and bowed my head. Her delicate brow furrowed slightly.

"My name is Tadg mac Nuadat." She flinched at hearing my father's name. I immediately held up my hands. "Rest easy. I am not here on his behalf."

Several in the crowd had placed their hands closer to their sword handles. I pretended not to notice. "Sétanta, would you like to meet my horse?" The boy nodded solemnly and pulled his hand from the woman's grip.

"His name is Gaoth. It means…"

"Wind," Sétanta interrupted. "I have heard of him. But I know of a faster horse." Gaoth tossed his head and whinnied.

"I think old Gaoth disagrees with you," I said, smiling.

The boy's words tumbled out, nearly too fast for me to follow. "Móralltach is faster, but Aonbharr can run on the water." I had seen the horses of Aengus Og and Manannán mac Lir run wild together at a summer festival many moons ago. They were indeed fast, but Gaoth had still run circles around them.

"Why have you come?" the woman asked.

"I am merely passing through. There is an errand that needs my attention to the northeast."

She drew the boy away and fully faced me. "And you are resting here this evening?"

Again, I bowed, then motioned to Gaoth. "With your consent, yes. We would both appreciate it." I added, "Your leader asked me to tell you that they will be along no later than Midday on the morrow."

She nodded and began leading the boy away. I moved to tend to Gaoth and my equipment. The members of the fianna rekindled their fires.

For the first hour, I sat alone, munching on salted venison. I had taken the tackle off Gaoth and brushed him down under the watchful eyes of Sétanta. Gaoth had eventually tired of my ministrations and wandered outside of the ruins, likely to graze. I knew he wouldn't go far.

Throughout the ruins, I saw people huddled around small campfires. The air had grown colder, even next to my own fire. It was cold enough that I had pulled Gaoth's saddle blanket off of the nearby stone wall and wrapped it around my shoulders.

Hearing a noise to my left, I looked over to find Sétanta settling at my fire. The boy was also huddled in a blanket. He moved dangerously close to the flames.

"Why is it so cold?" he asked me between shivers. I tucked his blanket in tighter around him and gently scooted him back from the fire. The woman emerged from the darkness behind us, watching my interaction with the boy. Her expression was wistful.

"I am Deichtine," the woman said, sitting on the other side of the boy. "I'm sorry if I was rude earlier."

I gave her a knowing smile and looked back into the fire. "Believe me… I understand." We sat in silence for a time, each of us staring into the fire. The flames were hypnotic, and I found myself suddenly tired from the two days of hard riding.

"Tadg…" Deichtine's voice was weak as if she had something caught in her throat. Startled, I looked over. Her eyes were wide open and full of fear. Her mouth was open in a silent scream. Her skin had taken on a grayish pallor.

Sétanta sat frozen next to me, his skin the same grayish color. My mind scrambled to make sense of what was happening, flashing back to the events on The Stern Beauty in the Straits of Segais only days before. The Bánánach had come!

I flung off my blanket, leaping to my feet. I slashed Vowkeeper in a wide arc around the surrounding darkness. The beasts were intangible and nearly invisible in the dark, save for their amber eyes. Even still, my sword met resistance as it carved through the air.

Screams echoed through the temple grounds. Other members of the fianna were battling their own Bánánach.

I continued to attack the darkness, doing my best to hold our perimeter against the nearly invisible creatures. I shouted "It is the Bánánach. Only magic weapons or cold wrought iron can defeat them!"

Staring intently into the darkness outside of the firelight, I saw three sets of glowing eyes. The Bánánach were simply biding their time, waiting for me to lose focus or tire. It was not a battle I could win, I realized.

I thrust my sword into its sheath and reached down to hoist the unmoving Deichtine under one arm. With the other, I snatched up Sétanta. I turned and began to sprint for the double doors. "Get to the temple!" I shouted as I passed the other fianna.

I felt the chilly air that surrounded the Bánánach just behind me. My arms and lungs burned as I desperately ran, still clutching the dead weight of Deichtine and Sétanta.

At last, I reached the stairs leading to the temple doors. I bolted inside, still holding Deichtine and Sétanta in my arms. Many others followed in behind me. The Bánánach slowed outside the doors, appearing hesitant to enter the temple. I slammed the heavy doors shut.

"Barricade the entrance," I commanded. Only seven others had made it inside the temple, but they immediately went to work, piling debris against the entrance. I didn't know if the creatures could phase through the thick stone walls around us. If so, no amount of barricading would save us.

Then silence. The world was quiet but for the sound of the wind blowing across the plains and the soft gasps of those whose lives were being sucked away just outside the temple doors.

To my utter horror, I heard a sharp crack from the stone pillars. At the same time, I felt the foundation beneath my feet shift. The temple was about to collapse.

CHAPTER 15:

TOO TIRED TO SLEEP

< CAI >

Day 14 of Midwinter, Nightfall
Túr Crochta, The Deep Realm
Annwn

Tethra's face gave away nothing as the Fomorians slowly left the great hall. She stood stern and quiet, and those who didn't know her as I did likely didn't see the rage behind her eyes. Finally, we were alone.

Letting down her guard, Tethra turned to face me, shouting, "Why would you do that?" I flinched in surprise. It was late, and I was tired from the day, not to mention emotionally exhausted by Corb's return and his challenge to Tethra. It hadn't occurred to me that my actions would have angered the very person I had been trying to protect.

Exhausted, I simply looked at her. I was, as always, struck by her beauty and strength. Sometimes it almost took my breath away. It had always been this way for me when it came to Tethra. I looked closely at her now, looking for the ominous haze. The tendrils still surrounded her, but the room was clear.

At my silence, Tethra's anger seemed to melt away. She held my gaze, her voice soft and serious. "I could have ended this today. You can't see the future, Cai. You said it yourself."

I felt a pang at her using my given name. She had called me "Béstin," the Fomorian word for "little beast" since our very first sparring match. She had told me, at the time, that I lacked form and finesse, claiming that my swordplay was that of a "mindless beast."

"Orna is faster than Corb's Fuilgeir," she continued. "And we both know that I am the stronger sword master." I knew she wasn't wrong, but I couldn't get the picture of Corb's sword out of my mind. It was huge, double-bladed, with the nickname "Blood Cleaver." It had only one purpose.

I reached for Tethra's huge hand and held it between both of mine. "But you will be trying to win. He will be trying to kill."

Tethra gently pulled her hand from mine. "He will abide by the rules of the duel, or any victory will be void." She was trying to hide it, but I heard the slight hesitation in her voice. She had grown up with Corb, and she understood his true nature even better than I. She quickly recovered, shooting me a scowl.

"You made me look weak."

"If anything," I began, with a half-smile, trying to ease the tension, "I made myself look weak."

She rolled her eyes. "I don't need you to fight my battles, Béstin."

"I know."

She turned away from me, gazing back to the still-warm ashes of her father. "Corb shouldn't even be here." She scoffed. "He claims he has brought back a huge treasure from Gorias."

I hadn't known that. "Do you know what it is?"

"Other than the Evil Eyes? No. I suspect he is saving the big reveal for an opportune moment."

Looking at her, I could see dark circles under her eyes. "You should get some rest. You look exhausted."

She shook her head. "You know, I miss the days when I followed you across Annwn to protect you… and now here you are, trying to look after me."

"I miss those days, too."

"Those days are gone, Béstin. There will be no more trips across the plains for us." Her voice wasn't cruel, but the words cut at me like a knife. "Those days died with my father."

My heart ached. I missed our nights traveling Annwn, smoothing her hair as she slept to quiet her bad dreams. We had shared so much in only a few short years, and my respect and affection for her had grown into something deeper and unbreakable.

She could see her words had hurt me. I saw my own pain in her eyes. Without another word, she left the great hall, leaving me alone with the dead.

"She's right," I admitted to the remains of my adopted father after Tethra had gone. "But you paired us, from my very first night in Annwn. You sent her after me in the Pool. Why?"

No answers came from the pile of smoldering ash, but I waited longer, just in case. When no answers came, I too left the room. Ill at ease and knowing I wouldn't be able to sleep, I wandered the quiet city. There were few out at that hour. Even those who had attended the king's funeral were home and in bed for the night. This wasn't unusual. The top-side chores that many residents had each day kept the underground city on a circadian sleep cycle. The night was quiet, giving me too much room for my thoughts and worries.

I walked down and down from the exit of Túr Crochta, not really knowing where I was going. Eventually, I found myself at the training area where I had first picked up a Fomorian blade. It would be at the center of these grounds that the duel would take place in two days.

The dueling ground was a sacred place to the Fomorians. It was a site used to adjudicate grievances and matters of honor. Only rarely had it been used for matters of rank, and never for matters of succession.

The circular pit was large enough for up to four fighters with melee weapons. The walls, made of aged stone, were about 15 feet tall. In the middle of the pit was the "Abyss," a dark hole that opened into the ocean, far below sheer cliff walls. The dark of the Abyss was complete, and no one who fell into the hole had ever returned to the light.

"The Abyss waits for us all," a mocking voice said from behind me. I recognized the husky tone, and my heart immediately started beating faster. In the stillness of the dueling ground, I was sure that he could hear it pound in my chest.

I turned to see Corb standing a spear's distance away. My eyes immediately flicked to his sheath, where I saw Fuilgeir at the ready.

"I'm not here to hurt you, Maccán. You are, after all... family."

I subtly shifted my position, angling my back away from the pit of the dueling ground. "Why have you come?"

"That is an open-ended question if ever I've heard one." The hiss of his voice reminded me of a snake, with each phrase coiling around the last as if for sport. "I applaud your efforts at the fortress city. Too bad you and father couldn't manage to bring back Nuada's head." His red eyes seemed to laugh at me.

My utter contempt bubbled to the surface, making my voice come sharp. "You mention father, but let us not pretend that you are here to honor his legacy."

He laughed. "Now your question makes more sense." He stepped closer to the pit, which put him closer to me. As he spoke, his red eyes continuously changed hues, typically a sign that a torrent of fire was coming. My already pounding heart sped up.

"You aren't wondering why I have wandered a sleeping city to find an outsider in the dueling grounds. No, you are more concerned with why I have chosen to return to MY home."

The weight of my sword hung reassuringly on my belt. "Your home? You were exiled, Corb. You know this." I was confident that this conversation wasn't going anywhere productive.

"… By a weak king whose mind was poisoned by a traitorous adopted son." He stared at me, hatred seeming to pour off him. "You may have fooled my father and my sister, but there is no rule in this for you, not while I draw breath."

I could see an amber glow beginning to creep to life in my hands, unbidden. My anger was feeding my energy boons, and I very much wanted to act on that emotion. I clenched my fists. "I have never wished to rule, only to help my family."

Corb's fiery eyes flared, matching the intensity of my energy aura. "Be careful, little beast. I am not so weak as my father or sister. I will kill you without hesitation. But…" His tone changed, as did the intensity of his glowing eyes. He leaned closer as if to tell me a secret.

"If you wish to fight against those who oppress us, I can give you a war like you have never seen. Fight with me, and I will allow you to unleash your power against our enemy. Glory will be ours." He extended his hand.

I froze, shocked. He wanted me to join him and truly believed that I was governed by my ambition. I supposed it was impossible for a mind filled with doubt and hate to expect anything but the same base-level motivations from others.

Disgusted and angry, I stared at his hand. I let the silence grow between us, waiting to respond until Corb's hand dropped back to his side. "First you defy a man that I loved. Then, you threaten a woman I love. If we weren't on sacred ground, I would cut off the hand you offered me."

The red glow came surging back into his eyes. I began preparing my Transform Energy boon, ready to modify the flame when it inevitably came, but it never did. Instead, Corb laughed, the fire in his eyes dying down. He continued to laugh, long and hard, all the way out of the training grounds.

CHAPTER 16:
MANANNÁN MAC LIR

Day 14 of Midwinter, Sunset
At Sea, Well of Wisdom
Annwn

The old man of the sea grasped my forearm in one of those old-fashioned handshakes I had seen in various period movies. I grasped his arm back, trying to make the foreign motion look natural.

I had told him about Fern's Shell of Promise. He said he was no stranger to the selkie items and knew exactly how they worked, which made one of us. Placing the shell in seawater would do nothing but communicate, on a subconsciously magical level, my exact location to Fern.

I reminded him that when the time was right, I would need the sea to hasten our reunion. Lir had agreed to my terms, but I could tell that he still thought he'd gotten the better end of our deal.

"How will I know where to find your brother… what was his name again?" I asked.

Lir turned as a figure stepped from the city into Tir fo Thuinn. The man had short, curly hair that looked wet for some reason. He was clean-shaven with youthful features that reminded me of

Ruadan. He wore a long rectangular cloth gathered at his right shoulder, leaving the left side of his chest and arm completely bare. In his arm, he held the weirdest-looking spear I had ever seen. It had four sharp blades at right angles to each other, with a point in the middle. It looked like a mace and a spear had a really weird-looking baby.

Lir gestured proudly to the newcomer. "Bren, this is my son, Manannán, Child of the Sea, Patron of Manau, Master of the Waves, Guardian of the Mist, God of Travelers."

I waved awkwardly. "I'm Bren. Just Bren... but I've been known to answer to other, less flattering things."

The boy-faced man smiled at me, but his eyes remained cool and appraising. "Búachaill is not an epithet that should fall unused." Clearly, he had heard of me. I hoped that was a good thing. Manannán extended his hand, grasping my forearm as his father had. "By the Sages, another Protector has not been seen since the Síorláidir Teutates vanished."

"Technically, I'm not a protector," I admitted, thinking about my Chaos domain.

"Yet, others seem to feel differently," Lir countered, his tone dry. "Assuming you didn't give yourself this title?" I shook my head.

"Father, a word in private." Manannán gestured to his father, and the two men took a few steps away from me. They spoke quietly for several minutes, Manannán looking troubled and gesturing to me. I focused my eyes on the city through the portal, casually stepping closer hoping to hear what looked like a soft argument.

From the scattered words that I was able to pick up, Manannán had convinced his father to let him take me to Murias before we headed east into the hills and mountains below Tech Duinn. Apparently, this was the last place Goibhniu, the Smith god, had been seen.

As Lir and his son continued their conversation, my thoughts shifted to Cai. I realized that by undertaking this additional quest I would miss the funeral of King Neit and the coronation of soon-to-be

Queen Tethra. I hoped, at least, that Cai would see my path across Annwn by watching from his... magic bowl thing. What was it called again? The name had reminded me of lingerie… a brazier, I think. This particular device, a Blaze Diviner, allowed Cai to remotely see what was happening in a particular place or around a certain person. Given that I didn't know how to shield myself from the effects of the magic bowl, I was pretty confident Cai could and would follow and approve of my current path.

Manannán embraced his father, their conversation apparently having drawn to a close. He stepped closer to me, placing a hand on my shoulder, and squeezing just shy of too hard. He gestured to the portal in front of us, pointing at the Deep Water port of Murias. "It is time, Protector."

I stopped before stepping through, remembering something. I turned back to Lir, raising my pilfered flask for him to see. He gave me a quizzical look before nodding, as if to simultaneously approve my taking of the flask and bid me farewell. I nodded back before stepping through the portal.

Manannán stepped through behind me. Looking back from where we had come, I realized that to any passers-by it would appear that we had emerged out of solid stone. I touched the side of the building. Where only moments before there had been a translucent sheen, now there was only a wall. My fingers felt around for the edge of a door or portal. Nothing.

"You won't find it by looking." Manannán placed his palm flat on the wall. His expression was a combination of admiration and fondness. "Every entrance and egress from Tir fo Thuinn requires a different key, so to speak."

"At least it's not complicated," I joked, trying to break through the other man's serious demeanor. "Will you teach me how to go back?"

Manannán shrugged. "I haven't decided yet, but ultimately that's up to you." Well, that wasn't concerning at all. I decided to abandon my attempt to make friends.

Instead, I pondered the building in front of me. It was nothing special or out of the ordinary. Huge blocks of the same fine-grained, light brown stone were stacked flawlessly upon one another to make this and what looked like all the other buildings of this neighborhood.

"It is limestone, in case you were wondering," Manannán said. "Look closely; you might even see patterns you recognize." I peered at the stone and realized that I did see familiar patterns. Most notably, there were tiny fragments of shells peppered throughout this particular block. "The limestone is particularly resistant to the lapping of the waves and spray of the salt on the wind."

Unfortunately, I saw nothing on the wall that gave me any clue as to how to get back into the portal room. Shrugging, I decided to get down to business. "So... What exactly are we doing here? And what should I call you? Should I use your full name? Do I need to include all of the titles when I address you? Honestly, even by itself, Manannán is a mouthful." I knew I was rambling, but the questions just kept tumbling out.

"Slow down, Protector."

"Stop calling me that," I snapped. "It's been a while since I protected anyone. Maybe just call me Bren for now."

Manannán's tone was light when he responded. "You feel as if the designation sets expectations too high for your future self?" He gazed over the edge of the stone platform, into the dark water below. Moving to his side, I peered down as well. My Dark Vision didn't seem to help me see into the opaque surface of the ocean. It seemed like a strange nuance of the boon.

Manannán held his hand above the water, which began to bubble and churn. I instinctively took a step back. I had already seen some of the sea creatures lurking beneath the surface on my travels from Inis Fer Falga. Who knew what the son of the sea god could unleash on Murias? I imagined enormous monsters with rows of teeth and countless tentacles and shuddered. To my relief, though, I watched as a small sailboat emerged. Water spewed from the small ship's recesses as it came to rest atop the surface.

"My currach," Manannán said proudly as if the vessel was a priceless artifact.

The thing was hideous. While I guessed from his tone that the ship had to be seaworthy, it looked like it belonged in one of those museums that exhibited random objects found in peat bogs or glaciers after thousands of years of neglect and decay. The ship had a black, wooden frame and what appeared to be canvas sides (also black). A single sail rose only six feet off the front bow. The thin mast sat at an angle, pointing toward the back of the boat.

"By the look on your face, I'm thinking 'currach' doesn't mean what I think it means," I said, trying not to laugh. There was no way this ship could handle the weight of one of us, let alone both. It looked like it was one hard breath away from dissolving into a pile of rags and sticks.

I was immediately proven wrong, as Manannán stepped down into the vessel and beckoned me to do the same. It didn't sink. Yet. He looked at me, his irritation visible. "What do you think it means?"

"You really don't want to know," I admitted, unwilling to admit I'd been pondering whether it was an Annwn word for a pile of crap.

"A currach is a sea vessel meant to travel fairly large distances in the rough waters of Ériu." He ran his hand lovingly across the sides of the small ship. "She has been a worthy ally."

I stepped into the ship, moving to sit across from Manannán in the low spot in the very middle of the boat. The minute I was seated, Manannán whistled sharply, a sound that seemed more appropriate to call a dog or a horse. Without a lurch, the currach turned and began to make its way toward the deeper open water. It skimmed lightly over the surface.

"Long distances, huh," I muttered, trying to imagine what it must have been like to spend days at sea, trusting my life to what seemed like no more than a little bit of animal hide and tar affixed to a small wooden frame.

"The sheet," Manannán said, handing me the edge of a rope, one of two in the oversized dinghy. I vaguely remembered the sheet could be used to move the sail side to side, while the other, the halyard, would move the sail up and down. I clutched the rope in my hand, feeling stupid and as if I was missing something important. Was the son of the sea god attempting to teach me to sail? Maybe I'd misjudged what I'd believed to be his fairly distrustful demeanor.

He pointed to the back side of the boat. "That is the tiller. It will help you steer the currach." Looking smug, Manannán leaned back against the side of the currach. "You will need both the sheet rope and the tiller to navigate what is to come."

I was immediately on edge. "I don't think I like--or understand--your meaning. What are we doing out here?"

"My Father risks much by trusting and aligning himself with someone so new to our world. I am less convinced you are worth that risk." He looked me up and down. "But I respect my father and his wisdom, so will give you the opportunity to prove yourself worthy of his faith." I sighed, preparing myself for more Otherworldly shenanigans I didn't feel at all ready to handle.

Ignoring me, he continued, his tone ominous. "This sunset you will discover why this sea is called the Well of Wisdom. If you survive, I will accede to my father's wishes and trust you to find Goibhniu."

A few moments passed as the vessel sailed deeper into Murias Harbor. I exhaled slowly, trying to shake the unease curling in my gut. "Let's do this thing Manny."

CHAPTER 17:

THE DROWNING POOL

Day 14 of Midwinter, Sunrise
Hook Head, Gorias
Annwn

We decided to ride Efa for the trek to the Sacred Cape. Both Bren and I had taken a shine to the chestnut Cob Nemain had given to Bren for his ride from Findrias to Gorias. I liked her because I could tell she was always ready to run into a fight. Bren liked her because she had unselfishly taken us through the night to our final destination. Bren appreciated the little things like that. He loved so easily. I missed him.

Morias rode behind me as I guided Efa through the dark. My Gloaming Gaze ability allowed me to amplify ambient light. It wasn't as effective as the Dark Vision boon, but enough that I could see very well outside at night.

The sky had just begun to lighten when we first heard the crash of waves against the cliffs on the southern side of Emain Ablach.

"Do you know why Hook Head is also referred to as the Sacred Cape?" Morias asked. I let out an exaggerated sigh.

"No, but I suppose you are going to tell me."

He ignored my sarcasm. "In a way, this is the most likely spot for Fintan's lost library."

"I thought we were looking for a laboratory," I said, guiding Efa up the slight incline to the promontory that would serve as our best access to the Drowning Pool.

"In the mind of a Sage, the two go together like…" he paused a moment. "Silversap and starlight." He seemed pleased with his analogy.

"I hate you so much right now," I muttered.

"In any event… This, my dear Ellyllon, is where the Old Powers first stepped into this world. The old gods: Danu and Donn, Eiocha and Taranis, et cetera, all stepped through to Annwn on this very spot."

"Did you just say 'et cetera'?" I asked.

"You know, Fíadan, I think sometimes my storytelling proclivity is lost on you."

"You think?" I timed my response such that he would be distracted from arguing at the sight of the view from the edge of the cliff face. It worked perfectly. The Sage was about to continue on his tale but instead gasped as he looked out from the tip of the Hook.

"Each time I visit this spot, I am overwhelmed," he whispered.

I found myself struck silent by the familiar, spectacular sight. Waves crashed high up on the straight drop beneath us. The smell of the sea and the mist from the water drifted past Efa's neck and brought me back to another time.

I closed my eyes, feeling the warmth of the sunrise on my skin. Efa stood, unfazed by the maelstrom beneath us. Even with my eyes closed, I could tell from the intensity of the crashing sound that the water of the great Wells had risen since the last time I had been here.

"The water is even more tumultuous than the waves of Segais…" Morias mused. "I suppose that makes sense. This is also a cross-water point of the two seas."

I forced my mind back to the task at hand. "So, tell me again, how I am going to get down to the Well?" Ambiance was great and all, but I knew without asking which of us would be taking the plunge. Morias was too… buoyant.

"I swam here once before, you know. It didn't go well."

"Normally, I would applaud your pun," he said, his merry eyes twinkling. I didn't laugh. "But I can tell from your tone that this is perhaps not a fond memory."

"My blue period, remember?" I kept my tone light, not allowing myself to go too deep into that particular memory. It was all darkness and all pain.

The Sage awkwardly coughed behind me, trying to fill the silence. I tried to flutter off of Efa but quickly remembered the state of my wings when a piercing pain shot through my back. I flinched, listing to the side. Morias quickly scooted back in the saddle, allowing me the space to dismount manually. The big man followed me to the ground and Efa wandered back away from the cliff's edge.

"I have a ring that should help you with your trip into the waves." Morias rustled through his robe, pulling out a massive clasp that held an impressive number of magical rings. He held one out to me.

I slide the ring on without fanfare. It was gritty and uncomfortable on my thumb and felt odd next to the Rings of Identification on the index finger of the same hand. I couldn't wait to ditch both rings and was planning to do exactly that at the first opportune time.

"Once you have successfully reached the well, and found the entrance to the library, I would ask you to place this Mirrorstone in a prominent location."

Morias handed me a second object, this one a dark, opaque stone with reflective surfaces. I studied the Mirrorstone closely. It was tiny, only taking up the palm of my right hand. I looked back up at Morias with a confused look.

"The stone has a mate." He held up a second stone that looked as if it might fit together perfectly with the one held in my hand. "I will be able to use the reflections as a projection into the library once you have placed it."

I shook my head and looked at Morias' robe with a new curiosity. "What else do you have in there?"

"I'm afraid that list would take more time than we currently have." He pointed down at the waves. "My dearest Fíadan...this is where I tell you the bad news."

I sighed, slumping. "How did I know there would be bad news?"

Morias pointed to the churning waves below. "The ring will automatically activate. But... it must be submerged for a full minute before the magic will seep into your skin."

"Are you saying I need to swim in those waves for a full minute before it does whatever it does..." I paused, realizing that I didn't actually know what the ring did. "What does this thing do, anyway?"

"The good news is that you will be able to navigate the waves as if you were one of the Cupbearers of the Sea god. The bad news..."

"... is that I might die before the ring activates," I replied, cutting him off. "Thanks for sharing that slightly relevant detail back in Gorias." I began to pace back and forth on the cliff face, glancing down at the violently tumbling waves with every turn. The memories of my last trip into the water came flooding back to me, even as I tried desperately to push them out of my mind. My breath began to come faster and faster.

Morias' voice came low and slow to my ears. "Give me the ring, Fí. I will go into the waves." I turned to find that Morias had begun to disrobe behind me. I was startled by his roundness...and as much as I wanted to take him up on his offer, seeing him like this was a reminder that he would not last a minute in the sea.

I shook my head, trying to physically force out the painful memories of my past weakness. My teeth ached from the pressure of grinding them together. I turned to face the sea. Before I could lose my nerve, I ran and jumped off the cliff.

The water hit me like a charging Fomorian, immediately blasting the air from my lungs. I found myself upside down under the waves. Below me, the water was a murky midnight blue. Thankfully, my Gloaming Gaze ability allowed me to see deep into the churning water. I could see the outline of the well in the amplified sunlight that trickled down into the depths.

I kicked hard toward the ancient bricks of the long-forgotten well. I swam furiously but futilely within the Drowning Pool, the currents bringing a flood of long-repressed memories of when I had first seen the well.

For years, I had tried to wash away my failure as a King's Guard in the rage of justified vengeance. I had bathed myself in the blood of any creature stupid enough to cross me. I killed changelings and fae alike…any who wished to do me harm. And in a moment of despair, my path had brought me here, to what had felt like the edge of the world. My isolation and depravity had left me weak and with a sole desire… to end my guilt and misery.

The waves had broken me then, and they broke me now, in the present. Tossed in the water, I narrowly missed being slammed into the rock of the cliff, saved only by the devastating rip current of a massive wave. I kicked again toward the well, trying to use the downward momentum remaining from my dive, but any progress I made was countered by the convergence of the waves.

I battled against the water, my lungs and the stump of my wing burning. I told myself that, just like before, I would survive. Then, I had kicked and clawed my way up onto the sharp rocks of the cliff face, gasping for air and terrified at what I had nearly done.

This time was different. Instead of seeking escape, I did my best to stay low in the water, trying to find the underwater currents that would suck me deeper toward my goal.

I knew exactly when my ring activated because I suddenly could sit upon the waves as if I were riding the wind. I controlled the currents around me, and I willed them to take me deeper, to the well on the ancient shoreline.

The burning in my lungs had disappeared. The briny hell around me gave me oxygen, and with it, I was able to see beauty in the chaos. I drifted, alone with my thoughts, deeper into the water and down into the well. I had survived the Drowning Pool a second time.

CHAPTER 18:

THE ABHARTACH

Day 15 of Midwinter, Sunset
Cruachan, Midlands
Annwn

As the sound of the cracking stone pillars rippled around us and dust filled the air, we ran deeper into Cruachan. I still carried the unconscious Deichtine and Sétanta under my arms. My shoulders had begun to burn from the weight of carrying their bodies, and worse, the pain in my lungs and ribs had grown agonizing. Every breath hurt.

I continued to run, mentally cataloging our limited options. Only seven members of the fianna remained. We could go back outside to face the Bánánach, but I had no illusions about our odds of surviving that battle.

We could choose to remain in the long entryway of the temple, where we'd likely be crushed by falling stones. Faint cracks were starting to become visible on the walls around us.

The temple that had stood for countless moon cycles was collapsing. Why now? Was it the weight of the small company of changelings that now littered the entrance? Could the auras of the deathly spirits chasing us be having some strange effect on the structure?

There was a third possibility that I didn't like...that the evil resting in the temple had awakened and was herding us closer to its cruel source. The possibility of that faceless and nameless evil consumed my thoughts as we descended deeper into the ancient structure.

"Lord," a voice called out behind me. A heavy thump followed, the sound of a body hitting the floor. I turned toward it, squinting into the dim corridor. Behind us, one of the women from the rear of the group now lay motionless on the ground. The man who had spoken lifted a long, glowing stick—once a piece of firewood, now our only source of light—casting a faint glow over the scene.

"She was gravely injured by the creatures before we entered." His voice was shaking.

Another man knelt beside the woman. He looked up and his eyes met mine. He shook his head.

"We must go," I said. Adjusting my grip on Deichtine and Sétanta, I turned away from the fallen woman and continued to move deeper into the bowels of the temple. It wasn't lost on me that eventually, the woman would turn into one of the Abhartach. We didn't have time to burn her body.

I thought back, once again, to my time on The Stern Beauty. Morias had explained to Bren what happened to the bodies of those killed by the Bánánach.

"They go by different names in different places. Sometimes they are the Dearg Due." Though Dearg Due was one of the names used for a female Abhartach, both male and female victims of the Bánánach all eventually awoke to become mindless blood drinkers.

They were supernaturally strong and fast, with heightened senses and teeth and claws that exuded a toxin that prevented their victims' wounds from healing. The beasts awoke completely feral, with a primal instinct that was sometimes their undoing. Despite exhibiting greater strength, the undead bodies themselves were actually weaker than they were in life.

I had heard nightmarish stories of Abhartach breaking down doors to reach a victim, only to emerge with broken and unusable arms on the other side. In their mindless hunger, the Abhartach would literally destroy their own bodies. Abhartach would never stop coming, unless their heads were separated from their bodies, or they were burned to ash.

The light of the man's firewood flickered; it wouldn't last much longer. I motioned to a shape against the wall behind him. The shreds of fabric looked to be the remains of a tapestry from an earlier time. The man picked it up and wrapped it carefully around his partially burning wood stick. The old fabric ignited, lighting up the corridor around us.

In its light, I could see that almost all the remaining fianna members were bleeding from multiple wounds. Many of them had an ashen gray hue to their skin, which appeared even more sickly in the light of our makeshift torch.

"We must get farther away from the entrance," I said.

At the rear, a man and a woman whispered. At my sharp look, they took a step away from the rest of the group. The man spoke up, refusing to meet my eyes. "We will remain here." He gestured at the woman, who leaned heavily on his arm. "Her leg…I must bandage it." Now that I looked, I could see the woman's thigh was drenched in red.

I shook my head. "No. We need to stick together."

"I can't farthing walk," the woman yelled out, her voice cracking. She released the man's arm and sank to the stone floor, leaning her back on the corridor wall. He crouched next to her and began quickly bandaging her wound.

"I will stay with them," offered another man.

Our tactical retreat was beginning to fall apart. The members of the group were either too injured or too scared to go on. They didn't know me or trust me to keep them safe.

I looked back at the body of the fallen woman and set Deichtine and Sétanta gently on the ground. They weren't going to like this part.

I drew Vowkeeper. The fianna collectively took a step away from me, but I ignored them.

"If we are to make our stand here, we must remove the head of our fallen."

Eyes shocked, the four fianna members left standing in the center of the corridor instinctively shifted to be between me and the dead woman. No one said anything, but the message was clear. They would not allow me to defile the body of their friend.

I considered the group. Except for the man with the torch, everyone had grabbed a weapon when the Bánánach attacked. Despite this, if they attacked me, I wagered I still had the upper hand. Father had insisted on my training beginning at a young age, and I had a nearly unmatched level of experience. Not only could I fight with any blade or bludgeoning weapon, but I could parry and defend against more skilled and more numerous opponents.

Even so, I knew that turning on one another would only leave us more vulnerable. I lowered my blade with deliberate care and exhaled, weighing our options. Heading outside was impossible— the Bánánach would tear us apart. Splitting into smaller groups would make us easy prey. And if we stayed where we were…

A scream came from the injured woman resting against the wall. The dead woman had risen and her jagged teeth were locked onto the neck of the man who held the torch. He gurgled in her newly clawed arms.

Utter chaos erupted from the remaining fianna. The three other men in the center of the hallway turned to attack the newly risen Abhartach suddenly in their midst.

The man who had been bandaging the injured woman jerked to his feet just in time to have his neck opened by the Abhartach's claws. His hands scrabbled at his throat, trying to stop the blood geysering from what I could see was a deadly wound. The Abhartach's first victim had already slumped to the ground.

The woman with the injured leg screamed and drove her sword upward into the creature's body. The monster impaled itself further on the blade as it lunged at her, sinking its teeth into her face. She began screaming, the sound muffled as blood from her ruined face ran into her mouth.

The blades of the surviving fianna sliced and stabbed at the creature as it continued to feast on the screaming woman. The three men had already cut off one leg and one arm at the elbow. Finally, one of the men swung wildly into the neck of the creature. Fortunately, the body of the Abhartach fell away from the neck where it had been attached in life. Unfortunately, the head of the creature stayed attached to the living woman who now had the blade of the man sticking halfway out of her neck. The killing blow had also doomed her.

An eerie quiet filled the hallway. It had been only seconds, but three more of the fianna lay dead. Before me, one of the men sobbed. The torch, still lit, was resting on the floor where blood was threatening to extinguish it.

"Pick up the torch," I commanded, my voice harsh. One of the men looked at me, then just as quickly scrambled to pick up the torch. I don't know what he saw in my face, but it must have been as terrible as the gruesome scene around us.

I felt completely devoid of emotion, in that calm place where my military training could take over. I knew the three men who had dispatched the Abhartach might think me cold or callous, but the truth was it was my desire to live that governed my actions. I had to survive in order to protect Deichtine and Sétanta.

This time, I would not be swayed. "Turn away if you cannot stomach what must be done."

Without a word, the men stepped aside, avoiding my eyes but allowing me passage to the bodies of the dead. I steeled myself and lifted Vowkeeper.

And that is when the ceiling collapsed and buried us alive.

CHAPTER 19:
DUELS & BLADES

< CAI >

Day 15 of Midwinter, Sunrise
Cai's Room, The Deep Realm
Annwn

I had eventually drifted off to sleep, dreaming of a series of bloody duels, all filled with flashing blades. In some, I found myself squaring off against faceless opponents in the dueling grounds. In others, I was merely an onlooker, watching an already in-progress fight. I tossed and turned, the dreams melting into one another.

The starring roles seemed to belong to the major Fomorian blades: Cathscian, Fuilgeir, Orna, and Fragarach. When I arrived in this world only a few years ago, I had felt overwhelmed by the names and bloody histories of each blade. But as I spent more time with the swords, and saw them in action, their meaning and purpose had become more apparent.

When I first arrived in Annwn, only three blades were in the possession of Fomorian leaders. Neit carried Cathscian, the "Battle Blade," the only blade not made of a cold iron or a cold iron alloy. Corb brandished the double-bladed Fuilgeir, known as the "Blood Cleaver." And Tethra carried her "Precious Gem," Orna.

Of the three blades, only two were currently being wielded. Cathscian had been damaged so badly in Neit's battle with Nuada that the sword had been retired. A sad end to a blade so legendary that its origins had been immortalized in the bard's tale, "The First Fomorian," then set to music and sung each Midsummer celebration. It had honored the coming of both Neit and Cathscian to the Otherworld. Cathscian's story had ended with the death of Neit.

In my dreams, I watched the remaining two blades flashing in battle. For thousands of years, they had been wielded side-by-side. For the first time, Fuilgeir and Orna would be pitted against each other on the dueling ground, with only the more skilled warrior emerging victorious. Despite my protests, I knew there was nothing I could do about it. Fomorian would battle Fomorian even while the Tuatha rallied their forces to destroy us all.

From a tactical standpoint, it was an interesting matchup. Fuilgeir made its wielder faster and stronger with every hit. But Orna had a memory. Not only did Tethra's precious gem herald the deeds of past battles, it learned from them. The sword empowered her to parry and counter similar actions from any opponent. It learned and remembered.

My mind subconsciously flicked to my own blade, Fragarach. I had only been in possession of the weapon for the last nine days. It had been a gift from King Nuada to his nephew, Lugh. When Lugh and I had faced each other on the banks of Lough Dearg, I had been forced to strike him down with the Spear of Victory. After, while the Morrigan cradled her dying cousin in her arms, Tethra and I had retreated with Fragarach.

Remorse and sorrow threaded through the edges of my dreams, but I forced them away in the half-awake/half-asleep gray area I floated in. War was coming for us. I reminded myself that people die in war. Despite its truth, there was a part of my mind that loathed myself for thinking that way. The part of myself that needed to be strong reinforced the reasons why Lugh's death had been necessary.

Yes, we had stolen his spear, but only because they had first stolen the cauldron. We were balancing the battlefield. Right?

I hadn't known Lugh but knew that his death would almost certainly bring Findrias into the war. Gorias, if they knew the truth about Brigid, would not enter the fray. That left only my people to battle the armies of Murias, Findrias, and Falias. Could the Fomorians successfully defend their way of life under Tethra's rule? Likely not without reinforcements. But could my brother sway the god of the sea to align himself with our plight? Could he sway Gorias? If so, perhaps we had a fighting chance.

The biggest question in my mind was whether these possible allies would remain allies if Corb were to defeat Tethra. He had aided Balor in the attack on the Heart-shaped Pool and the invasion of Gorias. Bren was out pleading for help for a victimized people that would be utterly and completely changed if Corb were to become our king.

I finally gave up on sleep. My head throbbed as it tended to do when I didn't get enough rest. My eyes felt gritty and hollow. I sat up, still damp from sweat, and reached blindly for Fragarach.

I thought back to the first time I had seen it. It had glowed a brilliant silver with my Identification boon. Such was the way with magic items in Annwn. The strongest magic glowed silver… until the items tasted the blood of the immortal Tuatha, then they glowed with a golden light.

I stood up and swung the sword in the air. The gentle whistling sound it made brought me comfort. The blade grew broader near the tip yet was perfectly balanced… an impossible feat that only the smith god could have managed.

The sweat from my body was drying in the cool air of the morning, despite the dampness of the stone floors of my room. The walls glowed with the dim light of the lichen that was everywhere in the Deep Realm. While my boons made it so I could see perfectly well, it had taken some time to get used to life underground.

I moved to stand in front of a polished obsidian mirror, staring at my reflection. A tired, dangerous-looking man stared back, heavy black scars standing out against the paler skin of my torso. I wondered if this was how Bren had seen me that night on the lake. At times like this, it was like the blackness went deeper than the surface, like the darkness of the branching scars was exposing the darkness contained within me.

How fitting, I thought. A part of me had always known the toll this war was having on my very core. Though I didn't know who I had been before the night of the Cold Moon, I knew that I had indeed been changed in my time in Annwn. If only I could use that darkness to save Tethra. I wanted, so badly, to take her place in the duel against her brother… my adopted brother.

But that would never be allowed to happen, and Tethra would never forgive me if I tried. I knew she would see it as a betrayal of the worst kind, a sign that I didn't have faith in her. But I also didn't trust Corb to fight fair. He had no honor, which made the mantra that all participants were required to utter before walking onto the sacred ground, meaningless. The words were simply "With honor, I stand, by the shore and sea. If the Abyss takes me, let it remember my deeds."

Tethra had taught me that there were only five rules in a duel. Breaking any led to automatic disqualification. The rules were as follows:

Honor:
Recite the honor invocation before battle begins.

Weapons:
Magic and ranged weapons are forbidden.

Defense:
Shields are allowed, but heavy armor is discouraged.

Interference:
Duels are between the declared combatants alone.

Retreat:
Fleeing or refusing to fight is prohibited.

There were three paths to victory. A combatant could force a submission, kill, or permanently disarm their opponent. Killing or sending a fellow duelist into the Abyss, which was essentially the same thing, hardly ever happened in a duel.

My mind whirled with worry. the Deep Realm had never seen a duel between the likes of Tethra and Corb. The very walls would shake, and blood would stain the ground for a hundred years.

Worry and inaction often went hand in hand in my estimation. Thoughts of the pending duel and the looming war were too much for my sleep-deprived mind, and I could no longer simply wait in my lonely room. The time for passive thought was over.

I rose to my feet, suddenly strong in my purpose. I would "stand" as the mantra said, next to Tethra, my friend, and hopefully, my future queen. We would spend the next day and a half preparing for what was to come. Though she was more experienced than me in swordplay, I knew that only I could prepare her to face the darkness inside of Corb. It was training time.

CHAPTER 20:

THE WELL OF WISDOM

< BREN >

Day 14 of Midwinter, Sunset
At Sea, Well of Wisdom
Annwn

A storm brewed on the horizon. As soon as we'd left the protection of the harbor with its view of houses and city blocks and entered the vast openness of the western ocean, I knew it. The clouds above looked ominous, and the churning water below had taken on an inky black shade I associated with fathomless deep.

I equated the deep with the unknown, a sensation made even stronger by the nothingness I felt on all sides. I felt...adrift, like the currach that was being tossed more and more by the waves around us. I knew I wasn't putting my best foot forward with the son of the sea god. Still, it was hard to remain cheerful given the seriousness of what faced us and, I admitted to myself, my impatience to get help to Cai and the Fomorians without having to complete whatever "test" Manny had in store for me. Still, I resolved then and there to give the mistrustful man a chance. After all, what's the worst that could happen to me here?

As if reading my mind, Manannán spoke. "There are worse fates on Mag Rein than death." Great. And just like that, my irritation returned.

"You're a real ray of sunshine, Manny, you know?" In my defense, Manannán was doing absolutely bupkis to help with the small boat. I struggled with the sheet and tiller, glancing up to see what looked like a hint of amusement on his face. As quickly as I spotted it, the expression was gone.

"Death is not always the worst-case scenario for we immortals, particularly on the sea." He gazed critically at where my hands clutched the sheet and tiller, looking as if he was about to comment on my…er, technique. In my defense, I had successfully made it out of the harbor without clipping another vessel.

I quickly spoke. "So…Mag Rein must be a reference to the two Wells?" No response whatsoever. I sighed, deciding I might as well face things head-on. "You might as well just tell me. When do the terrible things start happening?"

Manannán raised his eyebrows and tipped his head to the darkening horizon. "I see it," I snapped. My temper was close to a breaking point. "You had me come out here, and I'm pretty sure you knew this would happen. What exactly am I supposed to do? Steer into the storm? That doesn't seem particularly wise."

Manannán shrugged, relaxing even more into his seat while I wrestled with the small ship. "You tell me. But whatever you are going to do, you should do it soon. The wind and waves will only continue to increase in power."

He was right. The jib, the tiny front sail, was all over the place, and I was fighting the tiller so much that my arm had begun to cramp.

"I get it. This is the test." I pondered my choices. I could try to turn the currach around and flee from danger (which would make me a coward)…or I could sail directly into the storm (which definitely would make me an idiot). It was an impossible decision. It seemed situations like this were always set up by someone who liked lording their judgment over others. They always had a "right" answer in mind. I shook my head. "There is no good decision here."

Instead of replying, Manannán recited an all-too-familiar Irish proverb. "The storm makes the oak grow deeper roots."

"The storm also makes the oak into driftwood!" I retorted. Even so, I took his meaning and steered the ship directly toward the flashing lightning ahead. Around my waist, I felt an ever-so-slight buzz from Taranis' belt.

Manannán appeared completely unconcerned by the approaching maelstrom. He stared pensively into the darkness. "The Western Well always makes me think of Uncle Ogma."

I continued to struggle with the currach in the waves, but found myself curious enough to ask, "Uncle-God of Knowledge, right?"

"Yes. He is wise and full of wondrous stories and poetry. Some believe his great mind is fed indirectly from this very sea."

"I thought drinking salt water would kill you, not make you smarter," I said flippantly.

"Indeed… It is said the wisdom of Ogma was given by the salmon he attracted with his velvet tongue. The fish connected him directly to the weave itself and granted a sort of divine inspiration." It was a confusing story, to be honest, but of all things, fish making someone smart wouldn't be the weirdest thing I had heard in the past two weeks.

At that moment, I felt a sudden, strong gust of wind yank the ship off course. I found myself fighting even harder with the sheet and tiller. Seeming completely unfazed, Manannán stood suddenly. Without any fanfare, he pulled a flat and worn square of grayish leather from his pockets and folded it in his hands until it resembled the shape of a bag. Then Manny stuffed my loose belongings into it and set a foot on the gunnel with relaxed concentration.

"I will return the rest of your armor and your shillelagh if you survive." He turned to face the ocean.

"Wait! What are you doing?" I asked, panicking. "You aren't leaving, are you? You can't leave now!"

"Survive, god of Chaos. Be the quality that others have seen in you."

"How? What am I even doing here?"

"If you can understand the mysteries of the sea, I will find you after." With that, he leaped into the dark, turbulent water.

"You are the worst god of travelers ever!" I yelled to no one. The currach had lurched sideways, despite my attempts to pull on the ropes and tiller to hold it in line. I was fighting what felt like the full might of the ocean. The wind was now dictating the ship's orientation. It seemed that even my increased strength simply wasn't enough to steer it properly.

I had to be missing something. What had Manny said before he left me to fend for myself? Something about mysteries of the sea… I decided to stop trying to break apart Manny's cryptic goodbye, and instead focus on getting the ship pointed in a direction of my choosing. But where to go?

It was probably a bad idea to steer into the storm. But then again, I was here to prove something to the father-son duo, and I doubted the massive storm was a coincidence. With that in mind, I set about trying to orient the boat toward the flashes of lighting and the roar of… farthing hell, was that a funnel cloud?

The wind was too strong and erratic for me to even try to overpower it. Out of desperation, I let the wind guide my movements, without letting the gusts fully dictate the direction of the small vessel, which I realized picked up a fair amount of speed.

"Yes!" I shouted. I positioned the jib and the tiller such that I was at an ideal angle to propel myself forward, building momentum. With momentum came leverage and the ability to choose my own direction. I aimed directly at the monster of a waterspout sucking up the ocean before me.

As I grew closer, I felt the water from the top of the funnel falling all around me. There was "little bitty stinging rain and big old fat rain. Rain that flew in sideways." I steered the small currach in and out of the path of the tornado, but I knew eventually our paths would cross.

Have you ever been so fixated on a task that you could only focus on whether you can do something and not whether you should be doing that thing? That was my current frame of mind. I had been trying so hard to accelerate toward the supposed test of "quality" that I hadn't truly considered what was happening around me and how dangerous it was. Now only about a football field length away, I could see how massive the water cyclone was, and I couldn't look away.

A wave crashed into the currach, slamming me across the boat. I crashed into the opposite side, half falling out before Taranis' belt snagged on the side. Though my head and shoulders were actually down under the water, my belt, and dumb luck, had saved me from landing in the ocean, where I would have been without a boat, staring down the worst storm I had ever seen. I yanked myself back up, gasping for air.

I had temporarily forgotten about how dangerous the turbulent waters were. That mistake had nearly cost me everything. If I had died, I would have reappeared back at the Heart-shaped pool, miles from my current position. What would I have done then?

I shook myself out of my thoughts and moved back into position. I grabbed the sheet and tiller, watching as a wave crested close by. Using my newfound knowledge of how to work with the wind, I guided the currach into an arc that would directly intersect the wave's path.

The currach flew into the air, the new angle preventing the ship from being rolled by the oncoming wall of water. That was the key, I realized. I needed to use the wind and the instruments on the boat to steer myself into the waves. I would still be able to make my way toward the storm, but slowly and carefully. My primary goal was to not capsize before I reached whatever "finish line" Manny had in mind.

It was no sooner than I thought about the end state of this test that the water spout made an accelerated turn in my direction. "Ah, come on!" I shouted at the storm. "Really?!"

Powerless against the true power of the waterspout, I clutched the sides of the currach, holding on for dear life. At random increments, the boat was lifted into the air and then thrown back into the waves below. Despite the battering by the storm, I found myself mesmerized by the huge funnel looming above me. It seemed to stretch all the way into the heavens. For a split second, the whole world went quiet before I was sucked up into the maelstrom, currach and all.

CHAPTER 21:

NO ONE SHOULD BEITHIR

< FÍADAN >

Day 14 of Midwinter, Sunrise
The Sunken Well, Gorias
Annwn

One minute I was drifting downward into the brackish water of the well, beneath the waves of Hook Head, and the next I was emerging upward into the breathable air of a dark chamber. The well appeared much the same from this side, only there was no indication of the danger that lay on the other side of the egress. Fintan had come and gone in a different time, one before the flooding of the great Wells. Even still, I imagined that the first Sage likely had another way in and out of his library… laboratory… lair?

Emerging from the water, I found myself dry…a strange yet welcome enchantment, I thought. The well was at the center of a cylindrical room, surrounded by a spiral staircase leading up the inside of the walls. What was it with Sages and towers?

Unlit torches lined the walls of the staircase. Looking straight up, the darkness of the room kept me from being able to see the ceiling. I was reminded, in moments like this, of the limitations of my Gloaming Gaze boon. But there was no way I was going to try to light all the torches. It would take all day. Using my flint and steel, I lit the torch at the bottom of the stairs, intending to simply carry it with me.

Instead, I was pleasantly surprised to see the rest of the torches light themselves, in a wave leading up and away from me. It didn't warm the interior of the tower, but instead simply highlighted the age and neglect of the stairwell. Despite the limited signs of wear in the stonework, the dust and debris that had accumulated were impressive.

What was immediately apparent in the torchlight was the wide path leading up the middle of the winding stairs. It was clear of grime as if something had worn a path in the dust bunnies over time. And…that wasn't concerning at all.

"Hello?" I found myself saying out loud. I immediately felt stupid for alerting the entire tower to my presence. "Fintan… anyone home?" There was no reply, but I thought I heard a noise up a few levels.

I reached for my trusty Silverwhite blade, holding Swish in my right hand and Stick in my left. Something about having them out and ready to sing made me feel at home, no matter where I was. I began climbing the stairs.

"I don't know who's here, but if you jump out at me, I will definitely murder you." I knew that talking to my prey was a nervous habit of mine, but after hundreds of years doing it, I found it very difficult to stop.

Up on the first level, I found a living area of sorts. It was more wide open than I had expected. Several chests lined the walls, as well as bookshelves and a large statue of some kind of lizard. My eyes quickly fell back on the chests, and curiosity rose inside me.

"Um… I'm going to loot some chests now." I said aloud, now wondering if I was just talking to myself.

I flicked open the largest chest to find a collection of mostly rotten clothing. I grimaced at the smell and slammed it shut. I held my breath as I opened the neighboring, smaller chest. Inside I was pleased to find a collection of knickknacks that I knew would fill Morias with delight. I found a dark candle, four vials of different colored sand, a circular cipher wheel, a mostly crumbled map of a realm that looked vaguely like Annwn, a compass with a spectral needle, and a quill made of some sort of bone.

I cursed under my breath. Where were the weapons? Or the treasure? Then, I realized that this must have been Fintan's living quarters. Maybe he kept those kinds of things on another floor? There was plenty of the tower left to explore. As that realization came to me, I saw the arcane compass needle move out of the corner of my eye. It was now pointing in vaguely my direction, with the point of the needle moving slowly closer to my own location.

This device looked familiar to me. I remembered a similar device Urias had me experiment with while I served Bres and his family. What was it called again? The something "Dial…"

I thought back to when we had taken it on patrol with us. What did it do? I focused hard on the long-forgotten memories as the needle settled firmly on my position. My eyes went wide as I suddenly recalled its function. The memory came flooding back to me within the span of a heartbeat.

Urias had called the device a Heartbane Dial. The first time we had experimented with it, we had caught an assassin in the castle. The device was designed to point to danger, more specifically, to ill intent. I quickly rolled to my right as a massive shape whipped up behind me, crushing the chest I had been standing in front of.

Coming up into a fighting position, I stared at the creature in front of me. The reptilian statue was no longer in its original spot. It had quietly crept up behind me. My first thought was that I had set off some sort of protection spell, but when I got a good look at the creature, I realized my predicament.

The vaguely snake-shaped creature had two arms supporting its front-heavy frame. Its smooth, blue scales covered the whole creature, including its horns and massive tail. It had a flat, reptilian skull, with tiny white eyes that looked dead and buried inside of the protective scales. Its mouth was filled with hundreds of razor-sharp teeth.

This was a beithir, the most feared fae in all of Annwn. These things were what dragons would have had nightmares about if dragons had been real. In all of my time in Annwn, there had only been a handful of beithir sightings, and in the rare cases that the creatures had been defeated, it had taken a whole legion to defeat them. I was in serious trouble.

The beast's head moved from side to side, trying to figure out where I had gone. Its blue scales flashed with an electric light, making the hairs on my skin stand on end. The beithir opened its maw and lunged directly at me. I realized the creature must be using some form of static electricity instead of eyesight in order to find my position.

Again, I rolled out of the way. As I came back up into my fighting position, its massive tail slammed into me. I hit the side wall of the tower with a wet crunch and I saw stars. The beast roared in pain, and I was gratified to see that his tail had two bloody slash marks from where Swish and Stick had both found purchase.

The beithir let out a guttural hiss and my Fae Speech ability translated it. "For that, I will devour you slowly."

I didn't wait. I ran toward the creature, my head still spinning from my run-in with the wall. The creature's scales flared again with electric blue light, and I veered to the right as he sunk his teeth into the air around where I had been standing. I didn't stop and I didn't roll this time. Instead, I continued sprinting along the length of the beithir with Stick extended. The blade carved as I ran, splitting the beast's side. Its scales were hard, but nothing in this world was as hard and sharp as Silverwhite.

I felt pretty pleased with myself until I ran smack into the thick tail the beithir had instinctively brought around to capture and squeeze its prey. It surrounded me and immediately began to constrict in on itself. The gushing rent in the creature's side oozed its lifeblood inside the coil. Muscle, scale, and blood began to squeeze in around me.

I cursed. Had it been a few days earlier, I would have just flown out of this ever-shrinking circle of death. But with my wings in their current state, I was trapped. I squirmed and lashed out with my blades, stabbing them into the creature up to their hilts, stopping only when I felt the stench of beithir breath directly above me.

The creature flared with its electrical magic, and the cold eyes of the creature focused in on my position. It had left just enough space with its coiled body to plunge its mouth into the hole… the hole that I was trapped in.

Suddenly, the creature's body spasmed and another voice rose. The voice was one I didn't recognize, but again, my Fae Speech ability activated.

"I've never eaten blue food before." The voice was simple, wondering, almost detached from the dire situation that we all found ourselves in.

The beithir seemed to view the newcomer as more of a threat, as its coiled tail loosened slightly. It lifted its gaze away from me and flared its electric sight. Using the distraction, I dug my blades into the coiled mass of creature, then jumped, flipping myself up on top of the tail. My eyes searched in the direction of the new voice.

When I saw what had spoken, my heart sank. My mind reeled with the impossibility of the situation. There, in the room with me, stood another of the most feared creatures in all of the realms…an oilliphéist, its stinger exposed and dripping with a foul toxin.

"There you are," the oilliphéist said.

I looked from the beithir back to the oilliphéist, thinking about the absurdity of my life. In the split second before the two creatures could strike, I had already decided on my course of action. It didn't take long. It was the way I had lived every moment of my life. Gripping the girls tightly in my hands, I screamed and attacked.

CHAPTER 22:
TRAPPED!

Day 15 of Midwinter, Nightfall
Cruachan, Midlands
Annwn

I awoke with a start, unsure how much time had passed since the ceiling collapsed on us. I coughed, trying to clear the dust coating my tongue and teeth. The sound echoed loudly in the otherwise silent space.

It was dark, but I couldn't see stars. That could only mean we were low enough in the temple to still have some sort of superstructure above. I was guessing that only the sub-structure had collapsed.

My mind swam and spun around for a few minutes. It was only when I realized most of my body was immobilized that it seemed to settle in place. Peering into the gloom, I saw that several pieces of the shattered stone columns had pinned my legs, torso, and left arm in place.

I began testing the weight that held me down, first gently, then with all my might. But no matter how hard I pushed and pulled, I was unable to escape my dark prison.

My heart thudded painfully in my chest. The gnawing pain in my ribs and lungs was growing more excruciating with every breath. My mouth filled with a rich salty flavor, and I coughed again, spitting up dirt and blood.

There were no sounds from the fianna members. At the time of the collapse, there had been three alive, three recently killed, one slain Abhartach, plus the unconscious Deichtine and Sétanta.

All had been wounded by the Bánánach…which meant that any who had died, whether they perished in the collapse or had been killed by the Abhartach, were now a threat.

TADG MAC NUADAT

The voice in my head sounded bestial and raspy.

"Who is there?" I said aloud.

YOU ARE MY GUEST HERE. THANK YOU FOR COMING INSIDE… IT HAD GROWN DREADFULLY LONELY HERE.

The words were innocent enough, but the voice was mocking. I knew immediately who it belonged to…the creature I had feared, the one that changelings were afraid to mention too near to Cruachan. Its name was…

AILLÉN. IT IS NOT MY GIVEN NAME, BUT IT HAS BECOME WHO I AM.

I wasn't accustomed to having a conversation with another person in my mind. "I have heard of you," I said aloud.

YOU ARE AFRAID OF ME. BUT THEN, YOU SHOULD BE.

The voice sounded…amused.

I strained again but remained trapped. Trapped by the boulders. Trapped by the Bánánach. Trapped by those who would rise to become Abhartach. Now, I was trapped by Aillén.

My thoughts turned to Brigid and what would become of her if I didn't make it to Falias before my father. Then, there were Deichtine and Sétanta. Were they even alive? If they or any others of the Fianna had survived the collapse, their fate rested with my own.

SUCH AN INTERESTING MIND YOU HAVE. SURROUNDED BY DANGER AND DYING, YET THINKING ONLY OF THOSE WHO YOU MIGHT SERVE.

The voice chuckled.

"Get out of my mind!" I shouted into the darkness.

I CAN'T DO THAT. AH…THINGS ARE ABOUT TO GET INTERESTING. ALLOW ME TO SHED A LITTLE LIGHT ON YOUR CURRENT SITUATION.

With Aillén's words, the walls began to glow faintly, illuminating the wreckage of the passageway. The portion of the corridor that led deeper into the temple remained, but the way we had come was completely blocked by rubble.

I saw movement behind a large pile of debris. A figure emerged —the woman who had been killed by her fellow Fianna member. His sword was still lodged in her throat. And she was no longer a changeling. With a feral roar, the Abhartach charged me, her mouth gaping wide.

My body still mostly immobilized, I threw my free arm into her path. My hand groped at the sword. I felt a sharp sting as my hand slid down the blade toward the grip. Hot blood ran down my arm toward my body as the pain of the injury registered with my senses.

The creature raked its claws down my extended arm, snapping its teeth at me as it tried to get closer. The blood running toward my shoulder increased, but for the moment, it seemed I had just enough strength to hold the weight of the smaller woman off of me.

My injured hand finally found the handle of the sword. I instinctively jerked it with all my strength. The creature's head slid from its body, which thudded to the ground next to me.

It was quiet again. All I could hear was the beating of my heart, pounding in my chest. My arm fell back to rest on the ground, but I kept my grip on the sword.

Blood continued to drip from my hand and arm. The pool spreading out around me had grown enough to reach the back of my head where I lay panting. My ribs were screaming and every wheezing breath I sucked in came back out as a wet gurgle. My deep breaths weren't providing enough air for my depleted body and I had to fight the desire to simply close my eyes.

IMPRESSIVE.

The voice boomed again in my head.

YOU ARE A FIGHTER, AREN'T YOU? NOT SIMPLY THE SON OF A USURPER.

Ignoring the voice, I forced myself to focus on my surroundings. There had to be something I could do. Aillén continued, his tone still amused and mocking.

OH DEAR. I SURE HOPE THOSE OTHER CREATURES DON'T GET FREE…

With that, I heard scratching sounds coming from multiple areas in the passageway.

"Hello," I called, hoping to hear a reply from someone still living. No response.

ONLY TWO REMAIN ALIVE.

My eyes scanned the area of the floor for Deichtine and Sétanta. With the low light coming from the walls, I could finally see the boy. He was also pinned, but Deichtine lay nearby, miraculously free of the rubble.

NOW THIS SHOULD GET INTERESTING….

Ignoring the taunting voice, I dropped the sword to push against the debris that locked me in place.

YOU KNOW…I COULD HELP YOU.

Aillén's statement lingered in the air.

I fought against the fuzziness that was starting to creep across my vision. I was so tired. I didn't know if it was due to the recent blood loss or because I hadn't slept more than two hours in the last three days…or because I was dying. Every breath felt like knives. Even as I continued to push against the stone that pinned me, I could feel myself growing weaker.

The creature's voice in my mind crooned.

THEY WILL ALL WAKE UP SOON. IT WILL BE TOO LATE THEN.

I heard a small movement near where Deichtine lay. She slowly pushed herself into a seated position. The process was slow and painful to watch. She clearly had some internal injuries, as well as multiple cuts and bruises. Her skin was a sour color.

Her eyes fluttered open as she rested her body weight against a large-sized boulder. She met my eyes, the trapped body of Sétanta lying unconscious between us.

"Deichtine, help me." I could feel myself growing frantic. If she could just help me shift some of these rocks, I could escape and possibly eliminate the looming Abhartach. She and the boy would have a chance.

She didn't move or answer, only stared at me with dull eyes. The woman's arms lay limp at each side of her body. Suddenly, her head lolled to one side, revealing a gaping wound where a rock must have struck. She slumped, head dropping to her chest. A thin trickle of blood rolled out of her mouth as her body lost all muscle tension.

I watched in horror as the dead woman's arms started to twitch. Her head jerked with an involuntary spasm.

IT IS TIME FOR YOU TO DECIDE.

I desperately pushed again on the stone that pinned me, my bloody hand slipping and sliding on its surface. No luck. Deichtine's body spasmed again and then went still.

Her eyes snapped open, but there was a hollowness to her gaze. She drooled a bloody liquid and opened her mouth wide, showing a row of sharpened teeth with extended canines. Her ravenous gaze fell upon the body of the still Sétanta between us.

Panicked, I shouted, "What is it you want?"

ALL YOU MUST DO IS COME LOWER INTO MY TEMPLE. FREE ME.

The thing that had been Deichtine began to creep forward on her hands and knees. She crawled toward the boy with a feverish, hungry look.

"I'll do it," I screamed. I spared only a second's thought for the gravity of what I was agreeing to. Aillén was an ancient evil, one mostly unknown to me. But I knew it had been imprisoned here for good reason. What kind of evil might I be unleashing on Annwn?

"Free me," I gasped, black dots beginning to swim in my vision. "And I will come free you."

He laughed inside of my mind, and it resonated outside of my body and echoed along the walls of the passageway.

THE BARGAIN HAS BEEN MADE.

CHAPTER 23:
TRAINING DAY

< CAI >

Day 15 of Midwinter, Sunrise
Training Grounds, The Deep Realm
Annwn

"You look like chet," Tethra teased. She had never been one to keep her thoughts from me, no matter what they were. We walked together and headed for the training grounds.

I shrugged. "I feel like chet, so that makes sense."

Tethra, back in her typical braided leather armor, looked downright refreshed. In the meantime, I apparently looked awful. Thinking back to my dreams, I wasn't surprised.

She elbowed me gently. "You are much too worried about this duel, Béstin. I have trained with Corb all of my life. I know his weaknesses better than perhaps he does." We stopped in front of an isolated circular stone training area. The training grounds were similar in size to the duel pit, but unlike the duel pit, they weren't sunk into the ground. "True, he is bigger and stronger, but I have always been faster and smarter."

I placed my canteen on the ground outside of the carved perimeter marker, searching for the right words. "It isn't that I doubt your skill. It is what might happen if you lose."

"I am aware of our situation." Tethra began dropping all manner of weapons outside of the marked line. As I watched her prepare for our sparring match, I felt the knot of worry in the deepest recesses of my heart expand almost painfully.

Tethra dropped a final, wicked-looking dagger to the ground before turning to face me. "I know you think Corb is untrustworthy, but he is still kin. He was raised under the same strict rules of our father as I." She shot me a pointed look. "And you are not to do anything that would cast doubt on the validity of the final outcome."

I couldn't tell her that with every moment, I could see the tendrils of haze growing stronger around her. Some had begun to wind their way toward my own body. I met her eyes. "I know you would never forgive me…"

"…but?" She clearly could tell I was holding back.

"IF I saw him breaking the honor code, I couldn't promise to stay idle."

Anger flared in her unnaturally blue eyes. Her voice came out harsh. "You will do as I say in this matter, not only because I will be your queen, but because of the love you feel for me."

I drew back, shocked. For four years, Tethra had been the one person I could always count on. She had been the one to collect me from the Heart-shaped Pool. Her face had been the first I'd seen in this strange world, as I emerged horribly injured and without my memories. I was fiercely loyal to her and knew that she felt the same. We had eaten together and fought together. We had spent countless hours together, talking of the Fomorian culture and the world around us, talking about everything, it seemed… but we had never talked of love.

"Well, say something." Tethra stood still, her expression defiant. It would have looked cold and stern to anyone else, but not to me. I knew every curve of her face and could read her every mood. Right now, her eyes, while fierce, were pleading with me to respond. The silence felt heavy between us.

"You know that I do," I finally said. "That is why I need you to promise when you fight him, you won't treat him like a brother. He is your enemy. He is MY enemy. He is the enemy to all of our people."

She chuckled, breaking the strange, tense mood. "Are you really instructing a Fomorian daughter on how to do battle?" She raised an eyebrow as if daring me to argue. She stood still, her footing sure on the open stone floor. She looked like a cat who was biding her time until she lashed out with deadly claws. Orna was already in her hand.

I readied Fragarach, swinging my wrist to warm up. "I'm serious, Tethra. He will not treat this as a sparring match. Despite the traditional vows you will both say before the duel, this is not about honor for Corb."

She held up the sword in a salute that I knew indicated it was time for us to begin. When her attack came, I parried, knowing from experience that the only way to counter her incredible speed was to actually anticipate her actions.

"What do you think it IS about then?" she asked. Orna sliced through the air, almost blindingly fast. Fragarach met her sword with a clash.

"It's about power... over you... over our people. It's about taking power back from Nuada. And I think it matters little to him what is left after he is done grasping for it." I straightened from my fighting stance, willing her to listen. "He would burn it all down just to sit atop the smoking pile of ash."

Tethra took advantage of my pose, springing forward with her blade. I quickly recovered, barely managing to block her attack. My left arm would be feeling the effects of that blow for weeks to come.

"What is the Mná na Mara take on Corb's reappearance?" I asked. I darted in, feinting with my sword, then pivoted at the last second to deliver an unorthodox stomp to the top of Tethra's booted foot. She responded with a hard punch to the top of my head. I shook my head, momentarily dizzy.

"I see what you are doing, Béstin, but if you truly want to prepare me, grow bigger and stronger." Her eyes crinkled with laughter.

I charged forward, attacking with a flurry of blows. Our swords locked. While Tethra was bigger than me, I was more equivalent in strength to Corb than she was expecting. I leaned into my attack, finally forcing her massive blade crashing into her face. There was a crunching sound as her nose twisted, her eyes tearing with the sudden pain.

Pressing my advantage, I moved to deliver a brutal kick, hoping to catch her thigh and send her to the ground. Instead, Tethra snatched my foot from the air, using my momentum to toss me away. She wiped her eyes, narrowing them at me in irritation.

"The Women are under no illusions as to who Corb is and who he followed." Her eyes tracked my movements.

"Then why do they let this happen?" I demanded. I leaped at her as the words left my mouth, trying a repeat of my earlier move. Her sword whipped up to parry mine. Sparks flew as she slid Orna down Fragarach to the cross guard. The blade flew from my hand. I stared dumbly at Fragarach on the ground between us, realizing that both Tethra and Orna had known my attack even before I had. I raised my eyes to Tethra. She smirked.

"The Women can see his strength," she said, "and the only thing they value more than strength is honor. But many of them share his desire for revenge." She took a step back, gesturing for me to pick up my sword.

I took my time, thinking. I had been trying to fight as I thought Corb would, using strength and unexpected attacks to throw Tethra off. It hadn't worked. I knew he wouldn't be allowed to use the ranged fire attacks from the Evil Eyes, but the innate abilities of Fuilgeir would make Corb faster and stronger. I pictured the double-bladed Blood Cleaver and thought back to the added abilities it would grace Corb with. How could I imitate those conditions?

I moved to pick up Fragarach, crouching and rolling smoothly into a striking position. Tethra took up a defensive low-block stance. Using my Transform Energy boon, I slowed her kinetic movements the way I had done with the cannonballs and arrows on the battlefield of Brú na Dallta. While her movements remained slow, I slashed with my sword, scoring a quick hit to her ribs.

Tethra roared, clearly having felt her speed being diminished. But I didn't stop there. I spun and came at her again from behind. She turned, her movements still slower than normal. I moved in for a thrust, forgetting for a brief moment this was a training exercise. Even as I remembered, I forced myself to follow through with the powerful stab rather than turning my blade wide.

Tethra's eyes widened as she sensed the dangerous nature of my thrust at her torso. Before my sword could strike true, I found my legs above me. My back struck the ground hard. She had swept my legs out from under me. Looking up, I saw my blade pinned underneath Tethra's arm. We both were panting.

"I was trying to show you…" I began. The look on her face was terrible.

"You were trying to show me what it would be like to duel Fuilgeir. And you were fighting dirty." She took a deep breath and extended me a hand. "But you forget what I told you. I am the better sword master."

As I rose to my feet, she used the hand still holding mine to pull me in close. Her long arms wrapped around me. I stood in shock for a moment. Slowly, I let my arms rise to return the embrace. The side of my head pressed against her chest, and I could hear her heart race.

I let myself get lost in the rhythmic sound. I thought about the strength of the beat and the irregularities of the contracting muscles in her chest that made her immortal heart unique. I thought about the stamina inherent in a never-ceasing heart. A moment without one or two beats would stagger her. More than that would cause her death. Such a simple thing, yet so essential to life. She needed her heart, and I realized in that moment, just how much I needed it, too. "Tethra…." I began.

She released me suddenly, straightening to her full height. Her cheeks were flushed, whether from the unexpected embrace or the fight, I didn't know. She stalked to the boundary marker and began to pick up her equipment. "Come, Béstin. There is something you need to see." She began walking, clearly expecting me to follow.

We left the training grounds and traveled lower into the depths of the city. Eventually, the lights of the city and the echoing sound of her heart faded from my senses. They were replaced by the lapping of gentle waves, the darkness of the deep, and the now almost tangible tendrils of haze that flowed between us.

CHAPTER 24:

THE SALMON OF CAPISTRANO

< BREN >

Day 14 of Midwinter, Sunset
At Sea, Well of Wisdom
Annwn

I held tight to the currach as I sailed into the air, spinning violently. My sense of where the water ended and the sky began was completely upended. Anything that had been inside the boat had been ejected. The jib made a loud flapping noise that made me think it was badly damaged.

I was soaked from head to toe. It felt like I was standing in the middle of a rainstorm, only the rain was pelting me from every direction. Now that I was inside the water spout, I had the same sensations I'd felt riding a rollercoaster, though thankfully I was too disoriented to be motion sick. I couldn't tell you how long I was flung about, but at one point, the amount of static electricity increased enough for me to feel the humming of my belt over the wind and rain.

I saw the flash before I heard the sound. Somehow my body was slower to recognize the superheated plasma coursing through me than it was to nearly be ripped apart by the boom of thunder at point-blank range. While my logical mind knew exactly what the sound was, my human experience was sure that it was the end of the world, possibly the entire universe. The rumble pierced my brain and rattled my bones. Lightning blinded me.

Needless to say, I was not prepared to be heated to what felt like fifty thousand degrees. I knew I should be dead. Luckily, the bolt of electricity seemed to be attracted directly to my belt. I wish I could describe the feeling accurately, but I was neither melted nor caught on fire by the lightning. Instead, I felt full to the brim with power.

My eyes were still blind from the flash, but the halo of light I could see had changed from a bright white to a very familiar blue hue. I felt the energy stream from my body in all directions, and I suddenly knew what had happened. I had simply been a conduit for the lightning, taking it in, converting it, and sending it back out into the world. The belt had not only acted as a lightning rod, attracting the energy, but it had also increased the capacity of my energy reservoir.

Thanks to my regeneration, the blur that pervaded my sight slowly began to improve, and I began to see exactly where I was. Vision and a falling sensation came together to paint a picture in my mind. The short version was that I had been expelled from the funnel cloud and shot into the sky. The longer version was that I still clung to the damaged currach. Holes riddled the sides and bottom of the boat. The water spout and ominous clouds that surrounded the storm were dissipating rapidly, spreading far and wide from a position in the sky that I could only guess was where I had released the energy of the bolt back out into the world.

I was hurtling through the air in both a downward and outward trajectory. I estimated I was at least a thousand feet up into the air, and it was going to get pretty serious in about 10 seconds. If only I had chosen Mancer Savant as Cai had! My brother was able to control the speed of objects based on the amount of their kinetic and potential energies. While I could try it, I knew from painful experience that unfamiliar magic wasn't really the smartest thing to do when death was on the line.

Instead, I did the only thing I could think of. I created a thick protective energy barrier around me and the currach, filling the holes in the boat. I even placed a barrier between myself and the vessel. The sea came at me faster and faster. I felt a sinking sensation in my stomach as I hit terminal velocity before it all went black.

I'm not sure how long I was unconscious. Thankfully, none of the Bodach came for me while I was out. I supposed damaging your brain in a massive fall and going to sleep were two different things entirely when it comes to brain function. Of course, I wasn't thinking any of these things while I was out cold. It wasn't until I came to and the sun was coming up that I began running through the nuances of my unconsciousness.

My energy barrier seemed to have survived the fall, and my body had healed any of the injuries I had sustained in the storm. The boat, on the other hand, was trashed. The only thing keeping it afloat was my protective barriers. The jib sail was practically torn in two, and while I could turn the tiller, whatever was connected to the handle that lived beneath the water had broken off. I was adrift in placid water with no way to steer what was left of the currach.

The sky was no longer dark. In fact, at that moment, I could see the sunrise over the nothingness that lay to the east. That would have been the way back to Murias, had I had a working sail, or even a paddle. Everything in or on the boat had been destroyed or lost.

I drifted for a time, trying to keep my eyes on the eastern horizon so that I could find my way back to shore… provided a miracle appeared to deliver me there. I could feel my temper rising, threatening my normal cool demeanor. Just as I was about to lose it, I heard running water. I felt the currach begin to travel in a westward current.

Looking west, I saw the same thing that I saw facing east… endless water. Wait, no… not the same thing. There was the water and the horizon, but when I looked closer, I did notice a slight difference. To the west, in the direction of the rushing water, I could see some sort of hazy section between the placid ocean water and the sky. It wasn't until the sun rested on the western edge of the sky that I could identify what the sound and the haze truly were.

As I traveled with the current, I got a closer look at what would be my inevitable demise. Annwn didn't appear to be a globe at all. The Otherworld appeared to be flat, and I had nearly arrived at the western edge where the water plummeted off the side. Eat your heart out flat-earthers!

Despite my situation, I had to laugh. I guessed that I had at most 20-30 minutes before the boat literally fell off the side of the world. I needed to somehow reverse course.

My mind flew into action. I could probably shoot a blast of energy in the opposite direction and use it to propel myself eastward. But how much it would work and for how long, I didn't know. And eventually, I would need food and water.

Sticking my left hand into the water, I started to conjure up an energy blast. Before I could summon much energy, though, I was distracted by the sight of a large fish jumping from the abyss before falling back into nothing. It looked exactly like salmon from Earth, jumping upstream to mate... only this particular fish was the size of the currach I was currently sitting in.

The first time it jumped, it fell back down into the abyss. Its second attempt was more successful. The salmon made it up onto the edge of the Well before disappearing under the surface of the water. I tried to remember the story Manny had shared with me before he ditched me... something about his Uncle Ogma and the salmon of the Well. I was so lost in thought that I was surprised to look up only to find the fish had surfaced next to the currach and was staring at me.

"Um... Hello, large fish," I said, my voice cracking. "Fancy meeting you here." The fish appeared to be studying me. I frantically focused on what I could remember of Manny's story.

He had said, "Ogma's wisdom came from the salmon he attracted with his velvet tongue. The fish connected him directly to the weave itself and granted a sort of divine inspiration."

It occurred to me that velvet tongue was another way to say someone was a smooth talker. Had Ogma read the salmon poetry or something?

I decided it was worth a shot, and endeavored to take a stab at a stanza or two. After all, the fish was a captive audience and I could use some divine inspiration at the moment. My mind went to the first dramatic reference that the moment inspired. I cleared my throat and began.

"I would like to travel someplace warm. A place where the beer flows like wine. Where beautiful women instinctively flock like the salmon of Capistrano..." I paused, about to continue, when the fish splashed water into my face. "What?" I said, flinching back.

Okay, I thought. No movie lines, despite the obvious connections. Maybe some classic poetry...I cleared my throat again. "There once was a man from Nantucket..." The salmon slammed its head into the boat, rocking it. I fell back away from the side.

"Okay, okay! I'm sorry... Jeesh. You have NO sense of humor." I thought hard for something that wasn't just a collection of words. I'd never liked free verse, but writing rhymes wasn't something I could do off the cuff. At a loss, I thought about how Morias and I used to write silly haikus for our restaurant servers over the years...

> I am a lost man,
> Always letting down my friends.
> Now, I am alone.

The salmon shifted its position in the water so that it was looking at me from its right eye. It opened its mouth and I was briefly taken aback by the size of its many, many teeth. It let out a sound that I had never heard from an animal before, like bubbles being released or drops of water slowly falling into a pool. I didn't know what the giant fish was trying to communicate, but I took the gesture to mean that I should continue.

> Manny is a prick,
> His boat is the worst.
> Now, I am alone

I felt like I could keep going, now that my creative juices were flowing. But the salmon sounds increased, growing into a salmon song, one that I realized I could understand. It was strange, as the fish wasn't speaking words. Instead, it conveyed a feeling that my mind seemed to know how to parse.

We kept on like that for a time, speaking in different languages, but fully understanding one another. It was then, as I drifted closer and closer to the edge of the world, that I understood why this ocean was known as the Well of Wisdom.

CHAPTER 25:
DIFFICULT TOPICS

Day 14 of Midwinter, Sunset
Caisleán Saighead, Gorias
Annwn

"You could have at least cleaned off the filth. Your…appearance shows a lack of respect for the council." Macha stared down her nose at me from across the table of the council chamber.

I glanced down at the dried blood and salt on my arms and shrugged. "I always dress up for the people I like."

Macha appeared to take my meaning and stiffened. The rest of the council members just shook their heads at me… a gesture I had become quite familiar with over time.

Despite my snarky words, Macha wasn't wrong to point out my current state. Morias and I had just made it back from Hook Head. We hadn't had a chance to go to our rooms yet, let alone clean up. Erelith had found us as we were saying goodbye to Efa. Apparently, we were underdressed and late for the meeting in which we sat.

"Anyway…" Nemain said, breaking the awkward silence. "I am pleased that you and the Sage have returned from the coast without injury." She looked at the salt and blood crust that caked my arms. I could tell that she was thinking about retracting her last statement. Instead, she continued. "I trust that whatever urgent errand took you to the Sacred Cape has produced fruit?"

"Morias wouldn't let me stop to pick the fruit," I said flippantly.

"And this is why Ellyllon are not permitted to sit on the city councils!" Macha said in disgust. "It is impossible to have a linear discourse."

I opened my mouth to respond but stopped when I saw the frustration in Morias' eyes. His look implied heavily that I should stop talking. A vein bulged in his neck in frustration. I threw him a bone and just sat there, silent.

Finally, Morias turned his gaze away from me, turning to the tri-part sisters. "I believe Fíadan, with some aid from our former Prime Sage, has discovered the lost tower of Fintan the Wise."

Badb and The Dagda looked suitably impressed. Nemain and Macha did not.

It was Nemain who spoke first. "Why do you seek an old laboratory in our time of rebuilding?"

The Dagda spoke before Morias could. "Because he seeks to learn from the last period of destruction and rebuilding."

"That is correct." Morias' agreement was more succinct than I was used to.

"And what have you learned?" Macha said, following her sister's inquisitive lead.

I knew the question was for Morias, but it took all my restraint not to announce that I had reaffirmed my preference toward killing giant fae serpents than I did to listening to the flowery speech of court. Luckily, Morias filled the silence more quickly than I could retort.

"Fíadan has planted the Mirrorstone in Fintan's tower… and, might I add, has rid the premises of harm. Now that we have returned to Gorias, it will be my pleasure to study the famed contemporary of the Síorláidir."

Macha opened her mouth to ask another question, but Badb cut her off in exasperation. "To learn about the fall of the Síorláidir and the rise of the Tuatha… a turning point in our past that has marked an age."

"Until the Cold Moon…" Nemain's words trailed off.

"What is it that you think the Old Powers can teach us?" Macha asked.

"They are our forefathers." The Dagda replied.

"And mothers." I offered, drawing a smile from him.

Morias straightened himself in his chair preparing what was sure to be a rousing filabluster of information. I swear I saw him take in as much air as possible before opening his mouth to speak.

"The answer to that question is multifaceted." I sighed audibly, but he continued anyway.

"The finding of Fintan's tower is possibly the most important discovery of our time. We could learn about the very making of Annwn. We could learn about the sundering of the isles and the purpose of Uffern. We could discover the decline of the old gods and possibly learn how to avoid repeating it. We could discover how the Treasures were made and who ultimately made them. And selfishly, I might discover my own origins and purpose."

He finally paused to take a large breath. I saw everyone else do the same as if in some sort of sympathetic reflex. Macha was the first to respond and was clearly unmoved by the speech.

"We know all of those things, Sage. What we don't know is why you are taking time and resources away from the raising and defending of Gorias when we from Findrias are dedicating our sole focus to this endeavor."

"Because strife and war and murder require a new playbook." The Dagda's voice lacked its usual soft tone. "While we will forever be in the debt of our cousins from Cloudfair, I deemed it necessary for Morias and Fíadan to follow these ancient leads."

"It matters not." Nemain's face twisted in annoyance, even more than it usually did when I was around. "What matters is that we have now secured Gorias. From a military standpoint, Gorias is better prepared for an incursion than it was before the Fomorian invasion."

In my mind, I finished her thought. "Because no one has a better military than MY city. Gorias was not properly prepared before I whipped them into shape." True… those were my own internal words, but that sentiment had come through joint council meetings for untold years.

Nemain was staring at me. My expression must have betrayed my inner thoughts. I gave her the sweetest smile I could muster. I even batted my eyes.

Aengus snickered. He knew my thoughts all too well. "And the militia is fervently motivated."

"Yes," Nemain admitted. "And that places us precisely where we need to be as a council."

"Intermission?" I asked. I couldn't help it. Most of them ignored me again. Badb smiled again. Apparently, I was as funny as I thought even if the person knew exactly what I was going to say, which was saying something!

"Gorias must decide whether to answer the call that will inevitably come from Falias." Nemain paused and glared at the council members around the table as if daring anyone to challenge her assessment of the situation.

The Dagda didn't seem surprised. "The implication being that Gorias will be called to abandon its walls in pursuit of assembling with the combined armies of all four cities at the call of the Overking?"

Macha sent him a sharp look. "And where, precisely, would the walls of Gorias be without the aid of our Overking and those armies?"

I couldn't help myself. I laughed out loud. "So much for goodwill and altruism." Someone had to say it, and it seemed like everyone else was too polite. Or more likely, too politic.

Macha glared daggers at me. "The Ellyllon does not deserve the great honor the people wish to bestow upon her." Her farthing boons, not my rank in their world, was the only thing that kept me from jumping across the table and wiping that look off of her face. Even still, she visibly cringed at my murderous look.

"Yet it is the will of OUR people," Aengus said softly.

"Wait a minute. What exactly are you talking about?" I asked. "What honor?"

"The changeling guards and the Ellyllon wish to reinstate you as the official Captaen of the Queen's Guard."

"I am a King's Guard," I growled without thinking. That happened sometimes. My mouth often worked faster than my thoughts. I was immediately sorry, as the faces of Aengus and The Dagda fell, remembering the deceased former king.

"Fíadan…" Morias began with true sadness in his voice. "That is more than enough."

The echo of his words sat heavy on the room as I felt all eyes on me. I hadn't meant to cause anyone pain. I loved the noble house of Gorias and the family that ruled it. They knew that. But I had also reminded them of a different and painful time. The same painful grief they felt rose inside me as well, reminding me of my failure.

"And while we are discussing difficult topics," Nemain said, cutting the quiet of the room. "I have disturbing news that will be difficult for some of you to hear."

A faint smell tickled my nose. The metallic smell was as familiar to me as fallen cider apples on the southern Emain Ablach orchards. I frantically scanned the room for the source, finally spotting it. A subtle and barely noticeable drip of blood trickled from Nemain's nose, so small that she didn't seem to notice it. I glanced around the room, realizing that none of the council members seemed to have noticed…no one, that is, but Badb. Our eyes locked as Nemain continued, her voice ringing through the chamber.

"Bren Búachaill is now in league with his brother, Cai Maccán, and the Fomorian horde."

CHAPTER 26:
AILLÉN

Day 16 of Midwinter, Sunrise
Cruachan, Midlands
Annwn

I surged to my feet, the dead woman's sword in one hand, Vowkeeper in the other. The two swords flashed, decapitating Deichtine before she could harm Sétanta. The boy breathed shallowly, but he lived.

The remaining fianna had fared worse. None of the newly risen Abhartach had managed to free themselves. I found and killed them all. I didn't know what lay before the boy and me, but I now knew that there would be none behind us that wished us harm.

After freeing me, the voice in my mind had been silent. But the walls continued to give off a faint light as if Aillén were guiding me where he needed me to go. Sétanta was still unconscious, so I slung him over my shoulder, carrying him as I moved deeper into the temple. I had left the mundane blade behind. With my uninjured hand, I held Vowkeeper at the ready.

I shuffled deeper and deeper, fighting to remain conscious with every step. The toxin of the Abhartach's claws had invaded my body, and now even the injuries that had not been caused by the creature refused to stop bleeding. Jagged pain ripped up my side with every inhalation, and every few minutes I had to pause to cough up blood from what had to be a hemorrhaging lung.

I stumbled through the labyrinth of passageways. At each fork, the proper tunnel lit up, showing me the way. A few times, it was a hidden passage that I needed to find in an otherwise unremarkable hallway. If I hadn't been guided by Aillén, I would have never found his prison.

After what felt like hours, I came to a tiny entranceway to a tunnel that required me to crawl. I sighed. This was going to hurt.

Before long, I had gotten into a rhythm, but my body was beginning to shut down. I pushed on, only by the force of my will. Reach and pull. Reach and pull. Reach and pull. After every third pull, I hooked my feet under Sétanta's arms and dragged him behind me. The pain was agonizing. I found myself floating in and out of consciousness. Each time I awoke, I spat the blood from my mouth and began again. Reach and pull.

Eventually, I made it to a huge pyramidal room with other crawl spaces littering the walls. Between the small, dark tunnels were symbols in a language I didn't recognize. In the middle of the room was a massive dark shape. I couldn't tell whether it was a rock formation or a collection of some other sort of objects. The dark mass glowed with a reddish-orange light that radiated out at random intervals.

WARDING RUNES. MEANT TO KEEP SCRYING EYES OUT OF THIS PLACE.

This time the voice was not in my head. The creature was in the room with me, though I couldn't pinpoint exactly where. Its voice was deep and masculine.

I raised my voice to speak into the cavernous space. "Aillén… or is it? You say that is not your given name. Who are you really? Where did you come from?"

A cackling laugh echoed through the room.

VERY CLEVER. BUT IF YOU WISH TO SEE MY TRUE FORM, YOU HAVE ONLY TO ASK.

The large dark mass at the center of the room began to rise into the air. It wasn't hovering, as I had initially thought. At its base, I could now see scaly black structures that reminded me of bird legs. The structures lifted the black mass high into the air, where it began to unfold and extend six thin, feathered wings.

Deep, guttural grunts and roars came out of the creature's three bird heads as it rose up and up. At the end of the heads were beaks that reminded me of the hideous hornbills found in the marshlands of the great Wells. The beaks were long and curved downward, coming to a razor-sharp point at the end. Where the beast's three sets of eyes should have been were pits of glowing embers, giving the appearance that the creature was burning from within.

Aillén stood five times taller than a man and easily as wide. Even at a distance, I could tell that the creature dwarfed me. I glanced back at the small passageway that I had come through and where I had left Sétanta just inside.

IF YOU ARE THINKING OF GOING BACK ON OUR ARRANGEMENT, I WOULD CAUTION YOU AGAINST IT.

The creature didn't make a move in my direction. It continued to stretch out its limbs like it had been years since it had moved them.

YOU WILL NEVER FIND YOUR WAY OUT OF THIS FORSAKEN TEMPLE WITHOUT MY ASSISTANCE.

"I will not let you harm the boy." I rested my hand on the handle of my sword, wondering how quickly I could draw it in my condition, wondering if I even had the strength left to wield it.

The three heads of the bird-like creature laughed.

I DO NOT WISH HARM ON EITHER OF YOU, TADG MAC NUADAT. I MERELY WISH FOR YOU TO FULFILL YOUR PROMISE.

"To free you?" I asked. My vision seemed to be fading, and I felt myself start to list to one side. It took all my strength to remain standing.

INDEED.

Then, as quick as a bowshot, it launched itself toward me. Aillén landed a few arms lengths away with a loud crash. Dust rained down off of the slanted ceiling.

I feigned courage by standing my ground, but the truth was that his movement had happened so fast I didn't even have time to react. I drew my blade and held it at the ready. The sword felt too heavy in my trembling hand.

FREE ME NOW, AND I WILL SAVE YOUR LIFE.

His words convinced me of two things. First, he knew exactly how badly injured I was, and second, he didn't feel the need to try to convince me to uphold the terms of our arrangement. His tone was matter-of-fact, the cold amusement from earlier gone.

I shifted uncomfortably. No matter what he said, this was not the place, and he was not the creature from which to expect a healing boon. I would likely die in this buried temple, forgotten and unmourned by even my own family.

And after my passing, Sétanta would never find the light of day again. I had to try.

"What must I do?" I asked.

NOTHING. AND EVERYTHING.

The creature lowered itself onto its birdlike legs. Its words made no sense.

My body finally reached its breaking point. My saber slipped from my fingers and struck the floor with a hollow clang. The room had begun spinning. My ribs felt as though they were caving in. "Speak clearly," I rasped. "I can feel my heart failing me."

YET IT IS STRONG AND RESOLUTE, EVEN NOW AS YOU DIE. I HAVE WAITED A LONG TIME FOR SUCH A HEART. WILL YOU ACCEPT MY GIFTS?

I fell to my knees, my legs unable to support me. What kind of gift waited in the dark for a man at the edge of death? What kind of creature could be so evil it was sealed in such a place and yet survived for thousands of years? I had no answers, nor any other choices. "Yes," I breathed, "I accept."

Aillén rose again to his full height. His six wings flared open. The three heads craned back, and from each jagged beak, light began to spill. It was a yellowish-white fire, tinged with red at the edges. The three heads bent forward, and a torrent of living flame erupted from their mouths, converging on me.

I screamed in agony as the fire burned through me.

I felt as though I were being split apart. I felt my ribs shatter under the force of the flames. My lungs collapsed. My right arm, torn by the Abhartach, sizzled and split, flesh cooking and melting away in molten ribbons. The pain permeated every sense and stole my breath and voice. I felt myself creeping closer to death.

But beneath the pain, I felt…something else. Something was happening. The flames did not fully consume me. I felt a change in the fire as it began to remake the parts of me it had burned away. It shot through my body, remolding all of me. I felt each shattered rib snap into place, the bone healed and reshaped beneath heat and pressure. My newly forged lungs filled with fire, and then with a gasp, I felt myself begin to breathe again. The torn muscles of my arm knit together, reinforced by something stronger than sinew.

I felt myself rise within the fire that still burned around me. I had been broken down to the point of near death, then newly formed. I was…something whole. Something other.

Stillness came, and the flame receded. I looked wildly around the room, only to find Aillén gone. I collapsed on the still-warm ground. I had been healed, but exhaustion still crept over me, and I found that I could barely move. I needed rest.

Before I gave in to the darkness, the god of magic regaled me with facts that I already knew in my heart were true.

Name: Tadg mac Nuadat
Race: Corrupted Tuatha Dé Danann
Current Power Rank - Combined Level 96

Current Progression Status:
Combined Physical Progression +101
Combined Mental Progression +98
Combined Spiritual Progression +96

Domains Gained:
Judgment and Light

You must choose one domain classification...

CHAPTER 27:

LEDGE OF LIFE

< CAI >

Day 16 of Midwinter, Sunrise
Leic na Beatha, The Deep Realm
Annwn

"Where are we going?" I asked.

Tethra had led me deep into the supports of Leic na Beatha. We walked at the water's edge, the smell of salt water all around us. The water was calm, and the lone visible water line led me to believe that little current and tidal changes happened here. But this was an extension of the sea, without a doubt.

"Our father brought me here just before we sailed on Brú na Dallta. He told me he was afraid that the knowledge of this place would die with him." Tethra stopped at the end of the natural stone pier that we walked upon.

We had taken switchback after switchback down through the stone pillars that supported the city above. I had thought that I knew the city as well as any Fomorian, but I had eventually lost track of the number and direction of the turns. Now we stood at an unfamiliar dead end, staring off into the darkness of the tunnels beneath the Deep Realm. Seawater ran beneath and through it all.

Tethra stood silently next to me, as I turned in a circle, trying to take it all in. Looking up through the supports, I saw a view of the sprawling city from below that I had never seen before. It was a marvel that this vast society had sprung up, entirely hidden from the prying eyes of the Overking. The sight was a beautiful twisting maelstrom of flickering lights.

"Do you know the story of how father came to this realm?" she asked. "It was the kindness of the sea that rescued him. He told me that before the Tuatha and the Fomorian, there were those who sat upon the wind and the wave. He said the very forces of nature had names and would speak to those who would listen."

This place that we called home was a remarkable realm filled with magic and history. There were those who could not die. There were those that represented a duality of natural forces. There were fae in every land that represented each season, festival, and terrain. It was easy to believe there had also been a time when nature itself was aware and intelligent.

Tethra gestured to the room we stood in. "He called this place Leic na Beatha." The Ledge of Life.

I thought of the second verse of "The First Fomorian" song sung at the Midsummer celebration:

The waters turned to shadow, the deep began to shine,
The gods of Annwn opened the door, where wonders intertwine.

Though I had heard the bards sing the song many times, it was only now that I made the connection. The Tuatha wouldn't have even been conceived when Neit had come to the Otherworld, meaning the "gods of Annwn" weren't referring to the offspring of Danu. I turned to Tethra, silently asking a question.

As so often seemed the case, she knew what I was thinking. "Father mentioned only one name to me: Eiocha, goddess of the land and sea. He called her Tethra. It was she who opened the door from Ériu into the Heart-shaped Pool in the moment of his greatest need."

I smiled, thinking about the sentimentality of the hardened former king who had named his only daughter after the goddess who saved him. "A fitting namesake for a future Fomorian queen."

Tethra rolled her eyes. "All these years, our father has kept a secret from our people. I am the only one in all of the Deep Realm who knows this secret, and I wish to pass this information on to you."

I wasn't sure what she meant. Nearly everyone in the city above knew the tale of King Neit's coming to the Otherworld, and the story of her namesake wasn't something that seemed particularly earth-shattering.

Before I could ask for an explanation, Tethra stepped into the gently lapping waves before us. The water was shallow, and after only a few of her long strides, she came to a huge, isolated rock surrounded by water.

She placed her hand on the stone, seeming unsure of where to position it. Nothing happened. Her face flushed pink. "I've never done this before," she admitted.

She adjusted her hand slightly on the rock. After a few moments, the stone pulsed gently with magical energy. Tethra did not seem to notice.

"Something is happening," I told her. "I can see a dweomer coming from the rock." The stone's magic pulsed again.

Tethra squinted, then placed a second hand on the rock. The pulse of magical energy grew stronger, then held.

I stared at the glowing doorway that had formed on the surface of the stone. "How…? What did you do?"

Tethra's eyes were wide. "I don't know. I simply focused on my need to show you what Father showed me… Quickly! Come, before it closes." She walked through the glowing doorway, all but disappearing into the rock. I could see a vague outline of her beyond the light of the glow. She motioned me to follow, so I held my breath and stepped through.

I was surprised to find myself in a massive open space. Great walls of water rose on all sides. Multicolored dweomers sparkled on the surface of the water, but I had eyes for only the old man bowing in front of Tethra.

"Welcome back," the man said to her, his voice soft. He turned to me. "And you must be Cai Maccán."

I instinctively used my Identification boon on the man, who smiled and allowed my scan of his power rank.

Name: Lir Dofainn
Race: Tuatha Dé Danann
Current Power Rank - Level 75

Current Progression Status:
Physical Progression +84
Mental Progression +93
Spiritual Progression +89

Domain: The Sea

My hand found the pommel of Fragarach, but I didn't draw it. I was confused…no, shocked. The god before me was unarmed and appeared to be genuinely happy to see us. The last time I had stood face to face with a member of the Tuatha, it had been in mortal combat.

Lir's face remained calm as if he sensed my churning thoughts and emotions. "You just missed your brother. He is completing a task for me." When neither of us responded, he continued. "Welcome to Tir fo Thuin. This place was created by the first gods of the Annwn, the Síorláidir." He looked at me and winked.

I pointed at the dweomers. "Are all of these gateways to other places?"

Lir nodded and placed a gentle hand on Tethra's forearm. "Your father came through here many moons ago." Lir motioned to a purple-hued section of the wall that disappeared and reappeared farther down the wall. Looking closely, I could glean slight variations in the hues representing each portal. As they shifted and flickered, I found I could follow the movement of the various doorways by focusing on their specific hues.

I walked over to the portal in question and peered into the seawater. It was a strange sensation. I was looking into a wall of water that offered a gateway into a different body of water. On the other side, I saw the remains of an ancient shipwreck. The vessel and remnants of other vessels had been taken over by sea life and were only barely identifiable as sunken ships.

I gazed through the mass of fish and plants, my eyes catching on a faint glow just inside the portal. I reached my hand through, feeling the shock of cold water on my skin. My hand brushed over seaweed and the sharp edges of barnacles as I grasped for the glowing object.

My hand closed around the glowing shape. As I pulled it back through the portal, I began to see the object for what it was, a crude copper or bronze figure molded into the vague shape of a bull's head. My thoughts immediately went to the great bull's head of the Fomorian heraldry. Though I couldn't tell exactly what the object was, I knew the bull symbolized Neit both before and after he came to Annwn. I had found a lost item of the former king.

CHAPTER 28:
QUINTESSENTIAL SUPERHERO

Day 15 of Midwinter, Sunset
At Sea, Well of Wisdom
Annwn

The massive salmon swam off after my impromptu poetry slam. In exchange for my words, the fish had explained the nature of the Well. It seemed that my purpose on the water had been two-fold. I had assumed Manny wanted to test my strength and endurance, using the challenges of the sea as a litmus for how I would fare against adversity. But he had really been testing me and my merit. In the end, the wind and the waves tested my judgment and my ability to use the tools at my discretion more than any physical attributes.

The second thing I learned from the fish was that at one time, there had been many of its kind swimming the western waters. The fish had once brought with them imbas, divine knowledge that helped to feed the magic of the world. This very particular kind of wisdom had become beyond rare due to overfishing.

I watched the salmon go. It had pushed me out of the fast-moving westward current, and for the time being, it appeared as if I was in no danger of drifting off the edge of the world. But then again, this was Annwn, and it would be dark soon... who knew what the night would bring?

I wondered when Manny would come back for me, if ever. I would have ruminated further on that had the Dagda's voice not announced my new and updated boons:

Name: Bren Búachaill
Race: Síorláidir
Current Power Rank - Level 13

Current Progression Status:
Physical Progression +46
Mental Progression +49
Spiritual Progression +52

Domain: Chaos
Domain Classification: Battlesmith (Enhanced)

You have been gifted with the following boons:
Control Energy
Erratic Agility
Dark Vision
Pain Sponge
Spiritual Augur
Battlefield Forge
Imbas Forosnai

You have one blood-borne curse:
Mark of the Bodach (Permanent)

Innate Racial Abilities:
Rapid Regeneration
Advanced Identification
Magic Sense

Two magic items are in your possession.
You have acquired:
Seolán Neimhe
Cast Lustrum Shillelagh

Item abilities unlocked:
The Storm God's Reservoir- Seolán Neimhe (inactive)

It occurred to me that I hadn't really taken the time to analyze my boons and abilities. There was definitely a lot to unpack. Then again… I was floating in the middle of nowhere with literally nothing else to do. With that in mind, I decided to take a closer look at some of the newer additions.

Pain Sponge
Your capacity for enduring pain is nearly unmatched. You will continue to function with clarity and strength even when suffering catastrophic injuries that would incapacitate others. This ability does not negate the damage sustained, but it allows you to fight, move, and act, regardless of the toll on your body.

Battlefield Forge
As a Battlesmith, you possess an innate mastery of weapons and armor, allowing you to analyze and enhance them. This ability enhances your "Advanced Identification" boon, providing deeper insights into the strengths and weaknesses of any armament. You can also forge, repair, and sharpen objects without the need for traditional tools.

Imbas Forosnai - Language

The divine spark of knowledge within you grants complete mastery over language. You can speak, read, and understand every tongue in Annwn. Whether deciphering ancient texts, conversing with spirits, or reciting poetry to aquatic species, this boon ensures nothing is lost in translation.

The Storm God's Reservoir
You have become a conduit for the tempest, channeling the raw power of lightning into your being. This boon allows you to harness and unleash devastating strikes of electrical energy while significantly increasing the range and capacity of your "Control Energy" boon. This ability is enhanced by an item set - Seolán Neimhe.

Woah. The powers I had earned made me feel like a superhero. I mean… it sounded like I could literally shoot lasers and regenerate! That's pretty much quintessential superhero. And my mental stats were now higher than my physical stats, likely because of my chat with the salmon. If I could only fly…

I looked around the remains of the boat, feeling like I was on a stage. The water was still and the world was quiet. The moon was full and bright, making it feel like the heavens shone a spotlight on the currach.

If it really had been a stage where I floated, I would have been in the round. To the edges of my vision, on all sides, I watched as a wall of mist slowly approached. It was so thick that my vision couldn't penetrate more than a few feet.

"What did you do to my currach?" The voice startled me so badly that I nearly jumped up and danced around. Manny had appeared in his earlier spot. He appeared to be shocked by the condition of his boat… well, what was left of it.

"Farthing hell!" I said, trying to slow my heartbeat. "Where have you been?"

Manny shrugged. "I told you that I would give you a chance to prove your merit."

"And?"

"… And I did." Manny's frown turned into a smirk. He whistled a familiar tune and the boat began to transform before my eyes. The dark-stained canvas that made up the sides and bottom of the currach patched itself. The ragged edges of the torn jib sail knit back into a single piece of uninterrupted fabric. I felt the newly repaired tiller catch a current, turning the currach to the east.

Manny didn't say anything after the boat finished mending itself. He simply watched the sheet and halyard lines automatically change positions, as if being pulled by an unseen hand. I suddenly felt the need to prove to him that I was worthy to go on the quest for his father. "I understand now why they call this place the Well of Wisdom."

"Do you now?" He appeared uninterested and kept his gaze on the sea.

"At first, I thought I had the answer, after wrestling with the currach and flying into the storm." I paused, waiting for direct or indirect praise. None came. "Then I spoke to the salmon and realized how wrong I was... but I see now."

At that, Manny turned to give me his full attention. "You somehow ended up a full day's journey from Murias. And now you are telling me that you found one of the last remaining Salmon of Knowledge?"

It was my turn to smile. "So... did I pass your little test?"

Manny laughed, looking pleased with himself. Without another word, he steered the boat deeper into the mist.

CHAPTER 29:
BE THOU MY VISION

< FÍADAN >

Day 14 of Midwinter, Sunset
Caisleán Saighead, Gorias
Annwn

After the council meeting, I found myself wandering the castle, unable to bring myself to wash off the remains of the infernal serpents from Fintan's tower. The red flakes falling left a trail of dried blood everywhere I went, and my sepia-toned skin had a weathered look. It was itchy, but in light of the information Nemain had presented to the council, being filthy on the outside seemed unimportant. I felt filthy on the inside, too.

She had said she'd seen Bren on Inis Fer Falga, nobbin' hobs with his Fomorian brother, Cai Maccán, the one who'd likely planned the invasion of Gorias…the one responsible for the death of countless citizens of my isle. I couldn't wrap my head around it. Everything we knew about Cai and his adopted family pointed to him as some sort of strategic genius, capable of bringing destruction upon Falias and the sister cities. Yet he'd been defeated in Gorias, and Bren had fought against his forces.

Bren now deciding to follow Cai didn't sit well with me. Sure, he was naïve, even gullible, but not evil. Bren would be the first one to stand up against the wrongs I knew Cai was guilty of…wouldn't he? I was filled with sudden doubt. Maybe I didn't know him as well as I believed.

I wandered for hours, hearing people talk at me from every corridor and open space in Caisleán Saighead. I didn't take in or respond to any of it. I was lost in my own thoughts, and unwelcome memories crowded in, making me even more confused and heartsick.

With a start, I found I had unintentionally wandered to Uaimh an Bhróin, The Cave of Sorrows. I had sworn I would never return to this place, where the worst memories of my life hung on the wall, on display for anyone to see. Behind the series of doors in front of me lay the dead, magical ore of my fallen King's Guard sisters.

This place was both a tomb and a monument to my failure as an Ellyllon sworn to protect the king. We had battled fiercely against the coup, but all had fallen…all except me left to carry the pain of our failure alone. Even the king who saved me, rather than saving his position, was gone now. The undying man, killed by treachery twice over.

My hands shaking, I opened the door to the treasure vault, then the final door that led into the cave beyond. I walked down the narrow tunnel, stepping from finished to unfinished walls. I felt an immediate change in the air. Inside the rough passageway, I could smell the wetness and the minerals, as they seeped through the rock that surrounded me.

I stopped short at the bottom of the tunnel, and my breath caught in my chest. I wasn't sure what I had expected after such a passing of time, but it wasn't this. Instead of a forgotten, dusty shrine, I found a pristine and well-kept monument to the dead.

Rock shelves along the walls held the carefully placed remains of the Ellyllon soldiers I had once served with. I could see no dirt, debris, or other evidence that any time had passed since their deaths.

The Duinnite ore held the same vibrant white coloration I remembered. Everlasting flame canisters burned at the corners of each shelf, casting the crypt in a soft glow.

"Father came here first," a voice said from behind me. I turned to see the most beautiful man in all of Annwn. Aengus stood just behind me in the passage. "This room was his first stop after the reclamation of Gorias had begun."

I felt heat rushing to my cheeks, as it always did when the god of Love was present. But the normal hot feeling felt more muted than normal. My eyes found the floor, and I bowed my head to him. Aengus shook his head gently, then stepped forward to wrap his arms around me. He lifted me into a bear hug, pulling me deeper into his delicious, wonderful body. I sighed and melted into him, allowing the tears to come…allowing myself to feel all of the emotion I had been pushing aside.

The fallen Ellyllon. A dead king. Failed purpose. Bren's possible betrayal. Years and years of repressed pain and grief. None had been enough to break me. In the end, I cracked like the crystal in the ore around me, not because of my prolonged suffering. No, it was The Dagda's act of mutual respect and kindness that overwhelmed me. He had prioritized the revitalization of the cave even when the house around it had crumbled.

Aengus began humming as he held me. Occasionally, I felt his chest heave as I lost myself in the deep sound of his voice. It only briefly crossed my mind that he too might be feeling overwhelmed by the moment. Words grew out of his gentle hum. The song had an unusual sound, far different than the ones I was used to hearing in the taverns and pubs of Annwn. It felt as though it harkened back to another time and another place.

Be Thou my vision, O Lord of my heart
Naught be all else to me, save that Thou art
Thou my best thought, by day or by night
Waking or sleeping, Thy presence my light.

It was a hymn, I realized, an early Christian hymn from the first missionaries to Ireland. Among them had been the woman who had captured the heart of Aengus Og.

I lifted my head from his chest to stare at the cross he always wore around his neck. It glinted in the flickering firelight.

"Caer once told me," he began, "that we are only given burdens we ourselves can carry. No more."

I remembered her now, Caer Ibormeith, the mortal woman from the Lake of Swans. It had been quite the tale around the castle at the time. Aengus had stayed in Ériu with the missionaries much longer than many felt he should have…and fallen in love.

"Are you trying to convert me?" I joked, easing myself out of his arms and wiping my wet face.

"No, but there is wisdom in the words of the Christian god," he said with a shrug. "He taught love and compassion."

"Sounds familiar," I admitted. "But at the moment, I'm angling more toward hate with a healthy dose of vengeance."

He smiled at me. It was a loving smile like he knew better than I did what I was feeling. It was annoying, but I could never get angry with Aengus.

"I think there is more to learn from this hymn than the worship of the Christian god."

"You've been spending too much time around Morias these days."

Another smile, this one sad. "My sister-brother was not the best king. Bres angered the politicians because he was raw and untrained. He treated everyone in his life the same. He believed that he was their servant, not the other way around, and those around him loved him for it. Each family member, each Ellyllon became his light in the dark. Each became the lord of his heart."

"Is this a parable? What's your point?" I asked. I shot Aengus a mock scowl.

He paused a moment, maybe realizing that even he could only get away with so much. He stared into my eyes. "Who or what is the lord of your heart, Fíadan? I see how you grieve, and yet you continue to fight. Why?"

I drew Stick, using the blade to point to the inert ore on the shelves. The blade trembled in my hand ever so slightly and I quickly put it back down.

"Because I ain't done yet." I felt my face flush for a different reason. My heart pounded, and I felt anger rising, battling with the constant grief. I was working myself up into a frenzy, and when it came, there was very little I could do to stop the words from exploding out of me. "It wasn't good enough that they took his crown!"

Aengus nodded, surprising me. His expression seemed to will me to take it one step further. I cast my mind back to the night Nuada had come with his brothers and personal guard to Castle Arrow. It was supposed to have been a routine visit, but something had felt off.

Never before had so many Ellyllon and changelings accompanied Nuada across the Straits of Segais, but we didn't see the challenge coming, none of us, not even the Fomorian kin of Bres. This had been before they had been sent to live in the deep-water port of Murias. It was before they had become the enemies of Falias.

Something clicked in my mind, a piece of the puzzle falling into place. I realized the idea had always been there, tugging on my subconscious. Was the man responsible for stealing the crown also responsible for the death of my former king? If so, how had he done it, and why had he waited so long to finish the job? It didn't fit together perfectly in my mind, and yet…it made a horrible kind of sense.

I must have looked flustered and confused. Aengus kept his distance, but his soft words reached me through my haze of thought. "Now you see the truth…and also understand why I couldn't bring myself to come back into the castle."

I met his eyes and nodded. "Nothing makes sense anymore."

My mind reeled with the uncertainty of the future. What would we do in the coming war? Nemain was right. We would almost certainly be called to war against the Fomorians, and against…

"Bren." I must have spoken aloud. Aengus looked puzzled.

"Bren," I said again, this time more loudly. As if saying his name conjured him directly into my mind, I remembered our recent time together with more clarity. I recalled the battle on Wolves Hill and the time around the fire in the Midlands. I thought about saying goodbye to him outside the walls of the castle. Things were just… better when Bren was around. I was better. A smile broke across my face.

Aengus returned it. "I think perhaps you have more than one lord of your heart, Fí."

CHAPTER 30:
PAST CORRUPTION

< TADG >

Day 16 of Midwinter, Sunrise
Cruachan, Midlands
Annwn

I was in darkness. No longer was the pain of the fire consuming every thought. I was somewhere inside of myself, with the Dagda's voice still announcing my power rank notification. But there was another sensation too. My body felt full, heavier than usual, even in this limbo.

You must choose one domain classification...

Something was happening. I felt my mind speeding up the notification. I wasn't in control.

Psychopompic Justicar
Description bypassed

**Scion of Justice
Description bypassed**

**Warden of Judgment
Description bypassed**

**Greyblade
Description bypassed**

This was the moment I had imagined all my life. I had earned my domain. And now, after all of the work and the waiting, I was not the one choosing my domain classification.

You have selected- Scion of Justice.

**You have been gifted with the following boons:
Dawnpiercer
Blazing Mantle
Burning Pulse
Radiant Surge
Guilt-Sight
Penitent Brand**

**You have one soul-bound affliction:
Possession- Belenus (Corrupted)**

**Innate Racial Abilities:
Rapid Regeneration
Advanced Identification (anointment superseded)
Magic Sense**

**One magic item is in your possession.
You have acquired: Gealltóir, the Vowkeeper.**

Item abilities unlocked:
Scourge of the Fae- When wielding this saber against any fae, your attacks are twice as effective.

So many boons. It was impossible they all had come from a single domain. I had to have heard wrong. I had earned two domains? Justice and Light. How was that possible?

A cold dread washed over me as I remembered the affliction listed in the notification… Possession.

YOU ARE A MAN OF YOUR WORD, TADG MAC NUADAT. AND NOW, WE ARE FREE.

Though the three-head creature that had bathed me in flames was no longer in the room with me, its voice was back in my head, now even closer and more intimate.

"Aillén?"

ALLOW ME TO SHOW YOU WHO I TRULY AM…

Darkness came and went, and I found myself propelled into a vision of the past. Was this Aillén's memory?

Before me, I saw the familiar sight of the Midlands, but not as I knew them. The hills were gentle and sweeping, and at their center was…a grass-covered hill. The fire-breathing mountain of my day was nowhere to be seen. Yes, the promontory of the hill was expansive, but the elevation difference between the vision and present-day Tech Duinn was extreme.

The grassland colors were familiar. The greenish hues of Mag Mell were as rich and deep as I had ever seen them. Flowering trees littered the landscape. These trees bore the fruits that had made the region famous in Annwn for as long as the Sages had been making natural observations.

The vision took me along the green countryside before penetrating the expansive hill through a series of caves on the western side. I found myself inside the mound, having gone deeper and deeper through the caverns and crevasses. I was not alone but in the company of three others, a woman and two men. I didn't recognize their faces, and yet, somewhere inside of me, I sensed a familiarity.

I stood with the others at the edge of a spiraling vortex of water. It looked like a whirlpool in a massive underground lake, only the spiral traveled outward, pushing the water to the edges.

I studied it for a long while but could make no sense of how it worked. The water at the pool's edges splashed over, creating mini waterfalls that cascaded out onto the underside of the hill. The trickling of water flowed out into the darkness and away from my dream sight.

Within Aillén's memory, I knew this place, but I did not know its name. I knew that at the center of the whirlpool was the most sacred place in all of the realms. It was the very center of the world.

The memory shot forward in time and I saw rivers carved into the underside of the hill carrying the sacred water away from the source in focused channels. The rivers felt wrong, and unnatural to me, and sorrow flooded my senses. I could not tell if the nearly overwhelming regret and sadness was mine or Aillén's.

Before me, I saw the landscape change again. I watched as the ground split and liquid fire erupted from the rock of the hill. The mound rose into the air, beginning to take the shape of the mountainous region of my time.

The same threesome from the earlier vision was there, but they no longer stood at the pool's edge. Instead, they stood at the mouth of the volcano, where they appeared to be surveying the changes to the land.

In their expressions, I saw a blackness that I had never seen before. They wore it as one would wear a cloak. I watched as they transformed into terrible new forms. The woman grew and flew into the air. One of the men leaped into the fire and ash of the volcano, disappearing from sight. The second man was transformed. Beneath the blackness, I saw claws on his massive hands.

I didn't understand the vision I was being shown, but I knew there must be a reason Aillén wanted me to see it.

As the vision faded, I saw a distorted reflection of a man I didn't know. He wore a garment of black feathers. From his eyes, I saw the narrow hallways of Cruachan and watched as he barricaded himself inside that infernal temple.

The Cruachan of the vision vanished as a small hand pushed against my arm, shaking me. My eyes snapped open to see the real Cruachan stretching before me, unchanged. Sétanta sat in front of me. He had tears trailing down his cheeks. I wasn't sure how long he had been trying to wake me from the vision.

I wrapped the boy tightly in my arms and held him as he sobbed. He knew exactly what it meant that none of the other members of his fianna were with us. I murmured reassurances, telling him that I would protect him, but my words could not stop his tears. He continued to cry, his thin arms clutched tightly around my neck.

COME, TADG. I WILL SHOW YOU THE WAY OUT. AND WHILE YOU PROTECT THE BOY, I WILL PROTECT US.

CHAPTER 31:

DONN OF THE DEAD

< CAI >

Day 16 of Midwinter, Midday
The Deep Realm
Annwn

I sat on the edge of my bed. Shellshocked, I turned the object over in my hands. Had I really just reached through the portal and pulled an item directly from the ancient wreckage of Neit's ship?

Over four thousand years ago, Neit had used this same portal to cross into Annwn, where the magic changed his body. It had changed his sword, Cathscian, too. There were rumors that other items he had brought from Ériu had also been transformed that day.

Thinking, I rubbed my finger along the simple metal shape. Horns curved around and down in front of the metal bull's snout. It would have been easy to think that it was my Advanced Identification boon that allowed me to see the silver aura emanating from the brooch, but the glow had been there even before I had pulled it through the portal. Was it possible it had absorbed the magic of Annwn simply by being so close to the portal for thousands of years?

I smiled, feeling a lightening of my grief. Something about being the first person to hold this object since the former king made me proud, and I couldn't help but chuckle to think what Neit would have said if he could see me now.

And as always, when I laughed, coughed, sneezed, or even moved too quickly, sharp pain ripped from the permanent wounds on my back and side. Something had to be done about the Life Leak curse. It was distracting, painful...and slowly killing me. I thought back to my conversation with Bren about his ability to engage in a fairy trance and my failed attempt on top of the lighthouse.

Instinctively, I placed the brooch on the bed beside me and closed my eyes. Even with my eyes closed, I could see the haze around my body that represented future disharmony. Slowly and carefully, I sifted through the haze, bringing my focus to the energy that moved around and through me. Along my rib cage, the energy was a black, pulsing mass. The dark coils of energy leaked from me with every painful heartbeat.

My breath slowed as I sunk into the trance, losing all sense of time. I found myself hypnotized by the movement of the energy particles, which I had always thought of as part of the weave, as they cycled through my body and the environment around me. When the particles reached my wounds, the particles paused. The blackness of their energy invaded my consciousness, and I found myself slipping into another time and place.

Unafraid, I looked around. It was after sunset, but even in the darkness, I knew this place. Home. Hy-Brasil. Green mosses and grasses littered the hills. The air was damp, and I could smell the fragrances the rain unlocked in the earth around me. I realized then that I was seeing one of my own memories.

The vision spread out around me. I could see Bren to my right. I had just kicked him through the double-wide entrance of a mound. It was our mound, I remembered. We had spent many moons building it, and that night we had finally placed the keystone above the opening.

I watched as Bren disappeared in front of me, falling into the darkness of the mound. I now knew that he had been transported to the site of all geneses, the Heart-shaped Pool.

Pain flared in my side as the blackness of the energy in my wound became the blackness of the woman standing before me in my memory. Bren had told me this tale in the very room my body resided in. I was seeing what came after his memory.

A bitter cold seemed to stab into my body, before spreading out into all parts of me, even into the follicles of hair on my arms and the tips of my toes. In my vision, I stood, frozen, before the woman. Black extensions emanated from her. They wrapped around me, bringing spasms of pain.

I watched as a man and woman sprinted down a nearby hill toward me. Their faces seemed foreign and strange, but I knew I should know their names. The pain that wracked my body had overwhelmed everything that night. But now, inside the memory of my trance, the information came back to me.

I knew them now. They were our mother and father. I gritted my teeth, trying to grasp the names that swirled just outside my ability to recall them. I focused harder, feeding energy into the burnt ends of my mind, feeling it slowly wake up.

Briomhaith was my mother's name, and one I realized I recognized. Her dark hair swirled around a normally warm face that would have been unremarkable but for her full mouth and piercing green eyes. Now all her motherly warmth had been replaced by fierceness. She towered over my father as they ran, and between the size and the body structure that I had become so familiar with, I knew her to be a Fomorian.

The man beside her, my father, seemed to emanate a tarnished bronze glow from within. As he ran, a sleeve of chainmail appeared on his arms and chest. A staff adorned with a circular head appeared suddenly in his hand. He shouted a single word, causing a beam of light to shoot from the staff into the dark woman in front of me.

The vision fluttered in and out of my mind. As the bright beam struck the woman, she stumbled to the side. The agonizing black cords loosened, bringing sweet relief. Shocked at the sudden sensation, I swayed, toppling toward the entrance of the mound.

Time slowed in the memory. The lightning flashes behind the green hills seemed to take two or three seconds. Each long stride of my mother felt like an eternity. Only my father appeared to move outside the laws of time and space. He looked through the memory and into my real body. I saw him remove himself from the vision and smile. I knew him then, his real name, and more importantly, who he was.

My father, the father of Harmony and Chaos, was himself a Síorláidir. He was called "Dark One" by those brave enough to speak of him. He was the one who caused the ground to shake and the one who made mountains erupt in fire. He was the keeper of the dead and general of the Bánánach. Donn, the god of death.

I watched, outside of myself, as my limp body fell into the mound, disappearing. The blackness of the attacking woman dissolved in the nearly blinding light of my father's magic. My mother stood, tears in her eyes, in front of the doorway I had disappeared into. She trembled in her grief and anger.

In the distance, I saw a girl appear over the rise of a faraway mound. She was silhouetted by the flash of lightning, but even at a distance, I could see the green of her eyes. They were the eyes of her mother, my mother. The eyes of my sister.

My eyes snapped open, the vision ending. I sat in my real room, back in the Deep Realm. Neit's brooch rested on the bed next to me. I felt rejuvenated. The pain in my side was gone, though I knew it would return. The scars would never leave me, and neither would the curse, but I was relieved to know I had found a way to at least temporarily stave off the pain.

I thought about the vision…no, the memory that had come flooding back to me during the trance. Our mother's name was

Briomhaith. I knew now that she was a Fomorian, just as I knew that she shared a name with the lost daughter of Prince Elatha.

I realized that made me a Fomorian too, and not merely an adopted son. It made Bren a Fomorian, and it made our sister a Fomorian.

My mind whirled with this new information. What did it mean for my family? For the Fomorians? What had the god of death been doing in Hy-Brasil? Who was the woman in black, and why had she attacked Bren and me? There were so many unanswered questions.

I took a deep breath, trying to ground myself back in the present, in the goings-on of the Deep Realm. I opened my eyes, only to see thick tendrils of haze surrounding my body. I remembered suddenly what day it was.

There would be no relief in the present. It was time for the duel between Tethra and Corb.

CHAPTER 32:

INN FOR A PINT

< BREN >

Day 15 of Midwinter, Nightfall
Deepwater Harbor, Murias
Annwn

The Guardian of the Mist brought us into the harbor in record time. One moment we were on the edge of the world, which Manny called Tairseach, and the next we were back in Murias Harbor. What would normally have been a full day's trip had been completed in just a few minutes, roughly the time it took for Manny to—sort of—explain why he'd left me alone in the sea.

"You're telling me you conjured a storm just to see if I'd survive it?" I was too confused by his logic to be angry.

"Technically, Father conjured the storm," he admitted. "Though he only did it because I told him of my plan with the salmon at the Tairseach."

I realized I was, after all, angry, as my boot connected with Manny's chest, sending him flying over the side of the boat and into the water. The currach stopped immediately and began to sink. A few night fishermen paddling by stared at the sinking boat. Up to my ankles in seawater, I waved.

Dripping, the boy-god pulled himself up over the side of the boat. With a flip of his hand, he emptied the currach of water. He scowled at me.

"I have decided not to drown you," he said, "but I am tempted.

"I'm on a timeline, Manny!"

He sighed. "We all are, Bren, but the stakes for the Tuatha are a bit higher."

I thought about kicking him again but realized he might actually drown me if I did. "Whatever is happening here affects us all equally."

The boat shot into the canals of the city, pulling to a stop in a different place than we had gotten into the gods-forsaken currach.

"Where are we going now?" I asked, stepping out onto what I guessed would be considered a sidewalk in the waterlogged city. Manannán approached a nearby building and tapped on the plain, stone wall.

"Do you still want to know how to enter Tir fo Thuinn?"

I nodded and walked up beside him, facing the wall. "Are there portals in different cities or ports, or just this one?"

"The secret isn't WHERE to enter. You can enter from just about any location in Annwn. The secret is HOW to enter." He looked at the wall and bowed his head. "This truth is why the king will never be allowed entry."

"I don't understand," I said, totally confused.

"The first requirement is that you must have a NEED to enter. The second is that you must humbly request entry." He gestured to the wall. "Give it a try."

I did as he had done and bowed my head and knocked on the wall with a fist. "Uh… hello?" Manny nudged me to continue. "Can we please come in? I need to find Lir's brother."

Manny leaned in and whispered, "You don't actually have to say why you want to enter." I rolled my eyes at the magical know-it-all. But a translucent sheen did indeed appear on the wall, and we stepped through to Tir fo Thuinn.

Lir wasn't in the room. That made sense, I supposed. He couldn't spend all his time waiting for visitors. Manny walked straight across the room to another door. It took him only a second to find the right portal.

"We will journey to the western foothills of Tech Duinn." He disconnected a familiar, small bag from his belt. It was the grayish leather bag he had stashed all of my stuff in. Tossing it to me, he said, "You may borrow the Crane Bag for this quest. Inside it, you will find many things to help you along the way." He turned and walked through the portal. Unsure of what to do with the bag at the moment, I followed him.

The portal brought me to the back side of a small wooden structure that seemed to be in the middle of nowhere. There was a larger building next to the one we had used as our exit point. Around us, farther out into the wilderness, I could see we were surrounded by what New Englanders would consider mountains, but looming larger than those was a massive volcanic mountain that dominated the Eastern view.

"I never enjoy stepping through here," Manny said, making his way toward the larger building. "But it's even worse going back the other direction."

I followed him toward what I could now see was a tavern of sorts. The other side of the small wooden structure revealed itself to be an outhouse. I was going to make a joke about Manny taking me to all of the nicest places in Annwn but managed to resist.

Voices came from the front of the tavern, a tiki-style pub that was mostly open to the air. There was a roof, of course, but even that was different than I was used to seeing. It was probably 20 feet off of the ground. When I saw the clientele, I understood why.

Beneath a sign reading "Inn for a Pint," stood a familiar ogre drinking out of a large wooden mug. Garbánach. I looked over to Manny in disbelief.

"Here at Maurice's fine rustic establishment," he emphasized the "fine" part extra loud so the bartender could hear him, "all manner of fae are welcome. No violence and no provocation is permitted."

"Bren Callahan!" I heard the bartender say. Looking more closely, I realized I knew this bartender. He was the same man (if that was the right word for what he actually was) from the tavern in Port Cóelrenna. I didn't see how it could be a coincidence that I was somehow meeting the same bartender in a completely different part of Annwn. Some goofy Otherworldly nonsense had to be afoot.

"Hey, Maurice," I said. At the sound of my voice, the nearby ogre swiveled to look at me, his eyes blowing up like two enormous balloons. I could understand why. Garbánach was the same ogre that I had wrestled with only four days earlier. He had eaten me just after I swam ashore from the Heart-shaped Pool. When I reappeared only moments later, he had gotten a lesson in just how strong one of the Annwn immortals can be.

"Would you like two more of those golden lagers you enjoyed so much down in the Southlands?" Maurice asked.

I looked over at Manny and he shrugged. "That's a yes for me, Maurice, though it's not Callahan anymore. I guess it never really was."

The bartender considered my words and then smiled. "Good. It didn't suit you." He turned to another section under the tall ceiling, reaching up to refill a bucket I saw a bipedal turtle drinking out of. Now that I looked around, I could see that many of the patrons didn't have opposable digits. The drinking vessels appeared to come in a wide variety of types, everything from traditional mugs and glasses to the turtle's bucket and a few trough-like objects.

Manny approached Garbánach while Maurice and I continued to chat. At first, the ogre seemed unsure how to react, but whatever Manny said to him kept his attention.

"So, you're knobbing hobs with the noble types now?" Maurice asked quietly. His eyes suddenly flicked up to the shelled tortoise. "Mortimal! You know you're not allowed to leave your severed limbs where everyone can smell them." This place was so weird. Every day I was in Annwn, my bar for what I considered strange moved.

"The ogre says he will help us," Manny announced, coming back over to Maurice and I. "But I'm a little confused about his terms."

"Why? What in the world is Garbánach going to help us with?"

"This is where my uncle was last seen, according to Maurice here."

Maurice nodded. "The Smith lord was headed toward the fire-breathing mountain many moons ago"

"Do you know why?" I asked, before remembering that Tech Duinn is the only place in all of Annwn where the Duinnite ore could be found. "Was he seeking out more Silverwhite material?"

Manny gave me a nod. "That is my thinking too, though I'm surprised you know of such things, being so new to our world. Garbánach said he would take us into the shadowy crags of Tech Duinn where his people lurk… as long as you call off your pigs, whatever that means. By the sages, I have no idea what he is talking about."

Embarrassed, I didn't expound on my past encounter with the ogre. Instead, I thanked Maurice and wished him a good evening. We gathered our gear and my good buddy, Garbánach, then headed farther into the mountains.

CHAPTER 33:

O CAPTAEN! MY CAPTAEN!

Day 15 of Midwinter, Sunrise
Caisleán Saighead, Gorias
Annwn

The courtyard of Castle Arrow was filled with people. I hadn't seen it this crowded since Bres announced that the capital was changing to Falias. Guards and townsfolk alike mingled together as if they had just spent several days working together to put the castle back together…which they had. There seemed to be an unspoken comfort level among the guards and nobles with the presence of all of the locals. It was foreign to me, but it somehow felt right.

A makeshift stage sat back toward the keep. On it stood the city council members, a few members of the Queen's Guard (including Erelith), and Nemain's fiacha. I took my sweet time winding my way up from the crowd. I knew my presence was required for whatever pomp and circumstance they had planned, but I found myself in no hurry to stand next to the arseholes from Findrias. Over the last few days, I had gotten enough of that to last me the next millennia.

"My friends and relatives," The Dagda said. He spoke into some sort of magical twig that amplified his voice, and the crowd quieted.

Macha and Nemain stood impatiently behind him, clearly waiting for him to finish so they could say their piece.

"I have good news. Over the course of the last nightfall, I was able to repair our communication beacon." A cheer rose up from the crowd, though it felt muted, far below the uproarious volume level that a crowd of this size was capable of. I continued to wind my way toward the stage. Despite my trying to stay incognito, the people around me gave me a wide berth as I passed. I paused another moment at the edge of the townsfolk, steeling myself to be among the politicians again.

"So this is your moment," came Badb's voice from my right, startling me.

"Chet girlie, you nearly got a dagger in your throat!" I said, lowering my hand from Stick.

"I don't think so," she said. She looked calm and confident, and knowing her boons, I suspected she was right that she'd never been in any danger.

I peered at her. "I don't think I've heard you say this much the whole time you have been here."

"I speak when it is necessary," she replied. I paused, waiting for her to continue. She didn't.

"I bet you're a lot of fun at a party." No reaction. She was good. It made me like her... but only a little. After all, she was related to the other two black-haired devils up on stage.

"They aren't the devils you think them," she said. "But then, devils aren't really devils either, are they?"

"This is your version of necessary speech?" I asked, with only a hint of snark in my voice. The Dagda was saying something else up on the stage, but Badb and I were having our own private moment, so I hadn't really caught what it was. Still, it seemed to snag Badb's attention.

She looked back at me, her expression unreadable. Then, as she turned to leave, her lips moved silently. Just one word.

I blinked. Did she just call me a hellraiser? It was barely understandable.

"Hellraiser?" I whispered to myself, testing the word aloud. Was that supposed to be an insult? If it was… I kind of liked it.

The sound of my name shook me back into reality. At some point, Nemain appeared to have taken the magical twig microphone from The Dagda. I looked up to see her addressing the people in the courtyard.

"Thanks to your lords' work restoring the communication to Falias, we now know the Overking is calling for the formation of a grand coalition. He seeks a combined force of military vessels and personnel from the four cities. We join together to defeat the Fomorian horde!"

A great cheer erupted. My own heart began to beat faster, and I realized that I too was being influenced by Nemain's infernal boons. I fought the frenzy, realizing it was a little easier to do once I recognized its influence. All it took was to think about what she had said about Bren.

Oh, Bren, I thought. What are you doing with Cai? There must be a reason that doesn't involve betraying Gorias… or Falias.

The Morrigan, and likely all of the Findrias nobles, were obviously siding with the Overking, with no room for nuance and little thought of Gorias… or Brigid! Nemain had told us the Overking spoke of the former queen's need to rest after her travels. I thought it odd she hadn't returned to defend her city, or even after the invasion, to be with her people as they rebuilt…but his message said that she was with the city in spirit and would return to us soon. A brief pang of guilt at my own doubt and hesitation racked me. Shouldn't I also support Falias? Shouldn't we all?

But then again…I thought back to what Aengus had told me in the Cave. After the death of Caer, he'd left the castle, choosing to grieve alone. He had not returned until the recent siege, and when he had, he was different. Sure, he'd been withdrawn since the death of his beloved, but now he seemed watchful, almost tense. I assumed it was because he had come to the same conclusion I had. Though I didn't know how or why, I felt in my bones that the Overking was responsible for the death of Bres.

"You see? Even now she stands among you." Chet, Nemain was laying it on thick. I hadn't heard what preceded that puffed-up statement, but by the sounds of it, she was clearly ramping up to the culminating announcement about my reinstatement into royal service.

I looked up at Nemain. From here, she looked unusually pale. Dark circles sat below her eyes. And though her speech was definitely rousing the crowd, to an experienced listener, it was clearly lacking her usual fervor.

"Please join with me in welcoming our dearest Fíadan." As the crowd began to cheer, Nemain lowered the magical amplification twig. She beckoned me.

It felt strange. I knew there was a commotion going on around me, but my mind seemed to mute all of the noise and chaos. My legs carried me forward onto the stage.

The Morrigan handed me the twig and I held it loosely in my hand as I scanned the faces of those before me. Morias looked sad like he pitied me for the position I had been put into. I know it was because he cared for me, but I had never enjoyed being pitied.

Next, my eyes fell on The Dagda and Aengus. Both looked pensive as if they were still wrestling with the proclamation from Falias. Nemain leaned against Macha, holding a blood-spotted cloth to her nose. Macha supported her sister but managed to simultaneously look as though she was enjoying my obvious discomfort. And Badb…Badb had a wicked, secretive smile on her face.

Confused, I turned to the crowd. Many were still cheering and applauding. A few shouted "Captaen." My eyes flicked over to Erelith, who stood with an inquisitive look on her face. Where before I had only seen her naivety and inexperience, I now saw seriousness, as though she were weighed down by the gravity of the moment.

She nodded to me, in what I supposed was meant to be a show of support.

The crowd continued its frenzied cheering. It seemed that every moment I was silent only served to rile them up more. Even still, the longer that I stood there, the more awkward I felt. I raised the twig to my mouth, but nothing came out. Inspirational speeches had never been my strong suit, and my current swirling suspicions weren't helping. It would have helped if I had actually reached a firm conclusion in my own mind. Sure, I had conspiracy theories… but did that warrant a speech or action?

Flustered, I said the first thing that came into my mind. "You need to stop yelling. It's distracting me." My voice boomed across the crowd and they immediately quieted. I heard a small snicker from one of the council members behind me in the sudden silence.

"Thank you for coming to help me at the gate." The people remained silent, to my surprise. All eyes were on me. I shifted uncomfortably.

"Without you all… well, I'd be dead and the castle would still have those chetty green and gold banners waving over the courtyard." There was some laughter at that.

"But… you ain't brave, not really." I paused, thinking about how far down the rabbit hole I was willing to go. There were some confused looks from the crowd.

"Fighting with a mob at your back makes you feel brave, though. You know who was brave? My friend Bren." I pointed up on the wall to where Balor had held Morias captive. "Bren's not from here, but he fought for your castle and your queen."

A cheer went up at the back of the crowd. A voice called out Brigid's title, Breo-Banríon. Another took up the cheer, then another.

One of the council members muttered something flippant about my referring to Brigid as the queen, but I continued before anyone could move to take the twig out of my hands.

"He fought the biggest and ugliest Fomorian in order to save his fat Sage friend. And he did it by himself, alone, up on that wall, with no friendly mob to watch his back…just because it was the right thing to do. That's how we used to do things here." I could feel my face warming and my voice grew stronger with my anger.

"What are you doing?" said a voice behind me. I didn't bother checking which of the Morrigan sisters had asked the question.

"I'm not your Captaen… not anymore. You already got one." I glanced over to Erelith. She stood frozen in shock, but I was on a roll, so I kept going.

"A Captaen has to take orders… even when they know they are being lied to. I can't do that anymore."

A collective murmur of confusion echoed off of the walls of the courtyard. I turned and tossed the twig to The Dagda. I didn't bother to look for approval in the faces of the council members. I hopped off of the stage and made my way through the crowd, which parted for me as I walked.

I heard Nemain bark an order and turned to see her fiacha advancing toward me, hands on their weapons. Just as I was cursing myself for not having expected this, I saw Erelith and her Queen's Guard move to block the path of the fiacha. I wasn't surprised that Nemain or Macha hadn't liked my little speech but was surprised that Erelith would put her neck out for me like this. I knew that despite the infamous reputation of the fiacha, it was unlikely there would be any bloodshed in front of the townsfolk.

I quickly made my way out of the drawbridge, angling myself to the wharf. The whole time I had been up on stage, I had only one thought running through my mind. I needed to find Bren. I never thought I would have said it, but I truly believed Bren was the key to understanding the war and the events leading up to it.

Only one being in all of Annwn could be trusted to help me find Bren. That being was Fernawen of the Eastern Segais Reddeshorate. But first I needed to get to her…and for that, I needed to find myself a ship.

At the pier stood a lone Gorias naval officer. He seemed unsurprised to see me, almost as if he had been expecting me. There didn't appear to be anyone else around, which was very strange. Maybe they were all at the castle?

He saluted. "Hello, Captaen." I rolled my eyes.

"Are you here to stop me?" I asked, giving him a wicked grin.

He flushed. "I… I was told to offer you a choice of ships?"

"Wait, who… never mind. I don't want to know." I glanced out to the harbor, where I saw two small ships with flame-tipped sails side by side, waiting at their moorings. "What do you got for me there, chief?"

He straightened and gestured to the ships. "The Witchcurrent and Hullraiser are both crewed and ready to depart at your command."

I smiled, thinking back to Badb's whispered voice in the courtyard and pointed to Hullraiser. "Let's go! And tell the crew to expect a shadow in our wake."

CHAPTER 34:
EXODUS & HOMECOMING

< TADG >

Day 16 of Midwinter, Midday
Cruachan, Midlands
Annwn

The first stretch of the tunnel took the longest. Sétanta and I crawled through the same narrow chute I'd dragged him through earlier… only this time, he managed most of it himself. Mostly.

I had worried we wouldn't be able to find our way out, but the stone's surface glowed with faint luminescence. When Aillén had lit the way for me hours ago, the light was stronger, illuminating only the turns I needed. Now, a gentle shimmer coated every surface. I suspected the entity within me, whatever it was calling itself now, was softening its presence, trying not to draw attention.

According to my soul-bound affliction, Aillén's true name had been Belenus. The name was familiar, but I couldn't place where I'd heard it. Maybe during my studies under Morias? As I pondered, a low, amused chuckle echoed in my mind. Startled out of my musings, I turned my attention to my companion.

I had made the boy go first, quietly telling him which turns to take. He didn't know what waited ahead, but I did. The corpses of his fianna lay in a nearby cavern, mangled from when I'd put them down. He'd been unconscious then. But I wasn't taking him there. We would find another way out.

I WILL LIGHT THE WAY.

So Belenus could read my thoughts. Useful...but unsettling. I wondered how he knew so much about the structure that imprisoned him.

MY LIGHT SHINES THROUGH MINERAL AND ROCK. IT BENDS AND REFLECTS. I HAVE HAD THOUSANDS OF MOON CYCLES TO STRETCH THE LIMITS OF MY PROJECTION IN ORDER TO LEARN THE SECRETS OF CRUACHAN.

"I'm tired," Sétanta mumbled. Though his smaller size should've helped in the cramped tunnel, the Bánánach's touch still lingered. His skin had a sickly gray tint, and his eyes were dull with grief.

"I know. It isn't far now," I said aloud to the boy.

We crawled on for several more minutes, but at last, the tunnel opened up, letting us stand. I stretched, relieved to be out of the crawlspace. Sétanta swayed. He hadn't eaten or drunk in hours and looked ready to collapse. I bent and lifted him. He was lighter than I expected, and asleep in my arms almost immediately.

HE WILL PERISH SOON AND TURN. YOU MUST EITHER END HIM OR USE OUR BOONS TO HEAL HIM. DAWNPIERCER CAN BURN HIS AFFLICTION AWAY.

End him? I froze. That wasn't an option. He was just a child.

I hadn't yet examined my new abilities yet. We resumed walking and I focused on those specifics from my last power rank notification:

Dawnpiercer
Burns away illusions, shadows, and afflictions, revealing truth and exposing deception.

Blazing Mantle
A radiant aura of sunlight envelops the bearer in battle,

blinding nearby enemies and granting resistance to effects that would blind or obscure vision.

Burning Pulse
Unleashes a pulse of searing light, damaging creatures vulnerable to fire or radiant energy and repelling entities born of shadow, corruption, or darkness.

Radiant Surge
Become a streak of divine light, instantly traversing short distances through natural illumination. Ignore terrain and gain brief invulnerability during transit.

Guilt-Sight
Perceive the residue of guilt and regret on others as phantom impressions clinging to their form.

Penitent Brand
A radiant seal that exposes lies and hidden crimes.

Now that I looked closer, I could tell which boons were from Belenus's Light domain and which came from my new Judgment domain. Penitent Brand seemed to blend the two. Maybe it was tied to my Scion of Justice classification.

WHEN OUR BODIES MERGED, I LOST MANY BOONS. BUT YOU HAVE BEEN GIVEN LIGHT BOONS THAT I DID NOT POSSESS.

I focused on Dawnpiercer. On the surface, it looked like it would do exactly what Belenus claimed. What I didn't know was how much pain it might cause Sétanta. I thought back to how quickly Deichtine had transformed and realized I had no choice. I wouldn't let that happen to him.

I set the sleeping boy gently on the stone floor and covered his eyes. Focusing, I felt a burning heat transfer from me to him. He stirred but didn't wake. Pinpoints of light glimmered from his wounds as if radiating from within. I could see the outlines of his organs glowing beneath his skin. And then, the light faded. His skin was no longer ashen, but ruddy with health. He slept on.

For hours, we twisted through the dark halls of Cruachan. I carried Sétanta, slowing whenever I could to keep him from waking. Belenus stayed silent. Eventually, we came to an exit mostly clear of debris. He had kept his word. We were free!

It was still light when I pushed aside a rock at our exit. I heard a whinny from somewhere nearby and looked up to see Gaoth circling a large, familiar man on an even more familiar horse. Diarmuid sat astride Móralltach, of all creatures.

I recognized him then for who he truly was. He rode the mount of his father, Aengus Og. That's why he had called me cousin. That's why he had let me leave his camp, unscathed.

Around Diarmuid stood at least a hundred fianna soldiers, some mounted, some on foot. I was too exhausted to be impressed. I simply whistled for Gaoth.

When they saw me, Móralltach and Gaoth approached, parting the gathered men. To my dismay, Gaoth kept his distance. Diarmuid dismounted and came forward. Sétanta stirred and woke as I handed him off.

"It was the Bánánach," the boy whimpered, lips trembling. He buried his face in Diarmuid's tunic, his body wracked with sobs.

"The rest?" the leader asked me.

I shook my head. Diarmuid closed his eyes, letting emotion claim him for just a moment. When he opened them, he extended a hand to me. I took it, and we stood like that for several long moments. I saw gratitude in his eyes and knew that he saw sorrow in mine. Diarmuid nodded solemnly.

"I thank you, Tadg mac Nuadat. You've proven we can be better than our fathers." He looked back at his fianna. "We owe you a debt, cousin. Call on me, for any reason, and we will come."

He released my hand and took the boy to a group of waiting women. My gaze found Gaoth behind Móralltach. Both beasts looked uneasy, shaking their heads and keeping their distance.

"Come on, friend," I pleaded softly. "I need you to take me home." Móralltach turned and vanished into the crowd. Gaoth backed up, rearing. That nearly broke me. Gaoth had been my most loyal companion. Through years of battle, he had been the one creature I could always count on. I was his chosen. The only one he loved and trusted enough to ride upon him.

It was Belenus, I realized. Gaoth was afraid of him.

COME, TADG. YOU NO LONGER NEED HIM.

I knew what he meant. I could now travel upon the light itself using Radiant Surge. But Gaoth wasn't only a horse or a way to get from here to there. He was my loyal companion. With all my newfound power, I felt only sorrow. I sighed. Times were changing. And it seemed I was changing most of all.

"I understand," I told my oldest friend, my voice soft. "I know I am different now, and for that, I'm sorry." A sudden thought struck me.

"Go. Find Bren. He'll need your help before long."

Gaoth whinnied before turning on his hooves to gallop west. As he disappeared into the crowd, I whispered, "And he will take care of you."

I wiped my eyes and turned back to the fianna, where I found several of the soldiers staring at me. I must have been a sight...dirty, bloodied, bruised, and broken. Emotional. Resigned. Some may have even enjoyed seeing the son of King Nuada brought low.

But then again, their faces looked… surprised, maybe even fearful. Then I felt it, the feeling of the sun's warmth on my skin. It filled me with power. In a flash, I vanished. Belenus had activated Radiant Surge without my consent.

I felt myself flying across the land, streaking through light, crossing stretches of Mag Mell that even the fastest mount would have taken hours to cover. Five surges. Ten. Twenty. Ahead, I saw

Falias's beckoning towers. My home. Or at least, my current destination.

I recalled Bairic's words as I left Brú na Dallta. "War changes a man. Be sure it changes you for the better."

I didn't know Belenus's true goal, or what awaited me in Falias. Would my father declare war on me too, as he had against the fae and the Fomorians? Would it all end in blood?

Only one thing was clear to me as I flew toward the city gates, just as the last rays of sunlight vanished behind the towers. War HAD changed me, for good AND for ill. I realized it likely never changed a man any other way.

As I landed at the gate, the sentries stared at me in shock. Recognition dawned in their eyes. Despite the dirt and blood of Cruachan, I stood tall, a lord of Falias once more.

NOW IS WHERE THE FUN BEGINS.

CHAPTER 35:

THE DUEL

< CAI >

Day 16 of Midwinter, Sunset
Dueling Ground, The Deep Realm
Annwn

I was the first to arrive at the dueling ground. I watched as the Fomorian dignitaries and Mná na Mara filed in around the top of the circle. A few approached and tried to make small talk, but most gave me a wide birth. I was tense, and I knew I wore that tension on my face plainly for all to see.

I felt like a shell of myself. For hours I had been running possible outcomes through my mind. Even now that I was here, perched on the rim of the dueling pit, I felt outside of myself, more focused on my inner thoughts than what was happening around me.

Shrill pipes sounded as Corb made his way through the scores of people who had arrived to witness the historic battle. Looking around, I saw that behind the Fomorian nobles, it appeared that the entire city had come to watch. The tension in the air was thick, but not as thick as the haze surrounding my body from my Divination of Balance boon.

Corb sported the Evil Eyes helmet, surprising me. The rules clearly stated he would not be able to use the ranged magical fire in the duel itself. The Fomorian warrior was massive, with rippling muscles, dark skin, and glowing red eyes. His long, dark dreadlocks hung across his broad chest and back. Around his thick neck hung dozens of necklaces containing bones and decorative metal leftovers from past battles. As he passed me, he met my eyes. His mocking gaze held mine so long that I thought he might miss a step and fall into the pit.

Upon reaching the dueling area, Corb paused, turning in a circle and casting his red gaze at the crowd. They quieted, watching. He thrust his fist in the air. A cheer went up among some of the onlookers, and Corb raised both hands. The cheers began to spread, but they were cut off by the sound of a second set of pipes. Tethra had come.

She stalked toward the dueling pit. Her lack of fanfare or playing to the crowd was a sharp contrast to Corb's entrance. She wore her usual leather armor, which was nicked and scratched from past battles. Her hair had been freshly braided, likely by her mother, and around her shoulders, she wore her father's green cloak with a fastener that she had rescued from his funeral pyre.

My eyes locked on hers. I gave her a nod of encouragement. She took a deep breath and turned her focus back to the path in front of her. The Fomorians parted, clearing a path to the dueling ground.

Dubhlinn and Morvra stood just outside the dueling pit, their hands joined. The mothers of the two combatants would act as co-adjudicators of the duel, their faces impassive. Tension gripped the crowd.

The combatants faced each other, with the Abyss between them. Tethra shifted her weight from foot to foot, readying herself for what I knew would be explosive movement. Corb appeared to be breathing deeply, each exhale erupting a cloud of vapor from his nose and mouth.

Both combatants would have the opportunity to address the crowd. As the challenger, Corb would go first. I tensed, knowing he would play to the crowd. As predicted, I saw Corb's hand thrust into the air and the crowd fell silent.

"Comhthíreach," he began, his voice carrying. "Today I bring you good news from our battles in Emain Ablach. In the siege of Gorias, we took many casualties." He paused, letting the crowd soak in his words. "But that effort has afforded us a great treasure."

He pointed to a man who stood near Corb's mother, who I had not spent time with but knew to be called Indech. He was one of Corb's underlings. Indech pulled a golden object from the folds of his cloak and held it up at Corb's words. A collective gasp rippled through the crowd.

Light caught the edges of the pyramid-shaped object, which was roughly the size of a Fomorian skull. Though I'd never seen it up close, I immediately recognized it. In Ériu, it would have been called a pyramidion or capstone. Here in Annwn, the Tuatha referred to it simply as a beacon.

Each of the four major cities had only a single beacon, a magical means of communication for the vast empire of the Overking. They were the magical equivalent of the ancient act of lighting bonfires on hills and mountains to rally large groups of people living in the far reaches of a country. I immediately understood the significance. The beacon would enable Corb, or Tethra, to spy on Overking Nuada's plans to rally troops to their war effort. It could turn the tide in our favor.

"We have taken the Gorias beacon!" Corb bellowed. The crowd roared.

Corb turned to stare across the pit at his half-sister as the crowd cheered.

Tethra stood tall, seeming unfazed, though I knew better. I had seen the slight widening of her eyes when Indech had presented the beacon.

She drew Orna and the crowd hushed.

I saw Tethra's mouth begin to move before I heard her words. As I had expected, she had chosen not to address the crowd. She let her actions speak for her. Her voice rang as she spoke the words of the honor invocation that would kick off the duel. The crowd was silent.

"With honor, I stand, by the shore and sea. If the abyss takes me, let it remember my deeds." Corb's voice joined Tethra's after the first few words. When they finished, another cheer went up.

Corb drew the double-bladed Fuilgeir. Both combatants turned to the rim where their mothers were standing.

Dubhlinn moved to the very edge of the pit to address the warriors. "You know the Fomorian way. You have trained in the house of your father for time untold. To be permanently disarmed or to submit means defeat." She paused and her face grew stern. "To fall into the Abyss means certain death. Death means defeat."

My eyes instinctively moved to Corb. I could see the beginning of a smile at the corners of his lips. My heart sank.

Before his mother had even stepped back from the edge of the pit, Corb leaped at Tethra. She parried, and Orna and Fuilgeir clashed in a shower of sparks. The crowd cheered as the swords met again and again in a flurry of blows.

The movements and swordplay displayed below me were unlike anything I had ever seen. Fuilgeir's Blood Tide ability and Orna's Battle Herald ability seem to have remembered past sparring matches between the two. Corb moved with preternatural speed and strength, but Tethra moved to parry even before I could see the attack coming. It was like watching lightning flit in the night sky.

The clash of swords rang out and echoed through the training grounds. The very ground shook when the blades collided.

Corb's blows were strong, and punishing, but Tethra moved like a cat, graceful and faster than her brother. Orna slid Corb's blows away over and over, leaving Tethra with only superficial cuts. Her attacks on Corb were similar. Despite her speed, he managed to parry each of her slashes and avoid anything more serious than a minor wound.

The swords continued to flash as both combatants moved across the dueling pit in a seemingly unrelenting choreographed dance.

I could see the beginnings of fatigue from both warriors. Sweat, tinted pink with blood, dripped and splashed on the walls and ground.

If they continued much longer, Tethra would have the upper hand. While Corb's blows exerted more force, they also burned more energy. Tethra was simply turning away his blunt-force attacks, favoring defensive positioning. She was wearing him down while conserving her own energy.

The battle continued to rage, the minutes ticked by. I felt myself moving subtly with each of Corb's attacks as if my own movements would somehow aid Tethra. But Tethra didn't need my help. Corb was visibly slowing, and it was now obvious the tide of the battle had shifted in Tethra's favor. The gathered Fomorians could see it, and I saw the moment Corb realized it as well.

Enraged, he sent a brutal swing at Tethra, his muscles bunching with power. Tethra danced into it, smoothly deflecting Fuilgeir in a seemingly impossible move. The massive blade slid from Corb's grasp, flying nearly ten feet away and lodging in the ground.

Corb pushed away from his sister and ran to his sword. She pursued him more slowly, allowing him time to get to his blade. I clenched my fists, feeling a blast of panic. All Tethra had to do was reach Fuilgeir before her brother and the duel would be over.

Corb reached for his sword, and Tethra pounced, shifting from defense to offense. She chopped with a downward strike just as he yanked his double-bladed sword from the stone of the pit. He threw Fuilgeir up to parry in the nick of time, but the force of Tethra's blow dropped him to a knee.

Tethra drew her blade back, preparing another crippling blow. As she moved with the attack, one that would seal her victory, Corb's eyes suddenly flared with a hot red light. I leaped to my feet. The red flare had been the only visible warning before Balor had released the full power of the Evil Eyes in battle. The use of the magical flames was strictly against the rules of the duel.

Tethra faltered, instinctively shrinking back to protect herself from the expected torrent of magical flames. But no flames came.

Tethra's slight retreat gave Corb the breathing room he needed to recover. He rose to his full, massive height, dropped his blade, and surged the arm's distance toward Tethra. She lifted Orna so that the tip of her sword was in line with Corb's heart. Just before impact, Tethra imperceptibly shifted her blade. Orna thrust through Corb's side, the tip of the blade emerging from his back.

Gasps rang out from around me. The Fomorian crowd thought that Corb, impaled by Orna, was finished. I knew better. Even from here, I could see the angle of the thrust had missed any major organs. I knew it couldn't be accidental. Tethra knew exactly where to set her blade for a killing blow. She had chosen to spare her brother's life.

The half-siblings stood face-to-face. Corb grinned maniacally, despite the sword impaling him. His giant hand rose, locking Tethra's arms in place.

He reared back then delivered a brutal head butt to her face. I watched in horror as her eyes rolled back slightly from the force of the blow. Blood gushed from her fractured nose.

He released one of his hands to grip her throat, the other remained locked on her sword. She punched at him with her freed arm, the blows growing weaker and weaker as she ran out of air. Her legs failed her and she fell to her back.

Orna had still been lodged in Corb's body when she hit the ground, but he pulled it out with a grunt.

"Do you yield?" he demanded, standing over her with her own bloody sword. Tethra's head turned on the ground, her eyes finding me. I nodded, silently pleading with her to submit.

Instead, she tried to stagger to her feet. Corb delivered a brutal kick to her face, sending her sprawling back. He repeated his question. "Do you yield?"

Again, Tethra tried to stand, and again, he kicked her. Tethra's body fell completely prone. I heard myself scream her name in the sudden silence that had fallen on the dueling grounds. Without meaning to, I found myself at the edge of the pit, my hand on my sword.

Before I could jump in, I saw Tethra hold her bloody hand up, silently begging me to stop. Reason found me. If I intervened, it would not only mean defeat but also disgrace for the proud Tethra. I paused for a single heartbeat.

In that brief moment, Corb delivered a final, brutal kick- fueled by the full force of his massive frame. My breath caught as time seemed to slow. Tethra's battered body sailed through the air and plunged into the darkness of the Abyss.

CHAPTER 36:
OGRE AND OUT

Day 16 of Midwinter, Sunset
Shadowlands, Tech Duinn
Annwn

After hiking through the night and the following morning, we were finally nearing Tech Duinn. When we began walking again after a brief lunch, I realized I could smell brimstone. Though I knew it must be leaking from the top of the volcano, I could have sworn that the smell of molten rock and fire leaked out of the ground itself.

When I caught Garbánach staring longingly at the sulfur pools dotting our route, the ogre explained that he and his people used the more "bubbly" of the pools to cook their prey before eating. I noticed that he didn't mention using any of the other pools for bathing. That was not a surprise.

Though we went out of our way to avoid them, on one occasion, we were stopped by a pack of giants. Manny managed to successfully negotiate with them, explaining why we traveled with an ogre. It seemed you could differentiate the good giants from the Boggle (or "bad" giants) based on whether they lived in the highlands or the lowlands. Those that lived in the shade of the mountain, namely the fachan, trow, and ettins, were to be avoided. Ogres were technically not giants, mainly due to their smaller size, though they lived in the same places.

After a long day of travel, we found ourselves in the shadowlands, where Garbánach and his people apparently called home. After the sun set behind us, the temperature dropped rapidly, what felt like at least 20 degrees. Even worse than the cold was the menacing presence of the Tech Duinn looming over us.

Manny told us the volcano hadn't erupted since the Sages disappeared from Annwn, and the previous eruption had been 2,000 years before that one. Garbánach had frowned before talking of recent tremors that shook the ground near the mountain. When we pressed him for details, he had simply said, "Sometimes, the mother gets hungry."

Strange that his people referred to the mountain as feminine, when the rest of Annwn treated it as the House of Donn (the male god of death). Still, it was not the strangest thing I'd come across in Annwn and not the kind of mystery that was going to keep me awake after a long night and day of travel.

As Manny and I settled down to rest for the night, I realized Garbánach, seated across the fire, seemed ill at ease. He shifted constantly, peering into the darkness around the fire, as if he heard something we couldn't. Occasionally, his hands drifted toward his ears as if he wanted to cover them.

Finally, I couldn't take it any longer. "What is it, Garbánach? Do you hear something?"

"Garbánach hear angry sound, like buzzing in ears."

I exchanged glances with Manny. I was suddenly worried. Extremely worried.

"Have you ever heard it before?" I asked him casually, trying not to manifest my fears into reality like the Stay-Puffed Marshmallow Man.

The ogre nodded. "Garbánach leave home because of buzzing. Now it come back. Brother had it. Sister had it."

"Did you talk to them about it, Garbánach?" Manny asked.

"Couldn't," the ogre responded flatly, continuing to stare into the darkness.

"Why not?"

"Because Garbánach killed them."

I gulped. The buzzing that Garbánach was describing sounded like a rudimentary way to describe the collective hum of the Bodach's hive mind. I activated my Advanced Identification boon and skipped directly to the section of Garbánach's Power Rank information that pertained to curses. Nothing. No curses listed.

"Garbánach, do you know if there are any other ogres in your tribe… um… family that also heard the buzzing?"

"All." I felt a chill run up my spine. Did he mean all ogres were infected by the Bodach, or did he mean all of them were predisposed to hearing the hive mind? Or worse… Did he mean ALL creatures in the Southlands, not just ogres? I hadn't ever considered that before. But now, while I camped in the middle of giant and ogre-infested lands, I supposed it might be possible to be a minion of the Boogeyman without being subject to his curse.

"No go to sleep," Garbánach warned, affirming what I was afraid of. "The buzz make you crazy. Make you attack your brothers." He turned to face me, the tears in his eyes glistening in the firelight.

Manny looked at me, seeming confused. What he saw on my face must have been enough to spook the Child of the Sea, because his next words were sharp. "Douse the fire. Let's keep moving."

No one argued. We quickly put out the fire and packed our bags before setting off toward the mountain. I clutched my shillelagh as we walked. We had only hiked a few minutes before we heard the sound of drums coming from lower down the mountain. They were met by a second set of drums coming from somewhere off to the right. Then a third set joined in.

"Three hunting parties," Garbánach said.

"Sounds like they found our fire." Manny appeared to be judging the distance from where the first set of drums originated. "Garbánach, can you tell who is following us?"

"Trow drums. Fachan drums." He paused, continuing to listen. Then he sighed. "Searbhán drums."

Using my new Imbas boon, I understood his meaning. "Searbhán" was the term ogres used when referring to themselves. I also knew that trow were what Gary Gygax called "trolls," and fachan were one-eyed giants… So ogres, trolls, and cyclops. Oh my!

Manny stopped on the trail, so Garbánach and I did the same. The son of the sea god turned to face us, his face serious. "There is no chance that we can fight off all three hunting parties, but I may be able to lead some of them away."

"I don't even know where we're going, and you want to split the party?" Manny shrugged and reached for the Swan-bag hanging off my belt.

"Duinnite only forms near Uffern," Manny said, riffling through the bag. "There will be a cave or a fissure…"

"Garbánach knows cave. We not go there." The ogre looked to be weighing which option was more frightening, battling an army of giants or getting closer to the land of the dead.

Manny smiled as he seemed to find what he was looking for. He withdrew a fully intact violin from the gray bag, before reaching back in to pull out a bow. The thing was nearly as long as his arm. I looked down at the bag on my belt. How… ?

"I will lead as many of them away as I can." Manny held up the violin and bow. "They love string music."

"They like taste of string player more," Garbánach grumbled. "Will only work on trow."

"So that leaves us with the ogres and the fachan," I said, looking into Manny's eyes. "Thank you for your help. Get home safely."

"I will use the portals if I need to. Find my uncle and bring him back to Father." He clasped my forearm and shook it before turning to run into the darkness. From the distance, I heard the sounds of his violin playing Kashmir, a Led Zeppelin song I loved.

"It's you and me now, Garbánach," I announced. I turned back to face the ogre, but there was no ogre. Garbánach was gone. I sighed. I couldn't really blame him. But I suddenly didn't feel as good about my odds.

Something clicked inside me. I knew that, like Manny, I could find my way back to the portal room. Unfortunately, I would be no closer to finding Goibhniu and no closer to acquiring allies for Cai and the Fomorians. I knew what I needed to do. My eyes flicked uphill to the path that would take me higher onto Tech Duinn.

I let my Control Energy boon take over my visual senses. The energy in this place was strange. It appeared that the ambient energy in the area was being sucked into the volcano. It was just as I suspected. There were holes in the ground at random intervals that appeared to vent fumes and pull in energy. I looked farther up on the mountain and saw what I was looking for. There was a hidden entrance into the mountain that had been obscured from my current position until I used my boon.

Unfortunately, the entrance wasn't close. I estimated that even running at full speed, it would take me a few hours to get to it. The sound of the drums grew louder, pulling me back to my current predicament.

I immediately started sprinting up the path, using my newfound physical stats to push the limits of what a human body was capable of. I leaped over small rocks and used the large ones as launching pads. I was practically flying up the mountain, spending more time in the air than I was on the ground.

Behind me, I could hear only one war party. But while the drums of the other parties were silent from my new position on the mountain, the drums behind me sounded louder, like they were gaining ground. I thought about the longer stride of the much larger beings trailing me. Were they the fachan or the ogres? I supposed I would find out soon enough. I knew I wouldn't make it to the cave in time, so I did the only thing I could do. I turned and prepared myself for battle.

PART 2:

THE
ORDEAL

CHAPTER 37:
HULLRAISER

Day 15 of Midwinter, Nightfall
At Sea, Straits of Segais
Annwn

Hullraiser had set off at a clip. We had hoped to put some distance between us and any coastal cutters that might be following.

But before we could make much progress, a thick, dense fog had set in, with nightfall further hindering visibility. I found myself less concerned about who might be following us and more about the possibility of slamming into one of the numerous shoals that littered the Straits of Segais.

We sailed east toward the homeland of Fern and her family. Like most selkie families, they had formed a large, protected enclave under the waves from which they ruled their section of the wells. Fern's reddeshorate happened to be in the deepest part of the Ildatbach Bay, near the Well of Secrets.

Not a single member of the crew seemed willing to meet my eyes, but I could feel them studying me. I knew I was a sight, even in the darkness of the Crosswaters. It had been days since I had bathed or rested, and I could still feel the salt crystals on my skin from my swim at Hook Head. But… I could have been confusing salt crystals for dried beithir blood. Either way, I was gross, and I felt even more gross than I looked, which was saying something.

The crew consisted of a commander, a tide-master doubling as first mate, a boatswain, and six other crew members. I didn't recognize any of them, but they clearly knew me, or at least something about me. I wasn't sure that 'something' was good. I normally got a clear birth in Gorias, but the cold shoulder I was experiencing onboard Hullraiser felt even more frigid than the water of the Straits.

Normally, an Ellyllon in the service of a king or queen outranked all terrestrial or nautical military ranks. At one time, I would have been recognized as the highest-ranking officer on the ship. Unfortunately, now that I'd refused to reclaim my former title, I was just a fairy in need of their service.

I needed information, but also knew that it was important to exercise tact and avoid jeopardizing my relationship with the crew. This would be difficult.

"Hey! You! In the fancy hat," I shouted to the commander. "Why is everyone acting like I just strangled a cat? I didn't kill anyone…" I thought for a minute, then added, "today…"

The commander turned from the helm, where he'd been talking to the first mate, who was a stern, bald woman. Every patch of her exposed skin carried scars, and the curved blade at her hip added to what I had to admit was a pretty menacing effect.

The commander broke away from her after my outburst, coming to stand with me at the front of the ship.

"Yes, Captaen?" he asked, bowing slightly. "What can I do for you?"

"Fíadan," I responded, pointing at myself like he was an idiot. "Not Captaen.' What's your name… or should I just keep calling you 'Fancy Hat'?"

"Commander Maevin Scolt, my Cap… ma'am."

"And her?" I pointed to the first mate.

"Salka, the finest tide-master in service to Gorias. She…"

I cut short what I was sure was going to be a long elaboration on Salka's deeds and virtues by pointing to the short boatswain. "And him?"

"That's Cé Gwalch."

"Is he a Lubrican?" I asked, feeling my lip curl up in disgust.

"Yes, from Ildatbach." I could tell by the tone of his voice that he was confused by my visceral reaction.

I sighed. "Of course he is."

Most Lubricans lived in or around Port Ildatbach, and many of the vessels in the Wells had at least one as a crew member. They were seen as good luck in turbulent seas. And I hated them all. The Lubricans' unnatural affinity with the weave was a blight among all races in Annwn. But my view on the matter was not a widely held opinion.

"Is there something I can do for you, ma'am?" Commander Scolt asked, snapping me out of my unpleasant memories.

"Did Badb tell you to be ready to sail?" I asked suspiciously. I had been trying to process the whole turn of events from the previous afternoon, starting with Badb's whispering of the name of this ship in the Gorias courtyard. Had she made the ships ready for my escape before I even knew I was planning to escape?

"Lady Badb from Findrias?" he asked. "No… To my knowledge, she has had no interaction with anyone outside the keep since the siege."

"Then how did you know to expect me?"

I could see the man grit his teeth before answering. "I'm not at liberty to say, I'm afraid." Beads of sweat dotted his brow. He swallowed hard, then continued. "But know that we serve the Breo-Banríon, her kin, and those loyal to her."

I felt myself soften at his statement. "Badb told me to take this ship over the other in the harbor. Why would she have done that?"

"I'm afraid I cannot comprehend…"

"Cut the chet," I said more loudly than I should have, cutting him off. "You aren't stupid, so don't act like it. Make an educated guess."

He thought for a minute, then responded. "The Witchcurrent sits lower in the water. Hullraiser has a shallow draft, thanks to its wide hull."

"Does that mean Hullraiser is slower than Witchcurrent?"

He nodded.

"So, she told me to take the slower ship?!" I exclaimed, throwing up my hands. "I should have known…"

Commander Scolt drew back, clearly offended at my condescension. "Hullraiser may be… 'slower' than the Witchcurrent, but she has taken more unmolested trips across the Straits than any other vessel in the navy."

"She has a few other unique properties," said a new voice. Salka came to stand with us.

I rolled my eyes. "Yeah, I'm sure. Can you get me safely to the reddeshorate?"

The woman looked at her commander before answering. At his nod, she continued. "Aye. But for the moment, our progress is slowed by this fog."

"On the bright side, ma'am, there is not a soul that could follow us in the grey lady." Commander Scolt peered into the mist. True enough, I thought, staring at the fog that surrounded us. If a ship had been right next to us, even its lanterns would have been hidden.

I left Commander Scolt and Salka to their tasks and headed below deck in search of privacy. I stripped off my disgusting clothes and cleaned myself as best I could with the bucket of fresh water and rags that I found waiting in my quarters.

I then laid out the equipment I had collected since awakening in my old room back in Gorias. There was Swish and Stick, the Heartbane Dial, Morias' ring, aptly named "Wavewalker," and Bren's Rings of Identification.

I leaned back against the wall and ran my fingers over Bren's rings. He was out there somewhere, likely mucking things up. But I couldn't help but smile to myself thinking about how far he had come since that night on Wolves Hill when Morias and I had changed his life forever. Chet went sideways when Bren was around, but then, Annwn needed more of Bren's kind of chaos.

I hoped that if I found Fern, she could use her Shell of Promise to find Bren. I had trusted Nemain enough to deliver the Shell to Bren, but not enough to lead me to him herself. I knew where her loyalties lay, and as much as I wanted to hate her for it, I understood what it meant to be wielded as a weapon. She had her place in the hierarchy of the Tuatha, just as I had.

Bren was on a magically protected island. It was as if Bren, too, was in a deep fog, and only Fern's shell could cut through it. I didn't have any idea how we might fix our broken world, but once we found Bren, he would help us…I hoped. The Dagda had believed in him enough to send me to find him at the beginning. Morias believed in him, too. Maybe that was enough.

Chet, I was tired. Closing my eyes, I finally let my body fall into the much-needed trance. I found the flow of the magical weave around me, and I bound myself to it. I would allow myself these few moments of rest. Things would be better in the morning. After all, it couldn't get any worse.

CHAPTER 38:
WELCOME TO HIGHTOWER

< TADG >

Day 16 of Midwinter, Sunset
Market District, Falias
Annwn

IT HAD BEEN AGES SINCE I HAD TRAVELED USING RADIANT SURGE, AND I HAD FORGOTTEN THE EXHILARATION OF RIDING THE SUNBEAMS. THOUGH THE TRIP FROM CRUACHAN WAS LONG, I REVELED IN THE NEWFOUND FREEDOM.

THE SOUTHERN GATE SENTRIES HAD REQUIRED…SOME PERSUASION TO SHARE THE NEWS THAT OUR FATHER HAD BEEN HOME FOR A FULL DAY, NECESSITATING A CHANGE OF PLANS. WE WOULD NEED TO REMAIN UNSEEN, SOMETHING EASY TO ARRANGE.

"Stop it!" I screamed inside my own head as we walked into the central city. "You killed them!"

NO, WE KILLED THEM.

I shook my head in a helpless attempt to shut up the voice that I couldn't escape. I stared down at my hands, rubbing them as if I could erase the violence they'd carried out… violence I'd been unable to prevent despite sharing a body with the perpetrator. "Where are you taking me?"

WE ARE GOING TO THE MARKET WHERE YOU FIRST EXPLORED THE CITY WITH THE SAGE.

"Please," I begged silently. "I need to get to the tower where they are holding Brigid."

ALL IN DUE TIME.

"There is no time! Father will be cutting any loose ends before he finishes the war." I felt the alien presence's stubborn resistance to any change of plans, tinged with…was it longing I felt? It couldn't be.

I WOULD SEE THE FAMED CAPITAL CITY OF ANNWN. IN MY TIME, THIS PLACE WAS NOTHING MORE THAN A WAYPOINT IN A TRAIL SYSTEM RUNNING FROM WELL TO WELL.

Belenus ignored my pleas to stop, and I remained an unwilling passenger in my own body as we walked northwest into the market district. The stalls and shops of the purveyors went on for blocks in all directions, the colorful canopies representing where each vendor had traveled from. There were faded reds from Gorias, the once-brilliant color long faded by the sun. Other stalls held the distinct blue of Murias, or the deep green Findrias was known for. And of course, a majority represented the tan hue of Falias, the capital.

The central marketplace was named after Lir, largely due to the fountain at its center. In the grandeur of the city, the fountain seemed small and unremarkable, and yet it had always been considered the center of the market district.

My mouth watered at the smells from the various food vendors. I hadn't had anything to eat the previous few days other than dry, salted meat, but even so, the strength of my hunger surpassed anything I could remember feeling in the past. Before I knew what had happened, I found myself crossing the street to stop behind a small crowd that stood in front of a food stall of rotisserie meats turning over a fire. The stall vendor held a large carving knife that he used to carve slivers of the hot meat off for the waiting customers.

Judging by the size, most of the cooking animals would likely feed ten or twelve people.

Drawn to the crackle of meat and the hiss of fat, I drifted toward the fire, unable to look away. My movements were strange, predatory, and the crowd seemed to sense it. One by one, the townsfolk slipped aside, watching me with wary eyes.

I desperately wrestled for control, gaining a half-second hold that allowed me to flip a coin to the man turning the spit before Belenus crushed my will beneath his and ripped an entire chicken from the spit. He growled and buried our face into the hot meat, grease spurted onto my hands as he devoured the meat in huge chunks. I took advantage of his distraction to make my way out of the increasingly shocked crowd to an alleyway, my face and hands dripping with grease and chicken entrails.

"What are you doing?" I said in my mind between mouthfuls of meat.

I HAVEN'T EATEN LIKE THIS IN MORE TIME THAN I CAN REMEMBER.

I had to frame this in a way he would understand. "We are supposed to be keeping a low profile. Everyone knows me here, and you are drawing unwanted attention to us."

I watched myself lick my fingers clean of the chicken debris and the other filthy reminders of the past two days, namely, killing and crawling through centuries of dirt and grime. My thoughts overpowered Belenus' control of my body for a moment, and my stomach rebelled. I lurched closer to the alley wall, leaning against it as the partially chewed chicken shot from my mouth like it was being fired from a cannon.

GIVE ME CONTROL

"No," I said aloud, and watched as a passerby paused long enough by the alleyway to see the spectacle. I waved a hand at the man to move along. "You need to stop for a moment and listen to me. I have come here for a very specific reason."

I felt Belenus pause as if thinking. *YES. TO FREE THE FIERY QUEEN.*

"She is being held in the westernmost spire of the Watchful Crown."

AND YOUR FATHER?

"In the central spire," I said, wondering why Belenus wanted to know about my father. I had assumed he could read all of my thoughts.

I CAN. The voice seemed darkly amused. *BUT YOUR DESCRIPTION OF THE SPIRE WILL BETTER HELP ME NAVIGATE THE CITY.*

"Why do you want to know where my father is?" I asked, searching my pockets and bags for a cloth that I could wipe my greasy mouth and hands on. Belenus, surprisingly, seemed to be letting me.

WE MUST WREST THE SWORD FROM THE USURPER BEFORE WE LEAVE FALIAS.

I paused, cloth in hand. "Father will never part with the sword as long as he draws breath."

THERE IS A SOLUTION FOR THAT.

His message was clear enough, and I thought back to the way he... no, WE had dispatched the southern gate guards. "Despite everything, I don't wish to kill my father."

YOU WON'T HAVE TO.

"No!" I snapped, wondering if Belenus could feel my turmoil. "I won't let you kill him." My mind was quiet for a few moments before Belenus continued.

VERY WELL. WE WILL FIND THE SWORD OF LIGHT AND RESCUE THE WOMAN.

"Fine," I said quickly, hoping to mask the feeling of relief that had washed over me. "But why do you wish to find the sword?"

IF I UNDERSTAND YOUR PLAN, YOU WISH TO FREE THE WOMAN AND REUNITE HER WITH HER FAMILY ON THE FRONT LINE.

"You know that is precisely my plan," I muttered. Clearly, he'd been reading my thoughts again.

THERE IS NO POSSIBLE MEANS OF VICTORY WHILE THE USURPER POSSESSES THAT SWORD.

Belenus was right. I had pondered that exact thought from the first day I had set myself on this course of action. We needed to capture the sword, and time was short–it would need to be done before the war convoy left the city walls.

"I agree," I said. "But stealing the sword will be very dangerous." I heard the beginning of a crazed chuckle in my mind and suppressed an involuntary shiver.

LET ME HANDLE THOSE THAT STAND IN OUR WAY.

"These people are… were my friends. I won't kill the King's Guard." The voice in my mind was silent.

Finally cleaned of the worst of the grease and dirt embedded in my skin, we set off out of the alley. Even if I hadn't known my way around the meandering streets of Falias, all one had to do was look up. The Watchful Crown of the central city held the highest towers in all of Falias. In fact, it was how the city had earned the nickname "Hightower." It was also where Father ruled from.

From where we stood in the market, the three spires of the crown appeared to be the same size, with the central tower set back on the horizon. In reality, I knew the central tower was nearly twice as tall as the two others. In each of the three main towers there were other, smaller spires. Brigid would likely be in one of the smaller spires in the eastern crown.

Despite running across a contingent of soldiers heading south to the gate, we managed to avoid attracting any attention on our way. I wondered if Father had learned of the murder of his guards, but more than that, I wondered how we would achieve our goals without causing even more death and destruction.

Even as those fears passed through my mind, I heard another chuckle from Belenus that grew and grew until it felt as though my own thoughts were being crushed under the weight of the sound.

The laughter permeated my psyche in such a way that I felt myself on the edge of being driven mad.

I longed for the quietude of my own thoughts and my own struggles. But with Belenus in my head, silence was a luxury I feared I might never know again, especially in the trials that awaited us in the spires above.

CHAPTER 39:

BLIND RAGE!

< CAI >

Day 16 of Midwinter, Sunset
Dueling Ground, The Deep Realm
Annwn

Time seemed to stop after Tethra's body disappeared into the Abyss. A heavy silence had settled on the assembled Fomorian crowd, and not even Dubhlinn or Morvra, nor any of the other Mná na Mara, spoke. My own focus was locked on the smirking, bloody face of Corb.

Without having realized I was moving, I felt myself landing in the pit in front of the monster of a man. Though he was badly injured, Corb stood facing me, awaiting my approach. In his right hand, he held Tethra's blade, Orna. His own blade lay only an arm's distance away.

"Corb!" I snarled his name as I surged toward him, unable to find any other words. All I knew was that Tethra was gone. Forever.

The space between us narrowed, and the world around me seemed to go in slow motion. I caught a flicker of movement out of the corner of my eye just before I was slammed from the side.

Indech! Of course. I should have assumed that one of Corb's underlings would come to his rescue.

I crashed to the bottom of the dueling pit and managed to turn my fall into a roll that took me a few feet away from Indech's follow-up attack. I sprang from my roll into a ready position, Fragarach in my hand and ready to draw blood from the man if he remained between me and my target.

"Stop!" Morvra commanded from atop the pit. The crowd remained silent. Indech paused where he stood. I too remained still, feeling like a coiled spring ready to shoot forth with compounded force.

Dubhlinn's voice came next. "The duel is over." I understood her statement for what it really was, a command to stay my hand. But this was Corb's mother. Of course, she would want me to withdraw.

I glanced at Corb, seeing the weakness and fatigue behind his sneering expression. He had lowered Orna to the pit floor and was subtly using the blade as a crutch to remain upright. Tethra's strike had left him badly injured. Though he'd been able to shrug off the initial pain and damage, he had been completely run through, and the deep wound was taking its toll.

I activated the Perfect Aim boon that I had acquired through the death of Lugh, seeing Corb's body light up with possible strike points. He was injured and had lowered his sword. On top of that, Corb wore minimal torso armor, as was the custom with the highest-ranking Fomorian warriors.

Indech, who was in his own right a well-respected warrior, could tell that I was studying Corb. Without moving from his position, he caught my eye, growling, "I will strike you down before you ever get close to him."

I shifted the boon to Indech, seeing similar weak points in his torso light up…but it was his long, braided hair that truly caught my attention. I lowered my blade, feigning resignation. When I did, the boon highlighted the weakest areas of Indech's body. As I predicted, his hair remained his greatest liability in hand-to-hand combat.

"I challenge you," I proclaimed, lifting my sword to point at Corb. An audible clamor went through the crowd. Dubhlinn attempted, without much success, to bring the assembly back to order. I shouted to be heard over the growing noise. "As a son of our former king, I have earned this right!"

"You have no right, Maccán," Corb responded, his tone mocking. I knew he had highlighted my epithet to remind all present of my status as an adopted son.

I looked to the rim of the pit and studied the faces of Dubhlinn and Morvra. Ultimately, they would decide whether my challenge was legitimate. At first glance, Morvra appeared as stoic as ever, but I knew her well enough to see the grief that lay heavy upon her. Tears threatened to betray her facade of strength.

Dubhlinn's voice echoed off the walls of the dueling grounds. "There will be no further challenge. We have lost enough today."

My heart sank. If there was to be no approved duel, and in my heart, I knew there wouldn't be, I knew what I must do.

First, I would need to remove Indech from the equation before any more of Corb's supporters could enter the pit. Second, I would need to gain an advantage against Corb by seeking out Fuilgeir, which lay between us. Third, I needed to eliminate Corb.

My plan was not particularly well thought out, and I knew it was likely to end with my death. Given my domain, I couldn't truly die, but that wasn't common knowledge, and it didn't make a deadly injury any less dangerous for me or my people.

If I were injured to the point of death, my body would disappear from here and emerge in the Heart-shaped Pool back on the mainland…without my gear or my most valuable possessions, which would be here, with Corb and whatever army he intended to raise.

Each of these thoughts had come in only a fraction of a second. At that same time, Corb appeared to have realized many of the same things that I had.

"Yes," he said, his voice thick with mock sadness. "There has been enough loss today." Though he faced me, his voice rang through the pit, clearly pitched to carry to the gathered crowd. "If you cannot accept my rule, leave your spoils of war behind and go your own way."

I sucked in a breath. He was talking about the Spear of Victory. I hadn't brought it with me to the dueling grounds, but it seemed Corb now sought to claim the relic as his own.

"Why did you do it?" I asked him. I knew the answer, but I wanted to hear him say it…wanted our people to hear him say it. I activated a lesser-used ability of Fragarach, Trust Tongue, and continued. "Why did you kill our sister?"

I knew Corb, and I knew he would want to make a spectacle of this moment. He would try to spin Tethra's death as a necessary, selfless task he had taken on and a boon for his people. But I couldn't allow that. The magic of the sword surged forth, and where Corb would have otherwise spoken a sweet lie, Fragarach compelled him to speak only the truth.

"You and she were the only things standing between me and the throne." His eyes widened as he heard himself. I had not used Truth Tongue in any battle or sparring match since I had taken it from Lugh. "I simply had to eliminate her first, knowing you would do something foolish to avenge her."

He was right. I lunged forward, sidestepping Indech. He immediately swung his sword at me, but I slowed it enough to evade what would have been a devastating blow. I stepped under the swing, moving closer to his side…where I could reach his massive braid.

I knew that I was stronger than anyone currently watching the battle, even Corb, and I used that strength to my advantage as I wrapped my hand around the thick rope of hair. I yanked Indech off his feet and threw him in the direction of his new lord. He screamed as he dropped his sword and plummeted toward Corb.

I continued moving forward with part two of my plan. I rolled immediately after the throw and reached for Fuilgeir. As my hand reached for the blade, I felt stars explode in the side of my head before everything around me went fuzzy. I lay panting on the floor of the pit, realizing I had failed. Fuilgeir lay within arm's distance, as did Fragarach. I had dropped it in my pursuit of Corb.

I could see only a partial view of the dueling pit, as my head lay on the stone, swimming in disorientation. Indech was picking himself up somewhere beyond the boots of Corb, and Corb was being escorted away by several Fomorians I couldn't identify.

My head pounded as I felt rough hands lifting me and carrying me past the faces of Morvra and Dubhlinn. There was a coldness to their glares that I couldn't place in my current condition, but found disturbing all the same.

I knew then the fate I would be forced to endure. I would be taken back to Túr Crochta. Corb would either quietly murder me in the coming weeks or, worse, lock me away in an inescapable cell where I would spend the rest of my days remembering my failure. Who knew how long I might suffer alone within those solitary walls?

Rolling my head to the side, I saw that it was the strong arms of Ethlinn that held me tight. She was flanked by a score of other Fomorians, most, I assumed, who were loyal to Corb. I wondered if the blow that had struck me had come from her. Likely yes.

The world was still blurry, but I was beginning to think I wasn't going to black out...that is, until Indech surprised the group and hilt-punched me in the temple with his sword. The rest of the march to Hanging Tower was done in the darkness of unconsciousness.

CHAPTER 40:
CARRY A BIG STICK

< BREN >

Day 16 of Midwinter, Sunset
Shadowlands, Tech Duinn
Annwn

Things didn't look great. Sure, Manny's Led Zeppelin-esque musical stylings seemed to have successfully lured off the trow, and I could no longer hear the beating of ogre drums, only those of the fachan…which meant the whole party of fachan was still behind me. You might even say, they were fachan following me.

I hadn't actually ever seen a fachan, but the descriptions I'd heard didn't fill me with anticipation. The one-eyed giants were described similarly to the cyclops of Greek myth. Before Annwn, I'd marveled at how many "monsters" seemed to be standard from culture to culture and mythos to mythos. I now knew it was because these monsters were real, not the result of collective imaginations thousands of miles apart.

Unfortunately, the only weapon I had with me was the lustrum shillelagh. I was technically a living, breathing offensive threat even without weapons, but my energy boons, while incredible, didn't always do what I wanted them to do. I suppose that was part of having only been in the world for a few weeks. With time, I hoped my boons would level up, and more importantly, that I'd be able to wield them more reliably. I guessed there was no time like the present!

After a crescendo of Jumanji-themed beats, the first fachan crashed through the trees in front of me. He was followed by two more. I had the sneaking suspicion others were flanking me, given none of the three were carrying drums, meaning either the gigantic drummer boy hung back or was part of a second group circling me.

"Hello gents," I said in their language. "Don't suppose you are here to help me traverse the mountain?"

They didn't respond, seeming momentarily surprised by my cunning linguistics, but that didn't last long. They charged me, because… of course they did.

I assumed a baseball stance with the shillelagh, ready to swing for the proverbial fences. At the same time, I prepared to cast an energy barrier that would hopefully trip two of the giants. I was jerked out of my baseball stance mid-cast by the shillelagh, which yanked me up and sent me hurtling toward the fachan.

I'm not one to waste the element of surprise when a magic weapon gives me an edge in combat (if I had a nickel for every time I've thought that), so I swung hard at the fachan on the left. Thanks, shillelagh!

I was much faster than these creatures, even without the momentum of the flying weapon, and I landed a massive blow on the giant's knee. An explosion of blood and bone erupted into the air as he went down hard. I skidded past the giant, landing on my feet to see that the other two had also fallen to the ground, likely thanks to my energy barriers. Looking at the three groaning fachan on the battlefield, I felt pretty good about how the fight was going… but you know what they say, "pride goes before the fall."

A crushing blow from behind sent me crumpling into a pile on the ground. The missing drummer had apparently arrived. Dizzy for a second, I took rapid stock of my injuries. My right shoulder was out of place and several ribs on that side felt broken, but I remained conscious, thanks mostly to my Pain Sponge boon. Groaning, I erupted from the ground and swung the shillelagh directly into the nearby fachan's eye. He bellowed in pain and rage, swinging his bone sword blindly in my direction before falling to the ground and clutching his bleeding eye. I eyed the sword on the ground. So that's what had hit me…

Two of the four fachan were badly injured, and two were picking themselves up off the ground, still in the fight. With my right arm hanging painfully at my side, I readied an energy blast, but before I could fire it off, I felt a blinding pain on my other side. I landed painfully further up the mountain, feeling newly broken ribs on my left. I looked down to see my throbbing left thumb bent and broken at a gruesome angle. How many fachan fachan were there, I wondered.

My shillelagh was gone. I had apparently dropped it somewhere between where the fachan had done his best Arnold Palmer and where I now lay in a bleeding and broken heap. I reassessed my circumstances, realizing there were at least three semi-functioning fachan, one of them completely uninjured against one increasingly injured and definitely unarmed Síorláidir. Looks like I was going to need to magic my way out of this one.

The three mobile fachan began to run to my position, one of them pausing just long enough to pick up my shillelagh. The weapon jerked in the monster's arm, swung wide, and promptly smashed the neighboring fachan in the gut with the ball end of the stick.

The fachan doubled over for a brief second, then leapt up to pummel the first fachan, who shrieked about not meaning to hit him, his words broken up between punches.

The third fachan continued to charge towards me, holding its massive bone sword in its right fist. I (sort of) had a plan, but one that required a little bit of patience and a whole lot of luck. I mentally prepared to cast my energy barrier on my aching left side…

Then I simply had to wait until he swung… finally, as the creature drew back and swung his sword, I cast my spell.

The fachan wailed as his arm impaled itself onto my sharply constructed energy barrier, set just outside of striking range. He tugged at his impaled arm, his hand still gripping his sword, but I had constructed the spike with barbs that would make extricating his arm almost impossible.

I winced as I brought my own arm up as if I were a puppeteer and willed the barrier spike into motion. The fachan began beating himself in the face with his own sword.

The other two giants had finally stopped fighting and were watching in horror as one of their own literally beat himself into unconsciousness. "Stop hitting yourself. Stop hitting yourself." I repeated over and over until he finally fell to the ground.

I staggered toward the two standing fachan, feeling the bones in my right side snap into place. Their eyes widened in fear as my shoulder, too, slid upward and in to repair itself before their eyes.

Not breaking eye contact, I reached down and slowly, menacingly picked up the massive bone sword that the unconscious fachan had dropped.

"Let's do this, big boys," I said in my manliest growl.

They stood still, clearly considering whether continuing to fight was a good idea. In the end, I suppose they concluded that whatever prompted them to follow me up the mountain was more important than dealing with little old me. They charged.

As I braced myself, I felt a soft bump on my leg. Glancing down, I saw the shillelagh, positioned helpfully upright so that I could grasp it.

That was… weird. During my last power rank notification, the item hadn't appeared to have any abilities associated with it, but after its antics on the mountain, I was sort of expecting abilities like "Demon Possession" or "Sapient n' Sassy."

Grabbing the shillelagh, I grimaced as I felt the bones on my left side knit back together. I seemed to be mostly healed, which gave me a modicum of positivity going into what I was really, really hoping would be the final round of combat against the fachan. But… I also remembered the last time I felt this confident, things had gone awry. Not this time, I vowed.

I jumped, gliding high into the air, feeling the hair on my arms stand on end with static electricity. I brought the shillelagh down on one of the bone swords, surprised to see a yellow charge arc from my weapon to the fachan's just before the weapons clashed. The bone sword exploded, sending bone fragments into everyone present. The charged attack sent the giant tumbling back down the mountain.

The last fachan paused mid swing, eyeing me. After a tense second, he promptly turned around and ran as fast as he could down the mountain.

"Yeah, you better run!" I yelled. The injured members of the original hunting party did their best to retreat with him.

Something rustled behind me, and I spun around with the shillelagh held aloft. The familiar face of Garbánach stood not very well concealed in the trees. He was bloody from head to toe. And was that…flesh in his teeth? The ogre didn't say a word, simply standing there with a dazed expression on his face.

"Thank you," I said. I assumed he was the reason the ogre hunting party had not attacked me along with the fachan. "You had better…" Before I could finish my sentence, the ogre turned away from me, running back into the forest.

I felt a surprising pang of regret knowing that Garbánach was an ogre without a home. He would never fit in past the foothills of Tech Duinn, and he would never be welcomed back home for his past transgressions. What he had just done would likely only make things worse with his clan or tribe or whatever ogres called their family groups.

I sighed, thinking about the quest I was on. I thought about being hunted by giants serving the Bodach and about the dangerous and lonely hike ahead of me.

At the shillelagh's tug, I began to smile, realizing I wasn't truly alone. Fortunately, I had a demon stick to keep me company on my way up the volcanic entrance to the realm of the dead.

CHAPTER 41:
IT GOT WORSE

Day 16 of Midwinter, Sunrise
At Sea, Straits of Segais
Annwn

While I'm not entirely conscious when I'm tied into the weave through a trance, I'm also not incapacitated. In the past, when danger had presented itself while I was in the flow, I had been able to break away in time to defend myself.

There was one time with the Redcaps in the ruins of Dún na Fola when I almost got served as the main dish to the goblin king before I managed to snap out of my trance… the point is, I did eventually wake up, and I made the "Fortress of Blood" live up to its name.

But even compared to that night, my trance aboard Hullraiser was strange. First, I could tell, even in the midst of my rest and healing, that the trance was going long, which happens sometimes when I'm particularly tired or injured. But I also felt the weave change near the end of my trance, typically a sign that something or someone with a great connection to the magic of Annwn has moved into close proximity.

When I came fully awake, I realized I already had my girls out and ready to do some slicing. I was mostly clean and surprisingly refreshed. Salka stood in the doorway to my cabin. Her dour face looked even more grim than it had above deck.

"Let me guess," I said. "We have company." Salka nodded, and I hopped to my feet. "How many and did they come from Gorias?"

"You may want to see this for yourself." She motioned for me to follow her. Together, we exited my quarters and ascended the first few stairs to the main deck.

"Stop here," she whispered as my head poked out of the dim stairway into the sea air. "At sunrise, the mist began to burn away. We found ourselves in the middle of this…"

I turned in a full circle, seeing masts bearing the blue banners of the Murias navy on every side. We were surrounded. I was careful not to step fully onto the deck, as I peered more closely at the ships.

"There," I finally said, pointing at the Murias flagship. "We will be boarded by someone from that vessel."

Salka shook her head. Her expression was pinched with worry, making me suspect she'd never been through something like this before. "We are flying the flaming arrow of Gorias. For the moment, we have nothing to fear."

"Unless they see me on board." I reminded her.

Salka scowled, knowing I was right. "It gets worse. It's likely they've been notified about your exodus from Gorias…meaning we are farthed anyway."

"Why is that?" I asked.

"Because I'm afraid there is only one ship named Hullraiser in the Crosswaters."

"Chet," I muttered, thinking hard. I thought back to the feeling I had while coming out of my trance. "One of the Tuatha is on board the flagship."

"That makes sense. She's called the Seodra Nuada."

"Jewel of Nuada," I repeated. "Figures… but Nuada himself is likely back in Falias or en route to Falias to assemble his grand army."

"I'm less interested in WHO will be coming on board," said the stoic woman. "What's our play here?"

"I'm thinking!" I barked at her. "I barely got my sea legs back, and I'm supposed to be a master pirate all of a sudden."

She didn't say anything, but I could see the gears turning. "That's genius!" she said suddenly.

"It is?" I had absolutely no idea what she was talking about, but apparently I'd had a brilliant idea…if only I knew what it was.

"Neither party has done anything hostile, yet you are wanted by those loyal to the Overking."

"King."

"What?" she asked, still processing what she thought was my grand scheme.

"Don't call him the Overking. It makes me ill."

"Are you ever serious?"

"I try to avoid it," I said, without missing a beat. "Please continue explaining my genius plan."

"We can't just hand you over to them, and they will not allow us to leave without bloodshed."

I eyed the tall, bald woman and the blade at her hip. "I'm guessing you're against bloodshed?"

She gave me a hard look. "Does it look like I mind bloodshed?" I thought about commenting on the hundreds of visible scars but resisted. Barely. She continued, "We are outnumbered nearly fifty to one. We cannot cut our way out."

I shrugged. "Usually when I'm backed in a corner, I fight. What else you got?"

"We need to think like pirates here."

"Enlighten me," I snapped, impatient and sick of feeling like I was one step behind.

"We're going to smuggle you aboard the Jewel."

I wanted to say that my ideas were getting confused in the transfer process between my brain and her mouth, but the more I thought about it, the more I liked the idea. The largest port in the Straits was at Port Ildatbach. If the navy was heading there, its path would put me directly above Fern's reddeshorate. I'd be hitching a ride with the very people who were looking for me. It was truly devious.

"That really is the only way to go undetected," I said slowly, the plan starting to come together in my mind.

"That's right. They will board and search the entirety of the ship, most likely seizing anything dangerous or valuable as spoils." She shrugged. Clearly this wasn't an unusual event for ships stopped by the navy.

We looked at each other for a moment, then turned to run back below deck. Salka led me to the hold. Boxes and crates of armaments and food stores filled the room.

"It just so happens, we have a few containers that will fit the bill," she said, dumping several weapons out of a long crate. Reaching inside, she depressed two hidden buttons on each side of the base. A hidden compartment revealed itself. Inside were a few gems and several other items that I assumed were magical.

"How am I going to fit into that thing?" I asked, peering into the bottom of the crate. "It's long enough, but I'll have to lie completely flat."

Salka stared. "Do you have a bigger crate with a false bottom that you aren't telling me about?"

"Huh…" I remarked, looking back at her. "Morias is right. Sarcasm is incredibly annoying." I hopped into the crate, laying completely flat but with my girls tucked at my side rather than sheathed. It never hurt to be prepared, after all.

I glared up at Salka, waiting for her to close the specialized trap door that would seal me in. I hoped I could trust her…and I hoped I could figure out how to open the trapdoor from the inside when the time was right.

Just before she shut the lid, I asked, "What will you tell the soldiers?"

A slight smile came across her face. "That the annoying fairy we were forced to take on a joy ride must have jumped overboard when she saw them coming. When they can't find you onboard, they'll take a few crates for their trouble."

With a soft snick, the lid closed. I lay still, hearing her quickly pile the weapons and other items on top of the false bottom of the chest.

"If you can break away," I yelled through the wood directly above my face, "wait for me above the deepest part of the bay." There was no answer.

I thought back to Salka's last statement. She seemed all too genuine when she was relating what she would tell the commander of the Murias fleet. Then again, "annoying fairy" seemed like a stretch. "Joy ride" definitely was.

Despite her sarcasm and snide comments, I liked Salka. She seemed like the kind of salty sea wench that I could have a lot of fun with… unless, of course, she betrayed me, in which case, I would cut her from the northern cheek to the southern cheek.

For the time being, however, I had no choice but to trust Commander Scolt, Salka, and their crew. If the commander wasn't at "liberty" to discuss who had given him the orders to escort me across the Crosswaters, it had to have come from one of the two remaining lords of Gorias. They were the only people who outranked me in the commander's eyes. And if Aengus or The Dagda trusted them, then I would, too.

That trust prompted me to lie there, flat as a board and in total darkness, waiting for the greed of the Murias sailors to deliver me into their midst. Once there, I would find a way to escape undetected, slide into the sea, and make my way to Fern's reddeshorate.

If only I didn't have to pee.

CHAPTER 42:

SINS OF THE BROTHER

< TADG >

Day 16 of Midwinter, Nightfall
The Watchful Crown, Falias
Annwn

Father was not a trusting man. I could think of only two circumstances when he was separated from the Sword of Light: when he was bathing and when he was sleeping.

We had carefully made our way to the Watchful Crown under the cover of night, long after most of the citizenry had left the central city and fled to their homes in the residential districts or outside in the hills.

As we approached the central spire, we benefited from the protection of darkness but lost the ability to quickly move away from trouble on a sunbeam. There were also fewer people out and about that we could blend in with, meaning that if we tried to enter the main entrance, we would be spotted in less than a heartbeat. I stood partially hidden in an alleyway near the spire, stumped.

YOU COULD CLIMB THE CENTRAL TOWER.

"Are you insane?" I said back to the obnoxious voice in my head. The sheer walls of the tower reached high into the sky, far too high for me to climb. I felt a mild sense of amusement from Belenus.

YOU HAVE NOT FULLY TESTED THE LIMITS OF YOUR NEW PHYSICAL PROGRESSION STATUS.

I looked at the tower again, reconsidering. As much as I wanted to object, Belenus had a point. So far, since my possession by the Old Power, I hadn't done anything to truly stretch the boundaries of my previous physical limitations.

The base of the three spires was a sprawling central structure that turned into each of the different spires after the third story of large stonework. Handholds would be very difficult...

BUT NOT IMPOSSIBLE.

Before I could counter, I felt my legs rocketing me in the direction of the building as Belenus seized a moment of distraction by the guards. I felt my body leap, preternaturally fast, to land on a windowsill on the second story. Belenus was immediately off again, jumping from column to column, whether or not there were handholds. It felt as though he were simply commanding our body to hold its weight, suspended high in the air, by squeezing our arms and legs together. Friction combined with an unnatural strength made the feat more akin to something an insect would do on a smaller scale.

By the time I had wrapped my head around the things my body was apparently capable of, we had already begun our ascent of the central spire. There, the brickwork of the towers changed, the intricate decorations allowing for easy climbing, given my new abilities. We climbed and climbed, without tiring, until we reached the level below my father's quarters at the Crown, where I knew that he typically rested after a long day and night of battle planning.

Hanging from the wall on what must have been eight stories above the ground, Belenus made quick work of the window, cracking the masonry frame as easily as if opening an unlocked door. We stepped inside quietly, sliding the broken stones back in place as best we could so as not to arouse suspicions. I peered around the room, trying madly to get my bearings.

SOMEONE IS COMING.

We ducked into a shadowy corner as a half dozen guards walked by on patrol. None of them saw us or appeared to notice the signs of our recent entry into the most secure building in all of Annwn.

As the sound of their steps and quiet conversation faded, we quietly moved toward the suite our family used during long sessions at court. My plan was deceptively simple…make our way to the suite and hide within the rooms until Father entered and fell asleep, hopefully leaving the sword easily accessible. Once we had the sword, we'd sneak from the room and rescue Brigid…hopefully before anyone was the wiser.

Belenus was quiet in my mind. He seemed to understand and was going along with the plan, at least for the moment. For the first time all day, I felt as though I had complete control over my thoughts and body. I felt the speed and strength of my new domains, but I also could feel that one of the things I had lost in gaining my immortality was the ability to shape-change. I was surprised to realize that no part of me mourned that loss. My body felt alive and, dare I say, invincible.

As we drew closer to the long hallway that led to Father's quarters, I reviewed my next steps. Outside the entrance would be two guards that I knew very, very well. Given that one of those guards was currently missing a sword called Vowkeeper that was now in my possession, I suspected they would not be pleased to see me.

I had decided to act normally, and when I rounded the corner, I carried no weapon nor exuded any sort of hostile intent. I kept my expression calm and passive, and walked with my hands held out, showing that I was totally unarmed.

"I wondered when you would show yourself around the spires again," said the smaller of the two men. His name was Marc, and I knew him to be a loyal, though somewhat contrary man.

"You have something that belongs to me," said the other, larger man. Jolsten was father's favorite King's Guard, and the first changeling selected to be in the guard after father opted to transfer the responsibility in Falias from Ellyllon to changelings.

"An item that I came to return," I responded, giving a slight bow. "I apologize for having borrowed it, but it couldn't be helped."

"You look even worse than I was expecting," Jolsten said, taking a step forward and extending his hand for his blade.

I tried to retrieve Vowkeeper, only to find that my hand refused to move. Belenus obviously disagreed with my decision to return the man's blade. The three of us stood silently, the tension growing. Jolsten's eyes narrowed, and he dropped his hand, backing up a step. Marc placed his hands on the pommel of his own sword.

"Maybe you didn't understand him," Marc said, his voice tinged with annoyance. "You have something that belongs to him."

I strained again to move my hands to retrieve the blade. They remained in an extended position, open and remaining empty of weapons. My heart sank when I realized what was about to happen.

NOW YOU WILL SEE THE POWER THAT YOU POSSESS.

"No, please don't," I murmured aloud, my voice shaking. Marc's eyes lit up at the fear in my voice, and he set his hand more firmly on his sword. Jolsten, whom I had known all my life, took another cautious step away from me, clearly recognizing that something else was going on. He began to turn, taking a half step as if to run.

Before he could move out of my range, a massive horizontal column of searing light shot forth from my hands as Belenus activated Burning Pulse. Both men staggered as the flesh hit by the light turned a bright red. I watched in horror as blisters formed on their faces and hands. The men began screaming, wrenching with burning fingers at the suddenly red-hot armor they found themselves burning alive in.

"Stop!" I screamed helplessly into the vacuum of my mind. "Please stop!" But it was too late. The screams were already fading into low whimpers. With a few final moans of agony, Jolsten and Marc collapsed into smoking piles of ash..

WE MUST MOVE QUICKLY. SOMEONE INSIDE THE DOOR IS MOVING THIS WAY.

I was in shock. No amount of military training could have prepared me for what I had just witnessed… no, what I had just done. Belenus didn't wait for me to recover, but simply moved my limbs forward to the door and kicked it down. No sense being quiet any longer, I thought. No one nearby could have missed the screaming of the burning guards.

Inside the suite, we rushed past the foyer and headed straight toward the back of the floor. Before we could reach the bedrooms, I found myself face-to-face with Caicher.

"What have you done?" my eldest brother asked, his eyes wide. He held a short sword, but wore no armor or shirt, leaving numerous partially healed spear wounds visible on his chest. For whatever reason, Uncle Dian Cecht must not have been able to heal the wounds completely…which could only mean they had been made by Cai's Spear of Victory.

"Brother," I was able to manage, having wrestled the control of my voice from Belenus. "I am not the enemy that Father thinks of me. Please."

His eyes flicked behind me to the open door leading to the hallway. The guards had burned into nothing, but the smell of cooked flesh and ash had drifted into the room. Caicher looked at me with fear for the first time in his life. Gone was the cocky older brother who had teased and tormented me.

"It was you at the southern gate, wasn't it? What have you done?" He repeated his words, trying to wrap his mind around what had become of the little brother he thought he knew.

"Something happened to me…" My words suddenly stuck in my throat, as I found that I couldn't finish my thought.

"Father would have eventually forgiven you…after the war. Things could have gone back to the way they were. But now…"

Caicher's face was grim, but I watched as he mustered his courage again, his long habit of being the stronger of the two of us restored like an innate reaction. He assumed the poise of heir apparent and leveled his sword at me. "You will come with me."

I caught my breath at his words, fearing what they might lead to. At any moment, I knew Belenus could activate a boon and destroy any chance I might have of fixing things with my family. I held myself still, filled with fear. Seconds passed, and…nothing happened. No boons triggered. My hands didn't reach for my sword against my will. I found that I had complete control of my limbs.

"Please, Caicher," I begged. "Put that down and let me explain. I don't want to hurt you." I wasn't asking for his permission, and I saw the moment my brother realized it. I was giving him a chance to avoid conflict, and I saw the struggle on his face as he tried to reconcile this new tone with what he remembered of me.

"I won't ask again, little brother," he responded. "You have no weapon drawn, and I am the better dueler."

"Caicher, I don't want to hurt you, but…" I should have known better. I had triggered some sort of alpha response by insinuating that I could hurt him. He didn't wait for me to finish my thought, lunging at me. I stepped aside with ease, my newly enhanced speed and strength guiding my movements.

Years of training with my father and brothers had hammered in the quickest way to end a fight–strike first, strike hard, and leave your opponent unable to retaliate. So that's what I did.

My fist came down hard on Caicher's sword arm, a move I'd done a hundred times in training. I felt bones snap beneath the blow, startling me. My follow-up punch was already arcing toward his temple, and feeling the surprising strength behind my first blow, I tried to pull back, but it was too late. The side of my brother's head collapsed under my fist, his body flying back to slam into the wall.

Caicher lay in a heap against the wall, his skull shattered. His eyes bulged grotesquely from their sockets as he convulsed. His limbs jerked once, twice, and then fell still. My brother—the heir to

Falias and all of Annwn—was dead. I stared down at my still clenched fists. He hadn't fallen to Belenus, but to me. I had murdered my brother.

CHAPTER 43:

FOMORIAN TATTOOS

< CAI >

Day 17 of Midwinter, Midday
Túr Crochta, The Deep Realm
Annwn

I met my king and foster father for the first time only a few nights after the Cold Moon. My heart ached remembering that it had been Tethra, now resting broken at the bottom of the Well of Wisdom, who had brought me to the Deep Realm to recover from the injuries I had sustained in Hy-Brasil.

Though my memory is spotty of those first moments with Neit, I remember him looking at me the way a father would have looked at any of his newborn children. Yes, Neit had been a hard man in both voice and deed, but he had also had a softer side to him that very few people had been privileged to see. I remembered how my eyes had traced and memorized the creases of his wrinkles when I couldn't yet speak during my recovery.

My eyes had traveled along the signs of age and laughter up to the shaved parts of his scalp, decorated in traditional bluish-green ink. Despite not knowing their meaning, I had known immediately that the tattoos were important to him and to his people.

The three separate sets of knotwork seemed designed to catch the eye and add to his overall ferocious image. I later learned that these tattoos were important parts of the Fomorian leadership hierarchy. Any warrior, man or woman, was honored with a tattooing ceremony after an important milestone in their life.

I had awoken, as I had expected, in the Hanging Tower prisons. Ironically, I was in the same prison where Tadg had been kept in his short stint in the Deep Realm. Heavy manacles wrapped around my wrists and ankles, the chains barely long enough to reach from the wall to the bed that would serve as my only comfort.

There were no bars here, only chiseled-out lava tunnels of impenetrable stone. The thick door to my cell was fashioned of the cold iron that was nestled, in abundance, in the stalagmites and stalactites of the Deep Realm.

My head and other wounds inflicted by Ethlinn and Indech seemed to have mostly healed. It seemed that Ethlinn hadn't been trying to kill me, so much as stop me from attacking Corb. I supposed that I had, after all, gone against a direct order from the Mná na Mara. Dubhlinn had decreed that the duel was over and for the ensuing fight to cease. I had played into Corb's hands by going after both Indech and Corb, just as he had predicted I would.

I could hear the march of feet just outside my cell and straightened up just as Ethlinn opened the door. The large woman was mute, or at least, I had never heard her speak. The pervading belief was that when she had been forced to pick between life with her son, Lugh, and life with her mother and the Fomorians, she had done so grudgingly and at a deep, personal cost. I couldn't imagine the pain she felt at having to make that choice, or the pain she now felt staring at the face of her son's killer.

She stared at me, her gaze hard. Moments passed, neither of us moving or speaking. I could have shared my regret about what I had to do, but I knew my words would change nothing. She already knew Lugh had attacked Tethra and me in the wilds of Emain Ablach…and that my actions had saved Tethra's life. Even so, I knew that if I were in her shoes, I would have had less restraint when facing a loved one's killer.

I wasn't sure what she was waiting for until more Fomorians entered my cell. I wondered if her presence was mostly to ensure that I was still locked up. Then again, it might also be to make it painfully clear to me that I would lose body parts if I were to attempt anything foolish… like attack any of the people who had just entered my cell.

Indech stepped past Ethlinn, setting a chair directly in front of me. I noticed the chair remained just outside of my reach. An uninjured Corb sauntered to the chair, where he casually sprawled.

"Hail, Maccán." Avoiding his eyes, I watched as others filed into my cell. The newcomers held chemicals and instruments that I recognized as those that would be used in Corb's tattooing ceremony.

"I have come here to share important news of our war effort," Corb continued, as the men with him began to carefully shave the parts of his head where the tattoos would go.

"You've come to gloat," I snapped.

He chuckled, waving a hand at my chained state. "Gloat? You are insignificant and unnecessary to my rule. I do not need to gloat."

"Then why are you here?" I demanded. I believed him and found myself surprisingly curious as to what his answer would be.

He shrugged. "Because I can't kill you."

So, he did know what would happen if he tried to kill me. He continued, "But I also can't have you running around all over Annwn, exposing our secrets to the enemy."

"That doesn't answer my question," I said, raising my chin in defiance.

"The way I see it," he said, "I can either lock you in this box for all time, or…you can help us with the boons you stole from Ethlinn's son."

"What is it you think I would ever do to help you?" The men had completed the preparation of the bluish-green solution. They began jabbing long, iron needles into Corb's scalp, then quickly rubbed the solution across the small punctures. I watched the mark of a Fomorian king begin to take shape, my heart aching.

"Not just me," he said, preening at my interest in his scheming. "You would be helping our war efforts. Tomorrow morning, we will meet the combined forces of Falias on Mag Mór. We have heard, by way of the Gorias beacon, that the four cities are sending armies to the Great Plain so that we can finish this war once and for all."

"And despite knowing you will be hopelessly outnumbered," I said, "you are still planning to follow through with this?

He nodded, his eyes alight. "I know that they have figured out we have the beacon. They have broadcast this plan for all to hear, especially us. And we will answer the call."

Of course, he would answer the call. I was certain that King Nuada knew it, too.

"What I would like," Corb continued, "is for you to use those highly valuable boons of yours to assist with the war effort." He grimaced as the long tattoo needle reached a sensitive part of his scalp. He turned, snapping his hand out to backhand the man administering the dye.

"It doesn't matter what you do to me," I said. "I will never help you." Corb opened his mouth to say something, but I wasn't finished. "And you don't have enough men to contest the combined armies of the realm."

He thought for a moment, wincing as the tattooing resumed. "You have lived among us long enough to know that Fomorians always answer the call of war. You can either help your adopted brothers and sisters, or you will watch them die."

I looked feverishly around the room, searching for anything I could use as a weapon, but they had left me with nothing. No Fragarach. No spear. No armor. I had my Control Energy boon, but it was not trained the way Bren had trained his to shoot forth energy projectiles. With all my powers, I could do nothing to stop Corb, and he knew it.

I snarled, straining against the manacles that bound me to the wall, feeling the slightest bit of give to the metal. Ethlinn quickly stepped forward, leveling the tip of her sword at my throat.

"If he continues to strain against his bindings," Corb said softly. "You have my permission to remove the offending arm or leg."

I stopped struggling and looked up at the large, stone-faced woman. I couldn't get a read on her. I had never known her to follow anyone, with the exception of Neit. Had she simply transferred her loyalty to Corb, despite what he had done to Tethra?

Corb stood, despite the knotwork tattoos being nowhere near complete. If the artists were irritated by the constant distractions or interruptions to their work, they didn't show it. Instead, they quietly rounded up their equipment.

At the door, he turned back to face me again. "You have until Nightfall to decide. Think hard about what you are prepared to do for the people you claim to love." His laughter trailed behind him as he walked away from my cell, the others trailing behind him.

Ethlinn lingered for a moment, her dark blue eyes staring into my own. They reminded me of Tethra's, which had seemed a bottomless blue. The larger woman continued to consider me. I couldn't decide if she wanted to say something or was thinking about whether to follow through with the threat of cutting off an appendage.

She cleared her throat to speak, the sound gravelly from lack of use. "The Mná na Mara has come to a decision about your fate, Cai Maccán. Ready yourself for what is to come."

CHAPTER 44:
THE SOURCE OF MAGIC

< BREN >

Day 16 of Midwinter, Nightfall
Garbánach's Cave, Tech Duinn
Annwn

I had expected a power rank notification after my fight with the fachan, but none came. There was a gluttonous feeling, or more aptly a saturated feeling, that I now recognized as being on the edge of a power rank notification. I'd been looking forward to hearing the Dagda's sexy jazz voice in my head, but alas, the cave entrance came and no power up! Then again, there were also no further interruptions or altercations, which was nice.

The magical energies that I had seen leaking out of the mostly hidden cave entrance became nearly blinding as I got closer. This part of Annwn, the area near Tech Duinn, seemed to be erupting with the weave.

I had shut off my Control Energy boon hours ago for fear of going blind before even reaching the volcano, let alone entering it. But once inside, I didn't even need the boon to feel the ambient power leaking from every rock and stone of the mountainside. For someone like me, who was predisposed to the transfer of magical energy, the sheer volume of magic was downright distracting.

The tunnel I was in appeared to bend slightly downward. I didn't think I was all that high up on Tech Duinn, but even still, there seemed to be plenty of descent to tread. It made sense the more I thought about it. I had, after all, hiked uphill for hours just to get to the cave.

I alternated between descending and ascending for what felt like hours. To my utter confusion, the air seemed to be getting colder, not hotter. Strange, given I was literally marching into a volcano.

I hadn't seen any sign of a living being for a very long time, but I thought I heard running water amid the sounds of rocks shifting and general geographic indigestion. Eventually, I came upon an open space unlike anything I had ever seen.

The room seemed to be the origin of the water sound. A deep pool of water roiled and swirled, and the whirlpool swirled out instead of in on itself. Water appeared to be flowing outward away from the pool in all directions… all directions, including up.

I stared, dumbfounded. This room broke every law of gravity and motion—and probably a few others Earthbound scientists had invented to explain the natural world. Water streamed upward into the air and vanished from sight. The chamber walls were draped in waterfalls that cascaded over twin tiers of Roman-style arches circling the room. The arches climbed higher and higher, just like the water, disappearing into the mist above. It was strange and beautiful all at once.

I hadn't heard any reference to a strange primordial pool in my travels with Morias and The Dagda, but this place felt set apart… special. Looking around, I tried to follow the path of the water from the backward whirlpool up and onto the walls. From the waterfalls, it ran off through holes in the ground and walls. It ran under the arches in all directions, but the bulk of the water appeared to travel in three main channels.

My eyes settled on a path to the pool's edge, and I found myself shuffling down a set of naturally cut stone stairs to reach it. The water looked both refreshing and mesmerizing. It exuded magical energies that I had never felt in Annwn, not even when I was struck by lightning. I felt a nearly irresistible urge to reach out and touch the water.

The pool was beautiful and peaceful, and per usual, that's when something crazy happened…the possessed stick I had been carrying around began tugging me back up the stairs and away from the pool.

"Hey…" I said. I planted my feet to avoid being dragged by the shillelagh. "Stop that. I want to check out this weird reverse Charybdis."

I paused, hearing my own words. Charybdis. That was one of the Greek water monsters Odysseus ran into in the Odyssey. Was it possible that this thing was a water monster? It was Annwn, after all… Getting attacked by some sort of weird water, or Water Weird, would be right on course for this place. Was it possible that the staff was trying to warn me?

"Hey, staff demon," I said. "Is the pool dangerous or something?" It stopped pulling. "I'll take that as a yes."

Slowly, I backed away from the pool while keeping both eyes on the water. To my utter shock, nothing happened. So, this was what happened when you followed good advice and listened to that little voice in your head! It wouldn't make for a good novel, but it definitely seemed like it would keep me upright more than the alternative.

I had inadvertently backed up to a new position in the cylindrical room, not where I had entered. I stood just beneath one of the archways. The water fell from above, the resulting waterfall covering the passageway behind such that I could only partially see through to the other side, where I could see what looked like a faint light.

I pointed the shillelagh at the waterfall. "What about this water? Can I walk through this water?" No reaction. Shrugging, I set off under the archway.

The water felt strange on my hair and skin. It felt cool, but not just from the temperature. It was almost like it was rapidly evaporating from my skin. My skin prickled with goosebumps from the odd sensation, and a shiver rolled through me.

Ahead, I could see the outline of a room at the end of the passageway. It occurred to me that if each archway held another passageway from the pool room, there were likely a lot of rooms I'd need to explore.

I was most interested in the passageways that housed the largest of the water channels, but unfortunately, this was not one of them. Nope, I had "picked" this one based on the meddlesome actions of a certain possessed stick. Based on my luck, it would probably be the most dangerous passageway. Or not. I had absolutely no idea. Sometimes it didn't pay to be the god of chaos.

I walked further down the passageway, eventually reaching a room lit solely by the light of the liquid rock that surfaced in different parts of the space. Looking down from my vantage point, I saw a balcony of sorts. It was up against the farthest wall of the cave, isolated by the lava that ran in and through the rock walls. At the center of this seeming island was a gray stone kiln or oven. Nearby, tools in various states of disrepair were strewn about. Rubble sat upon all surfaces in the small space, which made me wonder if the shifting and churning of the mountain disrupted whatever went on here.

Looking around the rest of the room, I saw various weapons and armor racks, along with great empty urns. Was this a crude workshop?

My eyes snapped back to what I'd nearly missed, assuming at first it was a bundle of rags. In a cage hung an unmoving, emaciated man. My heart pounded as I looked closer, picking out details.

The man's reddish-brown beard looked overgrown from what I guessed had once been a well-manicured point well beneath his chin. Even in his present state, I could see that his arms held a steely, muscled strength that could only come from repeated and heavy use. His faded orange gown encircled his body, while still somehow giving the appearance of an apron.

The man's glistening eyes were locked on mine. He raised a shaking hand to me, letting it fall weakly after only a brief second. I watched as he took a deep breath as if building his strength. He raised his hand again, motioning as if shooing me away. What? Did he want me to...leave? I shook my head, knowing that if I were starving in a cage, I would want someone to come let me out.

I startled as a cold wind blasted through the passageway behind me. The man felt it, too. His eyes widened in fear.

"Hide..." the man whispered, his voice scratchy. "They come..."

"Damn it," I muttered, reaching to pull out my shillelagh. I felt suddenly exposed on the ledge where I stood, but I didn't see an easy path down to the man. If they (whoever "they" were) came from the room with the pool, the vacuous space that dropped into liquid hot magma behind me would leave me boxed in. I couldn't have that.

Making up my mind, I turned and leapt toward the large section of stone that held the rough smithy.

"No..." the man croaked out from behind me.

"How about a little positivity, dude?" I snapped, shooting a quick look his way.

Now that I was closer, I could see the man was in bad shape. What was the "rule of threes" for survival? Three minutes without air, three days without water, or three weeks without food, I thought. It was hard to know if the same rules applied in Annwn, especially if this guy was who I thought he was, but I was nearly certain the man had hardly eaten or drunk in many days.

As the temperature of the room began to rapidly drop, I realized what was coming. I was in Tech Duinn, after all, the gateway to

Uffern, the land of the collected spirits of death…the very place from where the Bánánach had been spilling out and ruining people's days. Morias had been troubled that we'd encountered the spirits of the dead outside of the large battlefields they were regularly found at. I didn't know what that meant, but at the moment, I didn't care.

The room had grown so cold that I could see the fog of my own breath. I didn't know what that meant about the number of evil spirits that would grace my presence, but being that I was on their turf, I suspected it would be a lot. I briefly considered freeing the man to help with the coming fight, but ruled it out just as quickly, knowing he was in no condition to assist with anything, much less wielding a weapon.

"Chains…" the man murmured, struggling to lift his arms again.

"I'll get to you in a second," I responded, turning my attention back to the waterfall passage I had come from. "I know you're locked up and all, but I'm pretty sure we've got bigger problems headed our way."

"No…" he said again, his voice stronger. He pointed over at a set of chains that led up into the ceiling. "Controls lava flow… forge."

I glanced up, understanding immediately what he meant. So, it was true, senior citizens, although slow and dangerous behind the wheel, could still serve a purpose.

"Thanks!" I said to the person I was pretty sure was the long-lost Goibhniu…the very person I'd been looking for.

I quickly moved to the chains and began yanking down on one side of the chain. A great gust of warm air blasted up in the forge, making the room immediately grow warmer.

This I could deal with…This I could use! I waited, tucking myself behind the forge, but in front of the smith god in the cage. I held myself still as the amber eyes, clustered in seven or eight sets, entered the room through the passageway above.

I thought back to what Fern had said to the spirits in the hold of the Stern Beauty when she stood over her captain. Seemed like a good use of the phrase to me.

"You can't have him, devils!" I yelled, brandishing the shillelagh, as the malevolent eyes came flying toward us.

CHAPTER 45:
JEWEL OF NUADA

< FÍADAN >

Day 16 of Midwinter, Nightfall
At Sea, Straits of Segais
Annwn

I had heard about Nuada's grand new naval flagship, the Seodra Nuada. Of course, I had intentionally avoided the christening ceremony. It had been so far away… and I had been so busy.

My mantra had always been to avoid stupid, self-important people and their self-important things, hoping that one day they would cease to exist. But even with all my intentional apathy, I had still heard about the ridiculously gaudy ship and its ostentatious figurehead.

The carved man on the bow of the ship was apparently supposed to be King Nuada. I'd heard it looked a lot more like his brother Lir, which some considered to be intentional since Lir had historically been the leader of Murias.

Whoever it was, the figurehead held a gigantic sword, meant to represent Claíomh Solais, the king's mighty "Sword of Light." What a bunch of dumb and self-aggrandizing nonsense. They should have stuck with either a mermaid, a barmaid, or a handmaid. That's some classy chet.

The plan seemed to have worked. A murmured conversation had been followed by the sensation of the crate being picked up and carried from Hullraiser. Before long, I'd felt the thud of the crate land in its new home aboard the navy ship. After what felt like hours, the ship had quieted.

To pass the time, I had gone into another trance. Back-to-back trances were not my usual practice, but it did help to pass the time. In doing so, I was able to look more closely into the fluctuation of the weave I had seen at the tail end of my last trance. Based on the flow of magical energy in the area, I had been able to see enough to know that someone or something powerful was close by. Now that I looked closer, I could see it was both a someone AND a something.

A very clear Tuatha signature was visible in the flowing of the weave. I wasn't surprised, given the flagship was so close to Hullraiser. Only a relative of Nuada would be allowed to command the Jewel, after all. But the interesting part was realizing that whoever was on board the flagship also carried what had to be a relic-level magical item. The two patterns of energy were close to one another, yet distinctly different.

I couldn't see the color differences of magical energies the way that some could. But I could see the pulse and movement of the weave as it changed based on the beat of a person's heart, and the static nature of item magic.

I racked my brain for what I knew about the four treasures. The Sword of Light was with Nuada. According to Nemain, the spear was with Cai, and I knew the Stone had been destroyed during the battle of Brú na Dallta. That left only the Cauldron unaccounted for.

Was it possible that the relic that had been stolen from The Dagda could be on this very vessel? If so, that changed my plans slightly. Gorias was owed justice for the loss of her treasure.

My mind spinning, I waited as long as I could stand before beginning to extract myself from my square prison. I hadn't heard voices for what felt like days. And though I had no idea exactly how much time had passed, I assumed it had been nowhere near that long.

The false bottom of the crate dislodged with much less effort than I had anticipated, and I did my best to silently shift the booty that remained on top of the hidden space as I made my way up to the true lid. I quietly cracked open the top to find that I was in a reasonably lit and well-furnished room. Given the spaciousness of the room and the obvious quality of the furniture, I realized I must be in the Commander's quarters… not what I was expecting.

From my vantage point, I couldn't quite see the entire room, but based on the reflections from the various mirrors and glass surfaces, I judged it to be empty. Quickly, I hopped out of the crate and re-fixed the bottom so that it looked the same as it had before my escape. If Scolt and Salka had kept my secret, I would keep theirs.

The room felt warm and lived-in, with the air of nobility that the Tuatha had become accustomed to. Red-lacquered dressers and a writing desk lined one interior wall, separated by a large map of Annwn. The red velvet blankets that covered the bed matched the color and pattern of the area rugs that littered the floor. The exterior wall had three large porthole-shaped windows dressed up by lacy white curtains.

On the desk, I found papers stamped with the personal seal of King Nuada. I pocketed them quickly without looking at them before I continued my scan of the room. My eyes fell on the bed again, and I drew in a shocked breath. It appeared the room wasn't empty after all.

I immediately recognized the sleeping young man under the velvet covers as the baby-faced Ogma, brother of Nuada, and god of the knowledge domain. With his short, curly hair and his lack of facial hair, he was almost identical to his nephew, Manannán. Ogma, however, had less tone to his muscles and a softness that screamed more "life of luxury" than "battle-hardened warrior." I wondered if that was why he typically wore more clothes than the Son of the Sea.

Ogma lay asleep in the plush bed that belonged to his tyrant brother. He appeared to have dozed off while reading, as a book lay propped on his chest and the lantern on the nearby desk remained lit.

His right hand was beneath the covers, but in his left hand, he clutched a small black and gold object. I couldn't believe it. There, directly in front of me, was the missing Cauldron of Plenty!

My Silverwhite blades glinted in the lantern light as I instinctively swung my wrists to loosen them. But I paused. What was I to do here? The cauldron was so close. I wouldn't even have to reach across Ogma's body to grab it.

But if I did, would the boy-god awaken and cause difficulty for me? Would he start yelling for help? It wasn't as though I could kill him, nor did I want to. What sort of magical shenanigans did this ancient adolescent have up his sleeve?

Taking a deep breath, I slid my girls back into their scabbards and thumbed the Rings of Identification.

Name: Ogma Grianainech
Race: Tuatha Dé Danann
Current Power Rank - Level 59…

The power rank notification was interrupted by a piercing pain in my belly. Looking down, I saw a bolt sticking out of my fae jack bodice just above my navel. Blood began to flow out of the wound and spill down my legs.

"Fíadan!" came the panicked voice of the boy-god, now sitting up in his bed. He dropped a tiny crossbow from his hands. "The appraisal startled me… I didn't know it was you! I swear it!"

My eyes met his horrified gaze. His expression portrayed a mix of confusion, fear, and clear remorse…But I didn't care.

Behind me, I could hear his words rousing the guards that were posted just outside of his door. There would be a dozen guards in the room in a matter of moments. Worse, this momentarily confused child of Danu would regain his senses soon and use all the boons of his domain against me. It was clear from his eyes that he wouldn't try to hurt me any more than he had, but that didn't mean I wouldn't end up his prisoner, and that thought didn't appeal to me.

Screaming, I snatched up the cauldron he had dropped on the bed and swung it wildly. There was a resounding gong as the cauldron bounced off Ogma's head. The boy-god fell limp, the momentum of the blow throwing him backward into the window, where the pane of glass promptly shattered.

Ogma, god of knowledge, toppled out into the night, wearing nothing but his pajamas. The satisfying splash of the water below was muffled by the sound of soldiers bursting into the chamber, swords drawn.

I felt the room begin to spin at that point, as my feet slid in the slippery blood I stood in. I turned to face the men, stepping backwards up onto the bed. The cauldron was still clutched tightly in my hands.

I wanted to reach for Swish so that I could properly defend myself, but my hands seemed to be moving in slow motion. I felt the sensation of pins and needles in each of my appendages growing as I stumbled backward to the open window before falling out into the dark water.

This time, fortunately, I would get to hear the sound of the splash. Unfortunately, the enjoyment of that splash would be short-lived, as my body and my consciousness sank into the depths.

CHAPTER 46:

THE ENEMY WITHIN

Day 16 of Midwinter, Nightfall
The Watchful Crown, Falias
Annwn

I stood over Caicher's mutilated body, struggling to breathe. I found myself getting lightheaded, and everything was swirling.

CALM YOURSELF, TADG. THIS WAS A NECESSARY ACCIDENT.

"Necessary accident?" I yelled aloud. I didn't care who heard me. "I killed my brother! I murdered my kin! I am no better than my father."

HE ATTACKED YOU. YOU CANNOT BE BLAMED FOR DEFENDING YOURSELF.

I sat down before I could pass out. I knew I needed to leave, but my mind could not get past the act I had just committed. I couldn't take my eyes off my brother's body.

THE GUARDS APPROACH. WE MUST DISPOSE OF THE BODY.

When I didn't respond or move, I felt Belenus take control again and approach Caicher. The room took on a red haze before my eyes. I felt heat and pressure in my face before it erupted out of my mouth, nose, and eye sockets, the sensation reminding me of how Belenus had first taken possession of my body back in Cruachan.

Caicher's clothing was instantly incinerated. His body began to sizzle and bubble, his skin, hair, and bodily fluids quickly evaporating into a dense cloud of ash that floated around and coated my armor like fresh fallen snow, even as I heard the sound of more guards approaching.

A foreign pain shot down the length of my leg bones at the same time I felt my muscles stretching. The skin of my hands and forearms darkened slightly, my fingernails a shade darker than the area around them. I could feel my body changing. The darkness that literally manifested inside of me brought me back to the vision Belenus had shown me of the figures standing on the mouth of Tech Duinn.

As the two guards rushed into the hallway, the same scene played out again. This time, I had enough control over my body to grab a pair of leather gauntlets off the men before they were completely immolated. I thrust my changing hands into the gauntlets even as I watched them darken and change further. I was becoming a monster. No… I was already a monster, and there would be no escaping my new reality.

Belenus took us back into the residence and out onto the balcony on the opposite side of the spire. I knew, through our telepathic bond, that more guards were approaching, but we had locked all of the entryways between the hallway and where we stood. It should be enough to buy us time… but time for what, I didn't know. There was no way for me–for us–to quietly steal Father's sword now.

From where we stood, I could see the entire city. Beside us stood the eastern spire, the western spire obscured by the tower I was in. Below me, I saw another balcony, this one on a level reserved for military command. A figure stood there, alone and unaware of the danger he was in, his back to us.

I FEEL ALIVE.

"By taking the lives of others?" I asked, rhetorically in my mind.

WE ARE BOTH KILLERS, TADG. DO NOT LET YOUR MORALITY CONFUSE THAT FACT.

"I know what I am…"

DO YOU? The presence of Belenus was mocking. *DO YOU REALLY KNOW THE TRUE NATURE OF ANYONE… EVEN ETHADON?*

My heart began to race at the mention of my brother. I forced our eyes back down to the balcony below me, to the man standing alone. He had turned to look out at the night, and sure enough, it was indeed my other older brother, Ethadon.

"Don't do it!" I pleaded, thinking of Caicher. Even his body had disappeared, unable to be mourned. He was just… gone. Forever.

I felt an unfamiliar power radiate from me as Penitent Brand, a boon I had never used before, activated. My finger pointed to Ethadon's back, and a bright red brand appeared on the back of his neck. He seemed completely unaware that anything was happening to him; however, upon first glance at the glowing red lines, I saw to the core of my brother.

I suddenly knew things about him that he had never told me. As a boy, he had stolen coins from a castle aide, using them to frame another. He had poisoned Bairic's pet hawk as revenge after a particularly grueling day in the stables. I saw that for all our lives, he had dulled my blades before sparring with me. He had used his power and influence not just for the good of the kingdom, but also for his own selfish desires and pleasures. The seemingly endless list of sins played through my mind until I intentionally stopped the boon's magic, unwilling to see more.

EVEN THOSE CLOSE TO YOU ARE NOT WORTHY OF YOUR PROTECTION.

My mind reeled. Rationally, I knew that every person, changeling, human, or fae would be tainted by at least some small amount of selfishness and insecurity, and those flaws often led to hurting others. But I was shocked at the number of small and large cruelties that my brother had inflicted on those he supposedly loved. My idea of who Ethadon was had been forever changed.

YOU SEE IT NOW.

I shook my head. "I see a deeply flawed man... but he is still my brother."

AND THAT SHOULD SAVE HIM FROM JUDGEMENT?

I didn't know what to say for that, but I could feel a feral instinct growing inside of me, like a cat before a pounce. I bit my lip and forced my hands to grip onto the railing. "I won't let you hurt him."

WE WILL DO IT TOGETHER. The voice seemed to take on a cajoling tone in my mind, as if it were reassuring me as to the rightness of the violent justice it wanted to deliver.

"No!" I said. "I will call out to him and warn him."

THAT WILL NOT PROTECT HIM.

I knew that he was right. I had met none other in Annwn that could perform the physical feats that we had done only moments before. Belenus had the strength to hunt down and destroy anyone in the central spire, with the possible exception of Father.

I wondered what else I could say or do that might sway Belenus, finally remembering another boon we hadn't activated yet.

"I am going to show you what it means to be mortal, even in an undying world," I said, activating Guilt-Sight before he could stop me.

We looked at Ethadon. The brand still glowed in the darkness of the balcony, but with it was now a lingering shadow, of sorts, that clung to his form. It overlapped with other shadows and floated, independent of the wind. The overlapping forms told another story to my boon-receptive mind. In them, I saw regret and sorrow for his cruel or selfish acts. For some, the grief was light and mostly forgotten, but for others, even those spaced out by countless moons, I saw deep sadness and remorse.

Through my eyes, both Belenus and I saw a deeply flawed man being held together by dissonance. All the killing and all the acts of insecurity over the years had created a lasting weight that Ethadon carried with him every day. Though I didn't know how Guilt-Sight appeared on other individuals, I could see the heaviness of the burden he had created by his many misdeeds.

"He is flawed," I said to the Old Power inside of me. "Like you and I. And he carries with him this burden that helps to remind him, every day, to do better… to be better."

Belenus was silent. I wondered whether he was going over my words again, coming to the same conclusion I had. While I suspected Guilt-Sight was a boon intended to help me dole out judgment based on guilty acts, I had instead used it to paint a picture of the whole man, rather than only his deeds.

When I saw movement in the eastern spire, across from us, my hopes were dashed. Belenus was not contemplating the morality of Ethadon, but trying to assess the danger level of whoever or whatever he was watching.

With our combined attention, we were able to focus on what I recognized as a familiar man with red hair. Ruadan, my cousin and son of the Breo-Banríon, stood quietly watching us just as we had quietly watched Ethadon.

I felt the primal hunter inside of me redirect its energy from Ethadon to Ruadan, but neither party made a move to attack. I sighed, strongly suspecting a fight would be in our future, given my role in the capture of his mother. At the least, there would soon be a reckoning.

CHAPTER 47:

A MOTHER'S FINAL LESSON

< CAI >

Day 17 of Midwinter, Sunset
Túr Crochta, The Deep Realm
Annwn

It had been hours since Ethlinn's cryptic command to "ready myself." What had she meant? Would Corb or his men plan to kill me in my sleep? I shook my head. They would know that killing me would be a temporary solution, a fool's errand at best...That is, unless they used the spear. A cold chill ran through me. Was it possible Corb knew the relics were god-killers?

There were no loud footsteps to warn me of the arrival of the Mná na Mara. At the barely audible snick of a key in the lock, I looked up to find only Dubhlinn slipping through the doorway. She quietly closed the door behind her and stood before me, just out of reach. I looked Corb's mother up and down, wondering if she had come to finish what he wished he could do himself. Though armed, she did not carry the Spear of Destiny.

"Cai Maccán," she began, as she slowly slid her sword from its sheath. She was human, even smaller than me, but her brown skin sat tight over rippling, sinewy muscles, making it clear she was no stranger to battle. Even so, the sword that she held looked massive in her small hands.

"The Mná na Mara have deliberated for hours over the best course of action for our people."

"And you volunteered to do Corb's dirty work," I said, my voice dripping with disdain for her son.

Fast as lightning, she came forward and slapped me. "The mother in me wants to run this blade across your throat, but you and I both know that would do no good."

Shocked at the suddenness of her slap, I held myself still, waiting for whatever came next.

"But," she continued, "a mother has a higher calling."

I looked closer at her, suddenly noticing the discomfort in her stance and the large blade she carried. It was Orna! How had Dubhlinn gotten hold of Tethra's blade?

I raised my eyes from the sword to meet her own. She nodded, seeming to know the question I couldn't seem to force past my lips.

"Corb presented it to Morvra in an attempt to quench the fire in her heart."

I laughed out loud and shook my head. "Nothing will ever quench that fire. I saw it in her eyes. She will never be parted with that ache in her heart… and neither will I."

"I know…" Dubhlinn began pacing the small length of the cell. "That is why what I'm about to do is so difficult for me." She carefully placed the sword against the wall before rummaging through her pockets and withdrawing a crumpled letter.

"This is what eventually convinced us of our course of action." The letter in her hands had been opened and pored over—by whom, I didn't know.

"What is it?" I asked the woman, suddenly afraid. Dubhlinn said nothing but held out the letter to me. She was well within my reach now but seemed to have no fear that I might attack her, take the key, and make my escape with Orna.

Looking down at the writing, I knew why. The letter had been written by Tethra. I snatched it from the smaller woman's hand and began to read.

Béstin, my beloved,

If you are reading this, I have lost the duel, and your worst fears about Corb were correct. He has killed me and taken the mantle of King.

The truth is, I believed all along that you were right about my brother. But I could not let myself believe that kin would slay kin, for any reason. Despite what I know of his character, and despite my own scars, I know that I do not have it in me to kill Corb. You knew this about me, and that is why you worried.

I suppose being right does not afford any relief in this case, because even writing this is breaking my heart. Thinking of a time when we will not be together brings me pain like I have never felt. Know that I love you, and I will continue to love you, even from the shadows of Uffern.

I wonder what your fate will be when and if you read this letter. In your grief, I fear that you will act rashly and end up imprisoned or killed. But you cannot...you must overcome! Our people need you, and you do not have the luxury of sacrificing yourself for revenge.

There is a truth that I never told you, Béstin. My father believed he knew your true parentage, and he shared that with me before he died. I kept this secret from you because I knew you wanted nothing to do with a political life...and perhaps, because I selfishly wanted to keep you for myself just a little bit longer.

Father believed that the children of the Cold Moon were the offspring of Prince Elatha through his lost daughter, Briomhaith.

If you ever loved me, and I know that you did, there is one last thing I must ask of you before I set you free. It is a heavy burden, but one that I know you can bear, because you must. Take your place as rightful king. Rule our people with the wisdom that I have seen in you… that my father saw in you.

Do this for me, and for our people, because they need you as I needed you. Do this for me because I love you, and because it is the last favor I will ask of you.

Yours forever, Tethra

Tears ran down my face as I finished the letter. My heart began to burn with renewed fire as I pressed the letter to my chest and stared at the woman before me.

Her face proud, Dubhlinn opened her clenched fist to show a key. With her other hand, she angrily dashed away her own tears. "A mother's higher purpose is to teach her child life lessons. The most important lesson of all is about consequences… My son has gone too far this time. YOU are his consequence."

She again held out the key to my manacles, but I did not move to take it, my mind still reeling. I felt broken and confused. No part of me could have anticipated what was happening.

"Take it," Dubhlinn said, more forcefully, before adding in a softer tone, "Comhthíreach."

"Countryman…" I felt outside of myself, as if I were watching my hand reach out to take the keys. As soon as I did, the proud woman seemed to shrink in on herself. Her shoulders slumped, and the small woman turned and left the cell, leaving the door slightly cracked.

Dubhlinn, mother to Corb, had brought me my freedom and the blade that she must know would kill her son. She had done it with the consent of the Mná na Mara. The purpose of such a group was clearer to me than it had ever been. The Women of the Sea were the balancing force for my people, no matter what it might cost them personally.

I had already known from my trance that Briomhaith, the woman in Hy-Brasil that I had seen on the mossy hills, was my mother. I knew that she was the daughter of Prince Elatha. What I had never truly considered was what this meant…that my parentage made me the rightful heir of Neit through Elatha, his first son. The question was, would I do as Tethra asked, and claim that right and responsibility?

I knew the answer. Tethra had asked it of me… so it would be done. I allowed myself one more brief moment of grief, then squared my shoulders. I quickly unlocked my shackles and stretched my wrists and legs. Even in the soft light of the lichen on the walls, Orna shone like the gem that her name implied.

I wrapped my hand tightly about the grip that Tethra had held so many times. This was the blade that should have killed Corb. Tethra might not have allowed herself to kill her brother, but I would not have the same hesitation. There would be no duel, no rules that would stay my hand. I would use all my strength and power to kill Tethra's murderer.

I knew what I needed to do, but also that Corb likely now had the spear. He would try to kill me, just as I intended to kill him. In fact, this whole scenario might have been a trap, a set-up for Corb to justify killing me. I realized it didn't matter. There was nothing else to be done.

I stepped quietly from my cell in Túr Crochta and began to travel the short distance to the throne room where I knew Corb and those loyal to him would be waiting.

CHAPTER 48:
DIVINE SMITH

< BREN >

Day 16 of Midwinter, Nightfall
Uisneach, Tech Duinn
Annwn

The Bánánach came in fast and straight for me. I instinctually focused on the forge in front of me and all that wonderfully hot lava running beneath it. Using my Control Energy boon, I rapidly raised the temperature of the lava around me, causing a great explosion from the forge as the Bánánach passed overhead.

A shrill, multi-octave cry that reminded me of The Exorcist movie came from the specters that had been blasted by the heat and rock. Huh, I thought. Fíadan had said that the most effective weapon against them was cold iron, but the molten rock seemed to be at least weakening them. Maybe it was the extreme heat, I wondered. They did seem to flourish more in cold environments.

I didn't even try to count the shrieking Bánánach as I ducked out of the way of the spray of lava, swinging the shillelagh. I felt the possessed staff score hits on several targets as I swung, but it was impossible to tell how much damage I was doing.

Something grabbed the shillelagh and began trying to pull it from my grasp. Ice-cold claws raked across my side, and I heard the bearded man behind me cry out in pain. This was getting out of hand quickly. I needed to find another way to hurt these creatures.

Despite my enhanced strength, the shillelagh was wrenched from my hands. It sailed across the room to fall, ignored, to the floor. Glowing amber eyes swirled around me. If I had done anything to impact their number or potency, it didn't show. Even worse, I had lost my weapon.

Rapidly thinking through my boons, I considered my options. I didn't have long to contemplate how the magic-rich environment might impact my energy magic...not that I ever did much contemplation before acting. I thought back to the success I had had against the fachan with my creative energy barrier. I was pretty sure I could outdo myself.

I focused on the overabundant weave energy swirling around me, much like the accursed specters, and worked to turn the magic itself solid. Great, sharp crystals of magical energy coalesced from thin air in wide arcs around me, imprisoning nearly all the Bánánach within the unmoving magical shards. The high-pitched wailing grew in volume as the spirits tore huge rents into themselves in their attempts to escape.

"Who are you..." The man behind me gasped before I heard the thunk of him collapsing. Great, now I was going to have to carry him out of here.

I forced myself back to my more immediate problem. Luckily, my control energy boon seemed to take almost no effort in this space. Unluckily, though the creatures were mostly trapped, a few looked like they could escape at any moment. Modifying the magic of my boon slightly, I increased the size and jaggedness of the crystals. The wails suddenly cut off as the amber eyes blinked out of existence. The room fell silent.

"That wasn't too bad," I said aloud, then cringed, looking around as if something might jump out at me. Nothing did. But now that the battle was over and my adrenaline began trickling away, I could feel the slashes on my left side. They were oozing blood and… whatever that white stuff was. I stepped over to retrieve the shillelagh, which had landed in one of the large urns.

As soon as I touched the weapon, I received a strange notification.

Your domain classification, Battlesmith, allows you the ability to modify this weapon with little or no equipment. This blade is a lustrum alloy shillelagh. Would you like to REPAIR or SHARPEN this weapon?

I mentally dismissed the notification, but was surprised to immediately receive a second one.

The water of Uisneach has unlocked an additional option. Would you like to unbind this weapon?

I paused. "Unbind?" Afraid of what that might mean, I dismissed the notification and fully pulled the hammer end of the shillelagh out of the liquid in the urn.

I wasted no time in finding the keys to the cage and removing the bearded man from his confines. His skin was badly lacerated by the claws of the Bánánach, and beneath the new wounds were too many scars to count. How long had they been keeping him here? And had they intentionally kept him alive? If so, that would present a new aspect of the Bánánach that I hadn't expected. Was it possible they were sapient, rather than the mindless killers I had assumed they were?

With that frightening thought, I placed an energy barrier over the passageway leading out to the weird pool area, which, according to my boon, was called Uisneach. I paused long enough to appraise the still unconscious god.

Name: Goibhniu Deoghabha
Race: Tuatha Dé Danann
Current Power Rank - Level 70

Current Progression Status:
Physical Progression +90
Mental Progression +79
Spiritual Progression +82

Domain: Smiths

That confirmed my suspicions. The badly injured man was indeed Goibhniu, Lir's missing brother. But I wasn't sure he would be able to make the trip back to Tir fo Thuinn in his present condition, and I had no healing magic or súg. I did, however, have a slightly unorthodox idea. Surprise.

As an energy manipulating extraordinaire, I was lucky enough to be able to enter a trance like that of the fairies. And though I hadn't quite mastered it, I had managed to plug myself into the flow of magical energy such that I would be able to restore both my health and my endurance. It was an essential skill for me now, given that the boogeyman guarded the entrance to actual sleep.

Over the next few hours, I experimented with the trance and the flow of energy. In the past, I had manipulated my place within the trance, not the actual flow of energy itself. I was now wondering if I could somehow plug the smith into that same flow and heal his body. This would be the first time I attempted to jimmy rig a trance, not just for myself, but for someone else.

That was the hardest part, actually. Attempting to manipulate Goibhniu's energy without his help or consent proved problematic. Even so, the room was so saturated with energy that I had some mild success. Opening my eyes, I saw the smith god staring back at me, his new wounds already scabbing over.

"I don't know who you are," he began, attempting to sit up. "But I have never seen anyone manipulate the weave like that. Not even The Dagda."

"I'm Bren," I said, knowing that wasn't going to mean much, if anything, to the god. "Your brother Lir sent me to find you. There's a war brewing between your brother and my brother."

He looked confused.

I continued, "My brother is Cai Maccán…and that makes me another child of the Cold Moon."

Goibhniu considered what I had said. "That doesn't explain why you are doing Lir's errand."

"Truthfully?" I asked. "We're looking for allies."

He scoffed. "And you think I would align myself with the Fomorians over my own brother?"

"I don't know what you are going to do," I responded with a shrug. "I didn't even know you existed two weeks ago. But I do know that your brother killed Bres with one of the Treasures and is keeping Brigid as his prisoner in Hightower."

His eyes narrowed, though I noted a lack of surprise. That was…telling.

"I have sensed a change in my brother," the smith god began. "That is why I have braved the dangers of the mountain once again."

"To find Duinnite?" I asked.

The smith nodded. "The realm needs more Silverwhite protectors." So, he DID see how messed up everything had become!

"Can I help you?" I leaned forward. "Can you teach me to make Silverwhite weapons?"

He looked at me like I was crazy.

"And while we are at it," I added, holding up my shillelagh. "Any chance you can explain what 'unbinding' means?"

CHAPTER 49:

THE REDDESHORATE

< FÍADAN >

Day 17 of Midwinter, Nightfall
Eastern Segais Reddeshorate, Ildatbach Bay
Annwn

I came to eventually, only this time, Morias wasn't there to make an inane literary reference. Instead, I opened my eyes to find a group of people I didn't know waiting for me to awaken, two women and two men.

It was dry. Did that mean that someone had dragged me back onto land? I suppose it would be possible for someone to fight the currents this close to the edge of the Crosswaters. If I had been closer to Gorias, I would have certainly drowned. Or would I, I wondered. Looking down, I saw both my magical rings where they belonged, snug on my fingers. Wavewalker was among their number, and the very presence of that ring made me question where I was.

I felt a moment of panic when I realized my blades and the Cauldron were gone.

"Where are they?" I demanded, trying unsuccessfully to sit up. Pain shot through my bandaged stomach, causing me to fall back on the bed. I peered through bleary eyes, realizing that the ceiling and walls around me were glowing slightly. Weird… but also not my biggest problem at the moment.

One of the women came forward and spoke gently. "They are near, Fíadan. Do not worry."

I recognized the woman's voice but struggled to form a reply. My vision was blurry, and it was all I could do to fight the sharp wave of pain that still rocketed through my guts. I could tell the bolt had been removed, but from the pain, it might have well still been sticking out of me.

The woman's voice continued. "I did not expect to see you again so soon."

Her words confirmed that we'd met before. "Come closer so that I can see you," I said.

None of the blurred shapes came any closer, and I realized they were frightened of me. No wonder they had taken away my blades. But why take the Cauldron?

"I'm going to give you something for the pain," the woman continued. "Then we can talk. Once you have come to yourself, I will return your belongings."

"I don't need anything for the pain," I said. I gritted my teeth and forced myself into a seated position. From the corner of my eye, I saw the group collectively take a step back. I focused hard on not passing out.

"Give me my stuff," I demanded.

The woman took a half step toward me as I wavered, trying to get a hold of the pain. When I finally looked up, I recognized the long, dark hair and freckles of Fern.

"Chet, lady," I chuckled. "I would have skewered you. Maybe next time, introduce yourself."

"Now you see why we took your blades," she responded with a smile. "They are here, along with the other item."

I shoved out of the blankets and struggled to my feet, struggling at first, but the longer I was vertical, the easier it seemed to become.

"Where am I?"

Fern extended her hand, as if to help me over to my things stacked nearby. I glared at the hand until she dropped it with a faint smile. "My people found you at the bottom of the bay, holding onto that blasted cauldron. Now you are inside the reddeshorate."

I chuckled. "At least I didn't let go of the relic. That would have been embarrassing."

A slow sense of recognition emerged on her face. "It sinks like an anchor, by the way. You are lucky you aren't dead."

"Not luck, I said, sliding my Silverwhite blades back in their sheaths. I patted them fondly, then held up my hand. "Magic ring."

Fern's eyes snagged on the other ring. "Why do you have Bren's ring?" she asked, a hint of worry in her voice.

"Don't worry. He's okay... I think." I paused, suddenly remembering the other people in the room. Now that I was upright, I could see them more clearly. There was a slightly older man and woman, and a second man who looked to be around the same age as Fern.

"Fíadan Ellyllon," Fern said formally. She stepped out of the way and offered a hand toward the other people in the room. "I would like to introduce you to my mother, Morlaithen, and my father, Caarunach."

The older couple took a half step forward to give me a slight bow. I noticed that they still didn't get too close to me.

I didn't bow back. I just gave them a nod. "Never thought I would get to meet selkie elders..."

Fern looked confused. "Wait...You knew I was the daughter of the reddeshorate elders?"

"Yep." I thought back to when Morias had told me on The Stern Beauty. I shrugged. "The Sage gave it away when he wouldn't let me call you a princess. I was very off put."

"But I'm not a princess."

"Bra-vay-doe, bra-vah-doe." I said.

The younger man cleared his throat and stepped forward. "I'm the brother that she often forgets about. You can call me Flide."

"I CAN call you any number of things," I quipped, moving closer to the Cauldron and taking hold of it again. "But what is your given name?"

"Flideion."

"You're right, I'll probably just call you Flide… if I call you at all."

Caarunach seemed to finally shake off his uncertainty at having me here. "Why have you brought one of the Four Treasures into our colony?"

I noticed Flide elbow Fern at his father's words. He gave her a nod.

"It's not the only Treasure in the colony, father." Fern reached into her pocket and held out one half of what I immediately recognized as the Stone of Destiny.

"You have got to be chetting me!" I said, not believing my eyes. The conversation I'd overheard between Ruadan and Bren in the Gorias council chamber suddenly made a lot more sense. Ruadan had coughed noisily when I'd said that The Dagda believed Bren and the Stone could help with the state of Annwn.

I slapped my forehead, groaning with the realization that when Fern had given Bren her shell, Bren had responded by giving her half of the Stone of Destiny. The other half was the one Nemain reported as having been destroyed in Brú na Dallta.

"I tried training with it," Fern continued, "when I was on my ship. But it doesn't seem to respond to me."

"We've seen how the Stone is meant to work," Flide added. "Bren used both Stones in Unseelie when we attacked him."

I chuckled, thinking back to Bren's state of disarray the morning after he had gone out on the town with Ruadan. I should have known the two of them would have gotten into some trouble.

"Listen, princess," I said with a little smile on her behalf. "A lot is going on around here that I need to catch you up on. To start, Bren's with his brother."

Fern startled. "He has a brother?"

Oh boy. This was going to take a while. I sighed, then took a deep breath, pain radiating through my stomach and torso.

"Here's the short version," I began. "Bren left to go train with Ruadan and ended up going back to Ériu. There, he got in a fight with the Bodach and came back to Annwn, where he rode to war with the Morrigan because Gorias was in the middle of getting invaded. The castle was taken, so we had to take it back. Things got messy. I lost my wing in the process and Bren died…" I paused.

"Only he didn't REALLY die, I guess. He earned his domain and then went with Tadg to where his brother is in hiding with the Fomorians. They fought with the King, and the Fomorian leader died. Meanwhile, Morias and I went cliff diving, where I discovered the lost tower of the first Sage. Everyone wanted to give me back my old title, but I told them to screw and left on a ship that got surrounded by the Murias navy. I found the Cauldron and then, if you can believe it, I got shot by Ogma, of all people! Who knew he could even hold a crossbow, let alone aim it and hit something? Anyway, I fell out the window, took an unexpected swim, and I ended up here with you all. I'm pretty sure Brigid has been kidnapped, possibly by the king… who might have also killed his own half-brother. So much for the gods never dying, right? Now the King is rallying an army to squash Bren, his brother, the Fomorians, and anyone who rides to battle with them."

I paused, thinking. "Yeah, I think that covers everything."

Fern and the others stared at me like I was crazy.

"That was the short version?" Flide asked, his eyes wide.

"Look," I said, looking directly into Fern's eyes. "You're the only one that can help me find Bren…and it is even more important now that we find him."

We both looked down at the Treasurers we held in our hands, and the weight of our next actions sat heavily on the room.

CHAPTER 50:
SO MYSTERIOUS…

< TADG >

Day 17 of Midwinter, Sunrise
The Watchful Crown, Falias
Annwn

WHERE DID HE GO? Belenus seemed equally surprised and frustrated.

"Ruadan? He is a slippery one," I replied in my head. "He will find us."

Before Ethadon had gone back inside, I had shut off both the Penitent Brand and Guilt-Sight boons. I didn't know if the brand would have been visible to others, but caution seemed the better part of valor, plus I was honest enough with myself to know that I also didn't want others to see what I had seen in him.

I had learned something interesting from using Guilt-Sight on my brother. One of Ethadon's regrets was how soon the army would be leaving for the battlefront. The army would ride hard to Mag Mór this afternoon. I knew that Nuada must have some sort of magical aid in order to move the entire Falias army so quickly.

THE SUN IS NOT COMPLETELY UP. THERE IS STILL TIME TO ACQUIRE THE SWORD.

Before I could respond, I saw a pulse of light from the roof of the main Crown building.

"It appears Ruadan would like a chat," I said. I was consciously avoiding any thoughts about the sword or our first catastrophic attempt to steal it.

IT COULD BE A TRAP.

"With Roo, that wouldn't surprise me at all. Be on your guard."

Though the sky was lightening with a brilliant palette of purple, the morning rays of the sun had not fully crested the horizon, meaning our boons could not yet carry us to meet with Ruadan directly. The sounds of commotion behind our position on the balcony came to my ears, and before Belenus could alert me to the presence of the guards, we jumped down onto the balcony below. From there, we jumped to a waterspout, then a windowsill. Again and again we jumped, and before long, we stood at the side of the red-haired and grim-faced lord of Gorias.

"Interesting method of travel, Grunt," he said, his usual snarky tone devoid of any affection. He partially reclined on a mostly flat section of the Crown, his pose casual. "Honestly, I thought it would take you longer to get down here, or I might have stood up. You won't be offended if I stay seated, will you? I'm really quite comfortable."

I DON'T LIKE HIM.

"He often has that effect," I replied in my mind, then to Roo I said aloud, "I'm pleased to see we are talking as opposed to trading sword strikes."

"We still might," he said, his expression hard even as his words and tone were flippant. "But I'm hoping that your good deed in Cruachan is a sign that you've experienced a change of heart and feel some regret over how you left Mother."

I drew back, shocked. "How do you know about what happened at Cruachan?"

He smiled wickedly. "Let's just say I'm well connected."

I felt a tingle as Belenus attempted to use identification magic to appraise Ruadan, followed nearly immediately by a strong sense of irritation at the lack of results.

Ruadan quirked an eyebrow at me. "Now, now, aren't you going to buy me dinner first? Besides, you should know by now that my ways are unknowable to all but me." He waggled his fingers as if doing a magic trick.

"It wasn't..." I started to tell him that I wasn't the one using identification magic, but I stopped myself, realizing how crazy it would sound. "Tell me how you know about Sétanta."

"I was there when you emerged from Cruachan. I was here when you arrived in Falias." He shrugged. "In truth, I have been following your progression since you left Deepwater."

"How is that possible?" I asked.

"If I told you that, I wouldn't be nearly as mysterious... and you know how much I enjoy that."

I shook my head. Inside, I felt Belenus assessing both our surroundings and the progress of the guards back up in the central spire. He was leaving me to deal with my cousin. That, I knew, was a good thing. Belenus was just as likely to destroy him as he was to listen to what he had to say.

Ruadan was eying me carefully. "You are different, Grunt. Something has changed about you." For all his frivolity, I suspected that Roo saw people much deeper than we'd ever given him credit for.

"I've been working out," I told him, trying to match his typical level of snark. It was a losing proposition, but he smiled, seeming to appreciate the effort. "So you knew that I was coming here?"

He nodded. "Yes. To free Brigid." He paused as if waiting for me to interrupt. After a few tense seconds, he continued, "I'm waiting for you to say that you are here to free my mother. If that's the case, we can be friends again."

I startled a bit before blurting awkwardly, "Actually, that is exactly why I am here."

"I knew it!" he said, slapping a knee before standing up quick as lightning. "I'm very relieved that I won't need to strangle you in your sleep." He eyed me again, thoughtfully. "Though, based on your recent changes, I suspect that would be harder than I had originally thought."

"And…" I started to say.

"Now, now, you were off to such a good start. Don't backtrack." He condescendingly shook his head and lightly tapped the wicked-looking dagger on his belt.

IF HE ATTACKS US, I WILL SEAR HIM TO HIS BONES.

"Don't threaten me, Roo. I'm not the king's grunt any longer," I said.

He peered closer at me, then smiled in what looked like genuine delight. "You earned your domain! Very exciting!"

"It's more complicated than that…" I paused, my words trailing off. I wondered suddenly how much Belenus would let me tell him. "There is too much to tell, and no time now to tell it. But if you have followed me since Bren and I parted ways, you must know that I have fallen out of favor with Father."

"Yes, of course. It's why I didn't immediately stab you when I saw you in the market…with the chicken." He gave a mock shudder. "You appeared to be very hungry after traveling so quickly from the Midlands."

I flushed in embarrassment, remembering the dirt, and blood, and grease that I had licked from my fingers in the alley. I tried to bring us back to the more important topic. "Roo…we need your help to steal the Sword of Light."

"We?" he asked, catching the slip of my tongue.

"Brigid and I," I rushed to say, trying to cover for my mistake. Roo's expression made it clear that he wasn't buying it, but thankfully, he didn't press.

"So you want my help to steal the sword… Are you proposing a trade of sorts? I help you, and you, in turn…will do the thing that you should do anyway?"

I knew that his question was a trap, but also that there was only one truthful answer to it. "Yes."

"Counteroffer," Ruadan said, motioning for us to walk to another part of the roof as the sun crested the top of our world and began to light our path. "How about you rescue Mother, as you should, and as you SAY you've come to do, I assume in an attempt to right your many wrongs, and then I'll think about helping you steal the sword?" I felt a wave of guilt wash over me. He wasn't wrong to doubt me.

"We don't have time. The army is setting out this afternoon for the battlefront."

He contemplated that. "What if Nuada decides he no longer needs to keep a political prisoner? What's to stop him from murdering my mother before they leave?"

"I've thought a lot about this," I said. "If Father had wanted Brigid dead, she would be. There must be a reason that he is keeping her alive."

"Such as?"

I shrugged, honestly mystified. "Maybe it has something to do with the war. Is it possible he's using her as leverage to bring Gorias into the fray?"

Ruadan shook his head. "No. If he admitted to kidnapping my mother, Gorias would already be at the gates of Falias."

I realized suddenly what this meant–neither the Dagda nor Aengus knew Brigid had been kidnapped and by whom. "Why haven't you told your grandfather or your uncle where she is?"

"Because Gorias would lose that fight... We wouldn't just be fighting Falias, would we? There is Findrias, which Gorias shares an island with, and of course, the navy of Murias, which would stop all trade in and out of Gorias harbor. We would lose in a big way."

I nodded, understanding. "Then there is another reason he's kept her alive, and I'm sure that reason won't change by the time the war begins."

He shook his head. "Your hunch isn't worth my mother's life. I'm afraid I'm going to have to decline your proposition, Grunt."

HE IS NO USE TO US. I WILL DEAL WITH HIM.

"No!" I said aloud. Ruadan flinched back, wrapping his fingers around the handle of his dagger. "There is another way."

I felt sweat beading on my forehead. I had to think of another way to get Ruadan to help us, or Belenus would kill him. "What if…" I said, thinking out loud, "You went for the sword, and I went for your mother… at the same time?"

He seemed to be considering my words, his keen gaze clearly noting the beads of sweat that dotted my forehead. I wondered suddenly if he had other appraisal magic that could circumvent my detection of identification magic. The truth was that no one had ever truly understood Ruadan's boons.

"I'm going to choose to trust you, Grunt." His brow furrowed, and he paused, looking directly into my eyes. "I can't promise that I won't fail. That sword is the most protected item in the realm." He narrowed his eyes. "But I do promise that if YOU fail, we will be on significantly less amicable terms the next time we meet."

I nodded solemnly. We spent a few more minutes discussing what would happen after we had both achieved our goals. I even asked him for a small favor, based on a theory I had about his constant knowledge of my whereabouts. When we finished, I held out my hand to shake, hoping he would sense my level of commitment. But Ruadan was already walking away, clearly planning the heist of the millennium.

CHAPTER 51:
VENGEANCE!

Day 17 of Midwinter, Nightfall
Túr Crochta, The Deep Realm
Annwn

It was late, near the middle of Nightfall, if I had to guess. There were no guards stationed outside of my cell door, and I saw no extraneous traffic coming in or out of the throne room.

I could, however, hear lively conversation coming from inside, and I felt no guilt in pausing to listen. It seemed that Corb and his closest allies were planning to assemble and move an army of Fomorians to Mag Mór. But how?

According to Tethra, King Neit had kept the secret of Tir fo Thuinn to himself until he had shared that secret with her and only her. How then could Corb possibly move an entire army to Tir Tairngire by morning?

I knew there were many thin spaces in the Deep Realm to Ériu. These spaces were the main way the Fomorians had been able to pass to and from the mortal world to procreate, after all. But I did not know of any thin spaces to other parts of Annwn.

Was it possible Corb had discovered Tir fo Thuinn? I shook myself out of my musings. The reality was that if the next few moments went according to plan, it would matter little.

I focused harder on the different voices coming from the room, trying to discern their number. Six Fomorians, plus Corb, if I had counted correctly.

It was likely they had my equipment and the Spear…which would surely be wielded by Corb. I wondered if I would be able to manipulate the relic with my boons. It was possible, though unlikely, and in a battle to the death, finding out the hard way that I couldn't slow the spear would have drastic consequences. As it was, my only weapon was Orna. But Orna had a memory…and it likely knew each of these opponents. I could rely on that ability.

The throne room was cavernous and cold. Braziers were lit at the bottom and at the top of the stairs, near the throne. Corb stared into one brazier I knew very well, the Blaze Diviner. I wondered idly who Corb was spying on, until he looked up directly to where I hid.

"I knew somehow you would come," Corb said. He looked back into the flickering flames. "It was the Mná na Mara, wasn't it? I shall have to do something about that group of women after the war."

The six other men began to make their way down the stairs, hands on their weapons. Corb remained at the top, reaching for the golden spear that could mark my doom. The spear was strong enough to pierce the strongest armor, not that I was wearing any armor at all. If Corb scored a hit on me with it, the sharp point would pass clear through me and return to his hand in the next moment. I had only one chance against its power.

I sprinted toward the men. As the first two reached the bottom of the stairs, I expanded and exploded the braziers to either side. Flames shot forth and engulfed both men. They screamed and attempted to smother the fire by rolling on the ground. Two temporarily out of the fight. Four obstacles remained in my path.

I activated Perfect Aim at the next pair of advancing men. The first swung his sword high in an obvious attempt at a killing blow. I ducked as Orna swung low, moving with a speed I had never experienced before. My Maximum Yield boon turned what might have normally been a deadly slash across the man's abdominals into a butter-smooth thrust that severed the man's spine.

I yanked the blade from the dying man's body, turning to face my next opponent. As I did so, I saw Corb make his first throw with the spear. Using my boon to control the speed of the charging man, I accelerated his pace to place him directly in front of me precisely when the spear would have stuck.

It shot through the man like it was passing through air, and I recoiled from its forward momentum, sliding low on the floor to the base of the stairs. The skewered man fell behind me, and Corb recalled the spear.

Two more Fomorians to go, not including Corb, and those two were almost upon me. I looked up to the chandelier hanging above me, even higher to the space above it where a high concentration of lichen was visible. With the candles in the chandelier, this space was where the majority of the light in the large room came from.

I did the only thing I could do. I squeezed my eyes shut and intensified the glow of the light until it felt hot from behind my eyelids. I heard screams from the two men, then a clattering as they stumbled and fell down the remaining stairs.

Lowering the intensity of light back to normal levels, I opened my eyes and sprinted to one of the many nearby stone half tables. The low tables, designed to be used as a chair or a table depending on what the moment required, were heavy and massive. I had never attempted to pick one of them up before. Throwing caution to the wind, I heaved with all my strength, hoisting the huge stone slab in front of me. A second later, I heard the thud of the spear on the other side and knew immediately that I had narrowly missed being impaled.

I ran forward, holding the heavy table as a shield. Orna was still clutched tightly in my hand between my palm and the table. I reached the first blinded man on his knees at the base of the stairs and paused long enough to kick him as hard as I could in the face. I heard his neck snap. The other man had stumbled to his feet, but one glance at his damaged eyes assured me he could wait.

I bounded up the stairs, taking two or three at a time, toward where Corb had previously been, still holding the table in front of me. Despite its usefulness as a shield, it greatly hindered my ability to see the room. Again, I heard a clang on the table. I jerked my face back as the point of the spear poked out directly in front of me before disappearing as it was recalled. I was shocked to realize I now had an eyehole!

Peering through the tiny gap, I watched Corb back up toward the throne. I charged directly at him, my arms increasingly heavy from the weight of the table. Corb growled in disgust and threw the spear to the ground before snatching up his familiar, double-bladed sword, the weapon that had seen him through countless battles.

"Fight me, Maccán!" he roared. The sound nearly covered the soft shuffle of one of his men attempting to sneak up behind me. Nearly. The man's charred, still-smoking clothing made it obvious that he was one of the men I'd assumed were already removed from the playing field. No longer needing it anyway, I heaved the stone table at him.

He faltered, dropping his sword without thinking and extending his arms as if to catch the massive object. It crashed down into him before it began toppling down the stairs. Each loud thud was accompanied by a heavy, wet noise as the man was crushed between the table and each stair that it slid down.

A quick recount, depending on the state of the men, left one burned and one likely blind Fomorian to go…and most importantly, Corb.

He stood his ground in front of me, Fuilgeir in his hand. Corb was a formidable fighter and nearly as strong as I was. Orna gleamed in my own hands, as if hungry for its final battle against Fuilgeir.

I closed the space between us, watching him carefully. As I expected, Corb's Evil Eyes flared to life, spewing forth a torrent of flames. He likely knew that I could deflect energy magic, but was using it anyway as a means of distraction.

What he didn't know was that I had another trick up my sleeve.

I had never attempted what I was about to do, but instead of turning the fire away, I used my Transform Energy boon to rapidly lower the temperature of the geyser of fire until ice crystals began to form. The column of flames became massive ice shards leading back to Corb's face. With my free hand, I grabbed a jagged shard and thrust it back to its source. Corb screamed as blood began to flow out of his ruined eye socket.

Corb stumbled back as the ice shard shattered. I didn't wait but continued to charge. I swung Orna with all my might. Corb managed to raise Fuilgeir enough to narrowly parry my blow, but the sheer force of my attack sent Corb flying back onto the throne. The sound of shattering bones filled the room.

Corb staggered to his feet. His eye continued to gush blood, and his body leaned to one side. He took a swaying step toward me.

"You didn't have to kill her," I said, waiting for him to come to me. "She was your sister… She was the best of us."

Corb smiled through bloodstained teeth. "That is why she had to die." He spat out blood and continued to lurch toward me.

I tensed, his words rekindling the burning fire in my heart. Jumping, I swung my sword high on his side with no vision. I landed on my feet, panting. His head thudded to the floor next to me, his body following seconds later.

I exhaled, feeling no relief but only bone-deep tiredness. As I assessed the canvas of red that decorated the throne room, a grim realization settled over me… This wasn't about justice.

As Dubhlinn had said, this was the consequence for actions that could never be atoned for. It was revenge.

CHAPTER 52:
PROTO-CELTIC PROTOTYPE

Day 17 of Midwinter, Nightfall
Uisneach, Tech Duinn
Annwn

"You are a Battlesmith?" Goibhniu asked, sounding surprised. He had improved enough to sit up on his own, but still looked like death warmed over.

"Yes…" I said, "But your reaction makes me feel a little self-conscious about it now."

"I'm also a Battlesmith," he announced. He looked me up and down as if considering. "But I have none of your energy boons."

I was surprised to meet another Battlesmith, but less surprised to find out that we manifested our power differently. In my travels around Annwn, I had only met one other person with similar boons. That person was the other half of my duality, my brother.

"So, you can sharpen and repair weapons with little or no tools?" I asked. It wasn't clear to me exactly how this domain classification worked, and I found myself filled with hope that Goibhniu might be willing to teach me.

The smith chuckled, the sound weak but filled with genuine mirth. "We are capable of so much more than that, child of the Cold Moon." He pointed at my shillelagh. "Is that weapon made of Lustrum?"

"An alloy," I said. "But when it fell into the urn over there, I was given an option to 'unbind' it… whatever that means."

Goibhniu nodded like this was nothing new to him. "Lustrum comes from Duinnite ore, the same as Silverwhite. It contains some of the other magical properties that Silverwhite possesses."

"What does that mean?" I asked. I was sure the ins and outs of the metals and alloys of Annwn would have been something I'd have enjoyed learning about, if I had any time between surviving the various things set on killing me.

The smith reached a shaking hand to the shillelagh, his touch reverent. "It means this weapon is bound to a soul, much like the weapons of the first King's Guard. Much like…" He paused and met my eyes before continuing. "Much like the Four Treasures."

My confusion must have shown on my face, because the smith continued.

"I studied the Treasures for years before growing my first Silverwhite blade. I didn't have the quantity of Neartór necessary to supply the King's Guard with satisfactory weapons, so I found a metal with similar properties."

"Silverwhite," I interrupted, suddenly understanding. "You used the Duinnite here, inside of Tech Duinn, to create the Silverwhite of the Ellyllon?"

"I did," he affirmed. "May I?" he asked. After a brief moment of hesitation, I handed him the shillelagh. He turned it in his hands, studying it closely in the light of the molten rock around us.

"This is…an interesting design. You said it gave you the option to unbind it?"

"Yes, but only when it was submerged in the urn there." I pointed at the urn the smith leaned up against, and he promptly turned to dunk the end of the staff into the water. When he paused, I could tell that he was analyzing his own magical prompts. He didn't turn to look at me, but kept his gaze locked on the staff.

"Would you mind, child of the Cold Moon, if we discovered what sort of secrets this weapon is hiding? I have never seen anything like it before."

I shrugged, and Goibhniu went to work again, interacting with his own boons. A vibration emanated from the shillelagh, rattling out into the walls of the room and causing Goibhniu to drop the staff to the floor.

We watched, rapt, as delicate fingers, then hands, began to poke their way from inside the shillelagh. Hands gave way to pale arms and finally a feminine head and shoulders.

A petite woman gasped in a lungful of air before frantically pulling herself the rest of the way out of the impossibly narrow staff. When she had finished the process, both she and the staff lay on the stone floor.

"I think that shillelagh just had a baby," I said to no one in particular.

The smith didn't respond, clearly mesmerized.

The panting woman looked up at us from the floor, then down at her hands with a panicked look in her eyes.

"It's okay," I said to her, moving slowly and cautiously to kneel next to her. "We aren't going to hurt you." I held my hands up, showing the lack of weapons in them.

"But what if I hurt you?" she said in a strange language that my imbas boon had to work to translate. I had understood some of what she said without the boon, but other words were unknown to me until it kicked in with the translation.

"Maybe try not to do that," I responded, extending my hand to help her sit up. "So… were you the reason the staff was possessed?"

"It wasn't possessed," Goibhniu interrupted. "She had bound herself to it."

"Right," I acknowledged. "What he said."

"I could perceive and interact with the world in a limited capacity," she began, then paused. A worried expression quickly overtook her face. "Tell me what happened to the others... to the other Síorláidir."

I glanced over to Goibhniu, who was studying the woman intently. She was lovely in her own way. Like Brigid, her face was youthful and pretty, but unlike the former Fiery Queen, she had a more innocent set to her lips. Her striking bone-white hair was set in thick braids, giving her an ethereal look.

"What is your name?" Goibhniu finally asked.

"Eiocha."

"Hey!" I said, thinking back on my time in Tir fo Thuinn with Lir. "I think I was in your armory!"

She turned her attention to me, looking me up and down. "That armor belonged to Taranis. But where is the rest of it?"

"I wasn't strong enough to wear it," I admitted, thinking I should try the straps and sternum disc armor again at some point.

She nodded, her expression pleased. "If he left his armor behind, then he was successful."

"Successful at what?" I asked. Goibhniu sat quietly, taking in each word that the woman said.

"I was the...prototype," she said, my language boon again needing a moment to correctly translate her words. "I was the first to attempt to bind myself to a weapon in an attempt to avoid the corruption."

"You certainly succeeded with the binding," I said, with a laugh, thinking about how the weapon had literally dragged me out of danger on the side of the mountain.

"What do you mean by 'the corruption'?" Goibhniu interrupted.

The woman looked at her hands with remembered fear. "Do you see it?" she asked, her voice high and panicked. "Has the blackness set upon my skin?"

There was nothing on her skin, save for the dirt and ash from the dirty floor.

"No," Goibhniu said, his voice calm and gentle. "We see no affliction upon your skin."

The woman breathed a sigh of relief. "Then, perhaps the binding was successful in cleansing the corruption from me."

"Hold on," I said, not understanding. "You bound yourself to the staff because you wanted to stop some sort of corruption, and there are others who did the same?"

She nodded. "Yes… There are likely four others."

Goibhniu and I looked at each other, realization dawning on us at the same time. Four others… Four Treasures. She was the prototype. I looked down at my belt. They likely had access to Neartór. The disc armor set was made of Neartór.

She continued, "Of those who had not yet been corrupted, there was Taranis of the sky. Teutates the Protector, Camulos the warrior, and Arianrhod of the moon."

"And what of those who had been corrupted?" I asked, thinking of the fear in her voice when she asked about the blackness. I remembered all too well my own fear as the blackness on the woman from Hy-Brasil had wrapped around me.

"Maponos of the summer court, Caileach of the winter court, Belenus of the sun, and…" she paused, tears forming in her eyes. "And Donn, despite all his love. He did it all for her. We all did."

Okay, that was a lot of information, most of which I didn't understand, though I did recognize some of the Old God names… the Old Gods who had apparently turned themselves into the Four Treasures. I wracked my mind for everything I had heard about them.

Manny had briefly mentioned Teutates the Protector when I first met him. I wore Taranis' armor. I also knew that Donn was both the father of the Tuatha and the god of Death.

I looked at the grief-stricken woman on the floor. What had she meant, they did it "all for her?" There was only one additional old power that I knew of that she hadn't mentioned.

"For who? Mother Danu?" I asked, unable to contain my question any longer. "What exactly did you do for her?"

Eiocha kept her eyes fixed on the stone ground in front of her. "We changed the pool. We sculpted the channels of living water here in Uisneach with our tools and with our magic… All according to the will of Danu. She was with child then." Her voice shook as if she were admitting to a terrible sin.

"It…changed us all, and it changed the very land that we now stand upon. Each of us was tainted by the desecration of the sacred water… each of us, but for her."

The prehistory of Annwn was slowly becoming clear to me, everything from the disappearance of the Old Gods to the creation of the Four Treasures. I wondered if the child Danu had been carrying then had been Bres, if it had been in those brief years before the Síorláidir had disappeared and the Tuatha had risen to power.

I had plenty of unanswered questions, like what had happened to the corrupted gods, and where Danu fit into all of this, and why what I now knew were two of the Old Powers had been chasing me from the first moment I saw the weave… the Bodach and the Cailleach Bhéara.

CHAPTER 53:
FLIGHT TO FIGHT

< FÍADAN >

Day 17 of Midwinter, Nightfall
Eastern Segais Reddeshorate, Ildatbach Bay
Annwn

"How did you know I would be here?" Fern asked me after I had fully caught her and her brother up on the state of Annwn. They had already known about the Slaugh Doctrine and the war against certain fae as part of Nuada's war on the Fomorians. But as their own people weren't on Nuada's naughty list, the selkies had generally been content to stay out of the conflict.

"I didn't," I responded. "I was just hoping that someone here would know how to get in touch with you. Why aren't you on your ship, by the way?"

She held up the Stone. "This… THING attracts the wrong kind of attention. Are you familiar with the Cailleach Bhéara?"

"The old Hag of Winter? Oh yeah," I said, remembering the fight on top of Wolves Hill in Ériu. I felt a sudden wave of nostalgia. "We had some good times, she and I."

"Are you serious? She almost killed us!" Flide had apparently decided it was time to participate in the conversation.

"No, she isn't serious," Fern interjected, shaking her head. "We had to abandon ship. That hammer of hers knocked down our mast and nearly capsized us."

"She is a stinker, that one…" I said, smiling. "But seriously, you probably should stay away from her. She's one of the most powerful foes I have ever faced. If it wasn't for Bren and that stone, I would have had a shallow grave in the mortal world."

"So how exactly are we supposed to get the Stone and the Cauldron to Bren, assuming that is your intent?" Fern studied the stone she held with a disdainful look. She clearly wanted nothing more to do with the relic.

"Simple. We need to go to where he is." I paused. "Or maybe where he will be?"

"Where is he now?" Fern asked.

"Or if that won't work, how are we supposed to know where he will be?" Flide added.

I looked between the siblings, thinking about which option would be better to pursue. The last I had heard, Bren was on the Protected Isle… or beneath it in the Deep Realm. That would likely take a while to travel to, even with Fern's help. But then again…

"Maybe these will help," I said, rummaging through my pockets. I pulled out the papers I had taken from the Jewel before Ogma had awakened and shot me.

Flide's mouth dropped open. "Father will not be pleased that you have these here!"

"What are they?" I asked. I knew they had the king's seal, but I hadn't bothered to read them yet.

Fern grabbed the papers from my hands and flipped through them quickly. "It looks like they are the war plans of Nuada." She looked up, her eyes shining with excitement. "They are assembling in Tar Tairngire, on Mag Mór." Those were the "great" plains north of Port Ildatbach and east of Mag Mell.

I nodded, thinking of the path of the naval ships from Murias. "The armada must be docking there. It makes sense."

"How does this help us?" Flide asked.

"I bet you a barrel of Gorias cider that Bren and the Fomorians will be assembling on that same battlefield," I said. I turned to Fern. "Will you be able to verify this with that shell of yours?"

Fern's cheeks flushed red at the mention of her Shell of Promise. Flide turned away in embarrassment. I looked back and forth between the two siblings, both looking uncomfortable. Had I just stepped on some sort of selkie cultural taboo? "Sorry if…"

"No, it's fine," Fern said, standing straighter.

Flide turned to face his sister. "Mother and Father don't know about your shell."

Fern didn't reply, instead turning to me. "I will only be able to locate him if he has submerged the shell in seawater."

My shoulders slumped. "How does that help us?"

"I never said that it would." Fern said, her tone tart.

"Well, chet…double chet. Farthing chet!" I paced back and forth, trying to think about what we should do. After a moment, I had made up my mind. "It doesn't matter."

"Why doesn't it matter?" Flide asked.

"Because if Bren isn't on the battlefield, we will give the items to the lords of Gorias."

"Won't that be the same as giving them to the king?" Fern seemed to be considering my words carefully.

"I sure hope not," I muttered. "Especially after I tell them where I found the Cauldron."

I thought about how Ogma must have been using the Cauldron for King Nuada. Someone had taken it from The Dagda and given it to the King and his close allies. That wouldn't sit well with Gorias.

"Mother and Father will never support a direct action against the king," Flide said to his sister.

"Then I won't ask them to. I am going with Fíadan." Fern's face was pale, but I recognized the stubborn set to her expression.

"Fern! You can't. What about the hag?" her brother asked. "She will kill you all."

Fern ignored him. "Do you have a ship?"

"Maybe. Probably…" I said in an unconvincing voice. "I told them to wait for me in the deepest part of the bay."

"That should be easy then," she said. "They will be right above us." She swallowed hard. "So, we are going to face the Hag of Winter, and if we survive that, we are going to war with Falias?"

She stepped closer to me, kneeling to look directly in my eyes. She looked vulnerable at that moment, so unlike the Fern I knew back on The Stern Beauty. "Promise me that this is the right thing to do."

I shook my head, unwilling to lie. "I never know if what I'm doing is the right thing to do. But I believe this is what Bren would want."

My words seemed to make a difference. Her face changed when I said that. She, too, had made up her mind. Flide, on the other hand, looked about as conflicted as a person could be.

He pulled his sister to her feet and clutched her arms. "I cannot let you go, Fern…" He choked on his words, unable to continue.

Well, chet, that complicated things even more. How would I smuggle Fern and the relics out of the reddeshorate, if both Flide and his parents were against us? Thousands of pissed off selkies would be a lot of blubber to cut through to reach the surface…and I had a suspicion that Fern wouldn't be happy if I used my normal "cut through it" solution to this particular problem.

Flide cleared his throat before continuing, "I cannot let you go alone."

Oh, I thought, moving my hands from where they'd drifted to my sheaths.

Fern hugged her brother tightly and leaned her forehead against his. "When we were back on the Beauty, and the hag nearly sunk us, I was afraid that my actions would kill you and the rest of our kin on the ship. I won't make that mistake again. You will stay here and protect Mother and Father. That is an even more risky proposition."

Before he could argue, she released him and then turned to move to the wall behind me. She placed her hand on a small indentation. At her touch, the color in the wall appeared to warm and glow brighter. I felt water begin to slowly climb up my feet.

"You'd best activate that ring of yours," she said. "It's quite a swim to the surface."

As Fern pulled her black cloak tight around herself, it began to almost melt into her skin. Her form changed too, skin darkening as her clothing was absorbed and transformed into short, slick fur the color of her cloak. Her dark eyes grew even darker as they changed shape within her newly furry and elongated face. Flide too was changing.

I glanced down at the water that was now up to my chest, catching a last glimpse of the two seals as they dove beneath the water.

"There's a kink for everyone, I guess," I mumbled, wondering about Bren's choice of woman. Then I dunked my head beneath the water, feeling the magic of Wavewalker take hold.

The walls appeared to shift and shrink back into the ground as the darkness of the water surrounded me. With the walls no longer in the way, I found myself in a colorful landscape of grand coral growing from the sea floor, each glowing with all the colors of the rainbow. It stretched for as far as I could see across the rocks and crags of the bay.

Seals swam in and out of the coral bunches, but only one that I saw was arrowing straight up. Using the power of my ring, I moved faster than the selkies of the reddeshorate, quickly catching Fern as she streaked toward the surface. In seconds, a solitary hull resting in the water above us became visible.

It appeared that Commander Scolt and Salka had successfully gotten away from the Murias fleet. Unbeknownst to them, they awaited two passengers who would likely bring all kinds of trouble to their crew and their ship.

CHAPTER 54:

A GOD SAVES THE QUEEN

Day 17 of Midwinter, Sunset
The Watchful Crown, Falias
Annwn

The king's army marched out late in the afternoon, much later than when Ethadon had thought they would leave. Watching from out of sight, I managed to catch a glimpse of my father riding tall in his saddle, his most valuable ally, uncle Dian Cécht, the god of healing, at his side. I didn't see Ethadon, but I was sure my brother was there, likely marching among his troops, thrice the size he would normally command. For all his faults, he had likely recognized the hole that my and Caicher's absence had left, and was amongst the soldiers, doing his best to keep up morale.

I strained to see any trace of Ruadan, but couldn't find him amongst the hundreds of changelings marching to war. I wondered idly if their late departure was Ruadan's doing. More likely, they were late because it took a very coordinated effort to move out so many soldiers in an organized fashion. In any case, Belenus was displeased with having to wait for Ruadan to uphold his part of the bargain. He grew even more displeased when it became clear his part of the bargain wouldn't happen within the city walls.

I BELIEVE RUADAN HAS SOMEHOW RETAINED HIS CHANGELING SHIFTING ABILITY.

"That will only help his cause on the trip south," I replied. As the day dragged on, we carefully surveyed the coming and going of guards from the eastern spire, learning the flow and rotation of the shifts. I knew some of this information already, but some nuances had changed, likely since Falias went to war. We had also used the time to think through and plan for Brigid's rescue.

Above the tenth floor of the eastern spire were four mini-towers, historically used to hold the crown's most dangerous enemies. We needed to get up to the tenth floor, then discover which of the towers Brigid was held captive in. We'd already ruled out simply entering through the ground-level entrances, which were heavily guarded at all times.

Unfortunately, the tenth floor was entirely windowless. We would need to enter through the windows of the ninth floor, which, of course, is exactly what I would have prepared for if I were in charge of the prison guards. Belenus seemed unconcerned, whereas I was worried we would end up murdering men and women that I knew and cared for.

As the last rays of the sun fell across the tower, we used them to propel ourselves to the window we'd chosen as our point of entry. We'd waited until just before the light faded from the city, ensuring no one would see the rapid climb. One minute we were at the base of the Watchful Spire, the next we were preparing to burst through the ninth-story window… or that's what I believed, until we paused outside the open window, waiting.

Belenus had full control over my body and held us completely still, studying the environment and threat level as the full moon rose high in the sky.

THIS IS A TRAP, he murmured in my mind.

"Almost certainly," I agreed, "but do we have any other choice?"

We carefully moved around the top of the tower, finding that the other windows had also been left open.

THE BARS HAVE BEEN REMOVED.

Belenus was right, the iron bars around the windows on this floor had recently been removed. I could still see stone debris from where they had been hammered out. It was not only a trap, but a painfully obvious one, far less subtle than I would have expected of my father or brothers, and all the more strange because of it.

THERE ARE TWO GUARDS INSIDE.

"Two guards we can handle," I said, suddenly worried. "Let me talk to them before you light them up."

I felt and heard Belenus laugh in my mind, a sound I was becoming too familiar with. It was reserved laughter, but I could now recognize it for what it was. Belenus wasn't one to laugh at a joke or a play on words. No, he laughed when something was about to go terribly wrong. I had a suspicion of who I was about to encounter in the tower.

Before I could move, however, Belenus triggered the domain classification description that I hadn't seen when I had earned my domain.

Scion of Justice

This classification reflects a domain centered on judgment, truth, and the moral weight of action. Unlike domains tied to raw elements or physical mastery, this classification manifests in a person's ability to perceive guilt, recognize dishonor, and weigh the hidden intentions of others.

Those marked as Scions of Justice are not passive arbiters but active participants in administering judgment.

"I think I understand your point."

GO INSIDE. I WILL GIVE YOU FULL CONTROL.

His unexpected willingness to forgo his own control filled me with dread as I stepped into the room. Within the sparsely lit, wide-open space, I immediately spotted the two men who stood back to back in the middle of the room in order to scan each of the open windows.

As I had feared, I was face-to-face with Ethadon and my younger brother, Gaible. Ethadon looked resigned, clearly having expected me. Gaible's face held an expression of utter shock. I wasn't sure if it was because he wasn't expecting to see me, the terrifying, visible changes in my body, or simply the fact that I had somehow entered the eastern spire through a ninth-floor window.

Gaible was the youngest of my brothers and fairly new to Annwn, having been brought to Ériu by our father in the brief period of time since the Cold Moon. He was still learning about the world of Annwn and had not yet been corrupted by our father's influence. He still had a childlike sweetness and looked up to each of his older brothers, me most of all, because of the small kindnesses I showed him. When we sparred, I taught him instead of embarrassing him, like Ethadon. In the delegation of duties, I had not given him the worst jobs, like Caicher.

It had been a cruel trick to set Gaible to wait for me. There was only one possible outcome here. If my brothers stood between me and Brigid, there would be bloodshed I wouldn't be able to avoid, no matter how much I wanted to. Belenus would see to that. I wondered whether Gaible's presence in the tower was Ethadon's idea or whether it had been Father pulling the strings.

"Brothers," I said into the quiet. "I have no quarrel with either of you. Stand aside."

"Did you kill him, Tadg?" Ethadon asked, his voice shaking. He had already slid his sword out of his sheath, though his stance was unusually awkward. I looked closer and realized his other arm hung limp at his side. I could see, under his armor, that his shoulder was wrapped in the fabric of the healer.

HIS COLLARBONE HAS NOT YET FULLY HEALED.

"Caicher's death was an accident," I said, approaching them slowly, not yet drawing Vowkeeper.

"What about Jolsten and Marc?" Gaible asked, his gaze filled with fear. His eyes were caught on Jolsten's hilt hanging from my waist.

"They attacked me," I said, pleading for them to understand. "I had no choice!"

"I felt you there, behind me, last night," Ethadon said. "I don't know what you did to me, but I haven't been able to rest since." His voice cracked, and I could see a slight tremor in his sword arm. My heart felt as if it was breaking.

"Please, brothers. Tell me which of the stairwells leads to Brigid's cell." I watched them intently to see if even a slight movement would give away the answer, hoping desperately to find her and escape without having to hurt either of them.

Gaible's gaze snapped to Ethadon. "Brigid is here?" From his tone, I could tell that he truly hadn't known.

"Shut up," Ethadon replied, his eyes never leaving me.

"I won't ask you again." As I spoke, I activated Blazing Mantle and began to glow with a soft light. The two men stood with their mouths agape as the light began to grow brighter.

Shaking off his surprise, Ethadon charged at me, swinging his blade. I reached up, catching his wrist mid-swing. I held it there, looking into his fear-filled eyes. Where he had once been stronger than me, I now held him still with ease.

I heard the sound of Gaible drawing his sword as he stepped around behind me. "Brother, please. Let him go," he said. I looked back at the young man. He swallowed hard, visibly scared, but held his sword firmly. He held himself well, and I knew that Father would be proud of him. I too was proud of him.

ACTIVATE PENITENT BRAND.

"Not on him...," I said to myself, trying to resist. "Never on him."

I was interrupted by a piercing pain in my midsection. Looking down, I saw Ethadon's injured arm holding the hilt of the dagger he'd lodged deeply in my abdomen. The dagger dripped with a black fluid that I knew immediately was poison. I paused for a split second in disbelief, hot anger rising within me. Ethadon had poisoned me!

My Blazing Mantle boon immediately flashed to the fullest extent of its power, reminding me of the great flash that Father's Sword of Light could produce. Ethadon screamed as he was blinded. Behind me, I heard Gaible cry out and drop his sword. From far below, I heard guards approaching, dozens of them, by the sounds of it.

"It's the one on the far left," Gaible's pained voice said. "They emptied the others earlier today." The boy was on his knees, his hands over his eyes. He removed them slowly, blinking, blinking as he tried to focus on me. "I didn't know it was her, brother."

I staggered toward him, stumbling as the poison that Ethadon had used on me wound its way through my system. Even with my extra healing, the poison was having the intended effects. My movements felt sluggish and clumsy. I concentrated, working hard to place my hand on the top of Gaible's head to ruffle his messy brown mop of hair.

"Don't let them ruin you," I whispered. "You are the best of us." He said nothing, his eyes still struggling to focus on where I stood in front of him.

Grunting, I slid the dagger from my stomach and bent to cut a shallow line down Ethadon's arm. It was a superficial wound, but I knew there was enough poison left on the blade that he would suffer a miserable fate…the fate he had wished on me. I knew that I should feel sorrow, or even regret for what we'd lost, but all I felt was anger burning through me.

Neither Ethadon nor I spared the other any last words. I turned from my brothers to stumble up the stairwell to the tenth floor and from there, to Brigid's cell. I staggered to the trapdoor, my breathing heavy and my vision hazy.

I winced as Belenus activated Dawnpiercer, and I felt the poison slowly burn its way out of my system as I lifted the door to Brigid's cell.

CHAPTER 55:

THE RED PARADE

< CAI >

Day 18 of Midwinter, Sunrise
Túr Crochta, The Deep Realm
Annwn

I had easily dispatched the remaining two Fomorians. I didn't hesitate, even as one of the men had begged me to stop. There were still hearts and minds to win over if I was to do as Tethra asked, and none of Corb's generals or closest allies would find a place in the general population where their whispers and deceit could root.

I glanced briefly into the Blaze Diviner and smiled at what I saw. Pieces moved in other parts of Annwn that would help our war efforts. Corb had been right in one respect. War would find us, regardless of when we chose to assemble. Corb couldn't have done it alone, but now…with Bren and his allies, perhaps there was a chance for us.

Pushing the power rank notification to the side, I quickly gathered my stolen belongings, including Fragarach and Neit's brooch. I worked quickly to gather the other things I needed, leaving the throne room even more gruesome than it had been only moments before.

Finally ready, I gathered the heads of the seven men, grabbing their hair in my hand. I made my way out of Túr Crochta, toward the training ground. I was painted in blood, and more blood followed me, the severed heads leaving a trail behind me.

As I walked, I passed many citizens on the way from the Hanging Tower. Many merely stopped and stared, but others, including the members of the Mná na Mara, fell in behind me as I walked through the underground streets.

Ethlinn, Morvra, and Dubhlinn walked in step just behind me. To someone who knew them as deeply as I did, Morvra and Dubhlinn were clearly grieving and sleep-deprived. To most, however, they showed no outward sign of turmoil or pain. These women were incredibly strong, and their quiet presence gave me strength.

To my surprise, before we had descended too far down into the city, the army came to meet us. In the lead stood Indech. His mouth gaped when he saw the bloody, dirt-covered heads of his friends.

"What have you done?" he whispered.

The streets were full now. It seemed that every citizen of the Deep Realm gazed upon the carnage that I held in my hands. I ignored the question and spoke in a voice amplified to reach each ear in the assembled crowd.

"I came to you as Cai Maccán, an outsider taken in by a great king. I became a friend, a general, and a servant of the Deep Realm. Here, I have lived… and loved."

The crowd didn't make a sound, not even Indech. They listened with rapt attention. I couldn't blame them, knowing I had presented them with quite a scene. Granted, I had also activated my Empathic Influence boon at the beginning of the march. That boon worked much in the same way as my other energy boons, only with it, I was able to manipulate internal processes to better connect with the people gathered on an emotional level.

"War will find us," I finally said. "The question is when and where. Corb would have marched you to your death against the four armies of the Tuatha. You would have faced that onslaught alone."

"You are a coward!" Indech yelled, trying to muster support from the army behind him.

I tossed the heads to the ground before him. "I am Cai O' Elatha, son of Briomhaith. I am the rightful king of the Deep Realm."

I raised my hand to touch the brooch I had discovered so recently in the wreckage of Neit's ancient ship. I activated the Eye-to-Eye ability, feeling myself grow two feet in seconds. My new size put me even with Indech.

The crowd began to murmur. Some were angry, I knew, some relieved, and some confused.

"I will not alter our course in this war," I said. "Nor could I if I wanted to. We are Fomorian, and we will answer the call of war, but we will also not hesitate to change our odds for the better."

Indech reached for his blade but stopped as quickly as he started. His mouth opened, dark blood running out of it. He looked down as if surprised to see the sword that had burst through his chest. Oirneth, one of Tethra's closest friends, slid closer, wrapping her arm around his throat as she whispered in his ear. His eyes widened in fear before glazing over.

Oirneth slid her blade from the dead general's back, letting his body fall to the ground in a heap. She stepped forward to stand in front of me and paused for a moment, searching my face for something. Apparently satisfied, she dropped to her knees in front of me.

I felt movement behind me and turned to see that the rest of the Mná na Mara had also taken a knee. A great wave spread forth through the crowd as each Fomorian took a knee.

I looked across the masses of my people, feeling the realization set in that I would be the one to march them to war. Despite the weight of that knowledge, I allowed myself to relax slightly and pulled up the power rank notification I had been avoiding.

Name: Cai O'Elatha
Race: Síorláidir
Current Power Rank - Level 17

Current Progression Status:
Physical Progression +48
Mental Progression +57
Spiritual Progression +54

Domains: Harmony and Harvest
Domain Classification: Mancer Savant

You have been gifted with the following Harmony boons:
Control Energy
Graceful Agility
Dark Vision
Energy Resonance
Empathic Influence
Spiritual Augur
Transform Energy
Divination of Balance

You have been gifted with the following Harvest boons:
Maximum Yield
Perfect Aim

You have one blood-borne curse:
Life Leak (Permanent)

Innate Racial Abilities:
Rapid Regeneration
Advanced Identification

Magic Sense

Three magic items is in your possession.
Fragarach
Orna
Bull Brooch of the Fomorian

Item abilities unlocked:
Trust Tongue (Fragarach)
Battle Herald (Orna)
Eye to Eye (Bull Brooch of the Fomorian)

One relic is in your possession.
You have acquired:
The Spear of Victory

Relic abilities unlocked:
Armor Piercing
Return to Sender

CHAPTER 56:

SHAFTED BY THE WEAVE

Day 18 of Midwinter, Sunrise
Uisneach, Tech Duinn
Annwn

Goibhniu, Eiocha, and I had discussed the Síorláidir for hours. We had filled her in on the current state of things in Annwn, and she told us of her suspicion that Maponos had become the Bodach and Caileach the Cailleach Bhéara. The remaining corrupted Síorláidir was almost certainly Donn, the god of death.

According to Eiocha, when they had diverted the magical water from Uisneach, the great wells had flooded. The central mound had become a volcano, and the spirits of the dead were collected in a place they named Uffern, a new sub-realm ruled by Donn.

I had been shocked to discover that Danu's reason for asking the Old Gods to divert the water in the first place was surprisingly simple: she wanted an easy way to and from Hy-Brasil. This was how the Heart-shaped Pool had been created, and Danu had quickly declared the pool off limits to everyone else.

My heart ached for Eiocha. Not only had she lost everyone that she had ever cared about, but the binding and unbinding from the shillelagh had stripped her of her own magical domain. The white-haired woman had shrugged off the loss, though, suggesting that its lack was likely why she had not immediately succumbed to the corruption that plagued the rest of her non-Treasure Síorláidir friends upon emerging from the staff.

Goibhniu, in turn, told us of his time as a prisoner in Uisneach. He spoke of "the big one," a hulking Bánánach who had led most of the torture sessions. He believed they had kept him alive because they enjoyed feeding off a Tuatha and had been careful to avoid killing him, which would have sent him to regenesis in the Pool, and therefore out of their reach.

Eventually, they both drifted to sleep, clearly exhausted. While they rested, I began experimenting with duinnite ore. Goibhniu had given me a brief overview of both the magical extrusion of Silverwhite from the ore and the living water of Uisneach. That was why there were so many large urns around the smithy.

I had found a large, pure piece of Duinnite and tried to activate my Battlesmith functions. The first few tries weren't very fruitful. In fact, I exploded several of the finest Duinnite crystals that Goibhniu had been collecting during those first attempts. The last of these explosions had woken the smith, who watched my continued attempts closely. Finally, I was able to get the prompts necessary to construct my own Silverwhite weapon.

> **Your domain classification, Battlesmith, allows you the ability to modify this crystal with little or no equipment. This Duinnite ore is enhanced by the water of Uisneach. Would you like to create a Silverwhite alloy or pure Silverwhite?**

I mentally selected the pure Silverwhite option.

> **Concentrate on the weapon you wish to create out of the Duinnite ore, and it will begin to grow.**

I concentrated hard, imagining a William Wallace-style claymore, ignoring the tiny voice in my head telling me that was the equivalent of purchasing a sports car in your mid-40s. I could almost hear the Internet trolls in my head as I watched the ore begin to grow. "Compensating for something?" the voice in my head snarked. Gah! I thought.

But it was too late. I watched glumly as the claymore began to shift again, shrinking down in size. I stayed like that for at least an hour, concentrating hard on making the claymore I wanted and growing sweaty in my frustration.

Finally, I gave up, accepting that what I had created reminded me of the disastrous single nunchuck that the Stone of Destiny had transformed into during the bar fight in Unseelie. It appeared the weave had a sense of humor.

> **Yang Stick of Growth**
> **A slim rod of gleaming Silverwhite, the Yang Stick of Growth adjusts its length at the wielder's command— extending smoothly from a discreet baton to a full staff in moments of need. Light in the hand but surprisingly firm, it responds best to confidence and a strong grip. Though undeniably effective in combat, its true power lies in leaving enemies stunned, and companions questioning what, exactly, the wielder was trying to prove.**

Farthing hell. Goibhniu was laughing so hard that he had tears streaming down his face. I scowled and pushed my newly earned power rank notification out of the way for the time being.

"Come on," I grumbled, pulling the pair of weak gods to their feet. "We need to get moving." I had tried to open the gateway to Tir fo Thuinn inside the smithy, but something about the magic of Tech Duinn seemed to be preventing it from opening. "We need to get clear of the mountain. Your brother is expecting us."

I had been worried about the trip out of Uisneach and was pleasantly surprised to find the way clear of any Bánánach. As we passed through the pool room, Eiocha pointed out the passageway that would lead to the entrance of Uffern.

"The Big One stands guard there," Goibhniu had added.

We made sure to give that passageway a wide berth as we exited, the smith god leaning heavily on me as we traversed the tunnel back to the cave entrance. Eventually, we came into the open air, but from where we were positioned on the western side of Tech Duinn, we were still shaded from the morning sun. The darkness of the mountain crags had me jumpy, imagining a fachan hiding in every shadow. I nearly dropped the smith when I heard a clatter further down the mountain.

"Stay behind me," I said to the gods, before remembering that both were probably significantly more powerful than I was. "The giants of the shadowlands hunted me on my way up the mountain."

I gently handed off Goibhniu to Eiocha, and, seeing him lean on the support of the much smaller god, began charging my hands with blue light. I had slipped on the shoulder straps of the Seolán Neimhe armor earlier and could feel the extra ambient energy flooding my body. I wondered idly what would have happened if I had completed the set and added the torso disc. I suspected strongly that I would have blown myself up again.

I could feel the gods behind me holding their breath as the rustling grew louder. I, too, took a deep breath in and held it, my tension ratcheting higher and higher as the mysterious creature's steps brought it closer. I bounced gently on my toes, readying myself. Whoever it was stood on the verge of receiving an energy blast greater than any I had ever delivered before.

Just as I was about to prematurely fire into the dark, I heard a familiar whinny. The light of my hands diminished slightly.

"Gaoth?" I blurted. I chided myself as soon as the words left my lips, knowing that if I was wrong, I'd just given away our position. But another whinny confirmed my initial thought. Tadg's smoky grey warhorse emerged from the shadows, bobbing his head in excitement at finding me.

"You don't know how happy I am to see you," I said, dissipating my energy magic. We approached each other slowly. I put both hands on the horse's head, touching my forehead to his. How had Gaoth managed to find me here in the Shadowlands, and what did that mean for Tadg?

I turned to the gods, my fingers clutching the horse's mane. "Do you mind helping my friends here down the mountain?"

"Hello, Gaoth," Goibhniu said, still leaning on Eiocha. Gaoth bobbed his head in greeting but didn't move any closer. It was clear that the two were familiar with each other. This might work! My hopes were immediately dashed as the smith turned to me and whispered. "I'm not getting on that horse. He's crazy!"

Gaoth whinnied and shook his head anxiously.

"I know. I know," I said to the warhorse. "He didn't mean it. Could you help me out here?"

The warhorse took a step back.

"Fine, Gaoth," I muttered. "What if I ride with them?"

The horse took another step back, and I glared at the smith. "I think you hurt his feelings." Eiocha and I stared at him, waiting.

Goibhniu sighed quietly and stepped nervously toward the horse.

"I didn't mean what I said," he mumbled through gritted teeth.

"I think you can do better," I said, crossing my arms. Gaoth snorted and nodded again.

"Fine. Gaoth, I'm very sorry to have offended you. Will you please forgive me?"

The warhorse bobbed his head and stepped forward to stand still while I raised myself into the saddle. Once I was seated, I reached and pulled the gods up onto Gaoth's broad back.

We rode for an hour before I finally felt the magical energy around Tech Duinn begin to normalize. I immediately opened a portal to Tir fo Thuinn, and acted out what seemed to be the beginning of a bad joke: Two Síorláidir, a god, and a warhorse walk into a magical portal room… Okay, so not a traditional joke, but funny all the same.

CHAPTER 57:
ALL KINDS OF TROUBLE

Day 18 of Midwinter, Sunrise
At Sea, Ildatbach Bay
Annwn

Hullraiser appeared unchanged since the last time I was aboard. While Commander Scolt looked surprised to see me, plus a seal who transformed into an admittedly beautiful woman, climb aboard the ship, Salka had merely given the older man an "I told you so" look.

Now dry, I took stock of my still regrettably injured form. I thought about the fights to come and grumbled to myself. How was I supposed to fare with no flight and a fresh abdominal wound? I supposed I would make do, like I always had.

The entire crew had come out to greet us, partly because I think they wanted to see the spectacle and partly because they were ordered to. Who knew how much they had heard about my little trip over to the Jewel and the events that transpired after? My guess was not much, as I assumed they had been well away from the rest of the fleet by the time Ogma and I took our little swim.

I wonder if the Murias navy had managed to find the boy-god in the black of night. I guessed that one of the numerous ships behind the flagship had noticed their floating lord... well, perhaps. He HAD been unconscious after all. No matter. Ogma couldn't drown, and the Cupbearers would likely have rescued him if he ended up too far under the Crosswaters.

Scolt eyed my bandaged stomach. "I see your little adventures didn't go unnoticed."

"And yet, here you are," Salka added.

"I couldn't stay away," I joked. "The two of you are such a hoot, I even brought a friend. This is Fern... Fern, meet Commander Scolt and Tide-master Salka, famous pirates of the inner sea."

Salka rolled her eyes, and Scolt simply shook his head at my words. I doubt either would have put up with being called pirates by anyone else in Annwn. But after our recent adventures, I liked them. I was sure they knew I was teasing. Well, pretty sure.

"Pleased to meet you," Fern said. She, too, was shaking her head, though I could see the hint of a smile. "I'm afraid we must repay your kindness with news that will likely be unwelcome." She looked at me expectantly.

"So... I've got some good news," I said with a bit of a flourish. At Fern's frown, I continued, "Fine... and some bad news."

"It's mostly bad news," Fern interrupted. She held out the Stone of Destiny so that everyone could see. I held up the Cauldron of Plenty.

The two sailors studied the objects and appeared to understand what we were showing them, but seemed otherwise unmoved. The crew, on the other hand, reacted more strongly to the gravity of the situation, muttering amongst themselves. At a sharp word from the boatswain, Cé Gwalch, the men quieted and straightened themselves back in line.

"You have had a productive two days," Commander Scolt commented. "What sort of trouble should we expect with these items topside?"

"The deadly kind," I said, smiling.

"The Hag of Winter found my ship, even in the open water," Fern added. "She utterly destroyed it, leaving my crew to swim for their lives."

I saw Salka reassessing me. Her eyes snagged on my wing, a clear indication that we'd have no air support to fight the hovering Old Power. Her gaze then flicked to the ballista on the bow, then to the mast. I knew she was anticipating the fight to come and readying herself mentally.

The Lubrican boatswain came forward, and I willed myself not to let my dislike of his kind show. He had red hair, like others of his race, and stood only a smidge taller than me. Lubrican always reminded me of a mini Ruadan.

"Sir," Cé said to Commander Scolt. "I must go below deck and ready the main mast."

Scolt nodded, and the little man ran off below deck. I had no idea what exactly he meant to do to ready the main mast for what we were likely to face. Typically, steadying a mast of a ship required adjusting the yards, stays, and other ropework around the mast. But trying to prevent a mast from being snapped by an enormous hammer was a fool's errand.

Then again, I remembered what Salka had said about Hullraiser…that she had a few other unique properties. I wondered what the Lubrican had up his sleeve.

"How long until we can get into port?" I asked.

"I would not recommend going to Ildatbach," Fern reminded me. "Not with all the Murias ships there."

"We can find a berth in Lough Solais," the Commander said.

"Cnoc Aine," Salka agreed. She turned and began shouting orders at the crewmen. As they hurried to their stations, I realized that most looked happy to finally be under sail. A few appeared frightened. I didn't blame them. My palms were sweaty in anticipation.

The small town of Cnoc Aine lay to the west of Ildatbach. It was named after someone that legend called a "fairy queen," whatever that was. I suspected a more accurate way to describe her was as the first documented spirit that chose to become an Ellyllon. She was still celebrated during the midsummer celebrations.

In any case, I found it ironic that we were sailing into a port known for celebrating a summer spirit while simultaneously being chased by the spirit of winter.

The journey would take all of sunrise and partly into midday. There was nothing for Fern and me to do, given the experienced crew.

Bored and ill at ease, I paced along the deck, watching the sky for any signs of the old woman. She had very seldom been associated with nautical vessels, choosing to keep to mostly mountainous regions. My run-in with her back in Ériu was actually the first time I had seen her up close…and that was too close for my comfort.

Fern stood near Commander Scolt and Salka. Occasionally, they would allow her to help in some way. There had been no sign of Cé since he went below deck, but the sailors didn't need his supervision as they moved smoothly from task to task.

The forced downtime gave me the chance to notice things about the ship I would have normally ignored or missed. One such detail was the main mast. From my new vantage point up close, I was able to see the intricacies of the wood surface. From a distance, it had appeared to be a smooth, dark wooden mast, but up close, I saw it was anything but. The grooves on the outside appeared to be actual living bark, with small blemishes and wood growth that wouldn't have been present in a traditional mast.

Looking up toward the crow's nest, I followed the line of the beam straight into the sky. I could see no discernible joints and fasteners. The mast appeared to have been grown into the proper shape. How was that even possible? Was it part of the "unique properties" Salka had referenced? Now I was even more curious as to what Cé was doing below deck to prepare for the battle to come.

And just like that, as if being summoned by my thought alone, the sky began to darken. The horizon that had been clear of storm clouds all morning grew dark. Thunder began to rumble, its sound so deep that I could feel the vibration in the boards of the deck.

The crew seamlessly shifted from their routine tasks into what I could only assume were battle stations. The sailor in the crow's nest made his way down to the deck. Not much sense in being at the highest point of the ship against a flying opponent, I guessed.

Two of the other crew members went to man the ballista. Yet another two turned a crank that slowly brought a large cannon up from out of the back of the ship. Commander Scolt took the helm, his expression forbidding. Salka drew her curved blade and stood at his side.

My blood vibrating, I unsheathed my girls.

"Where is she?" Scolt shouted, his eyes scanning the darkness around the ship.

"I cannot make her out," Salka called back over the sound of the now choppy water and rising thunder. Dark storm clouds had manifested out of the darkening sky, and a heavy mist lay thick around the ship. The crew stood tense, waiting.

In the heavy stillness, a thought occurred to me. Despite being grounded, I DID have a way to find out where the danger lay. I pulled out the Heartbane Dial, watching as the needle began spinning wildly. Was the hag flying circles around the ship?

Finally, the needle focused on a point just off the starboard side. I ran to the helm, pointing.

"There!" I shouted.

The soldiers swiveled the canon and the ballista in that direction, firing the moment the enormous hag came into view. With a surprised screech, she flew back into the darkness and out of sight. The crew let out a cheer. I did not.

The needle of the dial began to spin again before falling limp.

"Where is she, Fíadan?" Salka screamed, her eyes on the device. The crew quieted, waiting for her command…just as she was waiting for mine.

"I don't know," I said, shaking the dial.

With horror, I realized that I knew exactly what had caused the needle to go limp, unable to point in the direction of the threat. She was straight up! My gaze went to the sky just in time to see the hag's massive hammer crash into the mast.

CHAPTER 58:

LIGHT & FIRE

Day 17 of Midwinter, Nightfall
The Watchful Crown, Falias
Annwn

The room was dark, the lack of doors or windows preventing the light of the full moon from coming in. In the center of the room, Brigid lay unmoving on a stone dais. She looked peaceful upon first glance, but her absolute lack of movement was unnatural, as if her bodily function had been slowed to a fraction of its normal state.

Still, she was as beautiful as ever. Her golden locks tumbled across her fire-red dress. A white cloth served as a blindfold, and coarse ropes bound her neck, wrists, and ankles to the stone dais. The binding seemed unnecessary to me, but Father was nothing if not thorough.

Though it had been only minutes since I had finished purging my own body of the poison that Ethadon had hoped to kill me with, I could feel my strength beginning to return. Even without being fully recovered, I was fairly certain that Dawnpiercer would have the same effect on Brigid as it had on both Sétanta and me.

Dawnpiercer
Burns away illusions, shadows, and afflictions, revealing truth and exposing deception.

I stepped closer to Brigid, unsure what was keeping her immobile and asleep, but banking on the affliction's part of my boon. I glanced back at the trap door. There was nothing in the room that I could set on top of it, and I knew the guards were close behind me. Though it would be very dangerous for them to poke their heads up through that very narrow entrance, I knew that some fool would break the seal.

Moving quickly, I removed the white cloth from Brigid's face, then gently moved the coils of hair out of her eyes. A feeling twisted inside me, causing a moment's hesitation.

"No, Belenus," I said sternly. "We made a deal."

THEY ARE A BLIGHT ON THE REALM. ALL OF THEM.

"All of US," I said to him, reminding him that I, too, had earned my domain. The body he now inhabited was a part of the blight he referred to.

I focused all of my reserve strength and attempted to wrestle back control of my limbs while Belenus pondered my words. Finally, I managed to reach out to touch Brigid's arm. A surge of magic flowed from me and into her as I activated Dawnpiercer.

Her body convulsed as she took in a deep breath. Coughing, she sat up, fire in her eyes…literal fire. Seeing the flickering flames in her eyes, I backed up.

"Peace, cousin," I said, holding up my hands. I had rehearsed what I wanted to say on the ride from Murias, but everything had changed since then. The words I'd prepared disappeared, and in their place, a jumbled, but heartfelt apology emerged. "I made a mistake, Brigid, a very big mistake…But I am here to atone."

Brigid turned her fiery gaze from me, surveying the room. Her eyes lingered on the trap door. From below it, I could hear the commotion of the approaching guards. She seemed to immediately grasp our situation. "What is your plan?" she asked.

I opened my mouth to tell her that I had originally planned to sunbeam us out of the tower, but couldn't, since there was no sun at the moment, then stopped myself. She knew only Tadg the changeling, not Tadg the Tuatha Dé Danann…corrupted Tuatha Dé Danann, I reminded myself. She had no idea of the battle I was waging to hold Belenus at bay.

"We are going to have to fight our way out," I said, drawing Vowkeeper.

She nodded. "Where are we?"

"The eastern spire of the Watchful Crown…a penthouse with no view." I didn't know where my unexpected levity was coming from. Something about the hopelessness of the whole situation must have cracked me to the core.

Brigid studied me. Her eyes narrowed, and I realized that she could see the change in me, though I suspected she couldn't truly grasp what I had become. Seeming to come to a decision, she said, "You take the front. I'll clean up any who try to flank us."

I nodded in the nick of time, just as the trapdoor opened. In one motion, Brigid turned to face it, her red dress flaring behind her like flames. And as if an extension of her gown, a bright red flash flared to life, shooting from her to roast the top half of the guard who'd risen through the trapdoor. He crumpled back into the hole, his body smoking.

Brigid wasted no time walking to the lip and filling the stairwell with fire. She screamed, her voice filled with fury at her betrayal, her rage transforming into a searing flame that leapt and twisted from her. When she stepped back, the flames dampening, I jumped straight down into the hole in the floor. I landed amid a macabre scene of death and dying. Changelings wailed as they either attempted to stanch the flames on their friends or burned alive themselves.

Vowkeeper flashed as I walked through the carnage, bringing only more death. I whirled, my blade severing an arm here and a leg there. I recognized the face of a young man as he attacked from the side just before a fireball large enough to fill a quarter of the room rocketed him into the wall.

I gestured to the stairs, shouting to be heard over the crackling flames and the screams of the dying. "Each of the floors below us has a purpose, and we'll need to make our way through all of them. Immediately below us is a storage room, and below that, the general holding prison. From there, the barracks, then the armory, then the warden's office. Finally, the tribunal room on the fourth floor. That is the room we need to watch out for. There is a magic suppression field on the entire floor. All dangerous criminals are made to pass through it before they are imprisoned within the spire."

Brigid nodded. "I understand. The field robs them of their magic at the same time they are robbed of their freedom, whether they are criminals… or annoying relations." She strode to the stairs, leaning to pick up a warhammer without breaking her stride. It had been easy to underestimate her, given her flowing gowns and graceful demeanor, but seeing her now, I was reminded why she was known as the Fiery Queen. The hammer she'd retrieved had both a bludgeoning side and a side designed to pierce armor and flesh. She'd wreathed the weapon in flame, making herself even more terrifying.

I breathed a sigh of relief when we found the ninth floor was empty, Gaible and Ethadon nowhere to be seen. The same was true of the eighth floor–though I suspected it had been where the contingent of dead and dying guards had come from. The general holding prison had been emptied, just like the four towers at the top of this spire.

It was on the seventh floor that we encountered the next wave of guards. As we rushed into the room, I realized that I felt no remorse or guilt at what I had done and continued to do. It felt…odd. All my life, I had been plagued by thoughts about what was right vs. wrong, and lamenting any of my own actions that fell short.

For the first time in my life, I felt numb. I killed because it was necessary, and I felt neither guilt nor joy in doing it. I wondered, briefly, if I had managed to wrestle only my body away from Belenus, and whether the apathy I felt was really his rather than my own. I hoped that this was the case. The alternative was even more frightening.

A wall of flame pushed the soldiers back. As several tried to move around the flame, I activated Burning Pulse to either side of the wall. Screams echoed throughout the tower as the smell of cooked flesh filled the room. Brigid shot me a quizzical look even as she thrust the flaming hammer to impale the nearest enemy.

It went like this through the next two floors. On the fifth floor, Brigid's anger seemed to wane enough that she offered the warden, a man we'd both known well, the chance to let us leave peacefully. He would not step aside, though, and ultimately burned like the others.

Those who were left in the city were like lambs to our slaughter, with none strong enough to stand in our way. All the children of Danu were on their way to the front lines, meaning Brigid and I were likely the only people in Falias able to wield boon magic. The path of death we left behind us was incredible. The city would be burying its dead for days, if not weeks to come. I knew that I would never be allowed back into Falias after this, but I felt oddly unmoved by the realization.

When we'd finished clearing the fifth floor, I moved around the burning bodies to kick a window frame hard enough to send the window, the frame, and sections of the surrounding walls flying. We had no intention of entering the magical suppression floor; instead, we dropped through the shattered winnow onto the roof of the Watchful Crown near where I had met with Ruadan only hours before.

The streets around us were quiet, despite the smoke that streamed from the windows above us. A few people stood on the ground below, clearly having stopped to watch the light show from the eastern spire. Nearby, the other two spires loomed over us.

I pointed in the direction of the southern gate. "That is where we need to go."

"To escape the city?" she asked.

I fought to find the correct muscles to move my mouth to respond. Belenus, it seemed, was rewiring the way my nerves worked. Soon, I feared I would be unable to lock him out. As it was, I could feel his growing effect on my actions…and see it as well, I thought, looking down to the black feathers that edged out from beneath my gauntlets.

"To go to war," I replied.

CHAPTER 59:

MARCH TO WAR

< CAI >

Day 18 of Midwinter, Sunrise
Leic na Beatha, The Deep Realm
Annwn

The haze of disharmony clung to me well after the culmination of the Red Parade—someone's grim name for my march through the streets with Corb's head on display. I hated it. I knew how barbaric my actions had been, and how it changed how others saw me. I worried especially about Bren, knowing my lighthearted brother would recoil in horror when he discovered what I had done.

But appearances mattered, especially in the Fomorian culture. For years, I had been tolerated as a trusted advisor, but never fully embraced, despite the backing of my adoptive father. Now, in their eyes, I was truly one of them. I had proven my strength to these unforgiving, warlike people... my people. With Dubhlinn's unspoken consent, I had gambled that usurping the usurper in a brutal and undeniable way would carve out my own position within the Fomorian order, and the savagery of my actions had borne the expected fruit.

The army stirred around me as we prepared for war. Soldiers assessed weapons, sharpened blades, and adjusted armor. The murmuring of voices, the scrape of steel, and the restless shifting of feet filled the air like the low growl of a beast waiting to be unleashed.

Earlier today, I had named my generals—Ethlinn and Oirneth— my first official choices. Ethlinn still looked at me with coldness, but she had the respect of both the soldiers and the Mná na Mara. Her desire for victory, I hoped, would outweigh her desire for vengeance.

At last ready for our march to war, we gathered at the training grounds. I paused before the dueling pit, my heart aching for Tethra. I gazed into the Abyss, the memory of her body falling, hit me like a spear to the chest.

To my surprise, the entire army gathered in as well, each pausing to honor her in their own way before stepping aside to let their fellow warriors through for their own quiet moments of grief and respect. Some whispered silent prayers, others cast trinkets or tokens into the Abyss. Watching the solemn procession, I felt pride swell within me—pride that I had known her, pride that I had mattered to such a fierce woman, beloved by her people. For a fleeting moment, I longed for a world where stories ended with reunions and miracles. I closed my eyes for a moment, imagining her hand rising from the pit to clasp mine. But I knew better, and I opened my eyes as quickly as I had closed them. Tethra was gone. She would not return.

From the grounds, the army wound down into the bowels of the city. If any soldier doubted where I led them, none gave voice to it. They followed in a long zigzagging line, silent, steady, determined. The tunnels grew darker, the air colder, until finally we emerged at the water's edge.

This place, Tethra had said, was called the Ledge of Life, a name passed down from Neit himself. It was a fitting name for the cavernous space. The army paused, so quiet that the sounds of the waves lapping against the stone echoed from the damp walls.

I turned to face my generals and the Mná na Mara who had pledged to fight beside us. "Wait here. I need to prepare the way."

"We will wait," Oirneth said. Her face still bore the dried streaks of tears she had shed for Tethra at the dueling grounds. I nodded and stepped forward alone.

"Let's see if this works," I murmured, more to myself than to them. I had yet to attempt this without Tethra's guidance, though I remembered that she had said she focused on intent, on the need itself, when opening the portal.

I waded into the shallows, the water cool against my boots, and pressed my palm to the stone as she had done. My enlarged hand—still foreign to me—spread wide across the surface. I focused on my purpose: to bring this army through, to reach the plains of Mag Mór, to defend our people from those who sought to crush us.

The stone thrummed beneath my hand. Power pulsed outward in a deep vibration, a magical dweomer I knew that only I felt. The soldiers gasped as the glowing doorway appeared in the rock face, and I stepped through it into Tir fo Thuinn.

I had expected the chamber to be empty, but four figures stood within. Bren supported a gaunt man I recognized instantly as the smith god, Goibhniu, though he appeared pale and weak. In his hands, he clutched a steaming mug that appeared to be restoring his strength sip by sip. Beside them stood the sea gods, Lir and Manannán. Stranger still was the huge gray warhorse prancing in place behind the group, its coat shimmering faintly in the room's unnatural light.

"What's up, Broseph?" Bren grinned, clearly delighted to see me. "Check it out. Made some new friends."

I couldn't help smiling back. Though his odd Ériu words escaped me, I understood their meaning well enough from his tone. "So I see…" A thought struck me. "Any chance your new friends want to summon a few thousand soldiers?"

Lir studied me, then glanced into the portal still glowing behind me. "It is good to see you again, Cai Maccán."

"While I hate to correct a god," I said carefully, "that name no longer fits me."

"Ooh, that's a shame," Bren interjected. "Cai Maccán rolled right off the tongue. Problem with epithets—they trap you. No room for character development…"

Manannán sighed at my brother's levity. "Our armies are already mustering on the battlefield. They await yours."

"And they shall not be disappointed." I gestured toward the portal. "Bren…though now is not the time, we have much to discuss."

"Seriously? Like what? You can't just drop that and not give me a hint," he protested.

Relenting, I tried to summarize. "We are descendants of Prince Elatha…and the rightful heirs to the Fomorian throne."

Bren stood stock still, clearly trying to decide if I was joking. "Um…no thanks." He shook his head. "That one's all you." His lightness was maddening and grounding all at once. He made everything less dire, less heavy.

Feeling mischievous, I added, "We also have a sister."

Bren's eyes widened. A huge smile broke across his face, splitting from ear to ear. "That's awesome! When do I meet her?"

Lir held out a hand. "Bren. Cai. There will be time for this later." He gestured, and a regal woman I hadn't noticed stepped into view from behind him. She was slim, with white hair and features pale with the weight of countless ages. Her face was pinched with what looked like a bone-deep weariness.

"This is Eiocha," Bren explained. "One of the old gods. And I didn't mean old-old—just, you know…"

"Another Síorláidir," she murmured, her voice distant. Her eyes shifted from me back to Bren. "And you must be the duality. Yes… It makes sense."

"She turned herself into a stick!" Bren blurted. At my confused look, he added, "They all did. The Síorláidir."

Eiocha's solemn gaze settled on the spear strapped to my back. She extended her hand. "May I?"

At Bren's nod, I unshouldered the Spear of Victory and offered it to her.

"Camulos," she whispered reverently, her graceful fingers gently holding the spear. "God of War. The duality with Teutates, the Protector."

Manannán shifted uneasily, his eyes flicking between the portal to the Deep Realm and another portal shimmering at the far side of the chamber. He cleared his throat. "I must remind us all that while loose ends remain, the war will not wait."

"Tactful as ever, son," Lir muttered.

"Will it be enough?" Bren asked, his normal bravado seeming to falter.

"No," Lir admitted, his gaze resting on me. "The Fomorians cannot defeat the united cities alone. But there is a chance. When Nuada sees me upon the battlefield, he will seek parlay."

"Bren," I said, turning to my brother. "Fíadan has the Stone and the Cauldron. She travels with someone else, a dark-haired woman unknown to me."

"Fern?" Bren gasped, his hope plain.

Manannán frowned suspiciously. "How would you know this, Fomorian?" he demanded.

"He has a name, Manny," Bren snapped. "And they've got a Blaze Diviner in the Deep Realm."

The sea gods exchanged a glance, then both nodded, letting my words sink in.

"Then the pieces are indeed falling into place," Lir said softly. He looked to Goibhniu. "Are you well, brother?"

"No," the smith answered, his voice painfully hoarse. His cracked lips quirked in a smile. "But all the same, I would not for anything miss the look on Nuada's face when he sees the two of us standing with the Fomorians."

Despite the thick tangles of haze swirling from my Divination of Balance boon—thicker than ever, threads weaving and knotting themselves around Bren—I found myself smiling. Ominous as the haze around him was, my brother's presence had steadied me.

"You best retrieve your army, my lad," Lir said to me, clapping a hand to my shoulder. "This war can't start without us."

CHAPTER 60:

THE GREAT PLAIN

Day 18 of Midwinter, Sunrise
Mag Mór, Tir Tairngire
Annwn

Though Cai's army had been surprised to see some of the Tuatha in Tir fo Thuinn on our way to Mag Mór, I noticed relief on many of their faces as they realized they weren't in this war alone. It gave me hope.

We stepped out onto the Great Plain to find thousands of soldiers under the different banners of Annwn. Nuada himself led the Falias contingent but was accompanied by a hippie-looking man with a long beard. Lir told me this was Dian Cecht, the healing god. The blue banners of Murias were led by Ogma, another of Nuada's brothers. Findrias was helmed by Nemain and Badb, and Gorias by Macha and The Dagda.

I had been assured by Lir that Nuada would call for a parlay when he saw that Lir and Goibhniu had sided with the Fomorians, but even so, I felt sick to my stomach at the sight of the armies gathering. Was I really about to go into battle against the very man who had sent for me to stop all of this nonsense?

I estimated each army to have roughly 500 soldiers, with the exception of Falias. The capital had mustered twice as many soldiers as the others, bringing the number of enemy combatants to more like 2,500.

We, on the other hand, had only 1,000. Cai had seemed unconcerned, remarking offhandedly that any Fomorian was worth two of Nuada's best. But I had noticed that not all of the Fomorian soldiers were the enormous, muscle-bound type I had expected. Many appeared to be the adopted siblings and spouses of natural-born Fomorians.

I cringed. The armies of the great cities had armor and magic. They had the Tuatha and the Ellyllon. They had Nemain's fiacha. I was afraid we were walking into a bloodbath, and I could feel myself outwardly exuding my dwindling confidence.

Goibhniu stood to my right and Cai to my left on the front line of our army. Between us stretched the barren Great Plain. The smith patted me on the shoulder in a reassuring manner. His tone was light when he murmured, "At least you have your Silverwhite stick."

He was teasing me, of course, talking about the underwhelming Yang Stick I had constructed in the volcano. I forced a smile, then tried my best to look strong and confident like my suddenly weirdly huge brother. Cai intensely studied the ranks of the other armies, occasionally turning to whisper something to the tall women that he now stood eye to eye with.

Lir and Manny approached, each holding the reins of a horse. Lir had Gaoth, and Manny had a coal black horse that I didn't recognize.

"Aonbharr and Gaoth are long-standing friends," Lir said at my questioning look.

"More like sibling rivals," Manny smirked. "It seems old Gaoth here won't let Father ride him. Surprise, surprise."

Gaoth pranced with his front legs excitedly as Lir handed me the reins. "I want you to know," he said, looking over at his brother's grand army. "I haven't forgotten my promise. The strength of the sea is yours when you need it."

I nodded. I had found Goibhniu, but I now struggled with phase two of my own plan for using the might of the great Wells against the king. Looking over the soldiers ready to kill their own kin, I wondered if I had the stomach to put even more people at risk.

Before I could come to a decision, however, a great horn sounded, and to our left I saw a cloud of dust and pollen on the horizon. From within the cloud, I began to see a new army slowly coming into view. Shocked, I turned to my brother.

Cai was smiling, and I realized he had likely seen much of what was about to transpire in the Blaze Diviner before he had left the Deep Realm. "The fianna have come," he announced, his deep voice rolling across the Fomorian ranks. At his confirmation that the arrivals were friends, rather than foes, the soldiers calmed.

"Is that Ruadan?" Manny called out, looking in the direction of the approaching fianna.

"And another 300 men," Cai said. "Hmm…it appears he has also rallied the fae with the fianna."

Moments passed as both gathered armies watched the newcomers approach. Soon, it became clear that Ruadan and a second man were leading their men to side with ours. A cheer went up from the Fomorian ranks, growing in volume as the entirety of our armies joined in.

Ruadan thundered up, pulling his horse to a stop immediately in front of us. He winked at me, looking like his usual mischievous self. His companion, a man with a dark, prominent birthmark on his forehead, was more serious. Roo tipped his head to the man at his side. "Diarmuid, son of Aengus Og."

Introductions apparently over, Roo swung to dismount before our army. "It's been too long, Runt." I dropped the reins and wrapped him in a hug. He grunted. "But not that long." He motioned back over his shoulders to a pair that were making their way through the crowd of changelings and fae. "A couple of my traveling companions have been asking about you."

I caught a breath as Roy and Keely, the adopted púca parents of Jamie, whom I met on the Long Trail in Vermont all those days ago, soundlessly squished me into a tight embrace. There were no words between us; they simply made me into a Bren sandwich. But I didn't mind. I returned the affection.

Diarmuid's voice boomed behind me, breaking up the reunion. "So this is Bold Bren the Bare! Somehow, I expected more."

"We all did," Ruadan snarked. "But don't let looks deceive you, he's almost as slippery as I am."

"Somehow, I doubt that." Diarmuid smiled and clasped my arm before turning away to speak quietly with Manny and Lir. In a rush of words, Roy and Keely proceeded to tell me that they and many other fae who had fled to Ériu had heard about an uprising and come to pledge themselves to the cause. Jamie, the boy I had rescued from the Bodach, had not joined them at the front lines. He was safe with the rest of their extended púca family somewhere in New Hampshire.

As our army swelled in number and tried to reorganize itself, another horn sounded from across the plain. Representatives from the opposing army began to approach on their horses.

"The parlay has begun," Lir said, nodding to me.

Saying goodbye to my friends, I found Gaoth and climbed up. We would follow Lir and whoever else would go out to face the king. An old power rank notification caught my attention as we began our trot out to meet the opposing leaders, and I finally let The Dagda's voice fill my head with my newfound level and boons.

Name: Bren Búachaill
Race: Síorláidir
Current Power Rank - Level 14

Current Progression Status:

Physical Progression +50
Mental Progression +51
Spiritual Progression +56

Domain: Chaos
Domain Classification: Battlesmith (Enhanced)

You have been gifted with the following boons:
Control Energy
Erratic Agility
Dark Vision
Pain Sponge
Spiritual Augur
Battlefield Forge
Imbas Forosnai
Swell the Weave
Trance Healer

You have one blood-borne curse:
Mark of the Bodach (Permanent)

Innate Racial Abilities:
Rapid Regeneration
Advanced Identification
Magic Sense

Two magic items are in your possession.
You have acquired:
Seolán Neimhe
Yang Stick of Growth

Item abilities unlocked:
The Storm God's Reservoir- Seolán Neimhe (inactive)
Engorgement (Yang Stick of Growth)

CHAPTER 61:
OTHER UNIQUE PROPERTIES

< FÍADAN >

Day 18 of Midwinter, Midday
At Sea, Lough Solais
Annwn

Hullraiser shook from the impact of the hag's massive hammer. Crew members went flying; most were knocked to the deck from the force of the blow. Scolt and Salka were still on their feet, as were Fern and I. To my shock, the mast hadn't shattered from the impact, only bent.

"Fire everything you have!" Commander Scolt yelled. The crew hurried to reload both the cannon and the ballista. Salka sprinted to the main mast and began scurrying upward.

"What is she doing?" Fern shouted over the crash of water from the righting of the ship. "She's going to get herself killed up there!"

I sighed, then dashed over to begin climbing after her. Fern was right, climbing up to meet the hag was suicide. "You're crazy!" I yelled up to the tide-master. "But I like it!"

Salka didn't respond, seeming intent on making it up the mast before the hag could take another swing. She climbed with surprising ease and dexterity.

Below us, I could see Commander Scolt trying to steer the ship away from the flying menace. Fern had taken on Salka's responsibility of navigation. The dark-haired selkie remained in her human shape as she called out any obstacles in the water, which in this part of the lough were plentiful.

The crew had the ballista reloaded and were trying to lock onto the hag, who was phasing in and out of the grey clouds around the mast as the ship surged forward. Salka had made it into the crow's nest when the hag finally reappeared, coming from behind the tide-master.

"Behind you!" I screamed, hanging from the rigging of the mast. If only my farthing wings were working!

Salka turned to face the hag. In her hand, she held a long tube. As the hag drew back to swing her hammer, Salka pulled a lever, shooting a massive ball of fire from the end of the tube, which I realized was some sort of flare.

The fireball exploded on the hag's chest, the flames quickly spreading across her body. She screamed and disappeared into the low-hanging grey mist, the only sign of her a stream of fire as she rocketed around inside the clouds. Salka reached down for my hand, grunting as she pulled me into the crow's nest with her. Despite my small size, it was a tight fit.

"Can you reload that thing?" I asked. The stoic woman shook her head, tossing the smoking tube aside to draw her curved blade. "You know that won't do any good against that thing."

"We have to try," she said, turning to set her back against mine. "Get out those Silverwhite blades."

"You ain't the boss of me!" came my instinctive response. I rustled around in my pockets looking for the small object. My hands closed around the small piece of Mirrorstone I had broken off the one Morias gave to me. I had planned on saving my secret weapon for the next time I saw Bren, but I found myself wondering whether any of us were going to make it that long. Under the circumstances, I was pretty sure he wouldn't mind.

The flaming hag was visible again, circling us and growing closer and closer with each pass. I held the tiny stone in front of me, tracing the hag's path through the sky. It was surprisingly easy to follow her while she was on fire.

"Okay…" I began, unsure of how to broach my plan with Salka. "I'm going to do something that you aren't going to like." Salka didn't answer. "You need to go tell your crew not to freak out."

"Why do I get the feeling you are underselling that statement?" Salka hooked a long leg over the edge of the barrel, preparing to shimmy back down to the deck. I gave her a sheepish grin and shrugged. She shook her head and then disappeared from sight. I knew what I was about to do could go very badly, but I also didn't really have a choice. I would have to time things just right.

"Hey, you!" I screamed into the dark clouds, waving an arm to get the hag's attention. "All hail the Hag of Winter! Uglier than an ogre's arse, but just as full of chet!" I can admit it wasn't the most original insult, but it still worked.

The creature shot directly toward me, her hammer back behind her head, ready to crush me and the crow's nest and likely drive the mast directly through the bottom of the ship. Huh, I hadn't considered that particular approach.

With no time to reassess my plan, I activated the Mirrorstone. A heartbeat passed, then another, with no change. Just as I started to think I had made a huge mistake and doomed us all, a massive blue oilliphéist shot from the small stone to wrap itself around the hag, bringing them both crashing down onto the deck below. The hag lost hold of her hammer, which crashed through the top deck.

The weight of the hag and the oilliphéist pushed the boat down lower into the water, but it quickly rebounded back up, the motion nearly toppled me out of the crow's nest. I laughed hysterically as I watched the crew take Salka's hurriedly shouted orders. They drew blades and surrounded the strange pair, trying their best to stay out of the way of the thrashing tail of the oilliphéist.

I smiled, thinking of Morias. The Mirrorstone was supposed to be his way into Fintan's underwater tower. He had one half, and had given me the other half to put in the tower so he could project himself inside and study all of that sage-level mumbo jumbo. But then I had encountered the beithir, and more strangely, had encountered one very specific, very familiar oilliphéist.

It seemed that Monty had followed my scent to the cliffs of the Sacred Cape, looking for Bren, and had swam the perilous depths to enter Fintan's tower, only to end up in a deadly fight with the beithir. We had won, Monty and I, but only because we outnumbered the creature. Without the oillipéist, I would have died a grizzly death.

After that, I had decided I needed a portion of the Mirrorstone for a rainy day. In my defense, I did warn Morias that there was a friendly neighborhood death serpent currently in Fintan's tower… even if I hadn't told him I had broken off part of the Mirrorstone. Thankfully, it seemed to be working out for me. And thankfully, oillipéist were always ready and willing to fight and eat.

The hag shrieked in rage and pain. Monty had her completely wrapped up and was peppering her with a venom-dripping stinger the size of a long sword. By the time I had moseyed back down to the deck, the entire crew stood out of the path of the wrestling pair. Scolt and Salka stared at me, while Fern just shook her head.

"Now what?" Commander Scolt asked. I could tell by the tone of his voice that his real question was "Why did you let an oillipéist loose on my boat?"

I shrugged. "How quickly can you get to Cnoc Aine?"

"At this pace, Midday," Salka answered.

"Yeah, that's definitely not going to work." I gestured. "Monty can't hold the hag that long, and I'm pretty sure his venom is just making her more angry."

"Listen!" Fern interrupted from the helm. She was staring out at the sea. "Do you hear that?"

"Hear what?" Commander Scolt asked. The deck was strangely quiet. Monty held the hag still, or more precisely, the Hag had stopped struggling as she listened, too.

"That's just it," Salka said, reinforcing Fern's point. "I don't hear anything."

In the silence of the deck, I could hear…nothing. Not even the normal splash of the waves against the hull. The water sat eerily still, as if we had crossed into the doldrums, and even the clouds had vanished from the sky.

The hag shrieked, and the hammer flew from below deck into her hand. She pounded Monty once, twice, three times, until the oilliphéist loosened his grip enough for her to squeeze free. She shot into the air, seeming completely unharmed from her scrap with Monty, looking toward the coast (or where I imagined the coast would be). She hung in the air, motionless, staring off toward the northeast.

Commander Scolt and Salka retreated to the helm, and the crew began to edge back to man the ballista and cannon. A low rumbling started, the sound snapping out of the quiet that had gripped us. A not-so-gentle spray of the sea splashed onto my face as the boat accelerated forward. I clutched the railing for dear life as I heard Fern's voice yell in wonderment. "He did it. I know where Bren is."

CHAPTER 62:
TERRIBLE AND JUST

Day 18 of Midwinter, Sunrise
Granary Row, Falias
Annwn

For hours, Brigid and I fought our way toward the gatehouse that opened to the plains of Tir Tairngire, each of us wielding magic and melee weapons until our hair was matted with dried blood and our clothing pocked with singe marks from errant burning coals.

We were sweaty and tired, but we had done it. We had burned and cut our way through the Falias defenses, mowing down the city guard and any soldiers left behind by the departing army. We were more careful, the last hour or so, to avoid leaving an obvious trail of destruction in our wake, and as a result, were presently resting in the highest level of a barley silo on Granary Row.

Brigid looked out across the city, studying the wreckage of our handiwork. Lanterns and torches lit almost every thoroughfare between the southeastern gate and the Watchful Crown. The screams and moans of the dying echoed off the buildings to reach our ears, even as high as we were in our hidden perch. Fires burned across the city from where we had blown through those who wished to keep us prisoner. Hundreds who had stood in our path lay dead, with hundreds more lying injured in the streets.

I had expended boon after boon without tiring. Brigid, too, had fought at full potency until the very last fireball. Still, by the time we'd reached our refuge, the effort showed on her face, as did the wear of the days she'd spent lying in a magically induced coma. Inside me, I felt Belenus' primal engine continuing to pump power through my limbs, and I knew that he could have fought through the budding sunrise and likely into midday before even beginning to tire.

Even if the surviving guards still looked for us, which I doubted very much, they would be unlikely to find us up here. Though Brigid was careful to stand in the shadows as she looked out over the city, I knew this place was unlikely to be visited in the few hours before sunrise. In our youth, my brothers and I had climbed each and every one of the 25 granary silos on this street in our attempts to elude father's prying eyes. I knew from experience that we would be safe here for now…or more accurately, those that still searched would be safe from us while we remained in these silos. I also knew that I would not be safe from Brigid's inevitable line of questioning, now that we had a moment to breathe.

"Why, Tadg? Why did he do it? No…" she murmured. "I know why he did it. But why did you go along with it?"

I leaned back against the silo wall, feeling ill. "Because I was weak."

She hadn't expected the stark honesty of my answer, making two of us. I could feel her gaze on me despite the darkness, and though I guessed she had some sort of dark vision boon, I felt some comfort in being blanketed by the night.

I knew I had…changed since we'd begun fighting our way from the spires. With every death, I had felt myself transforming into more of what Belenus had become. Aillén. I realized, for the first time, what the vision had truly shown me. No one had trapped the corrupted Belenus beneath Cruachan. No, as he saw himself evolving, Belenus himself had mustered all of his remaining will and buried himself deep within those impenetrable walls, a last act of the good man he had been. I felt the feathers that now decorated my flesh from hands to shoulders and wondered if I would one day have the strength to do as he had done.

I arched my back at the piercing pain shooting up my body as it moved through another growth cycle, making me larger still. The pain rippled down my arms, and feeling the gauntlets tighten painfully, I tore them off to see the beginning of black talons. Brigid took a step back from me as I tried and failed to hold back the bestial roars coming from my throat.

When the pain subsided, I realized I couldn't make my limbs move anymore, yet move they did. I was again nothing more than a passenger, watching as the body I had controlled my entire long life was operated by a monster.

YOU WILL SOON SEE WHAT WE ARE.

"Stay back!" I said, forcing the panicked words out through gritted teeth. "I am not the man you remember."

The fiery queen's expression was one of pity. "I know without seeing you fully that you are changed, both for good and for ill." She twisted her hand in a slight motion similar to a snap–a motion I had seen many times before she used her fire magic.

"No, Brigid! Not in here!" I blurted. "You cannot light a flame in a granary silo." It was true enough that the space inside a silo was made up as much chaff dust as it was air, with particles of grain and flour known to explode around fire, but the real reason was that I wasn't ready for her to see what I was becoming, even as I knew I could not hide behind the dark for long. Behind Brigid, the sky had already begun to lighten.

"Listen to me," I began. I felt Belenus' amusement inside me, knowing it was likely the only reason he was allowing me to speak at all. "Gorias is riding to war against the Fomorians."

"What?" Brigid startled. "We would never…"

"Please. Let me finish." Each of my hard-fought words took twice the energy to produce. While Belenus seemed willing to let this play out, he wasn't making this easy on me. "So much has happened since we left Emain Ablach. Your home was invaded."

"Who would dare?!" she demanded in outrage. Flames began to flicker in her eyes as anger and worry replaced the hesitation that had kept her away from me. "Tell me what happened."

I sighed. "Balor and Corb led a rogue group of Fomorians into Gorias and were able to secure the city, though only temporarily. The Morrigan led their army down the Slí Draíochta, with Fíadan, Bren, and your father. Your brother led the townspeople to the gate, and their combined might won the city back."

The flames in her eyes died, leaving only pride. Fear and anger still simmered beneath the surface, but it was pride that won out. And love, I realized, love of her people and her family. It was a reaction, I realized, I had never seen in the stern countenance of my father, even as I had desperately longed for it.

"And now," Brigid finally said. "Gorias marches to war?"

I nodded. "They take to the field of battle at sunrise today."

Brigid turned to look at the rising sun, panic in her expression. "Why then do we sit here? We must join my people!"

If I could have held up a hand to steady her, I would have. Instead, it was Belenus who stood, though he continued to allow me control of my words. "I can get us there in moments, if you can trust me just a bit further."

She stepped closer to me. I now towered over her, and I could feel that the proportions of my body had shifted, such that my chest stuck out slightly. With every passing moment, it was more and more visible that I was becoming something "other." She met my gaze without a hint of fear, revulsion, or even lingering anger at having left her to rot in a cell. She smiled at me, unshed tears shining in her brilliant eyes, and moved her hands to gently cup my cheeks.

"If it is possible for a queen to be both benevolent and unyielding, then it is possible for a man to be both terrible and just. I am proud of you, Tadg."

She pulled me into an embrace, her arms wrapping around me. Strangely, Belenus made no move to push her away. Feeling the slightest bit of slack come into my limbs, I wondered if perhaps there was a portion of Belenus that hadn't been fully corrupted…a part of him that perhaps longed for the embrace of a loved one.

I lifted my arms slowly to return her embrace, fighting the urge to cry my pent-up tension into the golden coils of her hair. I relaxed slightly, content to simply hold her and be held in return. I knew that never again would Brigid and I share such a moment.

As the rays of sunlight fell on us more fully through the window, I activated Radiant Surge, taking us away from Falias toward the front line. I had no way of knowing if Ruadan had completed the tasks we had discussed, both acquiring the sword and bringing the fianna into the fray. I suppose I would find out soon enough.

War had indeed changed me, in ways I couldn't have foreseen when Bairic had spoken his fateful words only a few short days ago. I felt a surge of fear, knowing that war would continue to change me.

YES, IT WILL.

CHAPTER 63:

PARLAY

Day 18 of Midwinter, Sunrise
Mag Mór, Tir Tairngire
Annwn

I had never spoken personally to the king of the Tuatha. This meeting at the center of the battlefield would be the first time we would cross words. I was larger than he would remember, but I knew that would not intimidate the man.

Bren, Lir, Ruadan, and Goibhniu joined me for the parlay. Nuada had brought with him Nemain and The Dagda. I wondered what he was hoping to get out of this parlay. Perhaps he believed he could sway his brothers to join his side, or The Dagda to persuade Ruadan to do the same.

As it was, the Fomorians were unlikely to prevail in a battle against the combined forces of Falias and the other cities, even with the addition of the fianna and fae. If we lost the support of the elder Tuatha and possibly even the fianna, it would be a massacre.

Each of the opposing sides held one relic. I would need to be mindful of Nuada's sword when we met. That blade could permanently kill any of us...as could my spear. Nuada hadn't invited his healer brother to the parlay, and I gave myself a moment to wonder if an early offensive move against Nuada might be an option.

"I don't like that look," Bren said, shaking me out of my thoughts. "Maybe don't stare Nuada down like you want to stab him in the throat with your big pointy stick when we're trying to negotiate." I gave my brother a wan smile. It would have never worked, I knew, not with Nuada holding the sword.

We arrived at the meeting point, the five of us halting our warhorses, who snorted and pranced in place, clearly eager to participate in the battle to come. Across from us, well within spear range, I noticed, sat Nuada, Nemain, and The Dagda on their own mounts.

Before anyone could speak, The Dagda dismounted and crossed the imaginary line separating us from our foes. He carried no weapon and made no hostile motions, so we allowed his passage. Arriving at Ruadan's mount first, he placed a hand on his grandson's foot and whispered something that brought a laugh to both men. He promptly moved to stand next to Bren and Gaoth.

"I'm sorry to have to meet you again like this," the god of magic said. He rummaged in his cloak, eventually producing a black shirt made of some sort of tiny rings that he handed up to Bren. A dagger slipped out of the bottom, and Bren caught it deftly. "But Gorias owes you a debt that cannot be repaid simply by us returning your equipment."

He nodded to Lir and Goibhniu, returning to his waiting horse. Before he could make it, Nuada had started speaking. This was the moment we all had waited for.

"Greetings, brothers," he proclaimed, his voice booming. "Close relations and…" he paused, looking at Bren and me and seeming to parse out the relationship, then continued, "half-brothers."

Bren and I caught eyes, both of us processing his words and their meaning at different paces. I recalled the fragments of memory of our time in Hy-Brasil and what we had managed to piece together. But what had the god of death been doing in Hy-Brasil?

"I see by the look on your faces that you know it's true." The self- proclaimed Overking looked tired.

I studied the expressions on the faces of the first-generation Tuatha. Though all of them seemed to be hearing this information for the first time, Lir and Goibhniu seemed unsurprised, and The Dagda actively nodded his head.

"Did Mother Danu tell you this?" Lir asked his brother. "I have not heard her voice in a very, very long while. Why would she speak only to you now?"

"It is of no matter," Nuada said dismissively. "That is not what concerns us here today. I have no desire to kill my family in this fray."

"Nor do we," the smith god said, sitting tall in his saddle as he appeared to shake off his fatigue. "But something is amiss here, brother, and you know it."

"What is amiss is why a supposed king would want to kill his people," I blurted.

"Or his nephew-slash-half-brother," Bren added, trailing off in confusion as I suspected he tried to imagine Bres' family tree.

"Or imprison his niece in a tower?" Ruadan added. The Dagda's gaze darted between his brother and his grandson. Nuada didn't flinch, but sat with a cold expression. He stared back at his accusers, making no apology for his actions.

"Tell me she is alive," The Dagda said, his words stern as he stared down his brother.

"She is alive," a weak voice called. I turned my gaze from Nuada to regard the sickly woman slumping in her saddle. Nemain glared defiantly at Nuada. "That was the bargain, after all, wasn't it?"

"What do you mean?" Bren asked.

Nemain coughed fitfully, speckles of dark blood staining her lips a deeper crimson. When her spasms stopped, she drew a gasping breath. "I refused to bring Findrias to war if he harmed Brigid. She is his captive." She coughed again, the sound wet and hacking.

"I don't think you need to worry about Mother dear," Ruadan said with his usual smirk. How I had missed having him around! Despite his sharp humor, he had unseeable depths and always seemed to be one step ahead of the rest of us.

"You are always so sure of yourself, Ruadan," the Overking finally said. "Yet despite all your certainty, you were unable to rid me of the Sword of Light. Remind me how that attempt worked out for you?"

"As anticipated..." Ruadan quipped, his tone light and mocking. I suspected there was a story there, and the outcome had been dire. Fortunately for Roo, he always seemed to have yet another copy of himself somewhere else in Annwn. The one here was likely the version he'd had stationed with the fianna of the Midlands.

Nuada raised his chin. "I do not expect any of you to understand what I am doing, but know that I serve a higher power."

"Said every zealot pretty much ever," Bren muttered.

"You serve only yourself," I growled.

Nuada leveled his glare directly at me. "You are still young and unable to understand true responsibility. A man is nothing if he does not serve a power higher than himself. This is doubly true for a king."

"Who is this higher power," The Dagda asked, not taking his eyes off Nuada, "that would ask of you such horrible deeds? To hold the fiery queen captive? To force Nemain and me to stand at your side?" He shook his head, seeming to have come to a decision. "You are my brother, but Gorias cannot abide by these evil acts. We withdraw from this war."

My heart beat faster. Was it possible we could avoid unnecessary bloodshed?

Nuada sighed as if the weight of the world were on his shoulders and waved a hand to the armies gathered behind him. "I wish, with all of my heart, that things could be different."

Behind him, the four armies began advancing: Murias behind Ogma, Gorias and Findrias behind Macha, and Falias behind Dian Cecht.

"Stop, Uncle!" Nemain yelled, her voice faint. She was no longer the fierce warrior I had met in the hills of Emain Ablach with Bren. "The gambit is over. You have lost."

Nuada gave her a sorrowful look and shook his head. He reached out to place his hand on Nemain's bony shoulder. "It's too late, my dear. We have come too far, and she will not allow failure."

Before any of us could figure out the riddle in his words, the battlefield came alive with activity. The Fomorians, the fae, and the fianna erupted into a war chant, banging their shields so that the sound rumbled the very ground. Both sides charged, with us caught in the middle.

On a nearby promontory, a great flash of light erupted, flaring with such suddenness and brightness that the charging armies on Mag Mór froze to see its source. When the brilliance faded, two figures stood silhouetted above the battlefield.

"Brigid," The Dagda said into the eerie silence.

Ruadan laughed, long and loud, pausing long enough to say, "Tadg kept his word."

CHAPTER 64:
FAVOR REDEEMED

Day 18 of Midwinter, Sunrise
Mag Mór, Tir Tairngire
Annwn

The battlefield was a mess. Both sides had paused their charge at the unexpected arrival of Tadg and Brigid on the hill. Even the group of us in the middle of the field had turned to study the newcomers. Nuada's mouth hung agape. I felt the effect of Brigid's boons immediately, as my already sympathetic heart bent even more towards her presence.

But it was her companion that caught and held my attention. Tadg looked…off. His breastplate sat crooked on his torso, and his eyes were sunken in. He towered strangely over the tall Brigid, and even from this distance, I could see a strange darkness in his hands and arms, though the residual light from their sudden appearance lingered as a faint glow on the rest of his skin.

The Dagda galloped to Brigid's position, raising his arm as a signal for his army to stand down. I watched as Nemain, too, signaled her fiacha at the very front of the Findrias forces to back down from the battle. The movement seemed to drain all her strength, and she wavered in her saddle, listing and falling to the side. Jumping from my own saddle, I ran to catch her before she could hit the ground. I was shocked at how light she felt in my arms.

Familiar black veins ran up the length of her neck. My breath caught in my throat as I realized the cause for her state–the lethal poison from the athame we had shared during the géis ritual, where the three Morrigan sisters and I had sworn a magical oath to defend and support each other.

Nemain had betrayed her oath when she took up arms against me. That she had done so to save the life of Brigid didn't matter. Her bargain with Nuada, to lend her army to the fray if Brigid's life was spared, was costing Nemain her own life.

"Now you understand," she rasped, her eyes glassy.

I felt emotion catch in my throat as I searched for the right words to say. I hadn't known her long, and since I had met her, we had disagreed fundamentally about our path through this war. But I could also understand now why she had so ardently defended the crown and withheld certain information from Gorias.

I could not agree with her decision to sacrifice hundreds of lives to save one, and I knew that I never would. And yet, I understood why Nemain, who had believed her sole purpose was to serve her family, and by extension, her kingdom, had made the choice she had, given her sense of duty and her unique beliefs of virtue.

She smiled faintly. "You were right, as it turns out. I am more than a sword. I am the fiery queen's shield."

Tears filled my eyes as I scrambled for a way to undo the damage of her wasted body, knowing all the while there was nothing I could do. But she would recover now, right, since she had called her forces back? I watched for the slightest improvement, seeing none. She lay limp in my arms, her dark eyes staring up into the sky.

I looked to the Findrias army, searching for Badb or Macha. Surely one of them knew a way to reverse the damage from the Mark of the Géis, which didn't show up in my Power Rank notifications for some reason.

Thinking back to what I had done for Goibhniu inside of Tech Duinn, I recalled how I had used my Trance Healer boon. I knelt, still holding Nemain in my arms, and closed my eyes. The world seemed to fall quiet as I dropped expertly into a trance. Focusing on the flow of energy, I struggled to plug Nemain into the current as I had done with the smith.

A pain ripped through my body, and somewhere in the distance, I heard a scream from Macha. I forced more energy through, feeling it slide away from Nemain as if rejected. My Mark of the Géis flared, each attempt twisting against the weave. Nemain's aura remained faint. I forced still more energy through, feeling myself grow weaker as my own aura guttered out. At last, I had no more to give, and I collapsed at her side, the trance broken.

We lay on the ground facing each other. The sounds of the battlefield were still muted in my ears. Her eyes were calm and accepting. She gave me a faint smile before pushing herself up with a final effort.

"I still don't like you," she whispered, her voice rough but almost teasing. Her form rippled, feathers sprouting where flesh had been, and a heartbeat later, a raven took flight from my side, beating its wings into the morning sky.

I reeled, knowing that she had chosen her end. Macha would not survive from the poison of the athame. There had been nothing I could do to save her, and I knew there was nothing I could have said to change her mind about the path she believed to be right. I sat up, looking over the rest of the battlefield.

Tadg stood in front of his father, who had to look up to his son. Tadg was yelling at his father, but the words seemed muddled in my depleted brain. I watched as Nuada dropped to his knees, holding a suddenly grief-stricken face in his hands. I wondered what Tadg had said to him to affect him so, when none of our earlier words had made a dent.

Tadg was clearly angry, and I could see his body spasm as he spoke, almost as if he couldn't properly control his own movements.

My mind fought to catch up with the voices around me. "Danu…" Nuada had said. My senses continued to slowly recover, just in time for me to hear the older man's heartbroken voice.

"She switched her domain…Danu is now the keeper of Uffern." I smacked the side of my head, certain I had heard wrong. The goddess of life, mother to Nuada and all of the Tuatha, was somehow now the goddess of death?

The pieces began to click into place in my mind. Danu must have switched domains, just as I had done with Cai. I pictured the man in Hy-Brasil with my mother, details from that night in the hills with our mounds flooding back to me.

Our father was indeed Donn, no longer the god of death. And the woman who had attacked us after the creation of our brú, the one who wore the blackness of night, had to have been Danu.

My mind reeling, I stared at Tadg and his father. Only moments ago, Nuada had seemed to be the embodiment of strength. Now, he rested on his knees, looking like a broken man. He shook his head, pleading with Tadg. I couldn't hear all parts of their conversation, and found myself distracted again by Tadg's continued lack of control of his body.

"There is something wrong with her," I heard Nuada say. "She was different than I remember… Changed in some way."

Tadg's mouth opened, the sound of his voice changed, and unlike any I had ever heard before. It felt filled with disharmony and reminded me of something from an Exorcist movie. It sent chills up my spine.

FINALLY, SHE CAN JOIN US.

Those near us stopped what they were doing at the sound of the deep, malevolent voice. Tadg's body continued to wrestle with itself, falling to the dirt. Nuada staggered to his son's aid as Tadg writhed on the ground, his limbs flailing as he spasmed. He gently held his son's neck.

"Brother," I heard Cai say, worry evident in his voice. "Do you see that?"

I pulled myself to my feet, finally able to stand on my own, and turned to follow Cai's gaze to the top of the mountain. Lava spilled down the side of the cliffs, and I felt the first rumblings of an earthquake rumble under my feet. But it was the other thing that streamed from the top of the volcano that worried me the most. A stream of ghostly spirits shot forth, enough to rival the combined might of both armies.

"The Bánánach have come… She has released them all," Nuada said, still holding Tadg in his arms. He surveyed the battlefield as if seeing the thousands of living, breathing soldiers that he had gathered to Mag Mór for the first time. "What have I done?" he whispered.

I thought back to my earlier run-in with the Bánánach. Morias had been concerned that the spirits we had encountered on The Stern Beauty were so far removed from a battlefield, where they normally lurked in small but deadly numbers. Now, it seemed that the entirety of the pits of Uffern were spilling onto the plains and coming straight for all of us.

Pandemonium swept through the ranks. Thousands of soldiers broke into panic, crushed beneath the weight of ancient whispers about the Bánánach and the death they always heralded.

Cai's voice boomed over the mayhem as he called his army to his side. In seconds, he had the Fomorians, each brandishing a cold, iron blade, organized at the front line, ahead of pale-faced changelings, fae, and Tuatha. The Fomorians were the only ones that could stop the creatures, and my brother had seen it and acted.

I found Lir on the battlefield and rushed to him, rustling through my pockets as I ran. I yanked out Fern's Shell of Promise and the flask I had filled with the salt water of Tir fo Thuinn.

"I need to call in that favor now," I said to the god of the sea, who smiled gravely and activated his most powerful boons.

CHAPTER 65:

THE STRENGTH OF THE SEA

< FÍADAN >

Day 18 of Midwinter, Sunrise
At Sea, Lough Solais
Annwn

Hullraiser rushed forward, barely skimming the top of the water. The crew members held tightly to anything that was nailed down. Salt spray rushed across the deck, stinging my face. I was certain we had left the Cailleach Bhéara behind us, but I didn't dare turn my head to confirm for fear of snapping my neck from the force of the ship's acceleration.

"What is happening?" I screamed into the spray.

Fern, too, had a white-knuckled grip on the railing. "We are heading straight for Bren's position," she called back over the rush of wind. "I can feel it." Her cheeks were rosy and her eyes bright.

"Remind me to stay away from Shells of Promise in the future!" I shouted back.

"This isn't the shell's magic," she responded. "Something else is using the shell to bring us together."

"This IS Bren we're talking about," I called back. "At least now we can both throw up on him the next time we see him. It will be so romantic."

Ahead, I saw the horizon nearing…fast. Chet, I realized, we were about to slam into the continent of Tir Tairngire!

"Brace for impact!" Commander Scolt had given up steering in favor of dangling from the helm, but his shouted order came through nice and clear. I'll admit it was a nice gesture, but no one was actually able to brace anything, given we were all holding on for dear life as it was. Where was that farthing lubrican when you needed a spot of good luck?

I was tempted to squeeze my eyes shut as we thundered to the land, but if this was going to be my last moment of life, I wanted to see it coming. Still, I couldn't help but cringe back…straightening again in surprise as I saw the raised mass of land ahead of us cleave in two just ahead of the ship. The water skipped the flat hull of Hullraiser forward and upward to be level with the land.

We continued like this, moving so fast that we blew by the outskirts of Cnoc Aine before I could properly verify that it was indeed the town where we had intended to dock. In moments, Hullraiser had passed onto the plains of Mag Mór, where I knew the Tuatha would be facing down the Fomorians, and the children of the Cold Moon, the earth breaking in front of us.

I had expected a battle larger than I, or anyone in Annwn, had ever seen, but what I hadn't expected was to see the entirety of both armies standing together, the Fomorians at the head. The thousands of soldiers stood still…not fighting. Farthing hell, I thought, what was this? The mass of the army was facing the top of Tech Duinn, totally focused on it for some reason, at least, until they heard the very land under their feet crack as it continued to break a watery path for Hullraiser.

The ship began to slow, finally coming to a stop just behind the combined army. Behind us, the plain lay devastated. As it carved our path, the water of Lough Solais had exploded through the rock and dirt of the Mag Mór plains. The landscape of Tir Tairngire was forever changed. I swallowed, hoping no one would ask whose idea using the shell in the first place had been.

I hopped up to perch on top of Monty, motioning impatiently for Fern to do the same. She hesitated, a trepidatious look on her beautiful face at the idea of riding an oilliphéist for the first time.

"Monty, you won't bite Fern if she rides you?" I asked the oilliphéist in its hissing language.

He looked thoughtfully at the selkie. "I might."

I shrugged and beckoned Fern. "Monty said he would be honored to give you a ride!" She still hesitated. Sure, it hadn't been an EXACT translation, but I figured it was probably close enough. I rolled my eyes. "Listen, lady, I'm going to go see Bren with or without you. Are you coming or not?"

Looking suitably uncomfortable, Fern stepped up to sit gingerly behind me on the back of the oilliphéist. Once she was settled, I urged Monty to take us to Bren. The oilliphéist flew from the ship to the ground, landing with a heavy thud. Startled soldiers parted when they saw us, and we sped through the path they opened. Monty hissed and eyed the army warily, but none of them attacked. Either they knew who I was or they didn't like their odds, either of which was fine with me.

Before long, we came to the line of Fomorians and several of the Tuatha I had known for centuries. Brigid stood proudly among them, and my heart nearly leapt out of my chest with happiness. The Dagda was with her, as was Ruadan, and next to Roo was Bren. Finally, I was back among my people.

Bren ran up to meet us, his mouth open wide at Monty's present size.

"Oilliphéist apparently grow really fast," I said to him.

Before he could respond, Monty moved so quickly that Bren didn't have time to dodge. Fern and I fell to the ground as the young oilliphéist coiled himself around his former master.

"Why did you leave me?" While I was no expert in the nuance of the oilliphéist language, I couldn't help but notice the sadness in Monty's juvenile voice.

"I'm sorry, buddy," Bren squeezed out. Interesting. It appeared Bren was able to speak with his former minion, despite no longer being bound with him. "I'm a big idiot."

"I was all alone in that cave…"

Bren managed to wrest one arm free of the deep red coils to touch Monty on the side of his terrifying face. "I know. I'll make it up to you, I promise."

"Look!" Fern called. At the fear in her voice, I turned to look up the mountain, finally seeing what had held the attention of the combined armies. Thousands of the nastiest Bánánach I had ever dared to imagine were charging down toward us. Monty released Bren instinctively, giving a hiss that caused those nearest us to flinch back.

Fern turned to look back at Bren, her cheeks flushed. She had known the moment Bren had submerged her Shell of Promise in saltwater. How he had done that in the middle of Mag Mór, I didn't know.

Fern held up her hand, offering the Stone to Bren. He took two running steps to her, ignoring the stone completely as he wrapped his arms around the selkie, burying his face in her long, dark hair. Fern allowed her arm to fall and returned his embrace, squeezing him just as tightly.

"I'm sorry that I had to call you now, and like this," Bren finally said. "But there was no other way…"

"Shut up and just hold me a moment longer," Fern replied, squeezing my favorite god of chaos tighter. I could see her tremble as her eyes remained focused on the Bánánach over Bren's shoulder. She evidently had some residual fear from when she had narrowly escaped the Bánánach on The Stern Beauty that night in the Crosswaters.

When they finally released each other, he bowed and took the Stone from her hands. Turning, he saw me, a smile quickly lighting up his face.

"Fí! I've missed you, my friend," he said, looking me over. His eyes caught on my jagged wing, and I thought back to the last conversation we'd had, just before I stormed Castle Arrow. I had told him, "Not all of us will make it back. I'm prepared to die here." I knew that I was lucky to have only lost a wing.

What I said out loud, though, was, "You ain't so bad yourself, Shorty. But I'm beginning to question these people you choose to hang around." I nodded at the charging spirits.

He smiled that adorable crooked smile of his. "I have so much to tell you," he replied. "Save me some time after... all of this." I nodded, wondering if there would even be a time after this for any of us.

High above, the volcano exploded, sending fire and balls of molten rock high into the sky to arc in our direction.

"Shields!" a massive Fomorian at the head of the army snapped. He looked sort of familiar the longer I looked at him. Was that Bren's brother? I took a second look, thinking he was kind of handsome... not that I was into excessively large warlords. The entirety of the army raised shields into the air to deflect the incoming projectiles.

I watched as The Dagda raised a small twig toward the sky, and a thin protective barrier formed over most of the army. Seeing him reminded me of the prize that I now carried...the Cauldron of Plenty. It belonged back with the god of magic. I was pretty sure I had enough time to make it to him before the Bánánach arrived, but knew there wasn't enough to also make it back in time to stand with Bren and Fern.

That prompted a flurry of questions. Who would I choose to protect during the onslaught of supernatural gnashing and clawing? The Dagda, Ruadan, and Erelith huddled together near the red banners of Gorias. Bren and Cai would likely fight side by side. The other Tuatha were stationed near the bulk of their forces, and though

I saw Nemain's fiacha, I didn't see Nemain herself. The black-clad Ellyllon who had sworn an oath of protection for Nemain now surrounded Macha. Whatever. The old crow was probably chomping at the bit with all this bloody mayhem about to go down. I was certain I'd see her in the fray before long.

The most surprising sight was the bulk of the Falias army, led by Dian Cecht. Not only did Nuada not have the Sword of Light drawn, but he appeared to be kneeling on the ground with some soldier.

At a flash of red dress, I knew exactly where my presence would be best served. My queen! The Breo-Banríon pushed her way through the crowd, and I knew returning the Cauldron to The Dagda would have to wait.

I charged toward Brigid, halting as a roll of thunder sounded. A cutting wind poured from the newly formed channel of water behind us, making my heart sink. The Hag of Winter had finally caught up to us. Now, we would be fighting on two fronts.

The bulk of the army was still gazing skyward after the last eruption. I followed their eyes with my own to see a figure of a woman wreathed in darkness. Her eerie voice echoed in the wind as it commanded the Bánánach below and the horde of boggle I now saw pouring out of the forest behind our army…fachan twisted and lopsided, trow lumbering with cruel strength, all bent to her will. Danu had come, bringing ruin with her.

Brigid's crimson-clad figure stepped forward, her hair streaming behind her and her power blazing bright as a torch against the night. She fixed her gaze on the shadow in the sky. The Breo-Banríon would not bow; she would rise to challenge Danu herself.

My breath caught. I could not be in two places at once, and I found myself paralyzed, my heart torn in two even as my drawn blades itched in my hands. Brigid faced the Mother of the Tuatha, and the Hag of Winter bellowed from behind us, ready to spill certain death into our ranks.

Trapped in my indecision, I felt eyes on me, and I turned to meet the steady, certain gaze of Erelith. She had found me from across the chaos, and without a word shared, I knew that she would remain with Brigid, protecting our queen as I would.

Freed, I exhaled, my resolve sharpening like the wicked edge of my Silverwhite blades. With a fierce smile, I raised the girls high, feeling the deep wound in my stomach pull in protest.

"For the Queen!" I bellowed, even as my path took me away from her side toward the Hag of Winter and the death waiting in her wake.

CHAPTER 66:
MAMA SAID

< TADG >

Day 18 of Midwinter, Sunrise
Mag Mór, Tir Tairngire
Annwn

I felt the battle begin around me, but could not get to my own feet. I could scarcely breathe, let alone move, and I felt as though I was choking on my own tongue. My body wasn't my own anymore.

Learning of the fate of his sons appeared to have completely broken my father. I knew he was angry with me, but the anger he reserved for his own actions that had led to their deaths was far and away greater. He had left all three of my brothers behind, thinking that together they would overpower and overwhelm me. That decision had killed two of them, and now he knew it…and that it was only my mercy that had allowed the youngest of us to live.

It was obvious to him that something had overtaken me and given me the power to not only escape Falias but to rescue Brigid from the heart of his power center. I wondered, fleetingly, if he thought Belenus had been with me always, lurking. Perhaps he would rationalize his lifelong disappointment in me, convincing himself that I had wanted to be a dutiful son and was simply corrupted by an external force. I wondered if he needed to believe this to justify my actions against him, or his own.

The creature inside me, Belenus or Aillén, depending on how you referred to him, went still. I felt it too, an almost magnetic pull of another corrupted presence. The Cailleach Bhéara had come for the Stone and the Cauldron. Danu, the progenitor, had unleashed the Bánánach and the giants. There was Belenus…and another of the old powers that no one else could yet sense.

Bren and Cai faced the Bánánach, the Fomorians at their back. Brigid was positioned to take on Danu, Fíadan the Cailleach Bhéara, and the fianna and fae the giants. The remaining Tuatha and generals of the changelings from the assorted armies of Annwn were caught in the center, battling everyone.

A monster stood in their midst, and they didn't even know it.

MONSTER? IRONIC THAT THE GOD OF JUDGMENT DOES NOT WEIGH HIS OWN DEEDS.

"And that the god of light, his own darkness," I said in my mind. Outwardly, my body still spasmed and shifted between my skin and bones.

"This is my doing," my father said weakly, as he looked around the battlefield. I found I could no longer wrestle my voice away from Belenus enough to reply to him.

"It wasn't supposed to be like this," he continued. "She told me that only I was strong enough to help her save the realm from those who meant us harm. The Fomorians plotted and bred in their hidden places. The fae whispered of rebellion against you and your…" he paused, his voice catching, "brothers."

The broken thing that was my father rambled on and on about the lies and half-truths his mother had sold him. It was all plausible as he painted it, and all seemingly good-intentioned. But that is the way with war, I thought bitterly. The strong justified their actions and kept a scapegoat ready. But rarely did their violence yield the intended results. The only thing that war reliably produced was more death.

I understood why the new god of death had wanted this war. The answer lay all around us, as the spirits of death flooded forth from Uffern, ready to slaughter those in their path. Danu had wanted an army and had convinced Nuada to deliver it to her. Father recognized it now, too, but it was too late.

On top of all of this, the last of the Old Powers had arrived. The Bodach had come. The truth is that he had already been on the battlefield. He simply chose this moment to activate all parts of his hive mind.

Nearly a third of the changelings in service to the king heard the call and began to physically change. Coarse, long hair grew from under helmets. Gauntlets shattered as claws distended, breaking through them. At the center of the amassed army, chaos spread. Companies turned on one another. Brothers turned to murder brothers. Belenus remained silent in my mind.

"She is one of them. A corrupted Síorláidir!" Father said, finally realizing the magnitude of deception he had succumbed to. "They are all working together!"

He drew the Sword of Light and cleaved a Bodach in half as it reached our position. Another came in its place, then another. Father stood over my limp body, cutting each down as it attacked. Around us, it was impossible to tell friend from foe as the army savaged itself. Fire flared in the sky, and blue and red energy magic pulsed from somewhere on the battlefield. I heard Fíadan's angry war cries from nearby.

Father bled from several wounds as he continued to defend us both from the onslaught of Bodach. It was obvious that he would be overrun by the sheer number of enemies before long. I needed to get on my feet.

WHOM DO YOU SERVE, TADG?

"Let me up! Let me fight!" I screamed out loud. Father glanced back at me, confused.

WOULD YOU SERVE NUADA? HE IS THE WORST OF THEM ALL.

I tried again to seize control of my body, and found myself still unable to move. But Belenus HAD released control of my voice... was he going to release me fully?

I WILL, ON ONE CONDITION.

"What? I begged. "What else could you ask of me?"

ACTIVATE PENITENT BRAND ON YOUR FATHER.

My heart seemed to stop. I knew what Belenus was really demanding of me. Activating the brand now would enable everyone on the battlefield to see the depth of my father's depravity, the bargain he had made with Danu, the murder of Bres. Everything.

WHY DO YOU HESITATE?

"I don't know!" He had done terrible, evil things, I knew, but he was still my father, and despite his weakness and the depths of how he had failed our people and all of Annwn, I loved him still.

Father had five Bodach hanging on him, their claws digging deep rents into his flesh. He screamed in pain as two let go to turn toward me. I was still paralyzed on the ground.

MAKE YOUR DECISION.

Belenus's voice was cruel and demanding. I knew what he was doing–using imminent danger to rush my decision just as he had done in the tunnels of Cruachan. But it mattered little. I had already decided. My limbs moved, again under my control, as a red glowing brand lit the space between Father's forehead and the mass of people surrounding him.

Vowkeeper slashed again and again, killing quickly as I traveled the sunbeams to either side of my father. Before long, we had carved a space around ourselves. He smiled at me, his expression one of pride.

The battle continued to rage as Father and I danced in and around his soldiers. Each one that we passed saw the truth of their Overking and of the false war he waged against the so-called Slaugh and the Fomorian. I could tell that Father was confused by the looks he received, the sudden lack of support from his troops, and the suddenly twisted expressions on the faces of his brothers…but in the midst of battle, there was no time to parse such things.

The brand had illuminated the whole truth of Father's deception, from the killing of the sages to the kidnapping of Brigid. I knew that there would be hell to pay for my father if we survived the battle, but even survival was not guaranteed against the Old Powers. Bodies littered the ground everywhere I stepped.

Belenus continued to allow my use of our body. I felt fast and strong, and easily dispatched any enemy in my path. Father watched in awe as I used my new boons and seemed delighted at my newfound battle prowess. He had always valued power and loyalty above all else, and now I seemed the pinnacle of his dreams for his sons.

The irony was as thick as the mud and blood of the plains. I had at last gotten what I'd yearned for. I had earned my father's love and respect. I had wanted to see this look on his face so badly, and now that it was here, I felt…nothing. Not even sorrow as his seemingly endless misdeeds continued to stream into my notifications.

Belenus laughed so long and loud inside my mind that I was certain those around me could hear it. The sound seemed to permeate my whole being, and I found myself unsure which movements were mine or those of Belenus. It felt as if we were intertwined, his thoughts and desires flowing into me, becoming indistinguishable from my own.

Turning, I stared at the relic calling to me from the usurper-king's hand.

CHAPTER 67:

THE SPEAR OF VICTORY

< CAI >

Day 18 of Midwinter, Sunrise
Mag Mór, Tir Tairngire
Annwn

I knew immediately that something had gone wrong behind the line of my people. From the corner of my eye, I saw the changelings of the kingdom armies turning upon one another. For a heartbeat, I wanted to look longer, to understand, but the moment passed. There was no time for hesitation. The shrieking tide of Bánánach continued to bear down upon us.

The cold-forged iron of our Fomorian blades was all that stood between us and the death of every living soul on this field. We had sharpened our weapons for war against the Tuatha, yet now they cut down the spirits that plagued the Tuatha and Fomorian alike. I was proud that despite all the near-wars and betrayals of the past, I heard no grumbling in my kinsmen's ranks. Not one voice questioned our place. We knew the truth: step forward, or all was lost.

Danu hovered above the battle, her dark form weaving between torrents of Brigid's fire. The Gorias Ellyllon clustered tightly around her, shields raised, the glow of their weapons flashing as they turned aside every arrow, every spearpoint aimed at their queen.

At my side, Bren raised walls of shimmering energy, his barriers locking Bánánach in place long enough for our warriors to strike them down. Behind him, the Stone warped and shifted, reshaping itself under his will. He fought with the relic like it was an extension of his body, and I couldn't help but feel pride at how far he had come in such a short time.

Monty had begged to remain near Bren, but his former master had ordered otherwise. The oilliphéist had lumbered off with Fern on his back, heading toward the rear lines. I suspected they would meet with Fíadan soon, if they hadn't already.

As for me, I fought with both hands. In my left hand, I held Orna, Tethra's gleaming silver blade. In my right, I bore the Spear of Victory. It was not a natural pairing. Orna begged to be swung and cut, while the Spear longed to be hurled. Yet I had managed to find a rhythm: hurl, slice, stab, recall. Again and again, I threw the Spear far into the mass of spirits, fighting with Tethra's blade while it recalled. It would forever be Tethra's blade, I thought grimly. Even now, as I struck with it, I feared what might happen if I saw her form appear among the Bánánach. Would I have the will to cut her down?

The Bánánach came in countless shapes: hulking forms with twisted jaws, gaunt women with hollowed eyes, children whose mouths stretched too wide to show jagged teeth as they screamed their eternal pain. Each was unique, each was someone who had once lived and died. Ériu, Annwn—death knew no borders. As I cut them down, I found myself wondering whether this was truly the end of them. Would these souls simply rise again in some darker place, ready to be unleashed upon us once more? I slashed again and turned to shout down the line to my Fomorians.

"Take the heads of your fallen comrades! Don't leave them whole!" The abhartach would rise if we faltered, and then our battle would become truly unwinnable.

The clash went on and on. Our relics, our magic, and the bitter iron of our blades kept the tide at bay, but at a grave cost. Even the smallest of wounds on the soldiers appeared to fester almost instantly, the skin greying around the edges. That was the true curse of the Bánánach. Even as we seemed to gain ground, our victory poisoned us.

I staggered, seeing a familiar pair of amber eyes burning like embers. A massive Bánánach loomed above me, and even before my mind formed the name, I knew who it was. His form was larger, heavier, more solid than the others, as though his hatred alone held him together.

Corb.

I had just hurled the Spear of Victory deep into the horde, its light trailing like a falling star. My left arm swung Orna wide, carving a path clear, as I felt the pull of the relic returning to me.

But Corb moved faster. His misty hands shot forward, seizing the shaft of the Spear as it streaked back toward my palm. The relic jolted mid-flight, caught between us, my right hand gripping the shaft at last.

Corb's grip remained locked on the Spear, the weapon vibrating violently as though it could not decide which master to heed. The force of it rattled my bones, dragging me half off my feet. The spirits around us wailed and howled, but their cries seemed to fall away as we silently struggled.

The pull of him was immense. It was not only his strength, but also his will. My muscles burned, my vision blurred, my heart stuttered. Orna trembled in my left hand, eager to strike, but fell finally as I dropped the sword to yank at the spear with both hands.

The shrieks around us grew sharper. Corb leaned close, his face a hollow mask of fury. He pulled harder, trying to tear the Spear from my grip, and despite my efforts, my feet slid in the dirt, taking me closer to his maw as it opened wider than it ever had in life. I felt myself weakening and staggered, knees buckling. I poured the last of my strength into holding the Spear, even as I knew it was a lost cause. I could not stand up to the strength he'd found in death, not even with my own increased abilities.

"Corb!" Morvra's voice cut through the sounds of battle around me. The small human woman darted out of the line of Fomorian warriors, deftly snatching Orna from where it had fallen. She sprinted toward us, moving like the war-queen she had always been, shoulders squared, every step fueled by rage and sorrow.

The blade flashed against the pale light of the spirits, rising in a vicious arc, then smashing down through the tendrils of Corb's spirit that bound the Spear. The Bánánach that had been Corb shrieked, a sound that pierced marrow. The Spear lurched fully into my hand at last.

I lunged to my feet, intending to re-engage, only to stare at Morvra's continued assault. She held Orna with both hands and savagely swung again and again, battering into Corb's spirit form with ruinous precision. The cold iron tore jagged rents, each strike cutting deeper into the smoky body. He twisted and reeled under the weight of her onslaught.

Her face twisted as she struck at him. Not in triumph or fury, but grief. Grief for the daughter that Corb had taken from her. Corb clawed at her, his formless hands raking her arms and shoulders, but still she pressed on, her teeth bared in a snarl. She drove her blade home again and again, ravaging his huge form.

Seeing her begin to tire, I surged forward. The Spear blazed hot in my hands as I thrust it through Corb's chest, pinning his fractured spirit against the earth. The impact shook through my bones, the relic burning with a light that cut through the smoke and shadow of his form.

I held him, pinned to the ground with the spear, as Morvra's blade continued to tear through what was left of his form. Finally, his body convulsed violently, fractures spidering across it like glass ready to shatter. With a final crack, his spirit burst apart, scattering into a cloud of ash and fading light.

Morvra stood trembling, her blade trailing with black mist. Slowly, she dropped to one knee, her weapon digging into the ground to hold her up. Her head bowed in grief, and a low keening wail came from her. Around us, the Fomorians continued fighting, protecting her as she grieved again for her lost daughter. I stood above her, unable to speak.

When at last Morvra lifted her head, her eyes were bloodshot, and tears had cut clean lines through the dirt and blood that covered her cheeks. Her voice was soft, but carried clearly across the din.

"Cai," she rasped, extending the hilt of Orna. "Finish this."

I reached to grasp the sword tightly. In my other hand, the spear pulsed hot, alive with renewed fire, as though the sacrifice had seared new strength into it.

I nodded once to her, the only promise I could give. Then I turned, raised the Spear high, and hurled myself back into the tide of death.

CHAPTER 68:

THE STONE OF DESTINY

< BREN >

Day 18 of Midwinter, Sunrise
Mag Mór, Tir Tairngire
Annwn

I hadn't wanted to send Fern and Monty away, but had known they would be powerless against the Bánánach. Hopefully, they would be able to assist Fíadan with whatever enemy she chose to engage with. I had hoped that after Cai and I were done taking the brunt of the oncoming spirits, I might be able to check in on all of them.

At least Morias hadn't come to fight. Hopefully, he was safe back in Gorias, sipping tea or drinking his favorite cider. I felt a brief and nearly irresistible desire to go back to the days when it was just the two of us before all of this otherworldly craziness. But it was too late for that.

I hadn't been on the front lines long. One minute, Cai and I were trying to give the outnumbered Fomorians a fighting chance; the next, I found myself nearly overwhelmed by the buzzing vibration trying to pierce my mind. Such was the effect of the Mark of the

Bodach curse, but even so, the telltale hum of the Bodach had never felt this loud and clear, not even at Brú na Dallta.

I paused, thinking... Bánánach. Bodach. It occurred to me there were a lot of "B" bad guys here, but then, I didn't make this stuff up, and it was no wonder I felt confused sometimes as to which was the escaped death spirit from Uffern and which was the hive-minded copy of an Old Power / Old God / Síorláidir.

I clutched my head with one hand, guessing the sheer volume of the hum meant that there were hundreds of Bodach running around the battlefield. I knew, immediately, that I needed to leave the front line and draw them away from the others. Because if there was one thing I knew about all of these enemies, it was that they could spread their kind simply by injuring someone. If we managed to win this battle, we would have some serious cleanup to do.

I shifted to the north, stepping away from Cai and even Brigid. I found myself on the extreme opposite side of the battlefield from Fern, Monty, and Fíadan. My route had led me nearer to Nuada and someone that, if I squinted just right, looked kind of like Tadg, except uglier and more awkward. The king had a red glowing brand on his forehead that, upon first glance, filled my notifications full of his wrongdoings. And my, oh, my, was it a long list.

I hadn't seen many of Nuada's brothers since the battle had begun, but there was so much going on that I knew it was easy to lose people in the fray. I did manage to spot the very edge of the skirmish at the back of our army, where the fianna and fae were battling it out with the fachan and trow. From here, it appeared to be an even worse bloodbath than the front line. Changelings crawled over the bodies of friend and foe alike as they continued to fight.

A massive number of Bodach were killed indiscriminately as they followed me to the edge of the battlefield. Some of the creatures would be on me in seconds, others might take a while to get to me.

In my hands, I held the Dagger of Transmogrification, transformed into a single nunchuck, and the Silverwhite Yang stick of Growth. So, for once, it looked as though I had an actual set of disconnected nunchucks. They glowed with magical energy as I determined to use them as a focus for my boon magic. After that, it was up to me to control the Stone of Destiny. Assuming I could actually manage to control all of them at once, I would be a triple threat.

The first of the Bodach lunged at me, long hair matted with sweat and blood, claws swiping for my throat. Up close, they were even worse than I remembered. Their faces were twisted into something feral, their eyes shrunken like beads pressed into too much flesh, and their fingers were gnarled into sharp weapons.

I caught the Bodach's strike with my nunchuck and cracked the other end across its jaw. Bone gave way with a snap. As another Bodach rushed me, I willed the Yang Stick to its full length to drive the tip through its chest and fling the body back ten feet. Huh, I thought, looking at the Yang Stick. It appeared to be surprisingly effective when fully extended.

The hum grew louder, becoming low and guttural. The sound vibrated through my skull, so deep my teeth ached. The hive was talking.

"Join us," hundreds of voices said, layered into one.

"You again," I muttered, tightening my grip on the weapons. "You never call just to check in, do you?"

The Bodach spread wide, circling, but the hum pressed harder inside my skull. "She gathers the Powers and the Treasures to her to lead her grand army."

"What's that even supposed to mean?" I slammed the Yang Stick across another monster's ribs, then spun the nunchuck to crack it down. Nuada's brand had confirmed that his intentions had been anything but virtuous, plus I also now knew that Danu had been pulling his strings the whole time. Was the hive mind saying…

"Wait. Are you saying you're all working together? Seriously?" The hive mind shoved images into my mind. The Old Powers as they once had been. The first Síorláidir of the realm. Balanced. Equal.

Opposed, but not evil. The whirlpool inside of Uisneach and the way those first gods changed the flow of water to serve their purposes.

"No… HER purpose," the Bodach said in its humming voice of hundreds. "Join us or die."

I didn't have time to think. More claws raked at me, and behind them I knew there would be dozens more…too many to fight head-on with my nunchuck and the Yang Stick.

The Stone quivered in the air above my head, eager. At my thought, it shot forward, swelling to the size of a war club before slamming into the nearest Bodach. The creature's chest caved in with a sickening crunch as the Stone shrank again, darting back toward me.

Another thought, and it flattened into a wide disc, slicing through three more of the monsters before snapping back into a sphere. I barely had to guide it; each command I gave was met with fluid precision, as if the Stone knew what I wanted the second I thought of it.

A Bodach lunged for my side. The Stone stretched into a jagged spike mid-flight and punched clean through its ribcage, then snapped back down to the size of my palm as it zipped once more to hover over my shoulder.

The hive shrieked, and I willed the Stone forward yet again. I didn't let myself stop. If I stopped, the tide would bury me. I staggered north, dragging the horde with me, until a flash of light nearby caught my eye.

Nuada, cutting a path through the Bodach with the Sword of Light, his silver gauntlet gleaming as he swung. Beside him fought who I realized WAS Tadg, striking with a ferocity that surprised me. Father and son, shoulder to shoulder, their blades carving through the swarm and creating a space around their whirling blades.

Hope swelled, and I felt a smile start to curl my lips. At last, we might be able to turn the tide.

Then Tadg moved. It was quick—too quick for a changeling. Tadg's blade swept low, then up, severing his father's arm just below the elbow. Sparks burst off the sword when it clipped the edge of the silver gauntlet. Nuada roared in shock, clutching the ruin of his limb.

And Tadg… Tadg didn't hesitate. He reached down to tear the Sword of Light from his father's fallen arm and drove it forward, plunging the blade through Nuada's chest. The sword blazed with a flare of light so sharp that I had to shield my eyes.

The Bodach froze mid-step, the hive momentarily stunned into silence.

I rubbed my eyes, temporarily blinded, and switched to the same sort of energy sight I used when I was in a trance. With it, I saw the outline of Tadg looming tall over his father, the Sword blazing in his grip. Nuada staggered back a step, blood and light pouring from him, his face twisted with shock and heartbreak.

Tangled energy flared from Nuada as his life slipped away. Yet the greater horror was that the Sword of Light now belonged to the thing that I knew was no longer Tadg. What stood before me was a corrupted Síorláidir wrapped in Tadg's skin, moving him like a puppet in a flesh suit.

CHAPTER 69:

THE CAULDRON OF PLENTY

Day 18 of Midwinter, Sunrise
Mag Mór, Tir Tairngire
Annwn

Knowing that Erelith was watching over Brigid, I felt only mildly conflicted about facing off with the hag. Newly irritated at my inability to fly and the constant pulse of pain in my gut, I backtracked on foot to where Hullraiser had come ashore… and by ashore, I mean where we had been magically yanked out of the water and cut a huge farthing path through the actual continent of Tir Tairngire. Oh well.

Despite its insane path, the ship itself appeared to be unharmed, where it sat perched atop a mound of dirt and rocks. I wasn't sure how the crew would ever get it back in the water, but that wasn't a problem for me to solve.

The crew had scattered. Some were on land and some were still on the ship, manning the cannon and ballista. The lubrican, Cé Gwalch, had emerged from below deck and appeared to be checking out the damage to the living mast. He saw me approaching, complete with a dirty look, and gave me a faint smile before turning back to work at the base of the mast, a small drill in his hand.

Scolt and Salka faced away from the battlefield, appearing totally focused on the grey sacked corpse kite flying on the wind toward us. The Hag of Winter would be on us in moments, and for good and ill, we were far enough away from the main battle that we were on our own.

"Hello, little friend," said a hissing voice from behind me. I recognized it right away as that of the ornery, not-so-little oilliphéist I had summoned with the Mirrorstone.

"Bren sent you away from the front line already, huh?" I asked.

"In typical Bren fashion, he was trying to keep us safe," Fern responded.

I shot them both an incredulous look. "If you're looking for safe, I can send you back to Fintan's tower?"

"I'm not looking for safe," Fern snapped. "Neither is my new best friend here."

"This one keeps sitting on my back," Monty said with a sigh. "But no one will let me eat her."

I smirked and looked back to the horizon at the small shape in the distance that was getting increasingly larger. "We're in trouble here. Without someone in the air, we don't stand much of a chance."

"Can't you just magic up a solution for this?" Fern asked.

I started to shake my head before remembering that I was, in fact, carrying the literal Cauldron of Magic.

"Fern, you're brilliant!" I turned to face the crew, raising my voice. "Listen up, you hull-hugging fish sniffers!" I had always found that a smidge of insult aided in getting people's attention. Plus, I meant it in an affectionate way… kind of. "Get your salty arses over here and dip your weapons in this Cauldron!"

The crew members stepped forward quickly to do as they were told, Scolt and Salka in the lead. Both submerged their swords into the Cauldron, the weapons sinking lower than seemed physically possible given the Cauldron's dimensions. Fern followed, dipping her sword deeply into the tiny pot and withdrawing it.

I briefly considered dipping my Silverwhite blades into the Cauldron, too, but thought better of it because of their already magical nature. It would be like mixing ale and cider, I suspected. Something bad was sure to happen.

Cé Gwalch wasn't holding a weapon, which was just fine by me. The less I needed to interact with the lubrican, the better. He had finished drilling into his precious mast and was collecting something from the main trunk to put into a small vial. He took no notice of me. Lubricans, what a bunch of chuckleheads.

The Hag of Winter loomed closer, her tattered robe whipping in the storm winds. Her hammer gleamed grey, like her robe, and larger than Monty's head. I felt the same chill I had felt on Wolves Hill the first time I had faced her with Morias and Bren.

"Weapons ready!" I shouted. My blades thrummed in my hands, eager. Without thinking, I leapt into the air, crashing back to the deck with my gut and wing throbbing. Oh yeah. That. I was still grounded. Couldn't take the fight where it needed to go. Well, chet.

The others formed up. Salka bared her teeth, while Scolt muttered a battle mantra. Fern climbed up Monty's red coils and pointed her sword skyward.

The hag's laughter carried before her, dry and sinister. "Little lambs. Little nothings. I will break you and take your prize." Her eyes darted to the Cauldron at my hip, reminding me of her true goal.

Cé Gwalch scrambled to my side from the mast, clutching the vial he had been working on. "Take it!" he hissed, shoving it into my hand. "Súg of the mast. It is a special brew. It will mend you."

I blinked. He gave me a look, sharp and desperate. "Just drink, you daft crow!"

Before I could argue, the hag descended. Shards of wood shattered against the deck as her hammer came down, splintering anything that it touched. The crew scattered, cursing. Monty lashed upward, jaws snapping, but she batted him aside with one contemptuous swing of the huge hammer.

Oh for the love of…I pulled the cork with my teeth and drank. The súg burned going down, thick as honey, and then—heat pulsed through me, knitting sinew, straightening bone in my back. I groaned as my wing snapped, unfurling, staggering as sensation rushed back.

Cé gave a triumphant bark of laughter, cut short when the hag's second swing caught him full-on. He crumpled like paper and flew from the deck to land in an unmoving heap on the ground below.

"Dwal," I breathed. For all his smugness, the little bastard had saved me.

I spread my wings. The wind caught me and I rose in the air. Pain lingered faintly in my gut, but my wing was healed, and I was aloft, my Silverwhite blades catching what little light pierced the storm.

"Over here, you wrinkled chet-bag!" I screamed, diving at the hag's head.

The hag snarled, distracted from the crew below, her eyes locking onto me. Her hammer swung in a wide arc, but I twisted, throwing Swish and Stick up to spark against it. Every strike I landed sang through the air, each sharper and deeper than before. I laughed manically, feeling more alive than I had in a very long time.

Below, the others rallied. Fern leapt, her sword shining. Salka and Scolt slashed at the hag's ankles. Monty coiled again, his massive tail lashing to knock the hag off balance. But her eyes kept flicking past them to the Cauldron at my hip.

"You'll not have it," I spat, darting higher, slicing a jagged slash across her cheek. "You'll not have them, either." I darted further away, trying to draw her away from the others.

Her rage-filled scream shook the sky. She chased after me, her cloak beating a furious pattern in the wind, her hammer raising high and—

CHAPTER 70:
THE SWORD OF LIGHT

< TADG >

Day 18 of Midwinter, Sunrise
Mag Mór, Tir Tairngire
Annwn

Finally, the Sword of Light was mine. The usurper king stared up, betrayal and sadness in his eyes. The blade remained deep in his gut. Inside, I felt Tadg fighting to regain use of the limbs that I now fully controlled. I smiled, watching the light fade from his father's eyes.

As his life slipped away, the body I held grew and cracked, bones rearranging themselves. I wasn't yet the size and shape I had held in Cruachan, but I was no longer trapped in the deformed in-between. Black feathers covered my body, even reaching my face and the sharp, cruel beak. My curved claws were jagged and sharp, veritable blades made for rending flesh from bone.

Danu toyed with the former queen, buying us time to achieve our goals. We would bring together all of the Síorláidir, in body and in weapon form.

Caileach had already acquired the imprisoned Arianrhod in the form of the Cauldron. I had the imprisoned Taranis in the form of the

Sword. We would not bother with Eiocha. Without her domain, she was worthless to us.

Maponos, in his numerous forms as the Bodach, had Bren and the rest of the Tuatha completely distracted.

We still lacked Teutates as the Stone and Camulos as the Spear, but the new Síorláidir, the children of the Cold Moon, would bring them to us, unbidden. After the death of the Ellyllon, I was sure of it.

The giants and those they battled had mostly destroyed one another. That section of the battlefield was a grizzly mess of exploded flesh and broken bones.

Danu's voice, low, resonant, and commanding, cut across the field. "Enough. Come to me." I felt the inexorable pull of her summons.

Caileach raised her bloody hammer to her shoulder and turned, the grey tatters of her robe dragging through the gore. The multitude of soldiers that Maponos controlled grinned through the mask of their distended forms until finally the copies fell helpless amid the bodies of their victims. I flexed my new, half-formed wings, and together we moved toward the smoking horizon. Tech Duinn loomed, its peak lit crimson in the purple morning sky.

The survivors could not follow us there. Not yet. That was the design. We would allow them to lick their wounds and bury their dead. If and when they rose again to resist us, the battle would be on our terms.

Mag Mór seemed to sag in our wake. Screams grew distant. The clash of iron and steel dulled. Even the wind carried a hush, as it often did after a storm.

Tadg wailed from deep inside me, but I drowned the sound beneath the inferno that occupied the same space. I would not be captured again.

Power swelled inside of me as Nuada's boons were added to my own. Light. Judgement. Hunting. Beauty. I was the first Síorláidir to embody this many domains. I had no way of knowing exactly what would happen, but I laughed, feeling the domain power ripple through me as the notifications began.

Name: Aillén
Race: Corrupted Síorláidir
Current Power Rank - Combined Level 98

Current Progression Status:
Combined Physical Progression +105
Combined Mental Progression +102
Combined Spiritual Progression +100

Domains:
Judgment and Light

You have been gifted with the following boons:
Dawnpiercer
Blazing Mantle
Burning Pulse
Radiant Surge
Guilt-Sight
Penitent Brand

Domains Gained: Beauty and Hunting

You have been gifted with the following Beauty boons:
Radiant Countenance
Siren's Tongue
Glamour Veil

You have been gifted with the following Hunting boons:
Hunter's Instinct
Predator Endurance
Trophy Claim

You have one soul-bound affliction:
Possession- Tadg mac Nuadat

Innate Racial Abilities:
Rapid Regeneration
Advanced Identification
Magic Sense

One magic item is in your possession.
You have acquired: Gealltóir, the Vowkeeper.

Item abilities unlocked:
Scourge of the Fae- When wielding this saber against any
fae, your attacks are twice as effective.

One relic is in your possession.
You have acquired:
The Sword of Light

Relic abilities unlocked:
Never Miss
Blinding Blade

The four Síorláidir stood, once again, on the topmost ledge of Tech Duinn, staring down into the fire and ash. I was reminded of the first time we had stood here, after we had reshaped Uisneach and created the Heart-shaped Pool for Danu. The landscape of Annwn and even our very bodies had been forever changed because of Danu's will. After all this time, we still follow her commands.

We jumped and descended into Uffern as I let the description of my new boons play out in my mind. I hungered for the day when I could use them all to destroy any that stood in our way.

Radiant Countenance

Your form glows with an otherworldly brilliance. Allies rally to your side, while foes falter beneath the weight of your beauty.

Siren's Tongue

Your words drip with enchantment, carrying the power to soothe, deceive, or ignite passion in all who hear them.

Glamour Veil

You bend perception with a thought, donning faces of awe or terror until none can tell the mask from the truth.

Hunter's Instinct

No shadow, distance, or ward can shield your prey. You feel the pulse of pursuit as though the world itself guides your steps.

Predator Endurance

Your body surges with primal vigor, moving tireless and swift, as though every heartbeat were forged for the chase.

Trophy Claim

Each kill yields more than flesh; the essence of your prey lingers, a token of strength or gift of power bound to your triumph.

CHAPTER 71:

AFTERMATH

< CAI >

Day 18 of Midwinter, Midday
Mag Mór, Tir Tairngire
Annwn

We had begun the battle with nearly four thousand soldiers. By the time the Old Gods had withdrawn, just over fifteen hundred were left standing. Only half of my Fomorian Comhthíreach had survived, and many of those were horribly wounded. The fianna and fae forces had been nearly obliterated by the giants.

The plain had become a graveyard. Hundreds of soldiers lay unconscious in the mud, their armor cracked, their weapons scattered. I knew these were mostly those infected by the Bodach. Though they had been released for the moment, it was unclear when he would call them back into his service.

Nearly every survivor bore wounds. Those touched by either foe would eventually turn if they were not healed. I knew from Bren's curse that the Mark of the Bodach could not be undone, and I knew what that meant.

Oirneth was the first, and the hardest. She lay propped on the body of a fellow Fomorian, her blade clutched in a bloody hand. I stood above her, breathing deep to firm my resolve.

"My king," she said, her hand loosening on her blade. "Do what must be done. I am not afraid." Her eyes held mine as I swung Orna to cleave her head from her body. The Bodach would not have her now.

I felt my heart crack a little further as I shouted my orders. My soldiers called out to me at each of the Marked they found. My sword flashed again and again, heads rolling as I ended their cursed existence, keeping them from awakening as monsters. I forbade my people from carrying out the grisly task of executioners, and they trailed behind me, gathering the bodies for burning. Soon, a black, foul-smelling smoke filled the air.

The changeling soldiers and even some of the Tuatha looked upon me with a mixture of pity and anger. I didn't care. We had taken the front lines, saving the combined army from being swallowed whole by the undead. All now knew of Nuada's plot to wipe out Bres and the Fomorians. They knew the debt they owed us. But debts are forgotten over time. For now, the Fomorians had a tenuous peace with the kingdom. While many of the changelings and Tuatha likely understood the necessity of what I was doing, I would take no chances with my people. Any ire on their part would fall on me and me alone.

At last, the final Marked fell beneath Orna. I wiped the blade and sheathed it, looking out over the battlefield. We had lost so much.

Two of the four treasures, the Cauldron and the Sword, had been dragged into the volcano. Bren and I still held the Stone and the Spear, but I felt the Spear humming with magical energy, as if the relic itself knew its brothers and sisters were gone and longed to join them.

Our losses had been catastrophic. I did not know how many of the Tuatha still lived, but I knew Fern and Monty had survived their battle with the hag near the new lough that had pushed in from the wells.

Bren was inconsolable at the loss of Fíadan. Nothing remained of the last of the King's Guard but a brilliant white crystal that my brother hunched over. A colorful and clearly heartbroken Ellyllon sat at his side, her expression heavy with its own grief. Fern leaned into his other side, her arms wrapped tightly around him as he wept. Monty had coiled his scaled body loosely around the group as if to protect them from further attack.

In the distance, Goibhniu, Lir, and Ogma placed Nuada's body on the pyre they had constructed. Even as the flames consumed his body, the red brand remained on his forehead. They burned him unceremoniously, with no song or keening. There would be no Caoineag to lament his fall. It was an ignoble death for the man who defeated King Neit, and even his former subjects averted their eyes from the pyre, one of hundreds that dotted the plain. The air was thick with the stench of burning flesh and wet earth. Thankfully, the carrion birds had not yet come, though I knew it was inevitable.

I exhaled deeply, trying to release the tension that had knotted my spine for weeks. Had it been only two days since I had lost Tethra? The image of her falling into the Abyss stabbed at me, and I shook my head hard, as if I could force the memory away.

"Try as you might," a familiar voice said, "you cannot shake away the ugly."

Ruadan lowered himself onto the rock I sat on, mirroring my posture. His boyish face carried lines of exhaustion.

A weak chuckle escaped my lips. "I'm glad you aren't dead," I said, glancing sidelong at him.

"Third time was the charm, I suppose." His mouth quirked upward, but his eyes were heavy. I wondered how many of his doubles had died, and how many more were still out there.

For a time, we sat in silence, the kind born not of comfort but of shared exhaustion. Around us, the battlefield was quiet outside of the murmurs of soldiers aiding the injured.

Ruadan broke the silence first. "Do you think it was worth it? Any of it?"

My jaw tightened. "We had no choice but to fight."

"That's not what I asked." His words cut sharper than usual, and I searched my heart for an answer. Nothing came.

I watched, tired, as a Fomorian dragged another headless corpse to a pyre.

"Cai." Ruadan's voice was quiet as he watched. "Even if it was necessary, they will hate you for this."

"They already do."

"Maybe with time…"

"No," I said, and meant it. "But they will live longer, and that is enough."

Our brief exchange seemed to have steadied something inside me. Amid the ruin, I had felt an echo of the past, of the camaraderie I shared with Ruadan. Not everything had been lost.

At the edge of the field stood Brigid, her eyes fixed on us. She tilted her chin in the direction of Bren and the crystal he still held. I tilted the Spear in answer to her unspoken question. Sometimes words were unnecessary.

It was time to move again. I knew there were wounded who still needed care, and dead who still needed burning. I trusted that it would be done without me.

I rose to my feet, tightened my grip on my weapons, and moved to my brother where he sat next to the grounded Gorias coastal cutter. He lifted his head, his face pale and streaked with tears.

"Cai," he said, his voice hoarse but steady. "We don't stop here." Behind the sorrow in his eyes, I saw a deep well of anger.

I put my hand on his shoulder and felt the low charge of electricity from his armor. He rose to his feet, his expression hard. The crystal glinted faintly in his hands.

"We won't," I told him, watching the hazy tendrils that ran between us. The threads of possible disharmony, thicker than ever, led off to the northwest. Together we turned toward the smoking mountain that loomed over us. Fern, Monty, and the bright Ellyllon hovered behind us.

We would follow the Old Gods into the mountain's fire, and even into Uffern itself. Danu was not finished with her plan, whatever it might be. I knew, with a cold certainty, that neither realm would be safe while she remained among the dead.

A familiar pain stabbed through my torso, a reminder of how Danu had wounded me in Hy-Brasil. I closed my eyes, seeing the faces of fallen loved ones there. Every one of them had been a sacrifice to the god of death's war, and I felt my fury rise again.

We had a score to settle, and we would see it through, no matter what it cost.

ACKNOWLEDGMENTS

I should always acknowledge my wife first. She is the most well-read person I know and somehow finds it interesting to read and edit my books. I'm thankful for that fact, though I try not to dwell on it (and other things) too much out of fear the universe will somehow notice and redistribute the vast amount of grace and blessings I have received. Someday, you will write that novel I keep bothering you about and it will be fantastic!

I'd like to thank my friends Steve, Ben, Erick, and Frank for being my beta readers (and for playing D&D with me).

I'd like to thank my narrators Chris, R.J., Andie, and Neil. You have each been given gifts that I can only marvel at. Thanks for bringing my book to life.

I'd like to thank Soundbooth Theater for helping to expand my literary community with the advent of LitRPG Con, which they asked me to participate in. It was amazing and the amount of other authors I was able to connect with was game-changing.

Lastly, I want to thank Geneva and Kristen from The Legion Publishers. You guys are amazing and I'm very thankful for all of the marketing and advertisement work you have helped me with.

Overall, I'm just thankful to have written another novel. It is a lifelong dream, and I don't ever plan on stopping.

THE OG LITRPG FACEBOOK GROUP

To learn more about LitRPG, talk to authors including myself, and just have an awesome time, please join the LitRPG Group.
https://www.facebook.com/groups/LitRPGGroup

FACEBOOK GROUPS

Join these groups to discuss LitRPG with other fans!

GameLit Society: A place to talk to other GameLit readers.
https://www.facebook.com/groups/LitRPGsociety

LitRPG Books: This is a different group. Still a good place.
https://www.facebook.com/groups/LitRPG.books

SuperLit Book Club: Superpowers and loads of fun.
https://www.facebook.com/groups/SuperLit

LitRPG Legends: LitRPG, Gamelit & Progression Fantasy.
https://www.facebook.com/groups/litrpglegends

LitRPG Legion: A place to discuss your favorite LitRPGs!
https://www.facebook.com/groups/litrpglegion